The Rest of Our Lives

by
Dawn Connelly-Craig

Waverly House Publishing

Published by:
Waverly House Publishing
P.O. Box 1053
Glenside, Pa. 19038

Copyright © 2001 by Dawn Connelly-Craig

Lyrics of *A House is Not a Home* by Matt Dubey
excerpted with permission of Shazam Music

This novel is a work of fiction. All of the characters in this book are fictitious. Any resemblance to actual persons, living or dead, is purely coincidental.

All rights reserved.

Library of Congress Cataloging-in-Publication Data

Connelly-Craig, Dawn, 1966-
 The rest of our lives / Dawn Connelly-Craig
  p.cm.
 ISBN 0-9650970-4-8
  1. Afro-American families-- Fiction. 2. Dating (Social customs)--Fiction. 3. Divorced parents--Fiction. I. Title.

PS3553.O51169 R47 2000
813'.6--dc21
                                              00-043635

Cover design and illustration:
Kirk Gaines
Gaines Production and Associates

Printed in the United States of America
First Edition, 2001

DEDICATED

To every creative writing teacher I've ever had.

Your dedication has allowed me to go further than I ever dreamed possible.

* * * * *

From one of those teachers who dedicated his valuable time and attention to me, I gratefully received these comments on my book:

Passionate and psychologically intriguing, The Rest of Our Lives reveals the dynamics of family and relationships. Connelly-Craig's novel is engaging from beginning to end with intense vitality -- a must read.
                    Horace A. Morris, Lecturer
                    Howard University, Washington, D.C.

Acknowledgements

First and foremost, I will always thank God and all the ministries He has brought across my path. It is through these earthly angels that I have come to know that with Him, all things are possible.

I thank my girls, Ashley and Robyn, for needing me to show them that dreams can become reality. Thank you, Terrence J. Craig, my husband, for doing the playground duty and bedtime stories just so that I could focus on dreaming without guilt.

Deborah J. Watkins, you were my first real reader. You boosted my ego and kept me going by letting the characters become real enough, not just to read about, but to really care about. Roxanne Seth-Malone, my appreciation to you goes further than words can ever express. I am blessed to have a friend whom I love enough to admit that, yes, you can actually make me do things that I don't really want to do. William Jones, thank you for getting so caught up in my eight-hundred-page monster manuscript that you forgot about editing and allowed yourself to get caught up in the flow.

The support of my family and friends, especially the ones who have never read a word of this work but displayed their pride in my accomplishments, has warmed my soul on many occasions. Your belief in me has fueled my belief in myself.

I would also like to convey my sincerest gratitude to every person I've met who expressed interest in my work, well before it was released. For those of you who asked whenever we passed, "Is the book out yet?" I hope that you won't be disappointed.

My final thanks are to Waverly House Publishing for whispering the constant words of encouragement and praise. It has been real.

Also, thank you, Jewel, for pulling up a chair in my head and trusting me to tell your life story.

CHAPTER 1

"All right, sweetie, when I tell you to open your eyes, look straight at me. Don't even think about looking in the mirror!" Zora's voice was stern, and I obeyed her. The makeup artist scrutinized my face for a moment before turning back to her array of shadows and brushes, while I sat back in the chair, completely at ease. I figured this is what it's like to be a movie star. The ultimate sense of pamper.

Starting with the top of my head this morning, after only three and a half hours in the shop, I was now sporting a cute little bob, although at the moment the bangs that went with it were held off my face with a clip so that Zora could get a good look at her canvas. The facial and make-up job were literally the icing on the cake on this most serious of makeover days.

It must be that pampered, relaxed feeling that permits people to open up to stylists, and I was no exception - I had told Zora that the makeover was to surprise my husband who was away at school.

Zora turned back to me. "Now, I'm all for black men gettin' their education, and I don't mean no harm, but are you crazy? Wait before you answer - hold your mouth like this."

I smothered a smile and made an open O instead so that Zora could apply small brush strokes to my lips.

Satisfied with her handiwork, Zora snatched a tissue from behind her and continued to question me. "How can you say you have a good husband if he ups and leaves you and your baby girl to follow his dreams - *away* from home!"

"But, Zora, you just said that black men need an education to make it in life. And that's why Malcolm's in New York."

Zora put her hands on her ample hips and demanded, "Why should he get all the opportunities while you stay home and take care of the baby? And why couldn't he find a school right here in Washington? Last I heard, there was a ton of 'em!" Again, she turned back to her facial artwork, quite sure that I wouldn't be able to give her a satisfactory explanation.

It was cool. I had heard arguments like hers from plenty of people before, but out of respect I pretended to weigh her concerns. I glanced down at the little diamond on my left hand, moving it a bit to make it sparkle under the overhead lights. It was a Canardly diamond - so called 'cause you can hardly see it - but it was mine and I loved it. My voice was full of affection when I said, "Malcolm didn't want to go - I made him go."

Zora whipped around and leaned back on her heel. Her eyebrows rose and disappeared beneath the bangs of her carefully coifed auburn wig.

I tried to explain even though I knew Zora would think me naive. "You don't understand. I trust my husband. Malcolm loves me and Tia. He was the one who fought me tooth and nail when I tried to convince him that the school in New York wasn't that far from D.C. I told him we would always be a family in our hearts."

Zora pursed her lips and made a couple of little clucking noises before turning back to her tools.

I continued, feeling the ache of frustration from the past. "What else could I do? Have him pound the pavement looking for so-so jobs, taking what he could get? I know he'll be supportive of me when it's my turn - not because he owes me, but because he loves me."

Zora must have been softened by my confidence in my husband because she looked at me with a mixture of envy and pity. "Girl, I don't know, but hey, if it works for you, well then you are truly blessed. Me? I wouldn't trust no man no further than I could throw him. And I'll tell you what, I ain't about to put this old back through no changes for no man! Out of sight, out of mind!" She rolled her eyes and then stepped back into her professional mode. "Now, sweetums, I want you to look up and hold your face like this." Zora elongated the muscles of her face achieving that universal expression used when applying mascara.

"Yes," she crooned while blending in the eyeshadow. "This is the perfect color for your eyes. I'll put a few of these with your purchase and show you how to apply it yourself so that you don't have to come here whenever you want to look like a supermodel." She laughed and winked at me playfully.

"No, no," I said, raising my hands in protest, "if I want to look good, I promise - I'll come back to you."

I've tried to be a make-up kind of woman, but have never been able to get into the whole foundation, eyeshadow-blending thing. And I found out long ago that most lipsticks make the little facial hair I have stand out a bit - not that I'm an Aunt Bunny or anything, but my caramel-colored complexion makes the darker-colored hair on my body more pronounced. Fortunately, most men I've known seem to find my very faint, soft mustache and sideburns attractive.

Besides, chasing around after a two-year-old doesn't afford much time for putting make-up on and taking it off, so usually I was like, why bother? Lately, however, I had started thinking it was time to work on my appearance. After almost two and a half years, I'd finally stopped blaming the birth of my daughter, Tia, for the extra weight that I was carrying. No, the pudge around the middle and my thighs rubbing together were from hanging out in front of a computer terminal all day - the only exercise I was getting was when I schlepped out to pick up lunch.

So, instead of choking down some fast food garbage at my desk, I began walking and bringing food from home every day. Not only did that enable me to afford extras like this pamperfest, but I was able to fit into the jeans I was wearing today - they weren't from prepregnancy days, but they were one size smaller than what I had been wearing.

This morning, I had dressed casually, but with that carefully put together look - a cream-colored turtleneck tucked into my black, loose-fitting jeans for the first time in years. What really gave me the attitude of a serious diva were the boots that cost about two days' pay, but were worth it in looks if not practicality. They were ankle-length with about a two-inch narrow heel, made from this black leather that looked so soft that it put you in mind of cloth instead of stretched skin. Once I slipped into my black leather jacket, tapered at the hips with slightly padded shoulders, you couldn't tell me anything! Now my head wasn't so big that I had a hard time getting in and out of cars, but when you know you look good, you can't help but strut, and right now I couldn't wait to do just that.

"This is the end of the line, chickie." Zora was clutching three different shades of lipstick in her hand and held each up to my face. "Hhmmm." She tried to decide. "Since it's still morning sun, you should wear this, but this would look so much better this evening when you and your hubby step out." Switching them back and forth, obviously in a dilemma, she finally decided. "Well, I'll put the darker shade with your other purchases, but keep in mind that it's an evening color," she admonished. "If you wear it in the day, you'll look like a hooker!"

I nodded my head like I would really remember that once it got under my bathroom sink with all the others.

Then Zora said, "Be prepared!" and dramatically swung me around. If I hadn't known, I would have questioned who it was in the mirror. I had a chance to study the carefully applied foundation, the mascara that was heavy but not sloppy, and the way the blush blended in, making it all come together to create a flawless look.

Zora's face appeared behind my reflection as she explained her creation. "Now you'll notice that the foundation is a little lighter than you are, but that's in order to bring out the colors and highlights" - which was true - it did enhance the many colors that now made up my new look. The most defining feature was my eyes, dark and smoky with intensity. My naturally thick eyebrows had been trimmed, but Zora had filled them in with a little color pencil, making them look even more pronounced.

Zora asked, "So? What do you think?" The question was asked with that kind of superior attitude that says "I'm being polite because if you don't just love it, it's because you don't know anything which is why you came to me in the first place."

But I did love it, and my smile proved it. I was gorgeous! Just what I needed for my surprise visit to Malcolm in New York.

Satisfied, Zora turned back to the counter. "Now let me ring up your purchases. Did you want to get the eyebrow pencil?"

she asked over her shoulder, the item held between two carefully tipped nails.

"No, I don't think so." I fished through the little handbag for my credit card. After finally getting the bill down, I'd promised myself that I would be a lot more careful, and it had worked . . . until today!

Zora finished ringing up the hefty sale and handed me the package. "Good luck, doll." She said it with sincerity, but I knew what she was thinking. Not that it bothered me - I'd seen that look of caution in various faces over the last year and a half. I thought of my snotty cousin Dey who had made a comment that I was shortchanging myself for my family. Okay, yes, I thought, she has her masters degree, but will that degree ever hold up chubby little arms and squeal with delight when you reach down to pick her up? Does she have a wonderful husband and father like Malcolm? I don't think so.

The only thing that bothered me at all was that with responsibility, some of the romance seemed to have gone out of my relationship with Malcolm. I remembered the carefree days when he would come down to see me at school. We would wander around the coast during the day and spend the nights wrapped in each other's arms. I was pretty sure this makeover and a surprise visit to Malcolm would definitely rekindle that magic.

I headed toward the escalator, full of bounce and confidence, looking in every available mirror - not because I was vain, but because every time I saw my new image, my usual insecurities were suppressed, at least for the moment, and my ego was given a big boost.

I made it to Washington Airport just in time for my flight to New York, settled into my seat and stared out the window, excited, thinking of Malcolm and how he would react to my new look. "Calm down," I told myself, since it would be at least another two hours before I actually got to surprise him.

The flight attendant appeared and disturbed my reverie. "Hello? Would you care for something to drink?"

"No, thank you." My smile was on megawatt. *Three whole days of just the two of us. Me and Malcolm.* Don't get me wrong, I loved our child to death, but anyone who's ever had kids and had to work *and* go to school too will understand. Now throw in a long distance marriage, and you'll really understand my excitement.

I plugged into my Walkman, closing my eyes as soothing strands of Beethoven came to me, and thought about how Malcolm and I got to be a commuter family.

We'd just been buddies through high school, but senior year I noticed him in a new light when I saw him sitting on the steps that first day back to school, and he parted those sexy lips and said, "Hello, Jewel." My mouth fell open at the bass that filled my ears, but I never got up the nerve to tell him how I felt because of Stephanie. She was his first real girlfriend - popular and beautiful, busty and full of sexuality. She dogged Malcolm out every time she could, and all I could do was watch.

After that school year, we all went our separate ways. Malcolm stayed in D.C. and went to Howard, and I traveled south to attend Whitemore College.

Then it happened. Malcolm called and told me that he and Stephanie had broken up. We talked until five in the morning. My mother was hot when she got that bill!

It didn't take long for our high school friendship to evolve into a flourishing romance. We wrote and called each other almost every day, he came down to visit me at school a few times, and we were together whenever I was home for the holidays. When I got pregnant, yes, we were scared to death, but faced up to it and did what we felt we had to do. I decided to leave school, we got married and moved into an apartment together, and Malcolm got a part-time job and continued going to Howard, majoring in communications. Tia, our beloved daughter, was born, and we became a family for real.

It was my idea that Malcolm go to graduate school. When a white boy comes out of college, the doors start swinging open, but a brother has to make a serious investment in education just to get to the threshold of opportunity. Malcolm tried to stay positive, but I knew that it was killing him making just enough money to keep Tia in diapers and wipes and not enough for all the frivolous things doting daddies want to give their little princesses.

I took the reins and applied on his behalf to NYU's film school, but it took months of my pleading, cajoling, and even crying, to get Malcolm on his way to the Big Apple for graduate work. People like Dey thought I was crazy, but I wasn't, and now I'd be having the last laugh. In May, my husband would have his master's degree, and we would all be together as a family for the rest of our lives. I started getting butterflies in my stomach thinking about it as the plane made its descent.

The cabdriver found Malcolm's place, a big old brownstone rented out to grad students. I stepped out into the cold, ran up the steps, and slipped in as two students emerged. I climbed the three flights and then down a long hallway to Malcolm's door. It was fun to actually see where he lived instead of trying to imagine it from his descriptions. I knocked on the door and waited, practically jumping with excitement.

His voice, deep and muffled, approached the other side of the door. "So, what? You forgot your keys . . . ?" The door swung open, and there was Malcolm. I laughed at how he stopped mid-sentence, shock very evident on his face.

"Well, aren't you going to let me in?" His expression was priceless, and I was all grins as I do so love a surprise.

"Yeah," Malcolm said softly and then looked up and down the hall. "Where's Tia?" he asked, sounding alarmed.

"No, no. She's fine. I just came to visit you on your turf for a change." I walked into the living space. There was really just this big room that was divided by one of those Japanese panels into a sitting area and a bedroom.

On one side of the divider there was a little, dark green plaid loveseat in front of a large window, a big comfortable-looking chair in the corner, and a desk against the wall with a computer and a printer on a crate. Across from that was a huge bookcase filled with books and papers. The floor was covered with a big, shaggy, dark green area rug that looked like an invitation to stretch out. On the other side of the divider, most of the space was filled with a double bed, still unmade. I smiled to myself because I could never get Malcolm to understand why I made up the bed every day, even on the days that we were running late and we were just going to get back in it a few hours later.

His TV and VCR were sitting on top of a stand at the bottom of the bed with videos stacked neatly underneath. Most of them were of Tia. I had started sending them to him every week at his request and, in turn, he sent her videos about his life at school. They were so cute because sometimes he would read her a little story or just act plain goofy.

The bathroom was off the bedroom area, and I could still feel the humidity and smell the lingering fragrance of soap hanging in the air from the shower he must have just taken.

Turning to him, I took him in with sparkling eyes. It was still unbelievable to me that this handsome, intelligent, well-built man standing in front of me like a black Adonis was all mine. The possibilities the weekend offered swirled in my head as Malcolm leaned back against the dresser with only a pair of baggy gym shorts between me and what I knew to be the instrument of some intense pleasures. His bare muscular chest blended into the rockhard washboard abs, and the thighs were still tight and lean even though he hadn't been riding his bike lately. His black hair was curly from the shower, and there was still a little bit of soap that he always missed when rinsing off, just behind his ear. I ran over and gave him a big hug.

"Well, I guess you can say I really surprised you, huh?" I waited for the shock to wear off, but his body remained stiff. *Okay, Jewel, you know your husband well enough to see that he is not thrilled.*

Trying to set a tone, I started prattling. "Tia sends her love. She's staying with Mommy." *Maybe he's in a hurry to get to a class.* "Oh, hey, if you're on your way to class or something . . ." I began, now crossing over to the big comfy chair, "I can just sit right here 'til you get back. I've got plenty to keep me busy." I was going a hundred miles a minute because I was beginning to realize that this surprise was falling flat. "What's wrong?" I finally asked, worried that maybe this wasn't such a good idea after all. Malcolm was such a creature of habit, and perhaps I'd thrown him off his routine.

"Look, Jewel . . ." Malcolm began but was interrupted by the rattle of the doorknob turning. The rest went from slow motion to fast forward. This woman came flying into the room like a whirlwind.

"I forgot my notebook!" she announced, somewhat out of breath from the climb up. "Can't go to study group without it." A dazzling smile was hurled in my direction like a spell. The moment froze, and I got every detail of this beautiful creature. Tall and very slender, not skinny. No pudge hiding under her belt buckle like me or most women who've had children. Her complexion was toffee color with a strong jawline. A smile revealed straight and even teeth. High cheekbones gave her a regal air, but the nose that was small and cute gave her a spritish look. I noticed as she lunged across the bed that her legs, encased in a pair of faded jeans, were long and lean. The arm that reached for the book on the nightstand was graceful, the motion fluid. She's like a dancer, I stood there thinking. There was just a glimpse of bare midriff, but I could see no love handles impeding the smooth line from rib cage to hip. Her hair was pulled back into a neat bun wrapped in a scarf with just a few independent wisps of hair floating free. Her bright eyes were slightly narrowed in concentration beneath a pair of perfectly arched brows.

"Don't let me interrupt," she said, putting back the book and pushing off the bed, still scanning the room for the elusive item at large. Checking all around the bed, muttering that this was the last place she had it. "Do you remember what I did with it?" she absently asked Malcolm.

I don't know what he said or did because I couldn't tear my eyes away from this unexpected being.

Then her eyes brightened again as she zeroed in on the missing notebook. "Ah-ha!" She crossed the room to the desk where she reached down and picked up the book, triumphantly holding the prize over her head. Moving back to Malcolm, she gave him a warm kiss on the lips. Not the kind of kiss like one marking her territory, but one that says "this is a sweet gesture that I'm sure the receiver will appreciate." Wagging a finger under his nose, she warned, "Don't you fall back to sleep and miss this study class 'cause we need your brain!" and rubbed the top of his head with those slender fingers. The words she then directed to me were without a trace of cattiness - just filled with the ring of self-assurance that nothing was amiss. "I'm sorry I can't stay and formally introduce myself," she said apologetically, while standing there with her hand on my husband's shoulder, "but I'm really running late, and I gotta go." She turned back to Malcolm. "I'll see you later." And with one last fleeting kiss, she was gone.

It couldn't have taken more than two minutes, but I got the whole scene with every small detail down to the smudge on the sweatshirt that she was wearing. The H was smudged on Howard. I sat down slowly as my mind began to absorb what had just happened. I looked at Malcolm's hand. There was no ring. But I wasn't shocked. I mean that made sense. I looked around the room again and noticed that there were small snapshots of Tia but none of me. Nothing shocking about that. Then it hit me. She didn't even have a clue as to who I was! She felt so secure, she didn't even feel the need to question my presence. She belonged here, and I was evidently a guest.

Instantly, I saw the room with new eyes. The loveseat at the window holds the two of them cuddled up like spoons underneath a thick quilt, warming each other on the long evenings. There they are, sitting together at the computer desk, working on some papers. Going over issues I wasn't always quick to grasp when Malcolm discussed them with me, but was so eager to learn. The chair I was sitting on is filled with the two of them entwined, talking about their day.

Then, unwillingly my eyes went to the bed on the other side of the divider. That graceful hand is wrapping itself around my husband's neck. His hands are moving up and down her slender body, kissing that perfect mouth, running his tongue along that strong jaw now slack with shallow breathing. The bright eyes are half closed with desire. He's lifting the sweatshirt with the smudged H off her dancer's body, and now he's parting those long legs, slowly moving in to settle between them. That instrument that brought me so much pleasure is bringing a sigh of contentment past her lips as he grasps the firm butt and plunges deeper inside, and . . . "*NO!*" I thought for sure I had shouted it, but I think it came out more as a moan. I was feeling sick but I couldn't go into the bathroom. I was sure there were more private moments in there - them showering together, her watching him shave. Hanging my head to stop the images, I begged my mind to be still.

"Malcolm?" I turned up my face to him and pleaded silently with my eyes, *"Make this make sense."* In that moment, all of my fears were confirmed. Malcolm, my husband, stood there looking at me with such sorrow . . . or was it pity? Looking at the short woman with the carefully hidden paunch and the almost non-existent butt. The pathetic woman with the makeup that made her look more like a clown because he knew all the imperfections that it was trying to conceal.

Oh, God, I've got to get out of here! I stood up, unsure as to what to do. Turning back to Malcolm I still begged him telepathically because I couldn't form the words, begged him to tell me that there was another explanation other than the obvious, but he only sighed and looked away.

Get out! Get out! That's the only thought that made sense. *Just go. Your heart's breaking and soon there won't be enough blood pumping to help your body escape. When she gets back . . . and she will be back . . . you'll still be here. So run!*

Grabbing my bag, I rushed for the door, almost tripping and falling when the sole of my shoe left the rug and hit the hardwood floor. I yanked the door open and clumped down the stairs. Once I hit the street I just kept moving. I don't know if Malcolm called my name or if he was behind me. I could only hear what was going on inside my mind. *She didn't know who I was! No . . . am. No . . . was. Run! Just keep running.*

I stumbled again and almost ran into the traffic. Stopped by a red light at the corner, I was stuck, unable to keep moving which seemed absolutely essential to my sanity. Looking desperately left, then right, over the crowds, I searched for some direction in which to go. *If I have to stand still much longer I'll start screaming, and I know I won't be able to stop.* I felt the scream rising up my throat, pressing against my lips. One hand flew to my mouth to stop its escape while I stuck the other straight up in the air to flag a cab which pulled up as if by magic. I climbed in and shut the door, willing the cab to move.

"Where to, lady?"

In order to answer this person, I had to remove my hand but I was afraid that my screams would fill the cab . . . the city.

Then Malcolm would be able to find me, so I just sat there with my hand over my mouth.

The cabbie turned and looked at me over his shoulder. "You okay? You gonna be sick?"

I took a deep breath through my nose and was surprised at the calm voice that bypassed the scream. "I would like to go to Grand Central Station." And we were off.

I decided to take the train home because I was afraid Malcolm might show up at the airport . . . or worse, not show up at all. *Why should be come? He has a study meeting to go to.*

I put my sunglasses back on, although I thought the sun must have exploded because it was so cold and everything looked so gray. Paying the driver and rushing inside the terminal, all my effort went into finding the right ticket counter. *Don't think about anything but the basics.*

The next thing I know, this woman behind the ticket counter with a smile on her face is asking me where I want to go. *Why is she so happy? Can't she tell that my life is falling apart? That all my dreams are shattered and plunged deep in my heart like shards of glass?*

"Washington, D.C., please. Union Station."

Her fingers began flying across the keyboard, and she asked me if I wanted club car privileges.

"No, thank you," I stammered. "Do you have an express? You know, like non-stop?"

Again the fingers flew, and she told the computer screen that there was an express leaving in about ten minutes. She finally looked up at me, but with a frown. "You'll be cutting it close."

"I need to be on that train," I said from behind my barrier of dark glasses, pushing my credit card in her direction.

Again with the flying fingers, she searched for a seat. Not that it mattered. I'd strap myself to the top of the train if it would just get me farther away from that room.

"Fine. Will this be one way?"

"Yes." *Damn straight!* I stood there waiting for my ticket which she handed over with a fake "enjoy your trip" before moving on to the next poor soul.

Okay, I'm moving again. Feet go. Legs go. Running through the station looking for the right terminal, telling my body what to do over and over with each step. When I got there, the man was yelling the last "all aboard!" I practically hurled myself into his arms.

"Hey, young lady!" he said with a little laugh while giving me a steady hand. "For you, we'll wait." He must have noticed that my heart was bleeding because he gave me a funny look and helped me to my seat. His tone was that soothing, careful one you use - like when you see there is a small crack in something and you believe that if you speak just so, it will keep the crack from spreading.

I wanted to help so I sat very still and wouldn't allow myself to think until I could get home. There, I wouldn't have to worry about anyone getting hurt when the rest of me fell apart along with my heart.

CHAPTER 2

The train pulled into Union Station. I had made it through the trip without screaming or tearing my heart out, but I was tired, miserable, and sick. After just wanting to run and keep going, now all I wanted to do was stay curled up on the seat and go wherever the train went for the next few days. I sat there until the last of the passengers filtered out, and then I walked out into the bright and busy world of Union Station. At once, I was assaulted by memories. Malcolm, Tia and I had been here together less than a few weeks ago - we'd brought our baby here to see her first movie. Malcolm could barely take his eyes off his child as she sat very quietly amazed at how large the screen was and covered her ears when the sound first came on.

I've gotta get out of here. Should I call someone to pick me up? I could . . . no, I don't want to be with anyone right now. No one but Jack. He always knows how to give a girl a good time, especially when she's down, and he asks for so little in return.

I turned but kept my stare straight ahead so as not to make eye contact with anyone because that would lead to a smile and there was no way I could handle that right now. *Stick to the perimeter of the crowd and blend in. Try not to be noticed. Hard to do when you're leaving a trail of blood behind you. Blood streaming from a broken heart.*

I was so wrapped up in my thoughts that I almost didn't notice the tall man walking toward me, holding the hand of a little boy and staring at me as if he wanted to say something. *The last thing I need is to help some lost tourist.* I looked for an escape route. *Too late - here they come.*

There was an uncertain smile on his face. "Jewel?"

"Yes?" I asked, getting a little nervous because this was a big man. Not fat, but tall and very well built. If I weren't distracted by the fact that my life was falling apart, I would have appreciated the deep honey-colored tone of this strong brother.

Not the processed kind that you see in the store, but the dark, rich hue that hangs off honeycombs in a hive. He had long, even, neatly-coiled locs and a reddish-brown beard that was in handsome contrast to his skin tone. And while this man before me was nothing more than a combination of images processed by my mind, there were plenty of women noticing him, their eyes lingering on his broad shoulders and the long legs that stood parted and planted firmly in front of me. I tried to remember where I could have met him so that we could make our exchange and move on. His eyes were sparkling as if he had a wonderful secret which he was about to reveal, making him seem almost as youthful as the little boy with him.

"Jewel Webster?"

"Yes," I answered, only barely aware that he used my maiden name.

"It's me. Justin Baptiste!" Recognition registered in my eyes as he advanced excitedly, reaching out to give me a friendly hug. My body stiffened, and I held out my hand to ward him off, but he mistook the gesture for a handshake.

"I thought it was you! It sure is great to see you." Undeterred by the pool of blood I was sure we must be standing in by now, Justin took my hand in his, squeezing it tightly. "How have you been?"

How have I been, now there's a toughy. I just found out the man I love, my husband no less, is in love with someone else, which of course is okay because she doesn't know about me.

"I'm fine, Justin. It's nice to see you." I was wondering if I would get my hand back.

"Hey," he said, still beaming, but now his smile further lit his eyes as he turned to the little version of himself. "This is my son. Sam, this is Miss Jewel Webster. We went to school together." He said this as if it were a major accomplishment.

"Hello." The voice was so small that it threatened to get lost in the crowd of noise.

"Hello," I said and reached down to shake his little outstretched hand. "Never fall in love, it's fatal," I wanted to tell him, but then something in him made me think that he already knew. "He looks just like you did in first grade," I commented, stepping back into the past. Justin and I had gone through the first eight years of Catholic school together. Under other circumstances I would have loved to catch up on old times, but I really needed to get to Jack.

"Are you just getting here or meeting someone?" While we were in school, he'd barely acknowledged me, always running with the more popular bunch, and now he couldn't seem to just say hi and let it go.

"Yes, I'm meeting someone," I said, looking around, "and I've got to go." I tried to disengage my hand, ready to walk away.

"Hey." Justin reached into his back pocket. "Here's my card. Maybe you could give me a call. It's always nice to see someone from the old days." He glanced at the Canardly diamond. "I see you're married now." *Oh, for the love of God! He won't stop.* "Maybe we could all get together and have drinks or something?"

I stuck the card in my coat pocket and tried to hold back the bile that was rising in place of the scream, as he inquired about where I was living now and who I had seen. I cut him off, reminding him that I was late meeting my party and had to say goodbye. Bending down, I told his son that it was nice meeting him.

I left them and ran down the walkway to the liquor store where I picked up three packs of cigarettes and some other necessities before flying again. *Just a little further. You're almost home.*

Once again I was at the mercy of a cabdriver but instead of being able to just sit back and vegetate, I had to give this guy directions. Our home was a little out of the way, a garden-style apartment building sitting back on top of a hill.

"See that wishing well? You're going to make a left there and then a right at the mailboxes. It's the last building at the end." I paid the driver and headed up our sidewalk, relieved that none of my neighbors was coming or going. Being so close to the privacy of my own home, alone with Jack, made my feet race past the other three apartments on my floor. The apartment building was very well maintained, and there was hardly ever any loud music or voices in the hallway. Malcolm and I were so happy to have found a nice place to live, but the downside was that the rent made it almost impossible to save up for a house - but of course that wouldn't be a concern anymore! The thoughts were coming back now, and my hands began to shake as I tried to fit the key in the lock. Jack whispered to me that everything would be all right - to take a deep breath and relax.

Once inside the dark apartment, I just sat down on the tiled floor of the foyer, took off Jack's hat, and gave him a great big kiss. As the liquor poured down my throat, it dawned on me that less than twelve hours ago I had awakened happy and excited. Now I didn't think that I would ever feel that way again.

I needed a cigarette, despite the fact that I had quit smoking four years earlier. *I need that cigarette. I NEED IT NOW!* Because of Tia, there was no smoking in the apartment, so I headed for the balcony. The cold January air hit me in the face as I sat down in a corner with my back pressed against the glass and fumbled with the wrapper of the cigarettes. The first drag felt just as good as the last one I'd had four years ago.

Then the whole day came rolling back detail after detail with some very vivid images provided by my active imagination. *She's beautiful and he loves her. He didn't even try to stop me from leaving. How long has it been since he stopped caring or did he ever?*

It was going to be a long night, and by ten o'clock the pity party was in full swing. In my drunken and delusional state, a dialogue had begun among my head, my heart, and the remains of the bottle of Jack Daniels that had been keeping me company.

Look at yourself! The head was full of self-righteous indignation and was getting on my last drunk nerve.

Leave me alone; I have a right to do whatever I need to get me through this. Besides you should be grateful, because if it weren't for Jack here, you would be lost.

And I accepted Jack's warm company as we kissed again.

You should be ashamed of yourself. You don't deserve to keep the name that you were given. You were named after your great-grandmother Jewel Isabell Robinson, who . . .

Yeah, yeah, I know. Got her education, a college degree no less, raised three boys, one of whom she gave birth to while

crossing the Mississippi River running from the Ku Klux Klan because she and her husband refused to stop teaching cane pickers in the swamps of Louisiana. Yeah, yeah, I know the story.
    I took another drink. *Yes, I am a mess and if my great-grandmother could see me now she would probably change her name. But you know what she had that I don't?* I asked my needling mind.
    A spine?
    No. A husband!
    That shut the head up and I continued my long spiral into despair. Still sitting on the balcony with Jack and the cold night of January to keep me company, I watched the last four years of my life float by.
    I only asked that he never hurt me and this . . . this makes no sense.
    The phone began ringing in the house but I just ignored it, removing the cellophane from the second pack of cigarettes, amazed that the small pile of butts around me was all that was left from the first pack.
    Where was I? Oh yes, this makes no sense. I did everything. I was everything. His friend, confidante, mother of his child, his wife, lover.
    The head chimed in, *But don't you mean that he was **your** everything?*
    Shut up. I am not one of those women who gets so wrapped up in a man that she loses sight of who she is.
    Yeah, right. Of course you're not. Sure.
    See, that's what I didn't understand, because most importantly, right at the top of the list, I thought of Malcolm as my best friend. That's what wrenched my heart the most. How bad of a person could I be that the person to whom I had entrusted my heart would do something like this? If I hadn't gone up to New York, I would still be in the dark. Still running around trying to make things right.
    Isn't that what this is all about? My head asked again.
    Here you go. Now what?
    That you don't know how to listen, and now you know that everyone was right and you were wrong. Like that woman who

did your make-up this morning. You went around spouting how wonderful your life was and now it's in shambles. The head persisted. *You're afraid of what people will say - people like Dey, your mother-in-law, friends. That you were all wrong for him. That he was out of your league.*

Will you please give it a rest? You're the one that's going to have to pay for this tomorrow. I silently laughed, tipping the bottle again.

That's if you don't kill us instead. Is that what you're trying to do? Get a little sympathy from him? If you are it won't work, because you'll be dead! Hello?

Oh, please. I may be a sad drunk right now, but I am still a mother and nothing would ever make me forsake that little girl. Not a man, divorce, let alone humiliation. So shut up!

But I started getting up, grabbing Jack, because the head had made a point. *It is January and it is cold only I'm really too drunk to know it.*

The door buzzer was going off when I went into the living room, and the phone was ringing. *Boy, aren't I the popular one tonight!*

Suddenly the room was alive with the sound of my chipper voice on the answering machine, going out over the telephone lines in greeting. "Hello, you have reached the Stone residence." The tears were dripping off my chin as I remembered the day I had made that tape, inaugurating my new marital status. Oh, happy, long gone day! At the beep, I heard a male voice speaking to me.

"Jewel? It's me, Damon."

Oh, Malcolm's best friend . . . no, I'm his best friend.

"Jewel, I'm downstairs. That's me buzzing. I'm on my cell phone." As if to prove his point, the buzzer started going off again. "Jewel, I know you're in there. I saw you on the balcony when I drove up. Please open the door?"

Leaning against the kitchen wall, I pushed the button that allowed me to be heard downstairs. "Did you know?" I pushed the button to listen and waited for his response.

After a pause, he finally said, "Jewel, please just let me come in so that I can make sure you're okay?"

Pushing the button again, I could hear the sounds of someone either coming or going, completely unaware of the drama in progress. Funny how the world can go on without the sun. I asked, "Did you know?"

"Wait, I'll be right up."

Releasing the button, I reached over and extracted the little tape from the answering machine. The knocking began and crossing the living room, I asked the door, "Did you know?" and sat down on the step to wait for its reply.

"Look, I just wanted to make sure you were all right."

Men, I thought, slowly pulling the brown ribbon of tape from its plastic encasing. *They are such cowards. And they all stick together, like a pack of dogs.*

"Get away from my door," I said calmly, while holding the limp recording of the happy voice with the one-name residence in my hand. "You are not welcome here. You are not my friend." I got up and began to stagger across the room, back to my area of solitude. "Go home!" I shouted in that way drunks have when the alcohol has completed its purpose, and the pain can't be felt.

Settling down again with Jack, I went back to wondering. *How long has this been going on? Who else knew?* I couldn't call the one person who could answer my questions. What if *she* answered the phone, although that had never happened before. I *wonder why?*

What if he's with her now? Making mad passionate love because his burden has been lifted. What was I so afraid of? Why didn't I tell Malcolm off right then and there? Why didn't I tell that woman, no matter how beautiful she was, to get her hand off my husband's shoulder?

This time, the voice of my head was almost kind, but the words hurt nonetheless. *Because you were afraid that this person whom you've loved since high school, the father of your child, the one for whom you swore before God to forsake all others, would step in front of you and protect her. That he would send you away as the intruder, and that would have killed you. Trust me, you did the right thing!*

The phone rang again. Once, and then less than a minute later, again. My heart began to pound. It was the signal that Malcolm and I used when I first came home with the baby, and he wanted to let me know that it was he calling - before we got the answering machine. Stumbling across the room, ignoring my head which told me not to answer it, I grabbed for the phone.

"Hello?"

"So you're home." That voice, I love that voice.

"Didn't your buddy Damon tell you?"

"I just wanted to make sure that you were all right." He sounded as if he were getting ready to hang up.

"Malcolm, wait! We have to talk."

The sigh that passed to my ear was one I was all too familiar with. It was the one that said "I don't want to do this." "Look," he began, "I'll be home in a few weeks - we can . . ."

A few weeks?! Is he kidding? Besides, whose "home" is he referring to? I may need answers, but there is nothing that is going to make me change my mind.

"No, Malcolm, we need to talk about this now. There is no way this can wait another two minutes."

*Okay, my head started again, if you're really going to do this, here's the deal. No whining. No shouting. And do **not** let him hear you cry. We're going to do this with dignity.*

"Fine, then talk," he said belligerently.

"What's her name?" I tried to sound indifferent, but I was sure that he could smell my fear through the phone lines.

"Why?"

"Because I would rather refer to her by her given name instead of some other more colorful words that come to mind." *Oh, here comes the anger. I've been looking for you. Pull up a seat because I may need you.*

There was a hesitation before he reluctantly revealed, "Annette." *Annette. It would be something pretty like that. Does he call her Annie?*

"How long have you been seeing her?"

"A while."

"Is she there now?"

"No." I could hear the restraint in his voice, and it hurt. Like I was intruding on something sacred to him. *This is getting harder.*
"Does she live with you?"
"No." *Is that sigh because he wishes she could or because he's bored with this?*
"Is this the first time you've done this?"
"Done what?" *No, he didn't ask that!*
"Come on, Malcolm..." I began, but he stopped me cold.
"Yes, Jewel, I have been a good, faithful little husband until now." *What's he got to be angry about? He has it all.*
"Do you love her?" Turning up the bottle again, I took a huge swallow before he answered.
"I... I care about her," he said softly. This response nearly brought Jack spewing back up.
"Malcolm, you're telling me you threw away everything we had for someone that you just *care* about?!" I asked incredulously.
Malcolm exploded. "Damn it, Jewel! I've done everything I was supposed to do!"
Finally, a little emotion. They always crack when cornered. But what does he mean - everything he was supposed to do?
"Let's face it." Malcolm was shouting now. "I was the one who obviously didn't live up to your expectations - that's how I ended up in New York."
The world was swirling. "What - what are you talking about? When did I ever say that you didn't live up to my expectations?"
Malcolm shifted to that tight controlled tone that always made me feel like I was talking to a stranger. "Jewel, please, let's for once do something my way? Let's not get into this right now."
My fuzzy brain refused to let go. "Malcolm? We could have talked."
His voice became sullen. "No, Jewel, we couldn't. There's nothing I can say to make this right, and talking about it isn't going to help."
"Okay, Malcolm, you were unhappy." My voice was small and uncertain, the alcohol telling me that if Malcolm and I could

just have a conversation, everything would be like it was - that Malcolm would be coming home to me and Tia in five months and life would be good again. "You were unhappy, but that didn't mean you had to jump into bed with someone. Or were the feelings that I thought we had for each other something that I made up? Hello? Malcolm?"

After an eternity, his voice, soft and tired, whispered in my ear. "Look, things didn't work out the way we wanted, and I'm sorry. I've got to go." The line went dead.

Jack was sitting on the table, and I wondered why he didn't seem to be helping. *Why does my heart feel like a twisted rag? Why did Malcolm hang up? Why is my marriage over?*

I sat there on the floor thinking back. All the nights I stayed up typing Malcolm's term papers, well into the morning because they were due the next day. Forget that I would only get about three hours sleep myself. All the meals that I prepared because I wanted to make sure that he ate before heading out to his part-time job - meals that I rarely got a chance to enjoy because I had the baby to take care of. The vows when I stood up before the judge with God in my heart. *And this is it? This is all I get?*

Alone in the dark. No head cheering me on. No anger giving me strength. Just me and my tears, spilling over a broken heart, grieving for a lost marriage and the loss of a husband and friend I never really knew who had evidently left me quite some time ago.

CHAPTER 3

The smell of good food was all over the house since it was Sunday, the day that Lou (officially stepfather, but actually the major father figure in my life) and my mother have their weekly burn faceoff, each making their special dishes for dinner and vying for compliments.

Greens perfumed the air, complemented by the aroma of some kind of roast, and my glasses began to fog up after stepping in from the outside cold to the warmth coming from my parents' kitchen. The smell was good now but would only get better as the day went on. Lunch was never a consideration on Sunday because we all wanted to make sure that there was enough room for dinner - from the first helping of greens to the last forkful of dessert. Stomachs would begin to growl and tempers grow short in anticipation. We knew the agony was coming to an end when Mommy put the rolls that were rising under the tea towels on the counter into the oven to bake.

Despite the fact that I had a broken heart and a bit of a hangover, the smell of the comfort food began to work its charm. I felt fifteen again and that I could just drop my problems off my shoulders and leave them by the front door like I used to do with my school backpack.

"Hey, Mommy," I said in greeting, not wanting to look at her because I could feel that I was under close scrutiny. I was sure her radar had been up ever since I called Friday night and said I was home. Nothing goes unnoticed when it comes to Anna Lee Britt and her children.

Petite in size, my mother stands five foot nothing, but has enough energy and heart to make people look up to her rather than down. A few years back, she came home with her thick, shoulder-length hair cut down to a sleek fade that complemented her full, round cocoa-colored face - a face that can brighten like the sun when she's happy or cloud like a stormy day when she's worried or angry. Now, glancing up quickly, I could see the gray clouds gathering in her deep brown eyes.

"Hello, little kid."

I thought, "Okay, she's going to let me play this at my own pace," because usually her greetings begin with a criticism. Now don't get me wrong because I love my mother and feel very blue when I've gone more than two weeks without seeing her. And that's even if I've talked to her on the phone every day.

But usually when I come over, a greeting will consist of something like, "You're here before noon? The bed must have caught fire." Or, "That's a nice hairdo." (I wait because there is always more.) "And I hope that it looks just as good when you're stuck in bed with the flu, 'cause that's where you're headed if you keep running around in the middle of winter with no hat on." And I stand there sighing so slightly (I'm not crazy enough to suck my teeth or roll my eyes), thinking, "I don't care what she says because I don't have to wear a hat if I don't want to because I am grown." Now, I only think this, 'cause like I said, I'm not crazy enough to push and see just how grown I am.

"Is that roast beef or pork roast?" I asked, following my nose behind her to the kitchen.

"Roast beef." She checked her rolls and then started shifting her greens in the big pot. These were *her* things along with the yams that were sitting with the butter, apple slices, cinnamon, and nutmeg on the counter, ready to go in the oven for a quick browning. Lou would come down later and begin *his* things which would consist of fried chicken and my all-time favorite, much as that rankles my mother, potato salad. Yes, it is the very best and there is no one alive who can touch it. Not even his own mother who taught him how to make it in the first place.

"Where's Tia?" I asked.

"Trying to get your brother out of bed." My mother spoke with disapproval in her voice because of the lateness of the day. When we were young, we all got to sleep late on Sundays because we had to get up for school five days a week and for chores on Saturday. But there were times when the morning would start to stretch and Mommy would give us a little motivating shove to get us up. She would put on her gospel music, always beginning with the soloist, as she straightened up the house and fiddled with dinner. When she got tired of waiting for us to fall out of bed, she would change the music, moving to the choirs, and turn up the volume a notch or two until it was like having the whole congregation in the living room. That was the official message that *no*, you would *not* sleep the whole day away.

"Quinton! Get up, boy!"

Quinton was the baby. At fourteen, he stood taller than I and in my opinion was quite handsome. His sandy brown hair was all smashed and crazy because he was trying to grow it long enough for me to plait, and the little mustache that he had going still looked like peach fuzz. I could tell that he was going to be a big man like his father because he was all feet and hands, and definitely on the thick side for fourteen.

Mommy called upstairs again. "You're on your own for breakfast, and don't make my rolls fall." Provided that you got up timely, Mommy would fix breakfast for you. In Quinton's case, that was often forfeited for more sleep, which is really how he learned to cook.

She turned to me. "Your sister and Tamicia are coming for dinner. She said she had to stop by the office first."

Ashley is my older sibling by seven years and a single parent. She had been involved with a man whom she hoped to marry when they finished school, but he was still a fourth year undeclared sophomore by the time she received her doctorate and started to work as a child psychologist (which always amazed me because while we were growing up, her idea of therapy was to swing whatever was nearest to her hand upside my head). When Ashley started making wedding plans, the guy stopped calling or coming by. And when she confronted him, he said some pretty hurtful things that burned whatever bridges they had between them.

But Ashley moved on with her life. She became a foster parent to a little girl, Tamicia, who had spent her earliest years in poverty and chaos, badly neglected by her drug-addicted, teen-age mother. Ashley was eventually able to adopt Tamicia, and they'd been a happy pair ever since. As to Ashley's current love life, she had met an older man at a professional conference in Dallas; although they only saw each other occasionally, they seemed to be enjoying a new age, internet relationship.

When Mommy put the finishing touches to the dinner preparations and left the kitchen, I followed her into the living room. It wasn't the same house in which I grew up; my mother and Lou had moved out to the suburbs a few years ago where Lou had his own business, a small fleet of delivery trucks. The split-level rambler was perfect for the two of them, Quinton, and of course Chaka Khan, the family golden retriever.

"So," Mommy began, walking over and turning down her music, "do you want to tell me what this is all about now or wait until your sister gets here?"

"Might as well tell you now and her later 'cause I guess I should get used to saying it." Taking a deep breath, I blurted it out. "I'm getting a divorce." Once I had said it, it just sort of hung out there like a big bubble getting ready to pop.

Mommy didn't say anything.

I sat looking all around the room wondering if the words had actually come from me because it still didn't sound real.

Finally she spoke. "Are you sure?" *Why doesn't she sound surprised?*

I gave her question full consideration before answering. "Malcolm has someone else living with him - part-time, full-time - not that the details matter; he has hurt me beyond belief. Yes, I'm sure."

"Okay," she said in that "we'll talk more about this later" voice, "I'm not going to press you for details, but what do you plan to do about your daughter?"

"Well, I think Tia's gotten used to her father living away over the past year now, so I hope it won't affect her that much." I said this, wondering at the same time who was this poor family I was talking about.

Mommy shook her head. "No, I mean what do you plan to do about support, visitation, custody?"

"I don't know," I said truthfully. "I was hoping that you could give me some guidance since you've been through it." When I was five and Ashley was twelve, Mommy and our father, Angelo, divorced. In the beginning of the marriage, Angelo had been a model husband, but then he decided that he wanted the world and worked very hard to get it. He started his own business which always came first and wife and children a very distant second. Mommy did everything that two parents were supposed to do. Plays and school events had to be retold since Angelo was too busy setting up an empire. Mommy tried to be supportive, but Angelo didn't know when to stop even after they became quite comfortable financially. Eventually, he missed one too many of his children's birthdays, and that's when Mommy said enough.

Ashley missed him because she had been around in the early days before he became driven. Me? I couldn't miss what I had never known. But what really upset us at the time was that we saw our mother in a new light - a woman raising two little girls on her own. Mommy often looked afraid or worried, but she kept it together. I knew that, just like Mommy, I would have to keep it together for Tia now - not let her see that I was terrified. I had never planned on being a single mother without anyone to turn to whenever I was unsure.

"Do you think you'll have to fight Malcolm for . . .?" Mommy asked.

I was ready for that one and defended Malcolm. "If there's one thing I know, it's that even if Malcolm no longer wants anything to do with being married to me, he still loves Tia and will continue to support her."

Mommy looked at me like "are you finished?" before saying, "I have no doubt that Malcolm will support his child. I was asking do you think you'll have to fight him for custody?"

"Well, I . . . I haven't talked to him since Friday."

"I think you need to talk to a lawyer. Just make sure you have your ammunition ready, Jewel . . ." Mommy's voice became compassionate. ". . . because this could get ugly before it's all over."

I couldn't help but wonder why Mommy seemed far from upset over the loss of her son-in-law - again making me wonder if I was the only one who had been blind to the true nature of my relationship with Malcolm.

"MOMMY!" Tia yelled, taking a bumpy ride down the carpeted stairs into the living room. I looked at my pride and joy, and life had a purpose again. Cute little fat cheeks, huge brown eyes framed with dark but naturally delicately arched eyebrows. Her mouth still had that baby pouty look when it wasn't spread in a huge, toothy grin. She had a ton of hair that we fought over washing at least once a week, and unless you have a little African-American princess of your own, you would never believe that so much hair can be contained in two ponytails. Even though it was always a fight, I would never have thought of giving her one of those little perms. I loved her natural state. Sometimes I wanted to kill my mother for ever getting me started with all that straightening and stuff.

"Tia, you are going to kill yourself - flying downstairs like that!" I gave her a tickle, scooped her up in my arms, and held one of her little delicate hands. Everything about Tia was her name. Breathy. She was by no means a little sickly thing but more like a china doll with moxie. There was a passion and lust for life in her eyes that always made me feel great - like I was doing my job well. "Tia, where's your uncle?"

"I'm right here." The bass that appeared in my brother's voice earlier this year was still a little amusing to me.

"Boy, why don't you go and put some pants on before you come down here?" I asked as he walked over to the refrigerator in his baggy boxers and tee shirt.

Tia suddenly jumped from my arms, shouting "TAMICIA!" and running to meet my sister Ashley and her daughter who were just coming into the house. Tamicia was a velvety brown-skinned cutey pie. A real sweetie, with a loving smile and very quiet demeanor. At six, she was all arms and legs, with huge haunting hazel eyes that made you want to wrap her in your arms forever. Her hair was all braided up with pretty shells and beads, and I knew Ashley had spent many hours lovingly placing each one.

"Tia, let her go so Grammy can get some sugar," my mother said, stretching out her arms. Ashley smiled as she watched her baby. Gone were the days when my sister would have to explain to Tamicia that she didn't have to hide food for later or even be afraid to ask for seconds - that she was safe now after her early childhood of poverty and neglect. There were still nightmares and a lot of those hair sessions had their share of tears, but those two had a bond that nothing could break - not even if Tamicia's mother were to come back into her life.

I asked Ashley about that once - if it scared her. She said sometimes it did, but no matter how it turned out, she knew that Tamicia would call her Mommy for the rest of her life. Ashley had learned from our own lives that the badges and honors of parenthood have nothing to do with who was there at the conception - Lou was a testimony to that. Even if Angelo ever got his raggedy act together, he could never overshadow or devalue all that Lou had done for us over the years.

"Hey, people," Ashley said coming back into the living room after hanging up their coats. "Where's everybody else?"

"Quinton just went to get in the shower," I told her.

"And Granddaddy is still asleep," Tia said. Turning to Tamicia, she whispered. "Let's go and get him!"

Tamicia looked a little shy about that, but her little cousin wasn't having it and pulled her to the stairs.

Ashley watched the two little ladies scamper up the steps. "I just hope Lou is ready to wake up!"

"Oh, you know he'll love it," I responded. We all knew that Lou had the heart of a mother lion. It could be soft and affectionate one minute but ferocious the next if somebody messed with his family. And like I said, just because he was involved only in the conception of Quinton, never once had he introduced us as "Anna's girls" or "my stepdaughters," and never once was there an argument during which the words "you are not my father" passed our lips. We never considered ourselves to be half or step anything - just one big family.

We soon heard loud, shrill giggles coming from upstairs, which must have translated in dog to "Come on, Chaka!" because our Labrador went bounding up the stairs and in less than a second, the ceiling reverberated with the noises of a happy home filled with love.

"So what's up?" Ashley asked.

"I'm getting a divorce." I flopped down on the sofa, thinking that it definitely did not get easier. My sister sat down, exchanging a glance with Mommy. She didn't register any real surprise.

This was getting on my nerves, and I finally snapped. "Why isn't anyone shocked?"

My sister glanced again at my mother, and I asked, "All right, how many conversations have gone on between you two about my marriage?"

Ashley retorted, "Probably the same number that you and Mommy have had about me, talkin' 'bout, 'she should find a man who doesn't live so far away and start thinking about marriage.'"

"So . . . did you all see this coming?" I asked.

"No," Ashley said slowly, "but . . ."

"Wait . . . you all didn't like him, right?" I asked angrily, and this time the glance that passed between them said it all. For some stupid reason, I felt I needed to defend Malcolm and blurted out, "Malcolm is handsome, smart, a wonderful father, and the best thing that I ever brought home." *Now why did I go and say that?*

Everything Mommy had been holding back came rolling out. "How could I decide if I liked him or not? I never really got to know him."

"How can you say that? He was your son-in-law for almost two years and has been in my life since high school."

I really wanted to squash this before it could begin, but Mommy was geared up. "Yes, Malcolm was my son-in-law, but he never talked to me. I would try to initiate a conversation and - don't get me wrong - he was never rude, but he always floated on the boundaries of this family - like he didn't want to be included."

"It wasn't that, Mommy - he was just quiet." I was giving him credit where none was due. Actually, there were times that I would try to get Malcolm to participate in family discussions and sometimes pray that he would say something on his own, but he never did.

"Who's quiet?" Lou called out, coming down the stairs, carefully balancing the two little girls in his arms. "Hey, does anyone know these two waifs?" he asked, swinging them around.

"When are you going to tell Tia?" my mother whispered.

"Oh, today or tomorrow." *When I no longer feel like I'm going to throw up when I think about it which could mean when she's eighteen or so.*

The rest of the afternoon was spent in preparing dinner. When it was ready, my mother went to the bottom of the stairs and called up. "Quinton!"

Suddenly there was the thunderous sound of my brother's size ten shoes pounding down the stairs. After setting the table, everyone sat down while my sister and I grabbed plates to fill for the girls, but right away, Mommy and Lou said that they would do it. I looked at Ashley and smirked because for all our parents' talk about wanting to be free of children and have the house to themselves, we knew they were lying through their teeth.

Lou bent over toward Tia and Tamicia. "I made these drumsticks just for you little ladies," he said with great seriousness, "and they must be touched by my hands and your hands only." He then turned to my little brother and asked sternly, "What? You can't put on a decent shirt for dinner?"

We all looked over at the shirt that glorified some new gangsta rap group.

Blushing furiously, Quinton excused himself and went to change his shirt.

"And you'd better hurry up before all that's left is your mother's food," Lou called after him, sending a wink to my mother who then told the little girls to make sure that their grandfather didn't get any of *her* food.

Just as I was about to sit down, Tia asked, "How's Daddy?"

"Fine. He sends his love to you, and oh . . ." I sat down and gave her two kisses on each cheek. "He sent those, too." I thought to myself that *I* would never again get any kisses from Malcolm, and with that thought, suddenly my appetite vanished. But when Quinton came back into the dining room and flipped off my baseball cap, putting it behind his back as I grabbed for it, I knew that it was going to be okay. Even though the next few days, weeks, months weren't going to be easy, I congratulated myself for having made it through the minutes and seconds that had already passed. *Yeah, I may be a little woozy, but I'm still standing.* And raising my fork to begin the delicious meal, surrounded by my family, I knew I was not alone.

CHAPTER 4

The week dragged by very slowly. I called in and told the office that I had a bad case of the flu and was taking a few days off. I knew that didn't go over very well with those people since they came in no matter what - with all kinds of viruses and things. But, so what - they would just have to deal with it. I spent the time puttering around the apartment, getting Malcolm's things together to send by UPS to his lovenest in New York. His prized bike went out on the balcony where it could sit and rust for all I cared.

There was no word from him by Friday, and I took the next step in rebuilding my life; I went to seek legal counsel. The law firm was downtown off Pennsylvania Avenue. The elevator deposited me on the eighth floor, and I headed toward the end of the hall to the familiar offices that read Lipinsky and Craig. Douglas, the receptionist, announced me and said that Mrs. Craig would be with me as soon as she finished with her call. Douglas was a parolee, but always very poised and professional, having adapted well to this job that was a haven, somewhere between hustling and flipping burgers.

I sat down in the waiting area, declining Douglas' offer of coffee or tea, thinking about whether I was doing the right thing, but knowing full well that there was no turning back.

"Jewel! Hello." The founder of this small law office came striding down the corridor.

"Hello, Mr. Lipinsky." I stood and greeted the elderly gentleman.

"So! Are you here to take the busy Jasmine out to lunch?" he inquired good naturedly.

"Uhm . . . no. I'm actually here to discuss a legal matter with her." I was slightly embarrassed.

He frowned and asked if everything was all right. *All right?* Far from it, but I only wanted to recount the drama once so I said, "Nothing I can't handle."

He looked at me with kind eyes that were clouded with worry for me.

I liked Mr. Lipinsky because he was a man with a lot of heart. He had arrived in the United States right after the holocaust at the tender age of six, a survivor of the concentration camps where his entire family died, his mother just two days before the liberation. A Jewish family took him with them on one of the many boats that set sail for America, leaving a crippled Europe behind.

Abe lived in various foster homes after arriving in America. Growing up, he studied and worked hard and eventually put himself through law school. The day he opened his practice, there was no fanfare or anyone to help him celebrate his success. He merely went to the one-room office that he was renting in a cheap section of town, opened the door, and set to work.

Mr. Lipinsky's first clients were struggling African-American businesses, primarily founders of the U and 14th Street corridors. His rates were fair, and he treated each minority client not just humanely, but with respect, which was a luxury for blacks in that era. The African-American pioneers embraced the sharp Jewish man who represented them when no one else would. Most remained his clients, and to their ranks were added succeeding generations of would-be entrepreneurs.

Mr. Lipinsky took one of my hands in his old, gnarled ones and said, "If there is anything that I can do for you, young lady . . . but I know that you are in good hands with Jazz . . ." He was interrupted by the door opening from the other side of the reception room.

I was greeted by Jasmine Craig, Mr. Lipinsky's partner but more importantly, my close friend. "Hey, Jewel, come on in."

"Make sure that you two get something to eat later," Mr. Lipinsky ordered. "Charge it to the firm."

"Abe, we all get paid real well here . . ." Jazz began in a disapproving voice, but Mr. Lipinsky cut her off.

"What? You don't plan to eat something? Doug? You hungry today? Of course you are - you're still growing. Jazz, let Doug order himself something and charge it to the firm. And if you happen to order something for yourself, well then . . ."

Jazz folded her arms across her chest. "Abe, as I said, we all get paid real well to work here." Jazz directed her gaze at Doug.

She had taken him under her wing, making sure that he allocated his paycheck wisely, and at her direction, Doug had been brown bagging for some time.

Mr. Lipinsky headed back into his office before Jazz had a chance to continue the debate.

She smiled at the retreating back and asked Doug what he had a taste for before turning to me with her million-dollar smile. "What's up, girl?" She gave me a big old hug.

Jazz is about five feet, ten inches tall and solid. Her height was exaggerated by a pair of hunter green high heels to match her double-breasted business suit. New baby dreads were held back from her face by a colorful head scarf. She looked the epitome of a successful black woman. Mr. Lipinsky had hired her after their first meeting, sure that she would be the fire that would keep his little practice going.

In addition to her professional career, Jazz was also a wife and mother of six children, ranging from the oldest of thirteen down to the baby of three. Jazz claimed she wanted to have it all by the time she was thirty and damned if she didn't do it. Fortunately, her husband, Bryce, had been understanding of her goals. When she first started law school, it was Bryce who supported their growing family as a mechanic, working on the cars of friends and friends of friends until he raised enough money to open his own garage. Thanks to a wretched hoopty Malcolm and I once owned, we became good friends with the Craigs.

When Jazz completed the bar on the first try and started practicing, Bryce told her to put her money away for their future - that he was capable of taking care of his family and she could take care of them later when he was too old to bend under the hoods of cars.

I always thought it was awesome the way Jazz maneuvered home and work. Not one of her children ever felt neglected - she could swing a child on one hip, shoo another into the tub, while handing out advice to the teenager, and still keep on top of her legal caseload. Even though the children felt her love, it was Bryce who did the lion's share of raising them. He usually fixed breakfast and dinner and ferried the children to the doctor and piano lessons. But their somewhat unusual relationship worked. Bryce and Jazz - the two of them - did this dance that caused their kids to fall into the same rhythm, and a lifetime of family harmony came into being.

Right now, Jazz was in the middle of a brutal court case which took up most of her time in research, so I felt a little guilty coming to her; but my insecurities told me I needed someone who cared about me to get me through this, and I knew that she would never forgive me if I went to someone else.

Her dimples deepened when she smiled at me. "How did you know that I needed a distraction today?"

"Well . . ." I began as she shut her door, "I'm here as a client."

Immediately the warm and open smile began to fade. "Okay. Here, let's sit down."

We went over to the miniconference table that sat on the other side of her huge office.

"Okay," I said, taking a deep breath as she sat back watching me expectantly. "I need to know how to file for a divorce." My eyes never left hers, and hers never wavered.

She sighed. "I see."

"If you feel too close to the situation, I completely understand. I just want to know what to expect because this isn't like something I've been studying," I said ruefully.

"No, of course not. And of course I'll represent you."

"But do you have time? I know you have this other case you've been talking about."

"Girl, please," she said with mock indignation, "I am here for you. But, Jewel . . . what happened?"

I sat back and went through the whole sordid tale and then brought up custody. "See, my worst fear is that he's going to finish school, marry this Annette person, and then take Tia away from me." And that was it in a nutshell. That was the fear that had sent me down here. "Jazz, I'll be able to deal with losing Malcolm, but I cannot lose my child."

Jazz held up her hands. "Whoa! Let's take this one step at a time." She went over to her desk and buzzed her assistant. "Crystal, I need you to get the paperwork to file for a legal separation."

I began protesting that I wanted a divorce, not a separation, and I wanted to get this over with as soon as possible.

"I know, Jewel, but it doesn't quite work that way. To start with, you two can get together and hammer out the custody arrangements and child support. Since Malcolm is still in school I don't think that you'll have to worry about who will be the custodial parent, but you both may want to consider joint custody for Tia's sake."

I opened up my mouth, but Jazz read my mind, saying, "Unless you become a crackhead and leave Tia at the bus station for a week or so, there is no way that Malcolm can get complete custody of Tia. The only thing that will happen when he gets through with school and starts work full-time is that he'll have to pay more in child support."

When Crystal came in with the papers, I felt like I wanted to melt into the carpet. I mean it felt like everyone would know that I failed at keeping my marriage together - that everyone was judging me, whispering that I must have thought I had it all, and now look at me. I sat staring at the tabletop, willing myself to become invisible.

After Crystal left, Jazz began separating the forms. "Okay, first we fill these out, and I send them over to the courts to be filed. Next, Malcolm will be served with the same papers in New York at which time he will have six days to contest."

I snorted, knowing there would be no chance of that.

"I'll need the fee at the time of filing." She looked over at me as if it pained her to be charging me for this.

"How much does it cost?"

"Jewel, it varies." Jazz wasn't being coy; she was trying to be honest without scaring me to death.

"Okay." I thought about what bills would be going unpaid.

Giving a little shake of her head, she said. "Look, we can bill you so you can pay monthly." She rolled on, "Once everything has been filed, and if it goes uncontested, a year later it will be finalized."

Hello? Did she say a year!

"Jazz . . . a year?!" I was still sure that I had misheard, but she just nodded her head slowly.

"Come on, I was married in less than an hour and it only cost about thirty dollars!" I almost wailed. "Why . . ."

Jazz patiently explained that the delay was a cooling off period - a way to try and keep families together especially when children were involved.

"Even if your husband obviously doesn't want you?" I sat back, angry and frustrated at the unfairness of it all.

Jazz took my hand from across the table. "Jewel, I am so very sorry, but I will do everything I can to help both as your attorney and as your friend to get you through this." I looked up, realizing that it wasn't her fault, gave her hand a squeeze, and sighed.

Together, we set to work preparing to break down what was left of what the courts thought could be a salvageable marriage ... even though for me, it had ended forever seven days before.

CHAPTER 5

Despite my valiant efforts to block out the distractions of a not too typical day in the office, and yes, as much as I tried to skip over it, Valentine's Day was here again. I heard the receptionist at the front desk buzz Tammy to let her know that flowers had arrived for her.

Tammy's gushing voice trilled through the office. No one would ever guess that the producer of that annoying sound was a sistah. "Really?!" She performed like she was totally surprised. She probably had called her husband to make sure that the delivery was on schedule.

I thought to myself that too much emphasis was put on days like this - they almost had major holiday status now. I really felt that way, not just because there would be no flowers delivered anywhere for me today.

A rushed-looking delivery man walked in carrying a large bouquet of long-stemmed red roses tied off with a big red ribbon going around a crystal vase. I guess a balloon would have been too ghetto.

"Oh, my goodness!" Tammy's drippy, phony "I'm so shocked" voice echoed through the office, and the whole pack of Stepford wives came running. Now tell me, why would you want to send an arrangement like that if you planned to see each other later on at home unless you were both trying to impress everyone with how much you loved each other?

"Oh, Tammy, is that real crystal?" Sue, our resident haughty culture snot, would overlook the flowers and look at the container. Sue's bigotry wasn't based on color so much as on what you could afford. She thought that unless you were able to afford the very best, then you were underprivileged and therefore not worth her interest.

Very petite in a binge and purge kind of way, everything about Sue screamed high-priced chic, from the top of her frosted, feathered hair to the soles of her suede high-heeled pumps. At one time Sue had been the perfect trophy wife, but now despite her best efforts, the tarnish was showing. Having lost the battle with make-up concealers, she now spent her inflated salary on nips and tucks, doing everything she could to petrify the aging process. Sure, it hid the wrinkles, but the desperation it brought to the surface was far more revealing than any amount of candles on a cake. Besides, all the rearranging was not going to stop her husband from continuously dipping into the various fountains of youth around town.

But at least her husband is still with her!

And at what price? 'Cause you're on a serious trip if you think I would ever put up with that foolishness.

True. But, unlike you, at least she knows why he's stepping out.

Oh, please Lord, if You've ever loved me just a little, give me just a teeny-weeny stroke. Just enough to kill the cells in that annoying part of my brain!

"I don't know about the vase but these flowers are unacceptable." The disgust was evident in Tammy's tone.

Oh, here we go!

Paula tried to reason with her. "What's wrong, Tammy? Only two of them look closed, but the rest look fine." I could see the concern pulsing from Paula's big brown eyes. Paula was the nicest of the bunch. Very tall and healthy, she was the all-American girl type. Thick thatches of red hair, a dusting of freckles floating on a creamy complexion would have you guess her age to be way below her thirty plus years.

Dina made a comment that implied that perhaps Tammy's husband had not patronized one of the "better" florists. A self-proclaimed Jewish-American Princess with a lot of money, but no class, Dina lived in the richest of the suburbs and never drove through Washington after dusk, afraid that black gangs hunted Jewish people and carjacked their huge American-made tanks.

Dina would say such insensitive things - like the time we were talking about corncakes. She didn't know what they were so I explained that back in the day you would put corn or other fillers in the pancake batter to stretch it out. "Why would someone do that?" she asked, and I broke it down for her, that sometimes you did what you had to do to get by. Dina just sighed and said, "I am so glad that I never had to be bothered with anything like that."

Or the time, Dina came into the office by mistake, forgetting that Martin Luther King's Birthday was a holiday. The next day, she told her friends she wished she lived in Arizona! But Dina was typical of white people who feel free to spout the first thing that comes into their head. I had learned to put up with a lot of that sort of thing on my job. I remember the shocked silence from the whites when they found out I listened to Beethoven. And when they found out that my brother had turned me on to him, you could have caught a ton of flies in their open mouths - a young, black male who appreciated Beethoven? Just another reason why I was so intent on finishing school as soon as I could so I could get out of that office. Of course they nearly fell out when they found out I was studying medicine - they thought I should be happy to be in a deadend job in their office forever.

The next thing I knew Tammy was on the phone calling the florist. Glancing at Tammy, I tried to figure her out once again. I can't trust an African-American who has not one friend of her own race. When she didn't know who a very famous African-American poet was, one that even white folks were familiar with, well, I was through.

Once I tried to turn her on to one of the salons that I'd been to up in Rockville, but when I started giving her directions to the little Jamaican beauty salon, she stopped me quick, explaining that she didn't go to that part of town. Fine, she could let her hair keep breaking off for all I cared, going to those salons in the malls where you know they don't know anything about black hair.

"These are substandard flowers!" Tammy argued into the phone, insisting that her husband paid too much for them to look like this. "Well, did you look at them before they were sent out?" she asked, her voice dripping with venom. There was a pause and then she said, "Yes, that will be fine" and hung up, sitting back feeling very pleased with herself. "They're going to send out another bunch," she said smugly.

"Oh, Tammy, you are such a brat," Sue laughed.

"Come on, I need a smoke break behind all this," Paula said, and they all went like one big collective mind and got their coats and cigarettes, the sound of their laughter suddenly muffled behind the closing of the door.

I sat there shaking my head and turned back to my work. A little while later, the same delivery man came with a new arrangement, and this chick was still dissatisfied because there was no note of apology attached. Moreover, she felt she should be able to keep the original arrangement. When the delivery man said he couldn't do that, she offered him ten dollars for them, which he also declined. Tammy was steamed. "Fine! Just see if my husband ever uses your company again," she said, turning to get the original bunch. "Wait! Which is which?" She began laughing at her own stupidity. "Oh, here!" she said, thrusting the vase at him.

He turned and walked out of the office after Tammy dismissed him by turning her back on him and coming over to my desk.

"It must be hard having your husband so far away, especially on days like this," she began, but I knew that Malcolm didn't have to be in New York for this Valentine's Day to suck. I just smiled and agreed. I had decided I wouldn't tell them about my divorce since it was none of their business.

Tammy continued, her saccarine sincerity slowly giving me a toothache. "I was going to try to get him to sell me the other flowers at a discount so that I could give them to you."

I sat there with this blank look on my face. *Wait a minute, does she think that's supposed to make me feel better? Giving me flowers that weren't good enough for her? Am I supposed to be grateful that she's thinking about me, implying that my husband won't?* Tough choice since I found both possibilities to be truly insulting. But I am a lady so I took a deep breath knowing that she was doing this just to dig under my skin, because nobody could be this stupid on purpose.

"Thank you, but I don't think that I need anyone to look out for me on Valentine's Day or any other." I said this syrupy sweet. And with that I turned off my monitor and headed out the door to school knowing that my ingratitude would be the topic of the next smoke break.

The day went from bad to worse when I got to school. In light of it being Valentine's Day," my instructor began, "it only seems fitting that we have a little test on . . .," and he dramatically held up a blank diagram . . . "the heart." I sat there stunned. I knew some of it but not all. I turned and looked at my classmates on either side of me, and we all just sighed and tried to figure out how far this would bring down our average.

By the time I picked up Tia from Malcolm's mother and got her in the door of our home, I was so very ready for this day to be over. There was a card and a little teddy bear for Tia from her father, but of course nothing for me. Not that I expected anything - Malcolm's and my situation would present a real challenge to the greeting card industry - but it hurt nonetheless.

"Come on, let's get you into bed," I said, shutting the door with my foot since my hands were full with my sleepy daughter. I didn't feel like wrestling with her coming up the stairs, so I just carried her. Plopping her down on my bed, I took off her coat and hat and then my own. Tia scooted up to the headboard, and turning on one of her programs, curled up on the pillows with her new bear.

"Will you sit there while I jump in the shower real quick?" I asked.

She nodded yes, without taking her eyes from the screen.

"She's still sleepy," I thought to myself, and I started peeling off my clothes. "With my luck she'll try to take that nap Malcolm's mother said she wouldn't take this afternoon, and then I'll never get to see ER in peace because she'll be up all night."

I put the shower cap on my head and turned on the shower. Waiting for the hot water to kick in, I went back to my room to shut the bedroom door to deter any roaming tendencies that might surface in my child. Tia was still involved in the television but looking a little more awake, and I reminded her to stay right there or come in the bathroom if she wanted to keep me company.

Pulling back the shower curtain, I stepped under the nice warm water and sighed. All day I had avoided thinking about Malcolm. Not even with all the flower deliveries did I feel bad. Even if he had been here, he would never have done something like that. He just wasn't that romantic. "Or maybe he is," I mused, " . . . just not with me."

I placed the jets of the handshower right at the base of my neck, trying to relieve some of the tension. In the past, if Malcolm were home, I would be getting all dolled up and perfumed for him, I thought, as I lathered up my washcloth with plain old soap. He would be in there with Tia while I showered, and then we would play with her until she fell asleep . . . and then what? There had been very little romance lately and the sex had been just that - not really making love.

In the last few weeks I'd been forced to really look at what my life had been like with Malcolm, and there were a lot of things that I hadn't seen or only saw the parts that I wanted to believe in - like the fact that whenever we had sex it was always because I initiated it - no, be real, I begged for it. And it was always from behind, either doggie-style or the spoon position. At the time, I thought it was a more satisfying position for both of us, but was it because he couldn't deal with looking in my face during the act? Was it so bad for him that he didn't even think that he could fake it? When I really thought about it, I couldn't remember the last time we had shared a passionate kiss. That sent me ducking under the water to rinse the unpleasant thoughts from my mind - to run down the drain like the water, far away from me.

Sighing, I reached down and turned off the faucets, trying to shake the gloom that had been particularly heavy all day. As I was toweling off, I realized that I could still hear the sound of running water. Pulling back the shower curtain, I gasped at the sight that greeted me. There were at least two inches of water on the floor, and the toilet was steadily running over making the water even deeper. Right in the middle of all this stood Tia, her eyes huge and almost trancelike as she stood in her stocking feet watching the water pour onto the floor.

"Tia!" I said, stepping out onto the soggy floormat soaked with toilet water. "Don't just stand there in all of this!" I grabbed her by the arms and lifted her out of the lake of dirty water. Then the cotton balls came floating past me on the floor. "Tia, what did you do?!" I demanded and deposited her onto my bed.

"I was cleaning my bear," she answered in that voice that always implied that I was crazy for not noting the obvious.

"Didn't I ask you not to touch anything?" I responded sharply. "Now look at this mess!" I moved out of her way so that she could get a good view. "And do you know who has to clean this up?" I asked, throwing off the towel and pulling out a pair of underwear from my top drawer. "Me!" I said to the back of my little girl's bowed head. The phone began ringing as I pulled a teeshirt from out of my closet, yanked it down over my head, and went to answer it.

"Hello?" I answered, clearly annoyed, shoving my arms through the openings of the shirt.

The voice of my sister Ashley greeted me warmly. "Happy Valentine's Day!"

I sighed because I was really not in the mood for this.

"Where's my niece?" She was oblivious to my mood which only made it worse.

"If she knows what's good for her, she'd better be hiding," I muttered, looking around the kitchen for a mop but knowing that I really didn't own much of one, since we lived in an apartment with wall-to-wall carpeting.

"Why? What did she do?"

"She decided not to listen to me and flushed cotton balls down the toilet."

Ashley started to laugh, which really ticked me off.

"Well, she's just a baby," she began, but I didn't want to hear a supermom sermon, so I said bye and hung up the phone.

I went into the bathroom with my pitiful mop and tried to figure out where to begin. I bent down to pick up the soaking floor mats and looked for something to wrap them in to keep them from dripping across the apartment while transporting them to the washing machine. I grabbed the towel I had dried off with and used that and duck walked out to the washer hidden in the closet outside Tia's bathroom.

"Tia! Will you please go and sit down somewhere?!" I fussed at my child after I almost knocked her down, she was following so closely and quietly behind me. I slipped on my sneakers and used the plunger to unclog the toilet. Once I was sure it was flushable, I began the task of cleaning up the water. Pouring bleach into the standing water, I started mopping. "This is just great!" I thought after ten minutes of being stooped over.

I felt a little elation when I was able to push the mop through and not have the path cave in with more water. Push, squeeze, push, squeeze. It had a steady rhythm, and I was finished sooner than I thought. *I can't believe this. Malcolm's probably having a nice romantic evening with his precious Annette with no cares or responsibilities, while I'm here mopping toilet water off the bathroom floor with Tia.*

Then it hit me. *Where is Tia?* I checked in her room and didn't see her. Just as I was about to call out, I heard a little voice coming from out of her closet.

"You'd better stay here! You're bad!" Her tone was scornful.

I pulled open the closet door and peeked inside. There amid all of her toys was my little two-year-old, looking not much bigger than her dolls. She was holding her teddy bear and didn't look up when I stooped down to talk to her.

"What are you doing in here?"

"Hiding," she said, staring intently at the bear.

"Hiding?" Then I remembered. I had told my sister that she'd better hide if she knew what was good for her . . . and she had. *Way to go, Mommy.*

"Tia, come on out of there." She crawled out of the closet, and I pulled her the rest of the way until she was sitting between my legs.

"I'm sorry I yelled at you, duckie." I stroked the top of her head and then rested my cheek on it. "It hasn't been such a good day."

"Because you didn't get a present from Daddy?"

"No, not really. Daddy never knows what to get me like he knows what to get you. There's just been so much going on today. I'm afraid you think I was angry with you."

"You're not mad at me?" Tia asked, kicking her little leg up and down.

"No, not like you think."

"But you said on the phone that I better . . ."

I interrupted her. "I know and that was wrong. I shouldn't have said that. I'm not happy that you put cottonballs down the toilet because you know better," I said sternly, "but I am the Mommy and I should have watched you more closely." I gave her a squeeze. "Okay, you and I may as well take another bath," I said, rubbing her cold feet. Then I ran a bath for us in her bathroom with Mr. Bubbles and lit some scented candles. Settling down into the frothy water, I pointed out countries on the map that made up her shower curtain. She would always ask "where's daddy?" and I'd show her New York and Washington, and to her eyes they weren't so far apart. Then we visited Africa, Japan, Australia, with me telling her a little bit about each place. After the bath we climbed into my queen-size to watch the Thursday night lineup, with ER as the highlight.

Tia promptly fell asleep; it was way past her bedtime anyway. I knew that I should carry her to her own bed but she was so precious, and I really didn't want to be alone. I would be lost without her. It was funny because everyone wanted to come and get her for the night or the weekend - to "give me some space." I was like, for what? Tia didn't desert me. Why would I want to get rid of her? It was as if people thought that I couldn't handle any reminders of Malcolm around me. What they didn't get was that she was the best thing I ever got from him.

I snuggled down, cradling her in my arms like I did when she was a baby as exhaustion began to push me towards sleep. Just as I was dozing off, I felt a little kiss on my cheek and a whispered "Happy Valentine's Day, Mommy. I love you." I did what I would have considered unimaginable that day - I smiled.

CHAPTER 6

"Come on, girl, you have got to get out." My best friend, Robyn, was going a mile a minute, trying her best to sell me on the idea of a girls' night out with her and Jazz. Robyn was never down and felt like a good time was always right around the corner. Just the idea of it exhausted me.

Robyn, my girl. My partner in crime. My self-appointed guardian angel. We met when she was finishing up her degree and I was re-enrolling at D.C.'s community college. She was at the end of her second pregnancy, while I was just getting used to the idea of becoming a mother. She and her husband, Frank, were a model for me and Malcolm. A little older than both of us, we related easily to them partly because they also had started their family very unexpectedly with their daughter, Marquette. Now Marquette was twelve and their baby, Nikki, was three.

"Jewel?"

"Hhm?" I answered absently.

"Jewel, are you even considering the idea at all?" She was getting irritated.

"Of course, of course," I answered, only half listening. The rest of my attention had stopped on one of those infomercials for something that allows you to have the tightest, roundest butt in the world, not to mention slim hips *and* thighs in as little as twenty minutes a day without dieting or any other type of exercising!

"Well, what about it?" Robyn drilled. I turned over on my stomach, away from the television, and looked out the window and racked my brain for some excuse for my well-intentioned friend. Lying on the bed and looking at the budding trees standing in the dusk, I wondered if it had only been three months since Malcolm and I split up. On the one hand, my memories of it were so vivid, it seemed like yesterday, but when I thought about the day-to-day grind, and how depression can make you so tired, it felt like five years.

"You can't think of a reason, can you?" Robyn said smugly as if reading my mind, which annoyed me to no end.

"How about I just want to be left alone."

"Well, you've been that for about three months now," she dryly reminded me, "and my dear friend, you should at least try to remember what having a good time was like."

I sighed. It was true. I'd had no life since I filed for divorce, but I didn't seem to know what to do about it. I was twenty-three years old and had planned to be married for the rest of my life. I had cried on the shoulders of my mother and my friends, even tried to get up the resolve to get out and do my own thing - to pull myself out of this empty mourning - but I would lose my nerve and end up coming home and hiding out with Tia for company.

"Well, let me check my schedule . . ."

"Jewel, it's not healthy for you to put so much of yourself into Tia," she chided softly.

"But she's all I have," I said simply - and it was so true.

Robyn laughed. "Well, thanks a lot!"

"Oh, you know what I mean," I replied, moving through the darkened living room to go and check on my baby for the umpteenth time. "It's just that I've been through some serious changes in the last few months and still haven't caught my breath yet." As I pulled the blanket up over Tia's legs, I whispered, "And the last thing I want to do is jump out there into the human pool." I bent over and kissed Tia on her chubby little cheek.

"Well, it's not good for Tia to make her your everything."

This conversation was getting boring. I sank down in the papasan and looked through the balcony window. This had always been my stakeout spot because from here I could look out into the forest of trees or watch the cars pull into the parking lot. I used to sit here and wait for Malcolm to come home. Now I sat and waited for Malcolm to bring Tia home every other weekend.

Robyn continued her lecture. "Look, all I'm asking is that you let us take you out for a few hours. Cry on our shoulders or let us cry on yours," she said with her Robyn sparkle.

"Fine," I thought. Sitting in the dark, always waiting, was getting old.

"Saturday at what time and where are we going?" I conceded, and Robyn began squealing into the phone. "Don't you worry about any details - we'll take care of everything. You just be ready!"

"Yeah . . . ready for what though?" I asked suspiciously.

"Never mind," she gaily replied.

I hung up the phone and reflected on the last few months. It had been a wild ride. After the initial tears, I started getting myself together but it was hard. Whenever I thought about Malcolm, which was all the time, it still felt like someone had kicked me unexpectedly. He was like a friend who had betrayed me. And instead of talking to me, he simply moved on with his life as if I had meant nothing at all. For months, I'd been driving myself crazy trying to figure out what happened and kept tripping over what was real and what I perceived to be real. Because I worked so hard at believing we had the perfect marriage, it was very hard to face the truth.

Malcolm and I never did sit down and discuss what went wrong at all. In fact, for the first month of the breakup, we communicated through e-mail. I would explain to Tia that her father was coming down for the weekend and would stay at Grandma's with her - that since daddy was in school in New York, he didn't get to see Grandma and Granddad very often and this way he could see everyone at the same time. I didn't plan to deal with the issue of why Mommy and Daddy didn't live together until it came up.

When Tia would ask, "What about you, Mommy?" I just gave her a big old hug so that she couldn't see the tears welling up in my eyes. It was so sad that she cared more about my feelings than her father did.

Later I realized that it was a little silly to try to completely avoid seeing Malcolm. He and I would be Tia's parents forever and would have to learn how to deal with each other. I think secretly I wanted to see him - to see if maybe there were some way that we could get past all this even though I knew we couldn't. What I really wanted was for him to come home and tell me how sorry he was and that through some serious therapy we could work this out. But then I would get those mental flashes of him with that beautiful woman, and my fantasies became reality all over again.

I didn't know if Tia had ever met this Annette person and didn't want to deal with it. Right after I found out about this woman, I asked Malcolm to please let things move slowly. If she'd been a secret this long a little more time wouldn't hurt. I could have kicked myself after sending that particular e-mail, wishing that I could get to his computer first and delete it. It's very hard to be grown up when everything seems so unfair.

Picking up the cd remote, I hit play and the sweet melodies of Beethoven's genius came and surrounded me like the blanket I had wrapped around my shoulders.

Why won't Malcolm talk to me? I understood avoidance; he'd always done that, but did he want to completely erase me from his life? He never said a word when I sent him the divorce papers - just signed them and mailed them back.   *Oops! I forgot. Why should he talk to me? He's got a girlfriend! He's got a life! He's the one who walked away.*

As I headed into my bedroom, it came to me. *Wait a minute, girlfriend! Just because he has the answers, doesn't mean that I have to flunk the test.* I looked at my empty bed. The one that had been empty for way too long now and thought, "No, this isn't right. It's time to stop listening to my heart and get with the body parts that are making sense. My head needs grown up male stimulation - flirtation, compliments, and yes, a little ego stroking. And my body needs to have someone hold it just for a little while. I'll go back to being tough and strong later, but I deserve a break for at least one night. I can lie to myself. Make it a romantic adventure. Make it into whatever I want. Isn't that what I did with my marriage? So what if Malcolm doesn't want me, I'm sure that there are a dozen men who do.

That's it, I promised myself as I slid between the cold sheets and moved to the middle of the bed, arranging the millions of pillows I had so in that time frame between being awake and being asleep, I could think for just a minute that I didn't have to fill up this big bed by myself. And when I finally drifted off to sleep, it was with thoughts of moving ahead . . . even as my heart tried to keep me moored to the past.

CHAPTER 7

"Malcolm, you can't just come down and grab Tia whenever the whim hits you." I was trying to control the irritation in my voice.

"Jewel," he began in his patronizing tone, "I came into town early. I wanted to spend some time with Tia since you didn't let my parents bring her up to see me last weekend." This was, of course, a deliberate attempt to make me the bad guy.

"Malcolm, she was sick. Did you want her on a train to New York with a hundred and one fever?"

"Funny - she looks fine now."

"Well, that's the miracle of antibiotics. Malcolm, look, we have a routine, and I ended up making an unnecessary trip to your mother's because you had brought Tia here. Why didn't you just wait there?" I refused to go to the mat and ask why he still felt comfortable enough to use the key to this apartment.

Malcolm must have felt that an argument wasn't advisable because he switched gears. He grabbed Tia in his arms. "Little girl, now that you've had a bath, you smell so good I could just eat you up!" And he began nuzzling his nose in her neck while she squealed with delight. When she laid her head against his neck, I saw him close his eyes and hold her close. "Why don't you go and pick out a story for me to read you before I leave?"

"When are you coming back, Daddy?" Tia asked anxiously. She was just beginning to understand that her daddy would always be living somewhere else.

"Well, I'll be here for eight whole days . . ." Malcolm moved to stand in front of her bedroom door . . . "then again on this day. . ." he said, pointing to the calendar that he had sent, marked with his visiting days. "Now see this day?" He placed a big red circle around some day I couldn't make out from where I was standing. "I'm going to move back down here for good."

"Really?!"

"Yeah!" I chimed in, trying to sound excited. "So why don't you think about how wonderful it will be to be able to call Daddy to come and see you any time you want."

Tia cried, "Goodie!" Malcolm put her down, and she skipped to her room to get a book.

Malcolm turned his attention to me. "Why do you always have to do that?" he asked with more than a little resentment in his voice.

"What?" I asked, clueless as usual.

"Always make it seem like I'm just visiting?"

"Well, that's probably because you are . . . just visiting." The nice voices that we used in front of Tia were replaced by the hushed whispers of annoyance that we usually felt for each other now.

Trying to be blase, I said, "Frankly, I thought you'd be living in New York."

"Why? My daughter is here. New York was your thing. After graduation, I'll find someplace close to Tia."

"And is your Annette going to be joining you?"

"That's none of your business." *There's that wall that comes up whenever I mention his new love.*

"You think not?" I asked, raising my eyebrows ready to hand him a new script. "If Tia will be spending time with you, then Annette will be with her as well, so guess what? That makes it my business."

A sudden smile came on my face when I saw Tia come around the corner trying to balance a book that was almost bigger than she was.

"Daddy, I have my story ready."

"Okay, I'll be right there." Turning back to me, Malcolm announced, "I want to bring Tia back Monday night instead of Sunday . . . if you don't mind?"

"Okay. See, was that so hard?"

"Asking permission to spend time with my child?" And the attitude in his voice made me realize that this conversation, like all the others, would be impossible. I ignored him, and he went to read to Tia.

When Malcolm came out, I was on the phone with Robyn. "Yes, I will be ready at seven o'clock tomorrow. No, I won't have you come and not be here."

I hung up the phone, surprised to see that Malcolm was still waiting. "Is Tia asleep?" I asked, going to the kitchen.

"Knocked out."

My eyebrows raised when I saw him settle at the dinette set.

"Hey, Jewel, I'm sorry about this afternoon."

My heart was melting to the sincere apology in his voice, and I kept my back to him, as he continued. "I just miss doing the little things with Tia."

I bit hard on my lip to keep myself from reminding him who was responsible for the change around here. Instead I just shrugged and said, "No problem." *How difficult would it be to forget the whole thing? For Malcolm to move back into what used to be our room together, and we find our way back to being a complete family.*

"So you have plans this weekend?" he asked casually.

"Yes, Jazz and Robyn are taking me out tomorrow night." *Now, why didn't I let him wonder if it was a date?*

"That's great!"

His enthusiasm threw me. "And why is that so great?" I asked, feeling very annoyed.

"It's just that I think you should get out more, meet some people . . ."

"Look," I said, feeling like someone had just kicked me. "Since I've never asked for alimony, Malcolm, it's not like you have to be in a hurry to marry me off."

Malcolm sighed and sat thoughtfully lining up the salt and pepper shakers while I pretended to wash dishes. After a moment, he rose and left without a word. I stood with my hands still in the soapy water thinking that he could have cared - he could have acted like it mattered a little that I might find someone else. *Well, he doesn't, so get over it!*

* * *

The next night, Robyn had everything arranged for an old-fashioned girls' night out on the town. The plan was to head up to Baltimore's inner harbor area and paint the town red. I had my own ideas about the outing and had packed an overnight bag, along with a pack of condoms and very little forethought. It had been three long months, and it was time to get on with my life.

As I checked myself in the mirror, I realized that I was still young and not too bad to look at. My outfit of choice was a pair of Capri jeans and a white cotton tee shirt. I placed my manicured feet into a pair of white slouch socks and my new spankin' white Keds. The outfit showed off all of the crunches that I had been doing, as well as my athletic legs. Since the separation from Malcolm, I had lost about thirty pounds. The jeans enhanced my butt, which wasn't my best asset, and a push-up bra did wonders for my boobs.

I heard the toot of Robyn's truck from the parking lot, grabbed my stuff, and headed out the door. Robyn was grinning at me from behind the wheel, and Jazz called out, "Girl, you look fabulous!" I thanked her and climbed in.

The bass wafted out of the sunroof to mingle with the warm night air. Flying down Route 50, we fell into a nice, sisterly groove and before long, the road led us to the twinkling lights of Baltimore's Inner Harbor. We left the car on the lot and moved in the direction of the pier.

"Let's stop and get something to drink," Jazz suggested. Jazz liked to party and never missed a chance for fun. Tonight, after a stressful day in court, she was out to blow off steam. Her long, bare, Tina Turner legs began just under the top of a cute, denim miniskirt and continued down into some really high, strappy sandals, and men drooled as she sashayed past.

"So what does Bryce think of handling dependent care tonight?" Robyn teased before giving a wave and a loud "Skeeop" to a group of ladies passing on the other side of the boardwalk. With her hair pulled back in a ponytail, green leggings, pink oversized sweater, and pink and green canvas hightops, Robyn could easily be mistaken for a Morgan State soror, rather than an alumna.

"Girl, you know him. He wanted a big family, and I told him up front that I would drop 'em and keep on going. Anyway, when I get all involved in a case, I get ugly and they practically pushed me out the door!" Jazz laughed.

Thinking about what Jazz and Bryce had, I couldn't help but feel a tug of sadness - that should have been the way it was for me and Malcolm. I shook off the feeling, telling myself, "It didn't happen for me, and I have to accept that."

"I don't want to talk about nobody's kids, no husbands, jobs, dogs, cats, cockatoos!" Robyn announced. "Tonight is ladies' night!"

I could tell that Robyn and Jazz must have noticed my little melancholy. It touched my heart, and I wanted to let them know I wasn't so fragile that they had to avoid talking about their men. "Look," I said, "I love you girls, but please don't feel like you have to dance around issues with me . . ."

Jazz quipped, "Did someone say dance?" That's all she needed to hear.

Robyn and I fell in line, and the mood bounced back to carefree. We cruised around and came up to a large crowd standing around a group of brothers singing along with a speaker of music. They were doing the serious old school stuff, and we joined in patting our feet and clapping with everyone else. The crowd gave a little applause, and after the group broke down into some of the more sentimental tunes, we drifted off in search of a club.

Restauranteurs were trying to jump into the warm weather mode, and all their doors leading out onto the harbor were open. We went inside one that had a pretty good club beat going and pushed our way to a table.

"Let's order drinks before we get lost!" Jazz shouted over the music and signaled for the waiter.

"I'll have a double White Russian," I ordered.

"Ooh, girl! A double to start with? Don't hurt nobody," Jazz laughed.

I laughed back. "Hey! Don't start nothin', won't be nothin!"

"I'll have a vodka tonic." That was Robyn's signature drink.

The music was hot and so was the dance floor.

"Can't wait for someone to ask?" I heard Robyn laugh as I stood up. I shrugged and moved past the couples that were just standing around. When the music hits, I'm there. I headed straight to the middle of the tiny dance space that was packed with what seemed like fifty people all moving and grooving to the beat. One guy who was already dancing with someone gave me a quick up and down while chickie he was dancing with stood there with that "oh, no, you didn't" look. Jazz appeared to my left, moving like anything but a mother of six. She was dancing with a fine Chaka Zulu-looking brother who was trying his best to keep up. Soon we were all dancing and sweating and panting. I was in heaven, and the deejay was my guide.

I finally headed back to the table and spotted Robyn talking to a beefy-looking brother. When I sat down, she introduced him as Marcus.

"Hey!" I shouted over the music.

"Whuzup!" he shouted back in acknowledgement.

Robyn chimed in. "Marcus is from D.C., too, and guess what he does for a living?"

I shrugged.

"He's a detective." I could smell a setup and wasn't ready for Robyn to start making decisions for me, although the brother was on the fine side, if you really liked brawn. A nice, even shade of milk chocolate, with a clean shaven face to match his gleaming bald head, set atop a hulking mass of muscle that the untrained eye might mistake for fat. Had it not been for what seemed to be a naturally cheery disposition, he would have been an intimidating force to encounter.

I nodded while he spoke above the bass. "Yeah, it's funny how you run into more people from D.C. up here."

His eyes had a merriment that could be infectious. Smiling in spite of myself, I asked, "And what are you doing in Baltimore?"

"Me and my partner came up for a conference today and . . ."

I knew I was disappointing Robyn, but before Marcus could finish his sentence, I heard the sounds of my monster favorite jam, a combination of reggae, club, and all bass. "'Scuse me, but that's my jam!"

I was heading for the dance floor when this brother who had been watching me touched my arm. He was all right. Tall, dark, good body, so we hit the floor. Dude put his arm around my waist and just about lifted me off the floor as he wedged his leg between mine. I was like, it is way too hot for this, but I *am* out here tonight for a reason, and his attitude was one of a confident playa, so I went kind of loose and let him lead. Most guys that get all close like that really can't dance, and this guy was no exception. After a few bumps and grinds, I placed my hands on his chest which he mistook for hold me closer and gave me a squeeze. I smiled my prettiest, but gave a little shove. Dancing with a few breaths between us, I started to move. When I looked over, I saw Jazz laughing at me as she spun around. A few beats later my gaze caught Robyn in a serious peekaboo around this tall guy with a small waist, broad shoulders, dreads for days, and muscles you could see dance across his back when he held his hands above his head and gyrated his hips. I couldn't see his face, but whatever he was saying had put a smile on Robyn's face. I was glad to see that at least she was having a good time. *But then why shouldn't she - with a permanent body at home who knows everything about her - how to touch her, hold her, love her, while I'm out here doing what?*

I turned back to my partner who had this expression on his face like we were actually doing it on the dance floor.

Ugh! I gotta lose him because this is not what I'm spending the night with tonight. As much as I hated to leave the music, I excused myself and headed off the floor to go outside.

As I reached the door, I turned back and realized that the guy Robyn was dancing with was Justin, my old classmate! I went on out and just stood there, letting the breeze dry some of the dance sweat from my body and pondering this unexpected turn of events.

I didn't notice a presence coming up behind me until I heard a friendly voice say, "Now, this is too bizarre."

I turned and was face to chest with Justin. He was smiling down at me with the same kindness and warmth as in our last encounter at the train station.

"Hey, Justin!" I smiled, and we embraced in a friendly hug.

Stepping back, he fronted, "Girl, are you following me?"

I played along, saying, "Well, I could ask you the same thing!"

"First to see you at Union Station and then again in the same year after no contact in what - eight or nine years?"

"Stop. You're showing our ages," I laughed.

"No, I would almost think that you're still in high school - you look good." And his gaze spoke volumes about the sincerity of his statement.

"You don't look so bad yourself." Yes, definitely doable I thought to myself as I eyed him as unobtrusively as possible. He was about six feet two with that great athletic body. I noted his tasteful attire - the multicolored shirt like a black canvas on which the artist had brushed broad, colorful strokes, tucked into darkly colored slacks. A small crucifix hung below the hollow of his neck which was gleaming from the sweat he'd worked up on the floor. *Did he look this good when I saw him five months ago? Not that I was in any shape to notice then.*

"Thanks." His smile was so sweet and his eyes so warm, and I found myself leaning toward that warmth like a drunk trying to get out of the cold.

"So how long have you guys been up here?" Justin asked.

"Oh, about . . ." I checked my watch and was shocked to see that we had been there for almost two hours. "A while now," I laughed. "The time just sort of got away."

"Yeah, I'm 'bout ready to call it a night myself."

"Who said anything about calling it a night? I'm still gettin' my swerve on." I started doing a little dance move. "Me, I'm here at least until tomorrow."

"What? You don't have anybody who's watching the clock?"

It was an innocent enough question, but it cut me like a knife. I answered, "No, I'm my own woman, and if the dance floor is safe, I'm 'bout to head back out there." I turned to go.

"What do you mean, 'safe'?" he asked, trying to be heard over the music as we made our way back inside.

"Well, see that brother over there by the bar?"

"Yeah."

"He seems to think that he has exclusive rights to my dance card."

"Oh, we'll take care of that." Justin led me out onto the floor and started to move. He had been a good dancer in school and obviously hadn't lost a thing. We started to bounce, laughing and moving in time to the music. Then the deejay really read my mind - he started out with the Time's *The Walk* and we wopped on with the *Funky Beat* and somewhere in all of that he took us to *All the Way to Heaven* with Dougie Fresh.

Before I knew it, Robyn was standing beside me, informing me that it was time to hit the road.

"All right, I'll walk you guys back to the car." I was reluctant to leave because I hadn't thought of a way to persuade Justin to participate in my cause. We came off the floor and headed over to the table where everyone was in the process of grabbing bags and finishing drinks.

"Yeah, girl, I gotta get home to my little hellions. Bryce is good, but it's not too long before they all wrap that big old bear around their little fingers," Jazz said with mock disgust. "I'll probably find all of them, including him, asleep in front of the Nintendo."

We all started putting down money for the drinks and then headed out onto the boardwalk moving slowly toward the parking lot. A few minutes later we were joined by Justin and Marcus, and I realized Justin must be the partner he had mentioned.

"You want us to drop you off at your hotel, sweetie?" Jazz asked. "You know Baltimore can get a little crazy at night."

"No, I'll be all right," I assured her.

"You're staying up here?" Justin asked, and I just nodded.

"Well, hey, we'll walk you to your place."

Marcus said, "Naw, I'll have to see you later, man. I got some early morning business." Marcus said his goodbyes to us. "It was nice meeting you, ladies. Take it easy."

"How are you going to get back?" I asked my newfound companion.

"I rode up on my bike. It's in a parking garage. What hotel are you staying at?"

"The Marriott." I silently blessed whatever goddess was evidently running things tonight. This was getting easier.

Jazz had sized up the situation, and now she wagged a finger in Justin's direction. "Okay, as long as you be a gentleman and make sure that she gets up to her room. Then we won't have to hunt you down later." She gave me that "you go, girl" little wink. Justin and I waved goodbye, as Robyn put the truck in gear and they drove away.

"Well, let's get you settled in," Justin said, as we started back to the harbor where the activity was winding down.

"Are you sure? I mean, I'm not keeping you from anything, am I?" I silently crossed my fingers.

"No, I'm off tomorrow. What made you want to stay up here?"

"I just needed a change," I said evasively.

"A change?"

"Yeah, see I got this wacko stalking me in D.C., and I'm waiting for the restraining order to kick in."

Justin gave me a little look of surprise, and I struck a pose with my hands on my hips. "What? I can't have someone stalking me?"

"Naw, I mean . . . sure you can," he said, looking flustered, but then adding skeptically, "Are you serious?"

"No, but I did need a change, and we can talk about that another time. Let's head one more time around the harbor, and then I'll go to bed like a good little girl." I smiled sweetly.

We strolled around talking about not much. I didn't want to know him too well on a personal level because I was on a mission, and there was no need of getting too deep.

"What do you do?" Justin asked, maneuvering me around a small crowd of rowdy teenagers.

"Well, let's see," I answered thoughtfully, "I wear many hats. I'm a full-time mother first, a full-time student, and a full-time grunt."

"Okay, I understand the mother and student, but what's a grunt?"

"A grunt," I began, "is what is also known as a receptionist/secretary/administrative assistant."

He still looked a little confused.

"Let me clarify. Because I don't have my degree yet, I get to do the most work in the office - answer phones, take messages, xerox, type, arrange meetings - in other words, work that no one else wants to do, and when I don't show up for work, there is total anarchy, and yet I get to take home the smallest paycheck in the office."

He grinned. "I see you have a real love for your profession."

"No! Which is why I'm working on getting my degree."

"In what field? Wait, let me guess. Business? No? Computers?"

I shook my head again. "Physician Assistant," I said proudly.

"Hhmmm. Impressive. Why did you choose that?"

"Well, if I have to be a minority and work for the majority, I at least want to make a difference for people." The conversation was getting a little too personal for what I had in mind, but I was more than a little buzzed and continued to reveal myself. "The thing that I hate about working in this particular office is that they are so racist. One of them had the nerve to ask me if Malcolm was Tia's father - as if my baby's daddy just has to be lurking in the life of every black woman." I was ranting by now, mostly from the fact that my place of work really did make me sick, but also from the buzz, which probably was what caused me to let slip something way too personal when I said, "That's why I haven't told them about my divorce. You know how people get when they think you need them more than they need you."

"When did you get divorced?" Justin asked quietly.

That stopped me short. "What . . .? How did you know about the divorce?" I demanded suspiciously.

"Let me have a look at you," Justin said and gave me a careful look up and down. "Okay, you're a little farther gone than I thought. Let's get you to your room."

"Just what I was thinking," I murmured.

"Hhm?"

"Oh, I wish something would happen on my job to really freak them out." Alcohol was allowing me to jump freely from topic to topic.

"Where?" he asked.

"My job. Weren't you paying attention? I want to have something exciting happen - you know, like have some mob guy come by with his crew and say that I have to leave for the day and dare them to object." I started giggling at the idea of the bugged out faces of my office. "Then," I continued, wrapped up in my scenario, "I would come back the next day and not say a word. I could almost hear them now, 'Uh, Jewel, is there anything you would like to talk about?' What a bunch of morons." I snorted in disgust.

"Well, if you hate it so much, why stay?"

"Because I need it for now. A girl's gotta eat and pay the bills. Right now, it's my incentive to go to school almost every night."

"Where do you go?"

"The University of the District of Columbia," I said with bravado. "No cracks, please, because it's a first-rate school, but of course they don't see it that way because it's not a private institution - they think it's a place for the underprivileged."

I tried to take the focus off me and asked, "How do you like working for the force?"

"Not bad, but it isn't everything that I thought it would be either. When I first joined, it was to make a difference, but now I feel more like that guy who spent an eternity pushing the boulder up the hill - remember the one that we studied in Greek mythology from Mrs. Bergman?"

"Yeah." I grew nostalgic. "She sure was sharp. Oh, and guess what? I found out that Sister Josephine is still teaching."

"Oh, man!" Justin threw back his head and laughed. "That old girl was my worst enemy. She stayed on my case."

"Because you were so bad."

"Who? Me?" he asked in mock surprise.

"Yes, you!"

"Naw, you must have me confused with someone else."

"Not a chance! You were bad!"

When we reached the hotel lobby, Justin turned to me, saying what a great time he'd had and hoped we could keep in touch.

"Oh, no, you don't," I said, trying to keep the panic out of my voice. "You promised to see me to my room."

"Oh, right. Sure." I thought he sounded a little uneasy, but tough - I had invested all my time in him, and it was too late to look for a replacement.

While we waited for the elevator, Justin caught me staring at him. "Is something wrong?"

"Can I?" My eyes watched my hand move on its own toward one loc that swung independently from the rest. I fingered the twisted hair, amazed at the softness, not thinking about how intimate my action was.

"Jewel?" he said softly.

"Hmm?"
"The elevator is here."
"Oh!"
We headed up on the elevator, and I went deep in myself as I tried to work out a plan, all the same time feeling a little nervous about going through with it. The doors opened, and we walked toward my room at the far end of the hall. When we got there, I was sliding the little electronic key in the lock when Justin starting saying his goodbyes again.

"What, is my company that bad?" I joked, struggling to open the door. The green light finally began flashing, signaling that the door was open.

"No, not at all. It's just that..."

"Then come in and see the view I requested." I pushed open the door and held it aside for him.

He walked past me, and I took a deep breath and closed the door. *Here we go.*

"Wow! This is nice," Justin said, admiring the harbor view.

I reached over and turned out the lamp that sat on the dresser and stood next to him looking out the window. *Maybe he has a girlfriend.*

"You can't get the full effect with the lights bouncing off the window." I reached down and turned out the little sitting table lamp as well. *Maybe he has a wife.*

"Do you see any boats?" I asked, moving across the room and stepping out of my shoes.

"No, it all looks black - like there's nothing out there at all, just a void." *Maybe life just isn't fair.*

Slowly, my shirt went up over my head before I dropped it onto the bed. I knew he was saying something about sailing, but I couldn't hear him because my heart was beating so loudly in my ears as I undid the button on my jeans. Justin must have heard the sound, because he turned around. His curiosity turned to shock because my shirt is gone and I'm standing there in just a pair of unbuttoned jeans, socks, and a push-up bra.

Taking a deep breath and walking over to him, I put my arms around his neck. Nuzzling his ear and his neck I could feel his resistance. *I can do this. Malcolm found happiness in someone else's arms - now I can, too.* Running my hands down

Justin's back, I started pulling his shirttail out and jumped when I encountered his gun. But I was not to be deterred.

"Is that thing loaded?" I breathed into his ear.

"The safety's on," he answered absently. "But, Jewel, what . . ."

"No buts." I never noticed that his hands were still loosely at his sides.

"Jewel, what are you doing?"

There was no mistaking the arousal thick in his voice, and I became charged. "Don't worry, it will be all right." I wanted to kiss those full, slightly parted lips, but that would have made this intimate, and that's not what I thought it should be.

I finally felt him move, reaching up to undo my hands from around his neck.

"Look, why don't we slow down a little?" he asked, trying gently to disengage himself from me.

"No, don't want to," I murmured, as I ran my hands up his back under his shirt, around to his firm abs, and up to his chest. I was startled because the chest I encountered was hairy, and Malcolm's was smooth. *What?* Through the White Russian fog, I was confused.

I felt Justin's body push away, and I clung harder. I tried harder. Pressed my body into his. Tried to take his hands and lead them to my breast. I wanted to feel something, although there was no passion stirring in me - only a searing empty void that threatened to swallow me like the blackness outside the window.

"Please, touch me," I begged and looked up with eyes that couldn't really see. I was drowning, and this was the only person who could save me.

"Jewel, wait. What's going on?" Justin was struggling to get me to let go, and I was clinging to him like a child to a parent after being lost in the woods. I didn't know that I was crying. Didn't realize that agony was smeared across my face. I only knew that until I could get back at Malcolm, until I could do this, I would never be able to move on with my life.

"Help me!" It was almost a sob, and I continued to run my hands over his body. "Just do this for me! With me!"

"I want to help you, but you have to talk to me." He was speaking to me as if I were a trapped animal - cautiously and patiently - and I sensed that I was losing.

Panic took over, and I began pulling at his shirt, kissing his neck and trying to suck on his ears. Anything that would get him to take me. Take away this pain. Nothing could help me but him.

We were both breathing deeply and quickly. I had flashes going through my mind as I saw Malcolm and me in happier times and then I saw him and that woman, moaning, twisting, embracing each other in ecstasy. *Is someone moaning?*

By moonlight across the room, I saw my reflection in the mirror over the dresser, trying to undo Justin's belt buckle, almost clawing at it in my desperation. *I have to do this. Forget about how pathetic you look. Forget your dignity.* Finally I felt Justin's arms go around me as he lifted me up. In my relief, I sobbed, thinking that he was carrying me over to the bed.

"Don't worry. I have condoms in my bag," I whispered, so wrapped up in preparing myself for this first act of intimacy - no, sex - that I didn't realize he had taken me into the bathroom. Before my drunken brain could figure out what was going on, Justin had put me into the shower. As I reached for him, he turned on the showerhead. Icy water poured down on me, and I fought to get away. Pinning me against the wall with one strong arm which also prevented me from falling flat on my face, Justin told me to calm down. I started screaming. "LET ME GO! LET ME GO!"

"Not until you talk to me," he said over the sound of the running water.

I was shaking and sputtering, wondering through my haze if this was some kind of kinky sex thing. Then it hit me. *He doesn't want me!* First Malcolm and now him. *Jewel, you are so stupid!* I began struggling and spitting water because I just wanted to get out of there.

"Jewel, stop fighting!" he ordered.

"Let me go!" Water was going everywhere, but Justin managed to keep me pinned against the wall.

"I will when you stop fighting."

And I did. What was the point? I had lost.

Justin sensed the sudden change; he loosened his grip and starting talking again. "Now, I'm going to turn off the water and help you out? Okay? Jewel? Okay?"

Mutely, I nodded yes, although I was really hoping that he would leave me there to drown.

"Then we're going to go in the next room and talk. Okay?"

Again I nodded, too embarrassed to even look at him.

Justin reached in and turned off the water, oblivous to the fact that he was getting soaked himself. Cautiously, he began moving away from me as if I would bolt past him at any minute, but I had no energy for that so I just stood there dripping. A towel was going over my head and another placed around my torso. I watched the water going down the drain and wished with everything I had in me that I could just liquify and go with it.

"Come on," Justin urged, and I saw that he was holding out his hand to help me out of the tub. *God, this is so humilating!* When I made no move of my own, he gently took my arm and guided me out of the tub and into the main room, then sat me down on the bed and asked, "Does this have something to do with your divorce?"

I winced at that but nodded my head. *What was the point of denying it?*

"And I suppose that I was to be the one to help you get back in the swinging singles scene?"

I nodded again.

"Well," he sighed, "now that I know what my role is, we have a lot to talk about. Apparently I didn't leave a good impression of myself when we were growing up."

He was being so kind. I just wished that he would shut up and leave.

"Jewel, I want to help you."

I just sighed dejectedly.

Justin continued. "But this isn't me. I'm not a hit and run kind of guy."

Go on and rub salt in the wound, why don't you? Of all the men I could have encountered, this one has morals. Who would have thought!

"Look, I'm sorry. I made a very terrible mistake." My voice came out as a croak.

"Yes, you did, but I'm flattered that you chose me and not some lunatic out there - you must know how many crazies there are out there."

His reproach was mild but I still just wanted him to go. I had to end this fiasco. "Please, why don't you just leave? Trust me, I won't go down there and try to give it away again." Now I was sighing and with each breath I felt weaker and weaker, but my knight in shining armor wasn't having it.

"Jewel," he said, squatting down in front of me. "I would like to talk to you. Get to know you again? Help you if I can?" *Okay, not only does he have morals but a social conscience to boot.*

I started thinking about my escape. I'm so good at running away from things. I tried to look up but couldn't so I said to the floor, "That would be really nice, and yes, I really would like to have someone to talk to, but right now, I'm feeling a little queasy. Do you think you could get me a ginger ale from downstairs?" I didn't have to try to sound pitiful because I was already there.

"Sure, no problem," he said, sounding happy that we seemed to have a jumping off point. "Then I can check on my bike. Move it to the hotel garage, or would you rather I take you home now? We can talk back in D.C.?"

"Sure, whatever. I'll just lie down and get my head together," I lied and started to slide back on the bed holding the towel closely around what I was trying so hard to expose a few minutes before.

"Okay, I'll take the key in case you don't hear me knocking and be right back." And he was out the door.

I waited a few minutes and then got up and pulled on some dry clothes. I wrote Justin a quick note explaining that the room was paid for and if there was a charge from the garage to have them put it on my bill. Then I added that he should continue with his life as if this night had never happened. I left the note on the bed and sneaked out of the hotel, wrapping myself in a shroud of humilation, self-pity and extreme remorse. *Why don't things ever go the way I want?*

CHAPTER 8

When I rushed through the door of the office, our weekly staff meeting was in progress. It usually takes about an hour and a half - it's not that we have that much business to report, it just always winds up turning into a social event.

It's rough when you want to leave a job, but the pros outweigh the cons in a major way. The hours and the location enabled me to get to school, take three classes, and still get to my in-laws' to pick up Tia, get home, do a quick run to the playground, and then bath and story. But I was really tired of being regarded as a second-class citizen. As in most offices, people working in so-called support positions are treated with, at best, mild contempt.

Moreover, I hated working in a place where almost everyone was white, especially those in charge. I guess I really find it very difficult to trust whites for the most part. Like you can't discuss racial issues with them - or even movies and plays - without them getting all defensive. That says to me that if we were back a hundred and fifty years ago, I would be Kizzie and they'd be having me call them Massa or Missy. Why else would they feel that way about something perpetrated by their ancestors, rather than themselves, unless somewhere, deep down, they were in agreement? Sometimes at work, I closed my eyes and could almost see me in slave rags dressing or serving those people, and know which ones would keep a whip in hand and which would look right through me as if I weren't even worth thinking about.

As I slid into my seat, Steve, the big boss, gave me a look before saying, "So, let's say that we go around the calendar before we end this." *Okay, another thirty minutes to ooh and ah over the summer plans.*

"Jewel? Do you have anything to add to the calendar?"

I focused on the group that stared at me from around the conference table. "No."

"Oh, Malcolm's not taking some time to come down and see you?" Tammy asked as all eyes became glued to me.

Didn't I already say I had nothing to report for the calendar? I looked at her and said in a level voice, "I don't plan to take off any time from the office." The tone of my voice discouraged any more probing.

I was glad that I hadn't told them about my break-up. There is nothing more misunderstood than the single black mother - it would just be another way they would see me at a disadvantage - a prime candidate for ghetto poster child. They already assumed because we were African-American that my little family was hovering on the edge of poverty.

"Jewel, you have a call from a Detective Baptiste," the receptionist informed me as I went to my desk.

"Please take a message," I said curtly.

"She's not here right now."

I gritted my teeth because I really hated that girl. She was so unprofessional and inept. She would come in and spread all of her business - and everyone else's as well. I had dubbed her the badger - a stupid but dangerous creature which moves about life thinking only of its own personal gratification.

"He said that it was very important that you call him back." Her voice came screeching at me over the intercom.

"Uh, oh, what have you done, that the cops are calling you on the job?" Dina asked with that phony laugh tinged with the hope that I would really tell her.

"Ha! Ha! Wouldn't you like to know?" I countered in an equally phony voice.

My intercom buzzed, but instead of waiting for me to pick up the handset, the badger was yelling again into the mike. "Robyn Taylor is on line two for you."

Before I could even get out a hello, Robyn said in her deep, breathy voice, "I really think that since you got 'Miss I Can't Enunciate All My Words,' your organization has been drifting into slow decline."

I laughed. "You say that every time you call."

"But it's true. She sounds so . . . so . . ."

I stopped her as she searched for an adjective. "All right, now, don't go and get all highsidity on me."

"The word that comes to mind is clueless. Yes, girlfriend, we have a lingo but when you're the minority, you have to create that illusion of who you aren't but need to be to get by."

"True dat, true dat. But what can you do? Some people get it and some don't."

"So, what's up?" Robyn asked. "I got this strong telepathic urge to call you."

"It's the same old, same old, just a different day."

"Tell me about it. What's up for this evening? Do you have school tonight?"

"No. Just studying. Right now I'm attempting to learn medical terminology via ER."

"Where's the baby going to be?" *She thinks that she's sounding innocent, but I can already see where this conversation is going.*

"At home with me. Where else?"

"Well, I was kind of hoping that I could have her for a little sleepover. Nikki has no school tomorrow and would love to see her little soulmate."

"But I was thinking that Tia and I would do the facial thing together . . ." .

"Hey, Jewel, you have to let her be a little girl. She hasn't had a sleepaway since you and Malcolm broke up. You don't want to ruin her fun just because you're lonely." And of course that was it to a tee. I didn't want to go home to that empty house. I still hadn't defined a role for me as a nonwife, even though it had been six months since Malcolm and I broke up.

"So what's it gonna be? I've taken care of everything. It's my day off."

"Okay," I sighed, knowing when I was beaten. "But let me see how Tia feels about it, especially since she hasn't been away for a while."

"No problem. Matter of fact, I'm getting ready to leave here to pick up Nikki and then we can swing by and get Tia. Do you want to call Mama Stone and let her know?"

"Damn, you're really pushing this. Do you feel my child is that deprived of good company?" I was more than a little annoyed that Robyn felt the need to rescue my baby.

"Well, telling her that Cinderella gives the prince the best years of her life and then he turns around and leaves her for Snow White doesn't make for the best of mother-daughter talks."

"She has to be prepared." I half-laughed at the grim picture painted by Robyn. "I'll call and tell Ma Stone that you're coming to pick Tia up. But you have to bring her by here so if she decides not to go, she can come home with me."

"She'll be fine. But yes, of course, otherwise I know that you'll hunt me down."

"That's right."

Robyn changed the subject. "So have you heard from your friendly detective friend?" she singsonged.

"Don't go there," I warned.

"Why? You're the one who needs to get out. And didn't you say that he's been calling you?" I could feel her fingers holding my cheeks so that I would have to look her directly in the eye.

"No, I haven't spoken to him, and if he wants to continue to have conversations with my answering machine, that's on him. And by the way, I'm not lonely, and I don't have much time and . . ."

"A million other excuses." Robyn sighed with exasperation.

"I'll see you all in a little bit." I was equally exasperated. "Bye."

"This ain't over yet."

"Yeah, yeah, yeah."

"See you in about an hour, so look out for me."

"Will do."

I hung up with a sense of dread. My evening routine seemed like a huge void now. Thursday was my favorite day. It's the day before Friday, the hectic rat race is almost over, there are no evening classes, and ER is on the tube. And now all the events leading up to that moment special were ruined. I sat, submerging myself in the dull repetitive cycle of afternoon work.

Around two or so, the badger buzzed and informed me that Robyn Taylor was waiting for me downstairs. I rushed down the four flights and into the lobby where I was assaulted by my delightful two-year-old and her best friend Nikki, Robyn's three-year old.

I scooped them both up and hugged them tightly. "Who let these urchins in here?"

They both giggled, with fat cherub cheeks glowing, completely unaware of the bright ray of sunshine they brought to my day.

"Well, don't you look nice today, Miss Nikki," I commented, admiring her little denim vest with matching skirt. Her legs which were becoming coltish and losing some of their stumpiness came down into some very smart Buster Brown buckle shoes. That's one thing I admire about Robyn; she always allows her children to look like children. I remember one Easter we went all over town trying to find a suitable dress for her oldest daughter, Marquette. And it was a disaster. All of the outfits were straight sheaths that hugged her budding breasts and little fanny too close. It seemed that everyone wanted little mommy images instead of little girls, but with some mix and match ingenuity, Robyn managed, as usual, to create a suitable outfit for Marquette.

"I'm goin' to Auntie Rob's house!" Tia cried, full of little girl excitement. "We're gonna play nail salon!" My hopes of her wanting to spend the evening with me were dashed, but I was always so happy to see her excited.

"Nail salon, huh?" I gave Robyn a pointed look and said to her, "You know how I feel about that. Plus, Tia can't always keep her fingers out of her mouth yet."

"Girl, you know that it's all in fun and that this stuff comes off in the tub."

While we were talking, the smoking brigade came off the elevator, and I instinctively put myself between them and the girls, already knowing the scenario to come.

"Hi, Jewel. Ooohh! Is that your little girl?"

"Yes. This is my daughter, Tia, my friend, Robyn Taylor, and her daughter, Nikki."

Everyone said their hellos.

"Are you coming to see Mommy work?" *Hell no. Like I really want to show her what not to strive for.*

"No, they were just leaving," I said, moving everyone to the double doors.

"She looks just like you. And look at all that hair."

They all just sort of stared at my child and clucked around. Robyn said to me, "You have all the numbers where we'll be. We'll probably stop and get something to eat before we head home."

"No junk, please," I said, ever the mother.

"Are you kidding? We're going down to the wharf for some seafood."

"Oh, there's a fish market right down the street - I think they're pretty inexpensive." Tammy couldn't just eavesdrop on the conversation, but had to participate as well.

I gave Robyn a "here they go again" look.

"No, I'm taking them out to eat, like in a restaurant," Robyn informed her.

"You're kidding?!" Tammy looked like Robyn had said that she was going to eat them. "Are you taking anyone else?"

"No." Robyn couldn't see where this was going but I had heard it at least a thousand times before.

"God, there is no way that I could take two kids out that small by myself - and to a restaurant too? No way," Sue said, blowing smoke toward the skies.

Robyn was clearly annoyed by their conversation and told them in a somewhat condescending tone, "You can teach children while they're young and instill a positive attitude about good behavior - then you don't have to be afraid to take them anywhere. Come on, girls, let's go."

Tia stretched up for me to pick her up which I did in a big hug. Balancing her on my hip, I bent down and kissed Nikki. "Take care of my baby for me," I whispered in her ear.

"I will," she answered very seriously. And I knew that she would. She adored her big sister, Marquette, and wanted someone to take care of just like Marquette looked out for her.

I held open the door and helped the girls into the back of Robyn's new Mercedes SUV.

"You know you have to call me later so we can finish our earlier conversation," Robyn said and climbed in the truck.

"And what conversation would that be?" I asked, making sure that Tia and Nikki had each clicked in their seatbelts.

"You know and don't play dumb - I want to hear more about that *detective story* when there aren't so many big ears around."

"Yeah, yeah. Take care of my baby, and I'll talk to you later. You know that I'm gonna call, right?"

Robyn smiled. "I would think that something had happened to you if you didn't."

I shut the door and waved until they turned the corner and then went back into the building, running down a mental list of things I could do by myself this evening - walk home, take a long, hot bath after some toning work. As I stepped off the elevator and into the office, I was practically assaulted by the smoking brigade who all stood clustered around the front desk. *When do these people work? I mean first the ten- minute smoke break and then the mental break after and then the jump start needed to get back to work.*

"Your little girl is so adorable. And those pictures just don't do her justice," Paula said sincerely.

"Thank you." I gave a little smile and walked into the copier room. It needed toner, and as I turned to get it, I was surprised to find the smoking brigade standing around the doorway.

Tammy started in. "Tell me, was that the new Mercedes truck?" *Oh, so now they want to piss me off.* This chick was the most materialistic person I had ever met in my life. At one point I thought that she was just having an identity crisis, you know the slave that thought it was a privilege to sleep on the floor under Missy's feet. But then I realized that she was just a status seeker - unfortunately, she believes that white folks have all the status.

"Yes. It was a gift to her from her husband."

I knew I shouldn't have responded, but I was very proud of my friends and their accomplishments. Robyn had gone to school for computer engineering, and her husband, Frank, graduated with a degree in communications. At Robyn's initiative, they started a business which combined their skills and had netted them an extra hundred thou last year. So Frank decided to show his appreciation for Robyn's entrepreneural spirit by buying her the truck out of his share of the earnings.

"They don't still have that other truck , too, do they?" Dina must have observed me ride away with Robyn in a Grand

Cherokee in the past since I tried never to reveal my personal life to these folks.

"Yes, she and her husband have two now." I felt a ball of anger burning right in the middle of my gut.

"I wonder how much their lease payment is for a car like that? Do you know?" Tammy asked, leaning forward eagerly, the wheels spinning.

"I believe that it's paid for," I answered, glad that my mother had raised me better than Tammy's.

"Oh, I would tend to doubt that - those run pretty up there. Even the base models." This unsolicited comment came from Steve, the big boss who couldn't resist insinuating himself into the conversation. *What? Because **he** can't afford one, then it couldn't possibly be within the reach of a young black couple?*

"So I've heard. Excuse me, but I have to get to work." I was pissed, but slightly amused too. I knew they were dying to know if I was just frontin' or not, and I was pissed because I knew their first thought was probably drug dealing. *Oh well, I can't be responsible for their ignorance.*

I turned back to the deadlines and nonsense of work, letting my annoyance go by focusing on the job at hand. Every time I attempted to get into my scheduling program, I got booted out which always happened when I had more than two applications open. I was so engrossed in my temperamental PC that I didn't notice the two strangers coming over to my desk until they were right up on me. They both flashed badges.

"Excuse me, ma'am, but are you Jewel Stone?"

My heart skipped a beat, convinced that something had happened to Tia. There must have been an accident, and it must be bad since they didn't just call. I was slowly working up to hysteria and barely heard what the officer was asking.

"Jewel Stone - you live in Northeast Washington?"

"Yes! Did something happen to my baby?"

"No, ma'am, but I'm afraid that we're going to have to ask you to come with us."

By now everyone was standing around just outside my space, buzzing and whispering.

"What's going on?" I asked, completely baffled.

"We've been requested to bring you into the station for questioning."

"WHAT?!?" Questioning for what?"

The male officer handed me a folded up piece of paper that had way too many words, written in that combination of old English and law gibberish. What I did get was my name and that I was to be detained for questioning in relation to an investigation.

"This is crazy. There's some kind of mistake!"

"That may be, and we can talk about it down at the station." The female cop gave me a little nudge as she took my arm. Horrified, I looked at the curious faces of the people I worked with as they ushered me out of the office.

Paula followed us on to the elevator. "Is there anyone you want me to call for you?" she asked, patting me on the shoulder. The male police officer cut her off, saying, "Look, this may just be a routine matter so why don't we get down to the station and see if we can get it straightened out before we start making any phone calls?"

"Why, because you know that you made a mistake and that you could get sued?" Paula demanded.

"Now, now, this isn't an arrest - let's just see what happens," the female officer responded.

The elevator doors opened and we walked through the same lobby in which I had said goodbye to my little girl just an hour ago. *Oh, my God! What if I never see her again? Various cop horror stories besieged my mind.*

"Are you going to be okay? Do you want me to ride down with you?" Paula was speaking quickly because the officers were helping me into the car.

"No. I'm sure that everything will be okay. I'm sure that it's just a misunderstanding." My voice had that far off sound. The door closed, and I watched as the male officer walked around to the driver's side. We pulled off into traffic and headed uptown, arriving shortly at the precinct.

"Please sign in."

I signed my name on some register and followed the officers on to an elevator to the second sublevel. Once there, we followed a long corridor to a room that contained a metal chair and table where they asked me to sit down and wait. "The investigating officer will be with you in just a moment."

"I don't understand - if it's just questioning, why didn't someone just call me? I would have come down."

"Well, I can't really say. Just sit tight. You haven't been charged with anything." Then they were both gone, closing the door behind them.

I lost track of how long I had been there and jumped when the door opened. I wanted to appear confident and innocent, but I'm sure that what came across was pure panic. It took me a minute before I realized that the man walking in was Justin Baptiste. His locs were pulled conservatively into a black band. He was wearing a pair of dark gray slacks with a dove gray silk shirt and a tie that had strokes of burgundy and black with flecks of gold. On the side of his belt was his shield and around his neck he wore his police identification card and of course his sidearm was strapped in a holster just under his arm. My body relaxed as I realized that it was a friendly face and that all I had to do was convince him that there had been a serious mistake.

"Justin! I am so glad to see you. There's been a mistake! They brought me down here to answer questions, but I don't know anything, and I have to get out of here so I can . . ."

Justin placed his hand on my shoulder and tried to get me to settle down. *Doesn't he realize my future could be the next movie on Lifetime?*

"Wait. Wait. It's okay," he was saying over and over.

"Wha . . . what do you mean? Did they find the right person?" I asked, calming down a little.

"Well, no, because . . ."

The only word I heard was no, and I got upset all over again. "This doesn't make any sense! I can't be of any help to anyone, and I want to leave . . ."

"No. Listen," he started again, holding up his hands to silence me, but I couldn't stop.

"Justin, I'm afraid my pager won't work down here." I had left my phone at the office along with my purse. "My girlfriend has my daughter, and I have to be accessible to her, and . . ."

"I'm sure they're fine," he assured me calmly.

I was so wrapped up in what was going on that I almost missed what he said next.

"They're fine. I'm the one who has the questions." He looked down at me as he waited for it to sink in because I know that the expression on my face hadn't caught up with my mind which was still absorbing what it had heard.

"What . . . what kind of questions?" I asked, still in the dark but beginning to see a glimmer of light like when you crack open a door.

"Well, first off, why won't you see me? You never return my calls . . ."

"Wait. Why won't I see you?! What the hell kind of question is that?" Oh, it had sunk in now, and things were going to get ugly.

"Jewel, I was worried about you, and you kept avoiding me . . ."

"So you had me arrested?!?!"

"Detained. Look, I'm sorry, but I couldn't think of any other way to see you."

I reached up to hit him but realized that assaulting an officer could get me in trouble, and I didn't doubt that this guy was crazy enough to lock me up.

"You mean I'm free to walk out of here?" I demanded through clenched teeth.

Justin nodded, but went on trying to convince me that he had acted with reason until I cut him off.

"Look, you've taken stalking to a whole new level!" I said with a derisive laugh. "Now step away from that door and let me walk out of here, and I won't tell anyone about this . . . just make sure that I never see you again!"

Justin sighed and leaned against the door and tried again to explain. "I'm sorry, Jewel, but you know how you have something planned so perfectly and then when it comes to the execution, it kind of just doesn't go quite the way you thought it would?" He tried to make it light, but his words fell with a thud. Clearing his throat, he continued. "If you would just listen to me, I'm sure that I could . . ."

"What? Make me understand?" I asked waspishly. "Well, you can't!" I started to leave but could tell I would have to touch him to get past him which didn't seem like a good thing to do in my present state of mind. Instead, I put more distance between us by walking angrily across the room. "A person calls! A person may send a note or e-mail, flowers, even drop by unannounced! Go to a place where you would be likely to run into them, but this! . . . this is going over, *way* over the line." And for the next five minutes I ranted on, mostly because I was so relieved that I wasn't in some kind of trouble. When I was done, I just stood there shaking, close to tears, and an unexplainable embarrassment overcame me.

"Are you done?" he asked quietly.

"No." I really couldn't think of anything else to say, but Justin stood back expecting more.

"Is the door open?" I asked.

"Yes, but before . . ."

"Am I free to go?"

He sighed again. "Yes. Look, I didn't mean to hurt you or scare you . . ."

"That's the first thing you hear after someone makes you look like a fool. Did you get your jollies off? As if Baltimore wasn't enough for you?" I was so humiliated just thinking about that night, I ran out the door, trying to get as far away from this lunatic as I could.

Now I have no sense of direction and being upset didn't help, so it took me some time to get out of the police station, and when I finally saw the front doors, my anger had dissolved into depression. *Why would anyone want to do this to me?*

I stood on the sidewalk and tried to figure out what to do. In the panic of being taken away from the office, I had left my purse so I had no money. I could call Robyn, but I had forgotten my phone, too. I turned to run back inside to find a pay phone and almost collided with Justin.

Before I could pull away, he placed his hands on my shoulders in a firm grip and just started talking. "Now, you had a chance to say what you wanted," he began softly but firmly, "and now it's my turn."

"I don't have time for this, so let me go." I tried to twist away but he wasn't letting go. He wasn't hurting me, but I couldn't get away without making a scene so I stood there with that sistah look that says "say what you want to, but I'm not hearing it."

He took a deep breath and started. "First of all, I didn't do this to hurt you. Yes, I went overboard. But I've *tried* calling you. I've left a dozen messages for you at your office and at home, but you've ignored them. I've *tried* to casually run into you, but you go into your office through the garage and leave the same way. Yes, maybe to some degree what I did was stalking, but I would rather consider it as trying to get to know you. I knew it would be an awkward situation after Baltimore, but you didn't even give me - or yourself - a chance."

I flinched at the mention of that night because I wanted to forget that it ever happened.

"Jewel, I understand where you're coming from, but just get to know me before you decide that you don't want to know me. Y'know what I mean?" He tried to give me a lopsided grin, and when he didn't get a response, continued. "Look, all I know is that night in Baltimore, I saw someone in serious pain - I've been there, and I think I can help. Or were you just using me?"

"Yes, I was," I answered truthfully.

He looked hurt but tried to make light of it. "Well, that's what friends are for, huh?"

I could see that it had wounded him a little, and I couldn't figure out why. I was truly intrigued now. Sometimes I can wonder about things but keep them inside and try to analyze them by myself. This was not one of those times.

"Why did you do this?" My first question that wasn't actually hurled at him.

"Because I couldn't stop thinking about you since that day I first saw you in Union Station after all those years. Looking so pitiful. And then again in Baltimore when you were trying so hard to drive your demons away." He spoke softly and sincerely. "There's no rhyme or reason as to why we care and don't. If we could turn it on and off like that then you would have been over your ex-husband the moment he lost his senses. Well, that's the way I feel now. Like I did when we were in the sixth grade, and I couldn't figure out a way to make you notice me. I made an opportunity today, and I was hoping that you wouldn't beat me up over it."

Is he saying he used to have a crush on me?
Justin went on. "I don't know where these feelings are coming from or where they're going or if they're based on fact or fantasy, but I would like to explore them with you. Slowly, of course and I promise that if you say no, then I'll walk away and never bother you again. If you need time to think about it, I'll hold off."

I raised an eyebrow as if to say "suuure.'

Justin held up one hand, the other resting on his chest. "This is the most radical thing I've ever done. And yes, if you wanted to press charges against me, I could lose my job." Slowly his hands came to his side, and he said quietly, "Jewel, I guess you know that the next move is yours." He stepped away, and I was suddenly aware that the only thing keeping me from leaving were his words.

"Well, I'd better let you go." Justin started to walk away.

"I don't have a ride home," I called after him.

"What?" He turned around and walked back slowly.

At that moment a bus decided to come to a squeaky halt at the light. "I don't have a ride home," I repeated, trying to be heard over the din of the sad, protesting brakes.

"You need a ride?" Justin asked, cautiously coming closer and looking a little incredulous.

"Yes. All of my things are at the office."

By now he was standing in front of me. I was trying not to look in his face because I was terrified of what I might see.

There are two kinds of love. The kind like Romeo and Juliet where both hearts know without a doubt that they are meant to be together - that they can stop searching for that other half because it's right beside them. That's fantasy. The kind of love that a first real heartbreak reminds us doesn't really exist. Then there's the other kind in which only one heart has the confidence that things are going to be fine while the other heart is just terrified and wants to run, having been hurt one time too many and afraid that there won't be enough glue to put it back together when it breaks again. Guess which one I was? That's right, and when I looked into Justin's eyes and saw what could possibly grow, I almost felt sick. There was no way that I was going to fall in love again . . . but I didn't run away.

"I don't have any money because my wallet is at the office, and I can't go back there yet because then they won't have anything to talk about for the rest of the day." I was teasing now because my heart was racing. Justin wouldn't have gone through all this if he just liked me. No, for that you would call or inquire through mutual friends, and we had some. No, this was just the tip of the possible, and I knew it. It remained to be seen if we could fit without breaking or bending too much from what was to come.

Justin came closer. "I'll take you to dinner first. If you don't have keys, I'll get a hotel room for you . . ."

"No, that's okay. There's a spare set."

"Good. Let's go back in, and I'll grab my stuff." He moved aside, allowing me to set the pace.

"How about I wait for you here?"

"You might stop and think about what you're doing," he answered truthfully.

I gave him a little push and watched him jog back into the police station. *What in the world am I getting myself into?*

CHAPTER 9

Standing and waiting for what seemed like an hour but was probably no more than ten minutes, I started wondering why I was doing this. Yes, I did want to meet someone, but nine years is a long gap between two people who really didn't know too much about each other in the first place. What if Justin had gone over the edge and back since we left school? Sure, when we were young, I saw him every day five days a week for about eight years, but that didn't necessarily mean that I knew him. But we did take our first Sacraments together, and I did know his parents, so we weren't really like strangers or anything.

I was so caught up in the past that I wasn't paying attention to the motorcycle that pulled up or the person on it until he turned off the engine and called my name. I looked over, startled to see Justin sitting on the bike. Still I didn't make the connection that this was to be my mode of transportation for the evening.

"Have you ever ridden on a motorcycle before?" he asked while unstrapping a second helmet from the rear seat.

"No," I answered, looking at the hot-looking bike with all its chrome and thinking that there was very little protection between me and the rest of the traffic.

"Well, don't worry. I ride my son every now and then, and I'll pretend that you're him."

I'd always wanted to ride on a bike, but with my moment finally here, I was more than a little apprehensive.

I told Justin so, and he just grinned. "Everyone feels that way at first but you do get over it and trust me, I won't let anything happen to you." He held out the helmet and with some trepidation I placed it over my head and put on the leather jacket he offered.

"Listen up, because all this is important. First I'm going to start the bike. Then I want you to put your feet on these little pegs and climb on," Justin instructed. "Be careful that you keep your feet on them and not this thing." He indicated some part down there. Shiny.

"That's the exhaust pipe which is just like the one in a car." And I nodded, as he went on to explain. "It gets very hot and can melt your shoes off."

I looked down at my pretty cream-colored pumps, and looked for those little spokes harder than my previous glanceover.

"Don't panic over anything; if you do, definitely do not jump off, just squeeze me around the waist . . ." I looked at his lean, strong body. *Hhmm, I might be able to do that.* ". . . and I'll pull over."

We rode all the way down Georgia Avenue to Seventh Street, then straight into the wharf, and my mouth started watering. Justin turned off the bike and waited. Realizing that I was supposed to get off, I tried to do it as gracefully as possible and managed fairly well - you know, not kicking him in the head or anything, but I did do that little hop thing when I stepped off the peg.

"Well, that wasn't so bad was it?" he asked, reaching out for my helmet. I had a flash of what my hair probably looked like under there, but what could I do? I pulled the helmet off and handed it to him while trying to smooth down any hair that I knew must be standing straight up.

"It wasn't what I was expecting at all," I told Justin.

"Yeah, with the way you were squeezing me, there was no way that you would get thrown," he teased.

"I was not squeezing!" I said indignantly. "I was just making sure that if I went down, you were going with me."

We both laughed as Justin opened the door to one of the best seafood places in town, one of my all-time favorites with rich, dark woods and an expanse of glass along the entire wall facing the Potomac River.

Once inside, I excused myself and went to make any needed repairs to my hair and use the pay phone to leave Robyn a message as to where I could be reached.

When I rejoined Justin, he asked nervously, "So is everything okay? I mean is this okay for dinner?"

"Oh, sure. This place has my seal of approval." I felt pretty much at ease for someone who might be having dinner with a psycho.

"What, the food?" he asked.

"No, the restroom."

"The restroom!" I thought he must not be a lunatic, or my statement wouldn't have brought such confusion to his eyes.

I explained. "I think you can tell a good establishment from the bathroom - ever since I was a little girl, I've been checking them out."

Justin laughed. "I didn't realize I was out with a restroom connoisseur."

We stood there patiently waiting. Since it was still pretty early, the crowd was small. The carving stations were up, and the buffet table looked fresh and well-stocked with an assortment of vegetables, fruits, fish, ribs, baked chicken, and a huge pile of peel-and-eat spiced shrimp.

A young man who introduced himself as Girard came shortly and guided us to the platinum location, upstairs with a spectacular view of Haines Point. I got very comfy, and Girard took our drink order - a root beer for me so I wouldn't fall off the bike later and an iced tea for Justin, which made me feel greatly relieved since he would be driving the bike. Out of curiosity, I asked if he drank.

"On occasion, but not often since I have a job that pretty much keeps me on call twenty-four seven."

"Yeah, but doesn't the stress get to you? You know - make you want to kind of ease the tension?"

"I can pretty much leave it at the office. My son is my real job." And the smile went all the way from his sexy full lips to the twinkle in his dreamy brown eyes.

"I know what you mean," I said, laughing. "But mine can make me want to give *her* a drink sometimes. Speaking of which, I left word with Robyn that I would be here." I sat back while the waiter poured water and placed our silverware in front of us.

"Thanks," Justin said clearly so that the waiter could hear him. "You could leave her my pager number."

"Oh, that's okay. I have my pager with me, but I like to leave a number too because sometimes the airwaves are jammed during peak hours. Everybody teases me about being overprotective," I sighed. "And it's true. Funny, but true. Nothing has ever happened to her. Tia. My daughter," I explained, knocking on the wooden table. "I've never lost her . . ." (knocking wood again) ". . . she's the most important person in my life. And she's so little and depends on me completely - it seems like such an awesome responsibility."

"Yeah, they can't take care of themselves - that's for sure."

"But don't they act like they're here to take care of you?" We both agreed on that, laughing and dipping into a nice groove. "So where is your little boy?"

"My mother kidnapped him for the evening," Justin said in a tone that made his affection for both his mother and his son obvious.

The waiter came back for our order. Justin ordered the surf and turf, while I tried to decide between the crab cakes and the lump crabmeat dinner. I chose the latter.

"This is really nice, Justin," I said, looking around the room.

"Well, I hope you enjoy yourself, Jewel. You know - to make up for the over-the-top way of starting out?" He said this in a tentative fashion, testing the waters and having the nerve to look bashful.

"So what memories do you have of Haines Point?" Justin asked, his gaze directed out the window.

"Oh, lots. The first time I came here was when I was about five years old. Lou - that's my stepfather - brought me to try my hand at fishing."

"Were you any good?" He actually sounded interested.

"Why, of course." Grinning and sticking out my chest, I said proudly, "Caught a sun perch and even took it off the hook myself."

"Impressive," he said, raising his water glass to me.

"Oh, but it gets ugly after that. I was so proud that I went to show my fish off to some guys who were talking to Lou. Just grabbed the stupid thing, which by the way, wasn't dead yet, and boy, let me tell you, those fins that go up along the back of a fish are there for a reason. He lifted up his spikes and stabbed me in my little palm." I tried to sound pitiful. "It hurt so bad that I screamed and dropped him."

"Let me guess - back in the water?"

"Yep," I said, my laughter joining his. "So the only thing that I had to show for my first real catch was this." I held up my hand which still bore a very faint scar in the shape of an arc.

"Where?" Justin asked, straining to see.

"Right here." I put my hand on the table where he could lean over to get a closer look.

"I think that you've made this whole story up. There's no scar!" I was so intent on showing him my fishing wound that I didn't realize he was teasing me.

"Move the candle closer to my hand. Hey! Don't burn me!" I laughed, pulling back my hand, but he grabbed it, bending his head closer to look for the elusive scar.

"My story has validation in that scar," I said a little breathlessly. I wondered when he was going to let my hand go, but he seemed perfectly content to hold my upturned palm in his across the table.

"Maybe it's the lighting." He leaned a little closer toward me. His eyes were locked on mine, and I felt a serious blush creeping up my face.

"Well . . ." but before I could figure out how to respond, the waiter arrived with our salads.

Justin gave me a little smile and let my hand go. Nothing sleazy or suggestive, just nice, and we began to eat. The food was delicious and very, very filling.

"I haven't eaten so much since . . ." I sat there stumped because I really couldn't remember when I had eaten with such gusto. "I guess it's been a while."

"Since your breakup?" Justin asked quietly.

"Mmm, maybe . . . but that's another story for another time," I said without a hint of sadness.

"I'm sorry. I didn't mean to get all up in your business."

"But wasn't that the whole point of having me, as you say, detained?" I asked teasingly.

"Well, yeah, but I don't want to upset you." He looked over at me like he wanted to comfort me but didn't know how. Then there was our server again asking if we wanted dessert.

"Well, if I'm gonna pop out of this dress and really embarrass myself then it should be for a real good reason." I'll have the hot fudge sundae, thank you."

Justin sat shaking his head. "Where do you put it all?"

"Oh well, when it's free and since it might be my last good meal . . ."

He looked confused.

"You might just send me back to jail," I said wickedly. I expected him to laugh but he didn't. "Hey, I was just kidding." I felt I needed to assure him.

"Jewel, let me ask you, if I had asked you, like come down to your job and waited for you or come upstairs to your office, would you have gone out with me?"

I took a deep breath and said, "No, probably not."

"Then I'm glad that I did it."

"Well, I still don't understand it. I don't think that I need a bag over my head or anything, but why? Why me?"

"Because I meant what I said in Baltimore about really wanting to get to know you."

Justin said this simply enough, but to the cynic I had become, nothing was that simple. Every time I looked back to that night and how mortified I felt, I got angry, and it was beginning to show now. I put my napkin on the table and asked snappishly, "Look, is this a raincheck that you're trying to cash in on? If so, you're out of luck. It was a one-time offer."

Justin looked distraught. "No, that's not what I meant. What I want to know is what can I do to help you get over your ex-husband so that we can move forward?" *Help me get over Malcolm so we can move forward?* He was moving a little fast, but he had my attention as he continued, "Because I do really want to see you again . . . and again . . . but I know that we need to get past that first."

Turning this over in my mind, I responded, "Well, first off, we don't need to talk about Malcolm here, because this is one of the few places that I've never been to with him. I don't want to invite his ghost to come and haunt us over my sundae because that would really tick me off." I was watching Girard place this wonderful creation of ice cream and trimmings in front of me.

"Want some?" I asked, diving into the light and fluffy whipped cream that was way too thick to get past to the ice cream on the bottom.

Justin shook his head and sat watching me like this was just how he had planned to end up when he woke up this morning.

"No. That's okay. Did you want anything else?"

"No, I probably won't even be able to finish this." I spooned more of the decadent concoction onto my blissful taste buds.

Justin signaled for the check and waited patiently while I finished which didn't take very long. In my old days, before depression became my diet supplement, I could have put that whole thing away in addition to a piece of their midnight chocolate cake.

"Ready?" he asked.

"Yep."

On the way out, when we passed the phones, Justin asked, "Would you excuse me while I make a call to my Mom's? It'll just take a second. Sam worries if I don't check in."

I heard him greet his son, "Hey, little man!" There was a pause, and then Justin's deep, full laughter erupted.

I wandered over to the fishtanks to give him some privacy. I wondered what Tia was doing. I wasn't going to call, not wanting to spoil her fun . . . *oh, who cares?* I dug a little change out of my pocket and went back to the phones and dialed Robyn's number. Frank picked up on the third ring.

"Hello, Jewel," he said before I could even exhale.

"How'd you know it was me?"

"Because we have your little girl here for ransom," he replied, and I heard loud shrills of laugher float over the phone.

"Ransom, huh? Well, let's see how much you'll ask for when she wakes you up at three-thirty in the morning and tells you that she's thirsty."

"No problem," Frank said, "See, we keep her, which makes everybody happy. I get my next child which means Robyn don't have to worry about losing her figure. Plus this one's got most of her shots already." He was teasing, but I knew he wanted another child, and Robyn wasn't having it. She said that she wanted to get to know each child individually first, and that's why Marquette and Nikki were so far apart in age.

"Did you want to speak to Tia?"

"Well, I don't want to upset her or anything," I said in a rather unconvincing tone.

"Girl, quit trippin'!" I heard him call Tia to the phone.
"Hi, Mommy!"
"Hey, babe!" I smiled into the phone.
"You coming now?" she asked anxiously.
"No, not . . ."
"Good! I wanna come home *tomorrow*," she stated emphatically. I felt a pang of sadness, realizing that the apron strings were stretching already.
"Tomorrow," she reiterated in case I hadn't understood.
"Of course," I sighed. "I'll see you tomorrow."
"We gotta go get Marquette. She's trying to hide. Bye, Mommy."
And then Frank was back, "You want to speak to Robyn?"
"No, I'll call when I get home. I was just making sure that everything was okay."
"Right. Talk to you then. And Jewel?"
"Yes?" I asked, sounding bummed.
"Relax, she's fine."
I sighed because it was true.
Justin was waiting for me outside the little phone alcove.
"So do you want to take me to get my keys?" I asked.
"Well, if you've never really ridden a motorcycle before, you should let your food digest before climbing back on." He said it so seriously that I believed him, thinking that maybe he didn't want me throwing up all over him.
"How long should we wait?" I asked.
"I'm not sure. Why don't we just walk around some and see how it goes?"
I liked that idea because there were still a million questions buzzing around my head. This man had, at least for tonight, placed me on a pedestal, and I might not be there ever again.
We strolled toward the Tidal Basin. The Washington Monument was lit up behind us, as was the Lincoln Memorial before us. The branches of the cherry trees were heavy with new blossoms, ready to explode into the famous petals that last only a few weeks.
"So tell me your story, Justin."
"Who, me? My life is boring." Justin took my arm and guided me across the street. "You'd be surprised at how many

cars are pulled out of this thing every year," he said, evidently trying to change the subject.

I wasn't going to let him off the hook that easily. "Okay, mine is boring too, or so I thought, but apparently everyone's story can be of interest to someone, so let's hear it."

"How far would you like to go back? To sixth grade when I first noticed you? Or how about seventh grade when I first tried to get you to notice me?"

"Uhm, how about after that? High school?"

"Okay," he sighed. "I walked in Carroll thinking that I would be king of the hill and got knocked flat in more ways than I care to remember. After fooling around for the first two years, I got myself together for the last two. After high school, I went to California - USC on a scholarship. Met Sam's mother and then came home."

"Oh, no, Justin. That can't be it," I protested. "I want details."

"Fine, but when you fall asleep, just remember that you asked for it." Justin backtracked a little. It was in his junior year of high school that he suddenly realized how hard his parents were working to pay the tuition at the Catholic high school; Justin decided that it was time for him to do his part and stop hanging out and playing the class clown. He buckled down and went from a borderline average student to a fairly exceptional one, maintaining his GPA while playing first string football in his junior and senior years.

"My parents were so proud when I got that scholarship." He grinned in a small self-indulgence. "I was off to school, independent, on my own, and just like everyone else I lost my mind." He gave a little rueful laugh. "I immediately started hanging out with the jocks and that meant party time."

We were just crossing over the bridge that separated Haines Point from the Tidal Basin and stopped to look at the blossoms that stood out even in the creeping darkness with their rich and vibrant colors.

"Is that when you met Sam's mother?"

"Yep. Sheila," he sighed. "The best and worst person I've ever met." He told me they met at a party after one of the games and hit it off right away. She was from Texas, the darling little girl of a family with some money. "Sheila thought that I was good enough for her because I was not only a jock, but a pre-law student and seemed to have a future ahead of me."

Justin pushed off from the stone wall, and we started strolling again while he went on talking. "She was so beautiful and different." He seemed at a loss for words and then continued. "Well, it didn't take long before she had me wrapped around her finger."

So he falls easily? That's not very encouraging.

"I want to believe that she put roots on me, rather than think I could be that stupid. We had the ultimate college affair." Caught up in the past, he didn't notice how quiet I was, listening to his tale but at the same time thinking of Malcolm and that woman away at school.

"So the next thing I know she's telling me that she's pregnant and I need to give her some money so she can get an abortion. I always thought that as a guy I would be able to do that. You know, take the easy way out? But I couldn't."

Justin told me that he didn't tell Sheila right away that he was opposed to the idea of an abortion - he lost sleep, missed assignments, and basically drove himself to distraction while Sheila went on as if nothing were amiss - like she didn't have another person growing inside of her.

Our wandering led us to the fork in the small road that was the entrance to the park. Justin and I stood by the rail and looked out over the Potomac River, which was lapping against the side of the concrete barrier, far from reach due to low tide. I pulled Justin's jacket closer around me. The sun was all but gone, and the air coming off the water was a little cool, but I didn't want to interrupt him by suggesting that we head back.

"Finally I told Sheila that I couldn't give her the money - that I wanted us to have the baby. Well, that wasn't what she wanted to hear. First she tried reasoning, then cajoling - everything." Justin sounded weary, defeated, probably remembering how devastating reality can be to love. "Then when Sheila saw that her usual tricks weren't going to move me, she cried and cursed me, but there was nothing she could do since I was the only one who could get her the money. There was no way she could go to her parents. She wanted Daddy to believe that she was still his pure little virgin." His voice had a sort of sneer in it, but was that directed at the girl, the father ... or maybe himself?

"So after what seemed a lifetime, we finally worked out a bargain. I'd provide her with a place to stay so that word wouldn't get back to her family and then after she had the baby, if she wanted to walk she could. I would take care of the baby myself, and no one would need to know."

"And she agreed?" I was stunned.

"What choice did she have?" Justin held up his hand. "We were both to blame. I just didn't feel that another life should have to pay for our irresponsibility." Justin went on to say that he was pro-choice, that he respected the rights of a woman to her body, but that he believed the man should also be considered - if he wanted the child, the woman should have it and leave it with him.

"But that's not how it always works out," I said, trying to shed some realism on his male perspective. "So many times you have a guy that says that he wants a child, and then the next thing you know she's six months along and he's wondering if this is what he really wanted after all."

"Well, if he doesn't have the heart to stick it out, then they can consider adoption," Justin argued.

"Oh, that's a nice, practical idea for white society, but right now, there's a ton of African-American babies growing up in foster care, growing up thinking that no one wants them or loves them and white couples are going overseas to adopt children - and not just European, but Asian or Indian - anything but African or African-American. And then these kids turn eighteen and have to leave foster care, they're pushed out into society with no one to turn to." I was breathless when I finished.

"I'm just saying what was right for me," Justin said, a little defensively.

"Well, that's exactly why there should be choice. The father's feelings can be considered, but let's be real, it's the woman's responsibility to bear the child and take care of herself until it gets here."

We walked on in silence for a little bit, each digesting what the other had said.

"So don't leave me hanging. What happened?" I asked, breaking the growing silence.

"We followed my plan. Sheila told her parents that she was accepting an offer to join an acting troupe and would be sitting out a semester. Then I set her up in a little apartment in Palo Alto, withdrew my scholarship and worked like a dog so that I could keep a roof over her head, plus pay for her medical care, vitamins, food, entertainment . . ." He paused and I could see that, in his mind, the list went on forever.

"I thought that as the pregnancy progressed she would get a little excited but she didn't, and I tried everything. Went to the appointments with her. Bought all of her favorite foods so that she would eat properly. Rubbed her back when it ached. But it didn't matter. She never came around."

We had done a complete lap around the park and were heading back past the view of the Jefferson Memorial.

"By the time she went into labor we were complete strangers. You would have never believed that we were, together, responsible for her big old stomach. I don't know what she did when I wasn't at home but she never even so much as touched her stomach, even when the baby was kicking so hard you could see her shirt jump."

I remembered how special it felt whenever Tia moved. I would stop everything and silently beg her to do it again - and get all freaked out if she went more than an hour without moving.

"While she was going through labor, I tried to reach out and touch her, to be of some help." Memory of his helplessness and confusion made Justin's voice raw with emotion. "But I could have been on the moon for all she was concerned. She was completely focused on getting it over with. A nurse even asked me if she was a member of the Church of Scientology - you know, they don't make any noise when the child is coming into the world. It's supposed to be less traumatic for the child."

I had heard that also. *More power to them - everyone on the East Coast must have known that Tia was coming into the world!*

Justin continued. "Sheila was obsessed. Wouldn't listen to the doctors when they told her to stop pushing. That's how determined she was to get him out even though she was tearing. Finally, Sam popped out. All eight pounds eleven ounces of him. Twenty-three inches long."

That's a father's voice, all right. All full of pride like he had actually delivered the baby himself.

I cut in with the only conclusion to the story I could come up with. "So she took one look at him and fell in love, and you both wanted him so much that you had a big custody battle and you won - right?"

"She didn't even look at him," Justin said sadly.

"Well, not then - but later," I suggested, unable to believe that she wouldn't at least hold one of those tiny fingers.

"She wouldn't even let the nurses tell her whether it was a boy or a girl. She said that if they didn't get it out of the delivery room right then and there, she was getting off the table and walking out herself. She acted like she had just spewed out the devil's spawn."

I was wide-eyed and completely at a loss. "Was it just postpartum?"

"That's what I thought then - that Sheila just needed a little time. I guess she must be setting a record for the longest bout of depression ever 'cause she's been suffering from it for four years now." Yes, pain was still there, giving a definite edge to his words. "We haven't heard from her since. I stopped looking for that after Sam's first birthday."

I was stunned. *How can someone just leave their child like that - but of course I don't know the whole story - there's always at least two sides.* "How's Sam?" I asked, feeling really sorry now for this poor little boy who had no mother.

"He's just fine," Justin answered, the edge in his voice replaced with tenderness. "Never without love or care, and once I got it together, it worked out well."

"How did you do it? Did your parents help?"

"Not at first. My mother always told me if I was going to bring a child into the world then I'd best be able to take care of it. I waited a few weeks back at the apartment in Palo Alto for Sheila to show up - you know, hoping that she would pull herself together? And, man, those first few days were scary!"

I laughed with him, remembering how you bring a child home and really find out which things come naturally and which ones don't.

"I must have taken Sam to the emergency room one time too many in the first few days because a really nice nursing student said she would come by and check on me and Sam so that I would quit dragging him out at all hours."

I envisioned all the things that I went through during my first few days with Tia, and it touched my heart to be walking beside a man who had gone through the same thing. Not that I'm a sexist or anything, but usually when they find themselves at a loss, the baby gets sent to Mom.

"After Sam's six-week checkup, I felt I had waited long enough so I cruised past the campus and found out Sheila had gone to Hawaii with a few friends before the new semester. I left word as to where we would be and also sent a letter to her parents' address.

"My parents met me and Sam at the airport, and my mother took one look at Sam and fell in love. She wanted me to come home with him - I did for a little bit - just to get my feet back on the ground. I went to UDC at night and switched my major to criminal justice. I had a few temp jobs in a couple of law firms and realized that being in a suite with a bunch of people running around just trying to get someone off without looking for the truth wasn't what I wanted. So I finally decided to sign up for the police academy."

We were sitting at the end of the marina looking at the dark park across the street. Justin was sitting on a little stone bench while I perched on the back of it, absorbing the story he had told me. *He doesn't seem crazy or deranged - although maybe he's making the whole thing up. But what a story if he is!*

I couldn't resist. "So when did you become a homicidal professional stalker?"

"Actually, I'm still a novice," he said blithely. "Maybe I was stalking you when I ran into you at Union Station - then of course when I saw you in Baltimore - maybe they weren't coincidences."

"Justin, that is not funny!" It was a little disturbing that he could put that together so quickly.

"Whoa!" he said, looking at his watch. "I didn't mean to keep you out this late."

"What time is it?"

"A little before nine - you still have to get your spare key." He stood up and offered me a hand to help me down.

"Do you think that you can get me home before ten?" I asked anxiously. My show was like an addiction to me.

"Not a problem."

CHAPTER 10

"So then what happened? Did you work it out?" Robyn was swirling her little bony hips around lewdly.

"Are you crazy? Did you forget about what happened last time?" I still could not get over that rejection in Baltimore.

This morning I had called in absent from work and then went to Robyn's. She was still wandering around in her get-up-in-the-morning ensemble - a large, bright yellow tee shirt, purple leggings, and slouch socks in lieu of house slippers.

Robyn pressed for more information. "Well, did you at least get a little taste of him?" She was looking for some juicy tidbit, but I had to disappoint her. After Justin and I picked up my keys and raced to my house, I burst through the front door, grabbing the remote just as scenes from last week filtered past. Poor Justin had to sort of trail behind me, and I apologized, explaining to him that ER was like a really good game to a sports nut. He said "no problem" and sat down while I got engrossed in the first fifteen minutes of the show.

"Did you at least sit next to him?" Robyn was getting frustrated now.

"No. I sat on the papasan, and he sat on the couch."

"All that hard work down the drain," Robyn murmured under her breath.

"What hard work?" A thought crossed my mind, but just then the girls came tumbling down the stairs, each one giving kisses and leaving behind the faint scent of fresh soap and lotion.

"What do you want for breakfast?" Robyn asked as she inspected her troops, but Marquette was already reaching in the refrigerator for eggs and other ingredients.

"Mommy," she began in that lecturing tone that afflicts most girls over the age of thirteen who believe all parents suffer from Alzheimer's. "You promised that I could do this by myself." She reminded Robyn in a tone that said the whole conversation was embarrassing. I looked away and covered my mouth so that she couldn't see my smile.

"Oops! My bad." Robyn snapped her fingers as if just remembering. "I figured that you would have had enough of these two after last night."

"Tia? Did you give Marquette a hard time?" I asked sternly. Nikki was in the process of helping Tia climb up into a chair at the kitchen table.

"Tia?" I called a little louder in order to get her attention.

"No, Mommy. We were good. We just wanted another story."

Marquette defended the little ones. "Don't worry, Aunt Jewel, I only read them two extra ones and then made them go to sleep."

"I don't know, girl! I'm going to have to find out your secret. I usually have to go for at least four more, five if one is short, before I can get her settled."

Marquette puffed up with pride and began the breakfast ritual with renewed vigor. "Okay, what did you all tell me you wanted for breakfast upstairs?"

"Pancakes!" Nikki and Tia cried out at once.

"All right, then. Turkey bacon?" They both looked at each other like, well sure, and Marquette started moving around the large kitchen pulling out pans and plates, looking like a little Mommy herself.

"Don't use too much oil in the pan," Robyn cautioned, but Marquette was ready for her.

"Here, Mommy," she said, handing Robyn her coffee mug. "Why don't you and Aunt Jewel go upstairs so that you can talk, and I'll get the girls fed."

I turned my head and headed out the kitchen door because I knew there was no way I could hide the amusement that was all over my face.

"This way you and Aunt Jewel can get ready so that we get to the mall and back before rush hour begins."

"Well, can you believe that?" Robyn asked with a chuckle as we headed up the stairs to Robyn and Frank's bedroom. "My baby's growing up - big enough to babysit!"

Suddenly, Robyn looked a little sad, and I gave her shoulder a bump. "Hey, girl, just be happy that she just wants to watch 'em and not out trying to have 'em."

"Girl, you ain't said nothin' that I don't thank God for every night," Robyn said, getting up and tying her hair up. "But enough about that." And she demanded that I finish telling her what happened the previous night. "And don't say that after all that, you sent Justin home with just his thoughts for company."

"Yes, I did." I told her about how he sat and watched the show and waited until the commercial before asking any questions. Then we watched the news, and he left.

"Well, he was going to move slow, so I guess this is it," Robyn muttered.

"What is that supposed to mean?" My radar was picking up weird signals, and Robyn had this guilty look on her face. Suddenly, it fell into place for me. "You knew!" I shouted in accusation, jumping up and blocking her escape into the bathroom. "You set me up!"

"It was for your own good," Robyn screeched as she climbed up on her bed, hoping to escape me.

"So all of a sudden you've become my mother?" I dived at her from the bottom of the bed, grabbing her by the ankle and causing her to lose her balance and fall. She was struggling to get away from me, but I wouldn't let go.

"Who else was in on this, Robyn?"

"Just me and Ashley." She was already giggling even though I had yet to touch her feet. We always teased Robyn, saying she would give up the secrets of the universe if someone threatened to tickle her feet.

"Why?!" I demanded.

"Let go of my foot and I'll tell you," she panted.

"Tell me, or I'll start tickling you."

"If you do that then I won't be able to tell you anything!"

"What's all that noise I hear up there?" Marquette yelled from downstairs.

"I'm kicking your mother's butt!" I yelled back down.

The next thing I heard were little feet flying up the stairs, and in a flash Nikki and Tia were standing in the doorway.

I shouted, "C'mon! Help me!"

They came charging over and without even knowing the cause were clearly on my side. Soon we were all rolling around the king-size bed, laughing and tickling. Suddenly, Robyn jumped up and grabbed Tia around the waist and threw her over her shoulder, grabbed Nikki by her ankle, and dragged them both into the hall. Then she ran back into the room, slamming and locking the door behind her. We heard little hands banging on the door, begging to be let back in.

"No way!" Robyn gasped.

"Come on, Mommy," Nikki said in that singsong voice. "We'll help you this time!"

"Forget it!" Robyn responded while undressing and heading for the shower. "Now you have to calm them down for Marquette," she said to me devilishly and ran past before I could punch her.

"I hope you're all out of hot water," I grumbled on my way back to the bouncing door where Tia had her fingers sticking in between the bottom of the door and the carpet.

I yelled after Robyn. "Don't think that this is over by a longshot!"

"Of course not, dahling," she replied in her rich woman voice. "Just send the girls back down to eat, and we'll talk all about it."

I opened the door and told the girls, "She got away for now, but we'll get her later!"

"No, let's get her while she's in the shower!" Tia said.

"Yeah, we can wait 'til she puts the soap on her face and then we'll get her," Nikki chimed in.

Who are these demon children?

"No, no. We have to get you all some food first so you can get your muscles."

As we entered the kitchen, Marquette was putting the finishing touches on the table. I pulled back a chair for Nikki and helped Tia up on the booster seat.

"Aunt Jewel! I can do this," Marquette protested in a "please let me be a grown up for a minute" voice.

"Okay, okay." I backed out the door and went back upstairs to confront Robyn.

"So how did you fit into all of this?" I hollered over the running water.

"Are the girls eating? Did you want something to eat?" Robyn asked in a clear attempt to avoid the question.

"All right, Robyn, I can wait you out."

"Okay, I give up." She came out of the bathroom wrapped in a towel. "I'll tell you the whole thing because I thought we should have told you from the beginning." She moved around pulling underclothes from out of her dresser drawers. I waited in silence while she disappeared into the walk-in closet and came back out with a pair of sweats and a short-sleeved oversized shirt.

"You gonna wear your striped shirt? I'm gonna wear *my* striped shirt." We often joked about grown women walking around looking like twins. Robyn realized I had on a shirt very similar to the one she was holding.

"Oh, right," she said distractedly and ducked back into the closet again. "Like I said, it was my idea to tell you." Her voice was muffled as she rummaged around the back of the closet.

I could tell that my friend was trying to assuage me in the same way she now began to smooth lotion over her arms and legs.

"Anyway, I wanted to have like a party or something." Robyn was now pulling on one of Frank's undershirts, covering it with a button-down shirt and leaving most of the buttons undone. "But Justin was afraid that if we did then you would be too embarrassed and just leave." She was struggling into her hightops.

"How did he get in touch with you all?"

"He remembered Jazz was a lawyer and found her in the phone book. She put him in touch with me." Robyn was checking in the mirror to make sure everything fit right. *How could it not? She really should have gone into modeling.*

"So was my life that pitiful that you were willing to foist me off on what could be some looney?"

"He's no looney."

"And just how do you know?" I inquired.

"Because he seems . . ." Robyn was looking for the right word . . . "I don't know . . . sincere?" She looked over for confirmation while I mulled it around in my head.

"Besides, look at Romeo and Juliet," she pointed out, ever the romantic.

"Yes, they both ended up dead! And stop trying to turn this into a great romance. We had one date and that was not technically a date, it was a detention! He didn't say anything about calling me later or that he even wanted to see me again."

I laughed a little, knowing I was feeling somewhat disappointed because Justin had just said goodnight and nothing more. I mean he did say that he had a good time but was he being polite?

Brushing those thoughts aside, I stood up. "Come on, girl, let's go and get those little rugrats some clothes before they grow another two inches."

"That'll happen even before we leave the store," Robyn declared. She put her arm around my neck, and we headed out the door. "You still love me?" She bent her tall frame so that her head rested on top of mine.

"And why should I? You don't even think that I'm grown up enough to make my own decisions!"

"Of course not! That's what friends are for. Besides, you deserve to be happy." She gave me a little kiss on the top of my head as we headed into the kitchen to help Marquette straighten up. I found myself wondering if there would be a message from Justin on my machine. Part of me hoped not - I did want some time to think things over - right now it seemed like everyone was pushing me along, and it was making me very nervous.

* * * *

When Tia and I arrived home from the shopping trip, we were both exhausted.

"Mommy, look!"

Trying to juggle bags while looking for my keys, I glanced up. "What in the world?" There on the doorknob to our apartment was a beautiful hanging plant, a wandering Jew. We dropped the bags and sat down on the foyer step. Tia was playing with the leaves of the plant, and I pulled out the card.

"Who's it from, Mommy?"

"It's from a friend of Mommy's," I answered, smiling at the card.

Jewel, I had a wonderful time last night. You stay rooted in my mind. Hope with some attention that this can grow. Justin

CHAPTER 11

Seven-thirty in the morning was the best time to be at work in my office. No hassles. No noise. No telephones or demands. And especially no busybodies. After last week, I knew that these folks here were champing at the bit to find out what was going on. The good thing was that I didn't have to tell them a thing! Just because my abrupt departure was very unconventional, didn't mean that I had to share. It wasn't like there were any charges against me, and I had plenty of leave to cover my absence.

Walking through the door and turning on the lights, I wondered fleetingly if the whole incident might actually go undiscussed. *Yeah, right. Nope, knowing this crowd, it could prove to be a very interesting day.*

I threw my jacket in the corner chair of my space and turned to face the workday. Good grief, I had only been gone one-and-a-half days and yet my terminal screen was ablaze with yellow sticky notes. All this work waiting for me made me wonder yet again why I made the least amount of money in this office. No matter. I needed something to keep my head focused on something other than last Thursday night with Justin. Here it was Monday, and I was still getting unexplained heart palpitations just thinking about someone who might be a lunatic, a stalker, a homicidal killer!

Or maybe someone who's easy to talk to, has a wonderful personality, is a great listener, not to mention articulate, humorous, considerate . . .

Stop it, Jewel and get to work!

Did I mention FINE?!

Enough already! One day you're gonna learn that your heart is just too reckless to take seriously.

I opened my e-mail hoping that maybe there would be a pleasant note. *Now I know these people have lost their minds!*

My eyes had found a message welcoming a new staff member: This is to inform everyone that we are welcoming Bernadette Williams to our office. Bernadette is a single mother of two girls who just recently graduated from high school and is working on getting her certification . . . blah, blah, blah.

What ticked me off wasn't the fear that she might be my replacement - it was the overinformative message sent to the entire staff. I shook my head. What right do they have to spread this woman's personal business out there like that? Does her being a single mother have any bearing on her job qualifications? How 'bout tellin' us where she came from before working here? Or how 'bout just sayin' Bernadette will be working here and give us her start date? Let Bernadette decide how much about herself she wants known. See, this ticked me off because other people have come to this office and their bios were completely different from this garbage.

I sat in front of my terminal moving stacks of paper, further digging in my heels, determined to keep my business just that; my business.

Within an hour, calm had descended upon me as I started the daily grind. It didn't take long before I was completely absorbed in my latest project. The concentration level was so high that I missed hearing the front door open.

"Uh, hi, Jewel." All my eyes were able to take in was a glimpse of Dina rushing past my little cubicle.

"Hey, there!" My chipper voice followed her down the hallway. And so it went as the office began filling up. I went back to work, wondering who would be the one to stop and ask what happened. Funny thing was that everyone went running past my desk as if I had the plague. Tammy dashed past with a tight smile on her face but avoided eye contact which was fine with me.

Between the ringing phones and the search for the Monday morning rev, time was beginning to accelerate.

Bossman Steve came in around nine and looked startled to see me. "Uh, good morning, Jewel."

"Hey, Steve," I called over my shoulder. Barely looking up, I kept working because I'd long learned that his greeting was just a mere formality. Usually, the man was in his office before I could even open my mouth to respond in kind. Ah, but today was different. A few minutes later I felt his presence still lingering and turned away from my screen. Holding up my hands I smiled reassuringly. "I know what you're thinking," I began and saw the relief wash over his face. "That mailing that was due to go out Thursday? I pulled the file off your system, gathered everyone's e-mail and sent it this morning. All the information was included, and I saved the office some postage. What about that, huh?" My face was pleasant and my demeanor efficient, but inside I was cracking up!

The way my boss's face morphed from expectation to deflation was priceless. After clearing his throat several times, Steve thanked me and fled into his office where he hid for a good forty-five minutes or so, and I figured that was it.

My mistake was thinking that playtime was over, but it had just gotten a start. It took me a while to realize that the office printer outside my space was getting an awful lot of attention. Five times in less than fifteen minutes from Steve alone. When he made his sixth trip, I looked up and smiled, my eyes following him back into the office.

I waited a beat and then began silently counting. Four...three...two...one. BINGO! Again I let him know, by following him with my eyes, that I was aware of his constant presence. When the printer began whirling up five minutes later, I figured this was getting ridiculous. It was time to put him out of his misery because he was working my nerves now.

While he shuffled the papers around in his hands I started stretching. "Wow!" I said in his direction. "You miss one day and the evil gremlins come and pile work all over your desk!"

"Yeah," he agreed. There was an awkward pause while Steve looked for a better position to get this started. "Uh, Jewel, do you think that you have a moment?"

"Sure, Steve. What's up?" I figured that we could squash everything at my desk so that the walls could hear and life could return to normal.

"Actually I was hoping that you could step into my office."
"Okay."

I walked past him and sat down in the chair opposite his desk.

"I'll be with you," he said and disappeared.

I had just time to look around and wonder why his desk and office looked so clean and organized before he was back again.

"All right, now," he boomed, and I was surprised to see that he was shutting the door and even more surprised to see Sue pulling up a chair. *See, now they want to act real stupid.*

"Is there a problem with my time sheet?"

Both of them looked at each other.

"Oh, no. No," Sue rushed. "It's just about Thursday . . ."

"Yes, I'm charging that and Friday to my vacation time."

"Uh, well yes, but . . ." She was floundering because there was no reason for her to be a part of this meeting, and we all knew it.

Steve tried to diffuse the tension. "It's just that we need to know if you'll need any more time off in the near future?"

"Nope. Not that I can foresee." That was it. Pick up the dice. The game was already boring, I had won, and it was time to get back to work. Using a tactic picked up from some seminar training, I stood, ready to leave.

Steve knew that he wasn't going to get what he wanted, but wasn't willing to concede to going out like a complete punk. Leaning back in his chair, he feigned a composure that I knew he was faking.

"Jewel, we just wanted to make sure that this wasn't going to be a habit. If there are personal matters that need your attention, they should be handled outside of the office."

Raising my eyebrows, I responded facetiously. "Yes, next time I'll be sure to make that clear to the D.C. Police Department. Excuse me but I have to get back before those little gremlin devils take over my desk completely."

When I opened the door, there was the distinct scurrying sound heard from the disbandment around the receptionist's desk. Didn't matter. Sue would fill them in at the next smoke break. The joke was that she had nothing tell.

I would have done anything to have Detective Baptiste call me right then and there, and then for a moment the office faded. Thinking about the sound of his voice. The way Justin's eyes lit up over the candlelight at the dinner table as well as his overall personality made me realize I just wanted him to call for reasons other than stirring up gossip. The quiet phone sat on my desk. Too bad just wishing didn't make it so, but then again if "ifs and ands are pots and pans" then the world would be a kitchen!

CHAPTER 12

"Jewel, I can't believe you're from Washington, D.C., born and raised in Southeast. Growing up as a witness to the sound of percussion and the little bluesey chant that took Europe by storm, not to mention the good old US of A, and you're going to tell me you've never been to a go-go?!"

"Nope." I smiled.

"Come on, Jewel, Rare Essence got their start right in St. Thomas More's Auditorium. What about the Colosseum?" Justin asked incredulously.

"Nope."

There was a stunned silence on the other end of the phone.

It was late Wednesday night, and both of our kids were fast asleep while Justin and I were involved in what had become a comfortable evening ritual. After the stories had been read and our children asleep, one of us would call the other, and we'd sort of unwind together. It proved to be a great way to really get to know each other because even though Justin swore he'd known me longer than anyone else because of the eight years that we shared as schoolmates, it was obvious that we had orbited different planets.

"My mother wouldn't let me go unless I was accompanied by a responsible adult," I explained, stretched out on the couch, comfortable in one of my big nightshirts and big bear claw slippers. "And what responsible adult would want to go to a room packed full of teeny boppers all shaking their groove thangs?" I asked, raising my knees, crossing one over the other, and allowing my oversized foot to bob up and down. This is nice, I thought to myself. No need to be self-conscious - just go with the flow of the conversation. Many times, we'd be talking when I would glance at the VCR and be shocked that it read two am.

"I figured everyone who lived in D.C. would have been to a go-go at one time or another." He chuckled lightly.

"No, I got to see G movies and maybe go to a few skating parties."

"The funny thing is I always thought you were Miss Thang."

"Why would you think that? If I had been Miss Thang, I would've been hanging out with you and your crew."

"Aw, we weren't all that."

The smile in his voice warmed me, and I settled further back into the cushions. "No, your crowd just had the chains and the names of all the latest designers committed to memory."

"True, true," Justin conceded.

"So, tell me, were they anything like the go-gos today?" I was thinking about the live broadcast on the cable channel late at night. If anyone wanted to know where these new music groups were getting the hoochie mamas for their videos - the ones who don't mind being referred to as bitches and hos - they could turn on that show. Girls gyrating lewdly on the floor, up against the walls, the boys, any and everything, becoming almost hypnotized as the beat gets into its groove and the shirts and skirts begin to slide up. *Where the hell are their mothers?*

"No, back in those days if someone stepped on your spankin', brand new kicks," Justin recounted, "you stepped up and you and the crew would commence to have a good old-fashioned beatdown." I laughed because Justin's persona had reverted back to adolescence.

"Naw, man, it wasn't funny," Justin protested. "You could come out with some serious damage then, like your shirt could get ripped or your new jeans messed up. And you knew you weren't going to get another pair until your parents got paid." He laughed, caught up in nostalgia. "Naw, it wasn't nothin' like today. You handled your business like a man - with just your fists, and if some dude pulled out even so much as a knife or busted a bottle, well then he was labeled a punk!"

Justin grew quiet, probably thinking of the hundreds of homicides he investigated these days because somebody let a gun handle their business for them.

"But I figured you were one of those quiet girls that did her work from eight to three and then cut wild after school let out." Justin buoyed himself back into the conversation which seemed to be something he had to be able to do in order to deal with his job as a cop.

"And whatever made you think that I was anything other than a good Catholic girl?" I asked, feigning primness.

"Well, Nathan Green kind of gave that wildchild impression of you," Justin said in that detective way - as if there were more to the story and he was finally going to find out what it was.

"Oh, he did, did he?" I knew where this was going and decided to resist.

"Yeah, he made it seem like you two had something goin' back then." He was gently prodding, obviously trying to get me to spill everything that had happened almost eleven years ago.

"Well, whatever Nathan said, I'm sure it was a lie."

Justin pushed. "Well, he told me and some of the other fellas that he was your first." *Oh, that would explain my sudden popularity toward the end of my school career at St. T's!*

"Justin, that's ridiculous. We were in the eighth grade."

"So what? He just came up with that bold-faced lie about a sweet and quiet girl like you for no reason?"

"No different than the story about you and Monica," I shot back.

"First of all, Monica wasn't even trying to front as a nice girl, and secondly, it wasn't a story."

"Justin! Eighth grade! Don't you think that you were rushing things?"

"Well, what can I say?" he said sheepishly. "I got caught up in all the hype."

"And you knew what to do at thirteen?"

"Almost fifteen," he reminded me, and I was sorry I had forgotten that Justin was older than we were. It always made him uncomfortable that he was in middle school with us when he should have been in high school. His early schooling had been interrupted due to a car accident which left him with a badly broken leg and a lot of surgeries. When he recovered, his parents insisted that he return to the grade he had been in when the accident had occurred rather than be passed along.

"Now what about you? What really happened between you and Nathan?"

"Oh, that," I said dismissively. "Nothing as memorable as your first, I'm sure."

"So then he was your first?"

"No, no. Almost, but I just couldn't do it."

"So what made you want to try? You seemed so, so . . ."

"Prudish?" I supplied.

"No," he said giving a little laugh, "so . . ."

"Nerdish?"

"Is that what you thought about yourself?" he asked.

"Yep." And I did.

"But why?"

"Well, let's see, the glasses for starters." I started counting off. The fact that my mother wouldn't let me wear my hair in the flip or snatchback all the other girls were wearing. My fingernails - always trimmed just past my fingers and coated in clear polish only. Small gold hoops or stud earrings, not the big bamboo like everybody else. I paused, scrutinizing in my mind, the little eighth-grade girl in the plaid skirt and white blouse with the required little crisscross necktie, red knee highs, and black-and-white saddle shoes. The ponytail that I wore every day with the matching plaid bow in the back completed my picture from the mid-eighties. Yes, definitely a nerd compared to Justin's Monica who now stood next to me in my mind. Even though the uniforms were identical, it was obvious that Monica had a lot more to enhance hers. Her blouse always seemed to strain with her busty chest, and her skirt was shorter, revealing full legs and a firm round behind that looked like you could balance a tray on it. The comparison was dramatic.

"No, the word I was looking for to describe you was innocent," Justin said softly and then persisted, "So why did you and Nathan almost?"

I sighed, recognizing defeat. "Well, I liked to read, and my big passion was my sister's romance novels." I laughed, thinking about how my heart would beat a thousand times a second when Nathan first started showing interest in me, and how I painstakingly tried to make myself look more sophisicated. Soon, Nathan was waiting around to catch the late bus with me in the afternoons. The bus rides became the carriage rides that the characters in my books would take along winding country roads.

"So to make a long story short, I got so wrapped up in the romance that I invited him over the Friday that my parents were going to Virginia to visit some new outlet mall." Thinking back, I wondered again how I could have been so stupid. "When we walked home to my house that day, I told him to meet me around back in the alley so that our neighbors wouldn't see - as if they didn't have back windows," I said, giving a little laugh. "Anyway, while he was going around, I ran through the house, throwing off my uniform and changing into one of my good nightgowns and my ballet slippers - thinking that was what the characters in the book would do. When I let him in, I expected his breath to be taken away, and he would kiss me gently and carry me up the stairs."

"Somehow, Nathan never really struck me as that type," Justin said, interrupting the memory I was exploring.

"No, he wasn't," I said dryly, my voice going flat. "Nathan came in and complained that I took too long to let him in. He said nothing about my outfit or anything, just asked if there was anything to drink.

"I gave him a soda and then told him to follow me upstairs. It never occurred to me that he would be nervous. None of the heroes in the book were nervous, just overcome with desire. I was a little frustrated that he didn't seem to know how to act. He kept belching up each stair. He made comments about how big the house was and wondering when would my parents be home. I swept open the door to my room and assured him that it would be hours. Instead of pulling me into his arms he walked past me and just stood there looking around. Then he started to grab my stuffed animals and throw them in the air, one at a time. Sitting on my bed and striking a pose, I waited for Nathan to make the first move - to come and take me in his arms. But what really happened was he threw my bear in the air like a football and made a diving catch onto the bed. Then he sat up and started asking what was with all the ribbons and tried to look down my gown before stealing a kiss. My first kiss. Soon we were caught up in that, and he asked if we should get under the covers.

"Funny thing about that part in the books, first they were kissing and then the act, described as unbelievable passion, and then snuggling as he stroked her head as it lay against his chest. Nothing about how you got from the clothes to that end, so I nodded and we both pulled back the covers and climbed under. Hello?"

"I'm still here. Go on," he urged.

I continued. How Nathan started taking off his clothes and throwing them out from under the covers onto the floor. He asked about the door and I told him that he could lock it if he wanted to, so he jumped up from the bed and ran for the bedroom door and locked it while I slipped out of my panties, leaving on the gown in case he wanted to peel me out of it. When he turned around and came toward the bed, my eyes were glued to his white briefs with the little lump slightly protruding outward. Coming toward me!

"And at that moment I knew this was not what I wanted, but I didn't know what to do. So he came over and inexperience was definitely on my side because after he got out of his underwear . . ." I tried to stifle my laughter. ". . . no sooner did he climb on me than he exploded in a huge mess all over my sheets, my thighs, everything! It was awful!" Burying my face in the couch pillow, I howled at the memory.

"So that's all that happened?" Justin asked when I had regained my composure.

"Yes," I choked.

"And you didn't try again?"

"Are you kidding? I think it shattered all my romantic hopes," I said wistfully, "because it never got any better for me." Then realizing what I had said, I hastily added, "Not that I'm frigid or anything, just a hopeless romantic. I guess I'm still hoping for romance more than sex."

"Is that right?" Justin inquired intently.

Before I could make another attempt at damage control, I was startled by a light rapping on my apartment door.

"Hang on, there's someone at the door." I was more than a little curious since the downstairs buzzer hadn't rung. Standing on tiptoe, I looked through the peephole, and curiosity turned to wariness. "Uh, Justin, let me call you back tomorrow." There was a question in his agreement, but I didn't want to address it at the moment; I wanted to find out why Malcolm was knocking at my door, this late at night, unannounced.

* * * *

It still made me a little sad that I had been so suspicious of Malcolm's motives that night a few weeks ago. I had opened the door warily.

"Hi, Jewel. Sorry to come by so late," he said, stepping inside.

I stood on the stairs and let the emotional storm batter my heart. *When will it stop? When will I no longer feel like I'm slowly dying every time I see him?*

"Tia in bed already?"

I nodded, too nervous to speak. Finally, unable to stand it, I asked him what he wanted, and he thrust a small but weighty elegant envelope in my direction. The world stopped - it must be a wedding invitation!

Malcolm was going on about how he wasn't sure that what he was doing was protocol, but it was a sincere offer and he hoped that I would attend. Taking the bomb encased in white, I steeled myself for the damage. I read it once and then once more. Not a wedding invitation. *Of course, silly, we aren't even divorced yet!* It was an invitation to his graduation! I sat relieved, but then a melancholy swept over me. Sadly, I handed it back to him, explaining that while I was really proud of him, I just couldn't attend. It was a most important and anticipated event, but one from a different life - one that had ended that day I went to see him in New York.

Malcolm was quiet for a moment, then said, "I wouldn't even be getting this if it weren't for you."

"Thank you, Malcolm, but we are on separate paths now." He conceded. I think we both realized then that the pain of the past few months would always be in our way, but that on some level, Malcolm and I still cared for each other. It was a bittersweet moment that we knew better than to try to analyze.

So here I was now. The sky was blue and the weather very agreeable. A perfect day. My child was in New York participating in the achievement of her father, and I was standing at the entrance of the Zoo subway station, waiting to spend the day with Justin and his son, Sam. I couldn't believe

I had gone from being a reasonably happy, but delusioned, wife six months ago to a single mother dating a man with a child.

Justin's invitation to join him and Sam came as a surprise, and I didn't know what to expect. From what I could remember about meeting Sam at Union Station almost half a year ago, he seemed well-behaved but considering my frame of mind at that time, I could be wrong. Justin had told me that Sam was shy. To parents, that's sometimes a code word for rude.

What if he doesn't like me? What if I don't like him? There's nothing worse than children clinging to you, and you would rather they didn't.

I saw them coming up from the subway and was immediately impressed that Justin was holding Sam's hand because the stairs from the subway were so steep. It was like watching people come up from the center of the earth. Whenever I climbed them, I never looked back because I was always afraid of tumbling back down.

"Sorry we're late," Justin apologized. It's been a while since I've been on the train and now that they've added all those new lines, it's really a monster."

"Daddy got lost," Sam said with a little giggle. The look that passed between father and son was precious.

"Hey, little man, you remember Miss Jewel?" *Oh, yes, the crazy woman from Union Station.*

The little boy looked up with those big haunting eyes and shook his head a little.

We said our hellos, and his voice, a shy, almost-whisper, could scarcely be heard above the city's noise. *He seems sweet enough, but there is something so sad and old in that little face - an old soul is what the older folks would say.*

Sam looked around for a brief moment, taking in his surroundings, and then asked in a puzzled way, "I thought we were going to the zoo?" The question wasn't a whine, merely an observation of the obvious - where is it?

"You have to climb this big hill before you get there," I said as I squatted down to his level. "Have you ever been here before?"

He looked a little surprised to have me down on his level and just shook his head and then, as if remembering his manners, answered with a very polite "no."

"Then you are in for a treat," I grinned. "Let's get moving before the animals wonder where we are."

"You mean they know we're comin'?" Sam asked, surprised.

"Of course. I come up here all the time and talk to them." I had him entranced now. "I told them that you were coming, and they promised not to hide. Well, everyone except the bears. They are very unreliable. Do you know what that means?"

Sam shook his head and then remembered to give me a no.

"Well, it means that I can ask them to do something and they'll all be like 'Sure, of course Jewel, we'll be out just for you,' but instead they stay in their caves all day. When I ask them to come out because they promised and all, they start saying something like, 'It's cold,' or 'It looks like rain and I might get tangles in my fur.'"

I saw a little smile behind Sam's eyes as we started up the hill. "Are you two hungry? Did you want to get something to eat first?"

"No, I want to see the animals. They might think that we're not coming," Sam answered, looking worried.

"Oh, I wouldn't worry about that. They know that I would never stand them up," I assured him.

"Well, what do you say to Mickey D's?" Justin asked.

"No, Daddy. Can't we go afterwards - please?"

"All right, you're the man, Sam."

Walking along, with mc yakking all the way, I noticed those huge eyes on me every now and again, and I would turn and smile, and his face would light up. When Sam wasn't watching me, I was watching him. He looked so cute as he marched up that steep hill.

"So what grade are you in, Sam?"

"Kindergarten. My teacher's name is Miss Brown."

"Do you like her?"

"Yes, she's very nice."

"I never went to kindergarten," I offered.

"You didn't?!"

And even Justin was surprised. "Really?"

"Nope, I went straight to first grade."

"Did you know that's how I met your father - in school?"

Sam nodded his little head and huffed out a yes. "I think we're finally here," Justin announced as he panted up the last few steps before getting to flat land.

"As if you're really tired," I teased.

"You walk this every day?" Justin asked.

"Sure do - it helps keep me in shape." I was happy that Justin gave no leering looks that could have made me blush. I hate pretending that children can't figure out what you're talking about. It was clear that Sam sensed something was up here, and I wanted to make sure that it was okay with him.

Any doubts I may have had about me and this little boy flew away when I felt a small hand place itself in mine. Sam had my hand and was staring straight ahead, waiting for me to give the go ahead to cross the street. I felt a surge of elation. But what really made my heart soar was that when we got across the street, he didn't let go even when I loosened my grip a little. When I looked down at him, I could have sworn that he had just entrusted me with his little heart. From that moment what I had been afraid was going to be a long day to be endured turned out to be a blur of amusement. From watching the monkeys and trying to coax the bears out, we had a ball. Even when it was all over, and we had seen all that there was to see, the highlight for me was the simple act of holding hands with shy, little Sam.

CHAPTER 13

"So this is what's going to happen every time I make a mistake?" Justin asked, sounding a little exasperated which was fine because I was feeling really pissed myself.

"Mistake? Did I say *you* made a mistake? Oh, no, *I* made the mistake of sitting here for the last three hours, and you can bet I won't make it again!" I was moving like a whirlwind gathering my things. "I am so sorry that I even bothered."

"Jewel . . ." he started, but I cut him off.

"No, you're right, of course." Attitude was just pouring out of every pore of my being. *Why would he do this to me? He's the one who called me and asked me out. He's the one who dropped his keys off to me so that I could go to his apartment and not be stuck at the office, waiting for him to get off from work. So when he comes in three hours late what am I supposed to think? That he forgot his own phone number? No, I don't think so.*

I was standing in the middle of Justin's huge living room, where I knew every book on his bookshelf, the exact number of steps from the window seat to the bathroom and how long the water runs after you've flushed the toilet. No surprise because three hours is a helluva long time to wait for anyone to show up.

"Dammit, Jewel, I screwed up and didn't think to call, but don't do this! I can be but so understanding and believe me I have been, but . . ." *Oh, no, he didn't say that, as if he has been enduring a major hardship! Oh, now it's on!*

Sarcasm dripped from my words. "Oh, I'm so sorry that it's taken so much out of you. Well, fine. Forget it then!" And the whirlwind that was Jewel began again with me stuffing my keys in my purse and getting my hat while Justin dropped to the couch looking sad and pitiful.

Again, he apologized. "Look, I'm sorry. You have every right to be upset and I shouldn't have said that - it's just that I'm tired and frustrated . . ." He held out his hand to me, but I was still hot and stood looking toward the window at the same stuff I had seen since six o'clock.

"Yeah, frustration has a way of letting the truth come out, doesn't it?" I shot at him, trying to hurt him for some reason unknown to me, making me angry with myself. *Why am I tripping like this? We don't really have anything together - he's never even kissed me!*

"I'm sorry," Justin said again, imploring me with his eyes not to let this blow up any further.

Too late, I thought, with a major self-inflicted hurt attitude and said, "I told you this wouldn't work."

I was ready to hit the door, but Justin stood up and stopped me, saying wearily, "No, what doesn't work is me not calling to say that I'm going to be late."

"No," I cut in, sticking out my chin and holding up my head, feigning indifference. "You don't owe me a thing. Not an explanation nor an apology or anything else. I don't own you." I said this to the ceiling and when he didn't respond after a moment, I stole a look over in his direction, and he was staring straight at me. *Why am I doing this? I care for him.*

My anger dissolved into self-pity, as I walked us through what I was sure to be our final farewell. "Everything starts off great and wonderful, and people want to spend all their time with each other." I was now the one who sounded exhausted. "And then all of a sudden somebody needs space but is just too nice to say so. So they make up excuses so as not to hurt anyone's feelings instead of just saying, 'let's slow down.' Before you know it, BAM! You never even see it coming until you're standing all alone and completely lost." I sighed - a deep sigh - feeling very sorry for myself because I knew that it was over even before it got started. *I've been misreading this whole situation. We really were just friends. Single parents with something in common. God, Jewel, you are so stupid!*

"Are you finished?" he asked.

"Yes. Just let me get out of your way. I'm sure that you're tired and want to get some rest." I started moving toward the door, determined to really go through it this time.

"You know, you are very unfair most of the time."

"And why is that?" I asked, getting a little defensive.
"Because I'm doing you a favor?"
"And what favor is that?" He seemed mildly amused.
"I'm getting out of your way."
"Like Malcolm did for you?" The question was quiet but it hit with the force of a hurricane. When I didn't respond, Justin continued. "Look, leaving your ex out of this, you always get to say what you want and then try to run away. Like if you don't say it quickly and run then you won't be heard. Well, guess what? I hear you, but do you hear me?"
"I don't know what you mean. And as far as Malcolm goes ..." I began, ready to end this on the worst possible note, but Justin cut me off.
"If you want to go, it's completely up to you. But I don't want you to." Justin moved closer until he was right over top of me. "I'm sorry that I was late and didn't call. Next time I will. I'm sorry that you've been hurt in the past. If you allow me, I'll try to make it up to you but it's gonna take time. But look at this." He reached in his back pocket and pulled out his wallet and opened it up to his driver's license photo. "I can't apologize for being Justin and not Malcolm."
"I never wanted you to be Malcolm!" I protested.
"No, but you dish out punishment that I think you mean to be for him and not me. Your punishments don't fit my crimes."
I hung my head down real low at that one because it was true. "I'm so sorry. Maybe I came to you with a little too much baggage." I sighed. "I don't have any right to bring you into my problems."
"You're doing it again, and the funny thing is that I really don't think that you know when you are!" Justin said with a hint of exasperated laughter.
"Doing what?" I asked, really puzzled this time.
"You're trying to find some way to push me away. Now honestly ask yourself, is that what you want?" He held his hand under my chin and forced me to look into his eyes. There was a trust there - a readiness to give of himself.
"Is that what you want?" It looked as if he could almost read the conflict raging in my mind.

"No." My answer was soft and uncertain. It was hard to think with him standing so close, tilting my head up as if he were going to kiss me. I began to reach for him.

"Good, then let's go!"

What?! What happened? Why is he getting his jacket instead of kissing me? Now he's asking me if we still have time to make some show.

"We can grab some food first if you tell me what you want."

"Whatever you feel like," I murmured, feeling a little flushed and very embarrassed. *I must be reading this whole thing all wrong!*

"Come on, then. Let's do Chinese since it's not too heavy. I know a place that fixes it great not far from the club." He chuckled.

We moved toward the elevators and out into the chilly night. I felt a little better but still very unsure about what had happened back in the apartment. Then I realized that it wouldn't have stopped with just a kiss. Maybe Justin knew it too. *But why would that bother him so much unless he's turned off by me? Or maybe he just doesn't want to go that way yet. I'll give him a little more time to make his intentions clear, and then this silent crap is going out the window.*

CHAPTER 14

Sunlight streamed through the balcony window and washed over Tia and me in the silent apartment. We were stretched out in front of the sofa going through the stationery catalog that her grandparents allowed her to bring home. Its colorful pages, filled with all sorts of invitations and party paraphernalia, had kept Tia engrossed for all of thirty minutes now, which, for my child, was a record for anything that doesn't have music and quick cuts. Tia's birthday being only three weeks away is what had set her mind to finding the perfect decorations and party invitations. She was slowly making her way through the book, using one of my school highlighters to circle the stuff she liked. This meant just about everything including the big unity candles used in weddings as well as the feathered plumes you would use to recreate Mardi Gras in your home.

"Well, what about this one?" I asked pointing to her favorite dog character but she was shaking her head. "You don't like that show anymore?"

"No, I still like it," she said absently.

"Just not for the party?"

"Right."

Sometimes I try to probe a little deeper, trying to find out if there is a deeper meaning. Most of the time there isn't, although sometimes the rationale can be very funny. Once Jazz asked her second youngest who refused to be potty trained, if she had peed in her bed the night before. Noel looked very indignantly at her mother and said no, even though Jazz was standing there with a pair of wet panties between her fingers.

I was afraid that Jazz was going to try and kill her for telling such a bold-faced lie, but instead Jazz took a deep breath and holding the panties out for Noel to see, she tried again, "Noel. Did you pee in your bed last night?"

The little girl looked at her mother like which part didn't you get and told her, "No, I didn't pee in my bed last night. I peed in your bed!" I fell out.

"Well, what about Elmo?" I asked Tia since that was what I had decided on anyway.

"I love Elmo!" she answered enthusiastically. Which was good since I had arranged for a little birthday production by a group of actors who were friends of Ashley's and members of a children's workshop. They had put together a replica of the Sesame Street set, with costumes and everything.

"Mommy," Tia said, grabbing my hand. "Look at this."

"Tia, we have been through this book six times already."

But she was closing the stationery book and sifting through some other catalogs spread out around her. I smiled at the sight of her, no longer than a yardstick, lying on her tummy, her little legs ending in her favorite Elmo slippers. Leaning on her elbows, she carefully moved aside the discarded books until she came upon the one she was looking for.

"This one," she said, patting the space on the carpet next to her that I was in the process of vacating. Lowering back down, I looked at pages that were already covered with highlighted marks.

I feigned ignorance. "What do you need this stuff for?"

"Presents!" she answered brightly.

"Presents? You don't need any presents," I scoffed.

"Mommy." She gave me her little warning tone like this was an issue too serious to play with.

"Oh, I see, you mean the presents that you're going to give to me!"

"It's not *your* birthday!" Tia declared, scrambling to her knees. Placing her hands on her non-existent hips, she informed me, "You don't get presents when it's not your birthday. You're suppose to give 'em. To share," she pronounced carefully. I started laughing at her lecture expression. The little smile that was twitching the corners of her mouth and the fact that she had her eyes closed but the eyebrows raised in that superior manner just made me want to eat her up.

"But what about Grammy?" I challenged her, getting to my knees, ready to face off with her.

Tia opened her eyes in surprise.

"That's right. I always give Grammy something on my birthday."

She started to open her mouth, not really knowing how to debate this fact, and then started laughing at herself as she fell over on her side, defeated for the moment but happily so.

"Nah!" I said bending over in her face, my grin matching her own.

She stopped laughing and held up her index finger as if hit with an epiphany.

"See, there you go!" I pulled her up into my lap where I proceeded to tickle her while she squirmed and twisted to get away from my invading fingers.

"Do I get my present?" I stopped my assault waiting to see what she would say, waiting while Tia sucked in her breath and when she said no, I started all over again. Over her howling laughter, the phone began beeping.

"All right, you." I rolled her off my lap, her little body collapsed in a heap of quick breaths and giggles as she tried to recover. I went for the phone.

"Hey, girl, whatcha doing?"

"Hey, Robyn. What's going on with you?"

Tia dragged her toy catalog over to me and settled down in the space between my knees, as I sat on the floor with my back against the wall.

"Same old, same old." Robyn sighed.

I laughed and told her that the drama in my life would be too much for her to stand.

"Oh, I don't know, what's wrong with a little drama? My life is settled and boring. Hey!"

I smiled as I knew that Frank must be close by.

"Oh, please, Robyn. It's not all that - my life, that is."

"Yeah, right. I don't have a gorgeous, handsome, sensitive brother, who understands that the role of parenting goes beyond a quick two-hour visit and a monthly paycheck, chasing me around."

"Better not be!" I heard Frank shout in the background as he went into some playful tirade about how wonderful he was to Robyn. There was a time when this glimpse of happily married life would have really depressed me; now I just felt a little envious.

"So, Jewel, what I meant to ask is, what's going on?"

"I wish I knew," I sighed into the phone. I remained perplexed by the romantic signals being sent out by Justin. Whenever I began to think that we were heading down that road, it was as if we hit the border, and I didn't have the necessary paperwork to cross over. I asked Robyn what she thought.

"Well," she began reflectively, "maybe he's afraid of a rebound thing - getting hurt again."

"I don't know," I said doubtfully.

Then I speculated that maybe Justin had been protecting Sam. Not wanting him to be confused with a lot of women coming and going. Maybe Justin wanted Sam to understand the value of a commitment.

Robyn seemed to agree. "From what you've said and what I've seen, he seems to be a down-to-earth brother who's trying to be very careful about who he spends time with since it affects so much more than just the lives of two consenting adults."

"YEAH! Dat's right! The brother is representin' the feelings! Can I get a witness?!"

I laughed out loud at Frank shouting in the background.

My conversation with Robyn was interrupted by the beeping in the phone, letting me know that someone was trying to get through.

Robyn said she had to go anyway, and we said goodbye.

I clicked the button to switch lines. "Hello?"

"Jewel?" I found myself unconsciously smiling, glad to hear from Justin as was becoming the pattern, amused that Robyn and I seemed to talk him up. "Hey, Justin. What's up?"

"Are you busy?"

"Well, Tia and I were going through some books and I was talking to Robyn on the phone."

Justin let out a deep breath and started talking. "Jewel, I'm stuck at court waiting to give my deposition for this trial, and I can't seem to find my mother . . ."

I was wondering what this had to do with me since we didn't have any plans that night.

"See, the problem is that I don't know how much longer I'm going to be stuck here and . . ." *Oh, God. Does he think after last week that he has to check in with me whenever he's going to do something out of the ordinary? Oh, please, I hope not.*

I felt embarrassed as Justin continued, and I was ready to cut him off and let him know that this was not necessary when I realized that he had stopped talking and all that was rushing through the earpiece at me was the sound of an expectant pause.

"Hey, if you can't do this, I'll understand." *Do what? Great! Now how do I play it off like I was paying attention?*

"Jewel, are you there?"

"Y-y-yes, of course," I stammered.

"But if you do pick Sam up, I promise that I'll be there no later than seven. It's just that the aftercare closes at six thirty, and I hate to think of him there all by himself."

That's it! He wants me to pick up Sam! I let out a sigh of relief. "Sure, no problem. Just give me the address and I'm on my way."

Before hanging up, Justin apologized. "I am so sorry to put you out like this."

I assured him that it was really no problem and that I felt honored that he would entrust me with Sam. I felt a little guilty because I would have never even thought about doing the same with Tia.

"Ready, Tia?" I asked.

"Where are we going?"

"To get Sam."

She nodded as she headed out the door in front of me as if that were good enough for now.

Everyone was going home, and the city was in the second of its daily gridlocks. As we crept along bumper-to-bumper, I looked back at Tia, worried that she would become fidgety, but she had her little books and my highlighter so she was cool. Finally we started moving, and I checked my watch as I flew through the yellow light.

"Aawwww, Mommy!" Tia's warning voice came from the back, and I felt a twinge of guilt. I usually made a conscientious effort to be careful, especially with Tia in the car.

"Sorry, Tia, but I was going too fast to slam on the brakes." And it was true especially since the guy behind was riding my bumper. If I had stopped he would have been sitting in the front seat with me.

"Then slow down," she admonished, before returning back to her book.

"Yes, ma'am." And I did.

At the center, the director gave me a really hard time about picking up Sam, saying that they had strict rules and that I could only take him if she had prior consent from the parent to release him to me. Fortunately, it turned out that there was a message from Justin which someone had forgotten to give her, so after making a copy of my driver's license, Sam was turned over to me, and I introduced him to Tia.

Once we were all settled in the car, I headed home. "Sorry about the holdup, Sam, but they wanted to make sure that you really know me and that you feel okay going home with me and Tia for a little while. Do you?"

"Yes," he said quietly. Glancing back into the mirror I quickly made my own assessment - no problem - Tia had his undivided attention, going over her present list, asking him what he already had. Since the rush hour had died down a bit, we made great time in getting home.

Tia stepped out first and went straight to the curb just like Malcolm and I had taught her, with Sam following close behind. When we arrived in the apartment, Tia started dragging him away.

"Tia, let him get his bearings first!"

"I'm okay," Sam assured me, and they both disappeared into her room.

I checked the answering machine. The first message was from Malcolm which I fast forwarded in case he mentioned any details of Tia's party. The second was from Justin saying that he was leaving the courthouse and should be here shortly.

I placed some chicken in the broiler, put a big pot of water on the stove to boil, and searched the cabinets for some sauce. Blessing my good fortune, I was satisfied with what I had put together by the time I called the kids to dinner.

Placing their plates at the kitchen table, they both seated themselves and seemed to be impressed with dinner. At least I didn't see any curled lips or upturned noses.

"I hope you like garlic bread, Sam." The heat from the broiler had made the bread crispy, and the smell of garlic and butter was heavenly.

When I turned around, both children were in the middle of prayer, and I was so touched by the sight. But soon they were both gobbling their dinner as if it were the first one they'd ever had, and I was glad that I hadn't stopped off and grabbed some fast food junk.

"Mommy, you have messages," Tia announced around a mouthful of food.

"Yes, I know," I said, pouring them both a glass of fruit punch soda. "And don't talk with food in your mouth, you'll choke."

Sam and Tia exchanged looks that said, "Aren't adults so cute!"

I had started cleaning up the kitchen when the door buzzer went off, startling the kids who were eating steadily with an occasional "watch this," followed by the sound of slurping up noodles.

I went to the intercom. "Yes?"

"Is this Jewel Webster - oh, I mean Stone?" The woman's voice caught me off guard for a second. "Yes?"

"This is Barbara Baptiste, Justin's mother."

"That's my Grandma!" Sam sang out, just as shocked as I was.

"Oh, hello, Ms. Baptiste. Please come up when you hear the click." I was tempted to change out of my jeans and tee shirt or at least slip back into my shoes, but there wasn't time. Instead, I smoothed my hair back into my scrunchie and went to greet her in the hall at the top of the stairs.

"Hi!" I called out, listening for her approach. I debated as to whether or not she would be insulted if I met her halfway to help her the rest of the way. Even though there are only three flights, it can sometimes seem that you've been climbing forever. As I struggled with my dilemma, I saw her turn around the last flight, and decided that she didn't look any the worse for wear. Come to think of it, she didn't look much different from the last time I had seen her at our eighth grade graduation.

"Well, you look pretty much like you did at St. Thomas More, so I'm going to assume that you're Jewel!"

"Yes." I smiled as I went toward her, offering my hand.

"That's good," she breathed as we walked toward the apartment. "That climb gives me a chance to work the kinks out of my legs." She looked great in beige slacks, which were just a few shades lighter than her skin tone, and a white silk blouse tucked into the waist encircled by a thin gold belt. Her flat beige shoes made an echoing click as we drew closer to the light coming from the end of the hall. "Is Sam still here?"

Her question was answered when the normally reserved little boy came barreling out straight to his grandmother who lifted him up in a hug.

"How did you know Sam was here?" I asked. The light caught her chestnut brown hair that was stylishly cut into a very short bob parted on the side.

"From the day care center. I thought this was a good chance to come by and say hello." I knew that there was more to it than that, but it was cool, especially since she didn't seem to be trying to peek into the rooms on the sly.

"I wish that I could say that my house doesn't look like this all the time, but that would be a lie." I gathered the catalogs that Tia had dropped on the floor when we came in.

"It looks fine to me."

"Please come in and sit down." I suddenly felt a mental push from my mother to remember my manners. "The kids were just eating a little dinner. Would you care for anything?"

"No, thank you, but it sure does smell good."

"It is good, Grandma!" Sam said, as he and Tia went back to finish their plates.

"And who is this little lady?" Mrs. Baptiste asked, looking in Tia's direction.

"I'm Tia Jade Stone." Tia enunciated this perfectly.

"And what did you eat, Lady Tia?"

"Well," she began coyly, "this is really my second dinner. The first one was spaghetti at my Grandma's house."

"Honey, you just keep eating like that while you can; before you know it, you'll be trying to talk yourself out of even one meal a day! And what did you have, Sam?"

"Chicken, cucumbers, noodles, and bread." He had to recite it from memory because there was nothing but a little sauce left on his plate.

Mrs. Baptiste raised her eyebrows in amazement. "I am impressed. Most working women would have stopped for something quick and easy."

"Oh, it took less than twenty minutes, and I didn't mind." I shrugged it off modestly.

"Well, thank you again for going out of your way to pick up Sam for Justin."

"It was no problem at all. I think that Tia liked the company." The two of them had disappeared again to Tia's room.

"I think that I can say the same for Sam," she said ruefully. "It almost breaks my heart that he's not just an only child but so alone in other ways as well."

"I know, but he seems happy. Quiet, but happy."

"Yes, Justin is doing a wonderful job." Her voice rang with pride. "But what kind of grandmother would I be if I didn't come meddlin' just a little?" She smiled mischievously.

My expression must have been completely duh because Mrs. Baptiste winked at me and said, "I just couldn't pass up the opportunity to meet you once it presented itself to me in the form of your license and address at the day care center."

I thought of my own mother and knew that she would have done no less. I offered Ms. Baptiste something to drink.

"No, thanks. I'd better get Sam home before it gets too late and my husband wonders where we are."

"Well, I hope that your visit put your mind at ease just a little."

"Oh, my, yes."

"Because I would love to be called upon for services any time they're needed. Or at least for a visit because I know that Tia will ask me about Sam every other day until she sees him again." I laughed.

"So this is the first time that the children have met?" Mrs. Baptiste sounded a little surprised.

"Uh . . . yeah." I felt a little awkward trying to explain something that I was still very unclear about myself, but the older woman knew when to stop, enabling us to establish a comfortable ending for our first meeting and setting the tone for the next.

"When Justin comes . . ." but she was cut off by the buzzer. I knew it was Justin before even asking.

Sam and Tia came running out, and Mrs. Baptiste told Sam to gather his stuff.

He moved a little slowly, and I was afraid that Tia was about to cry. "Is that Sam's daddy coming?"

"Yep." I stooped down to see if I could get an emotional reading.

"He has to go?" Tia asked unhappily.

"Uh-huh."

Sam and I both stopped short when I opened the door and Justin came into the room . . . minus the beard and mustache I was used to!

"Daddy, you shaved!"

"Well, son, a man always tries to look his best when he's going to meet a pretty girl."

Justin picked up Sam who immediately observed, "You smell good, too!"

A person would have to be color blind not to have seen the blush creeping up Justin's face. He cleared his throat and turned to his mother. "Hey, Mama, what are you doing here?" Justin kissed his mother's upturned cheek.

"Just trying to help you out a little, but it seems that Tia here had everything under control. And if you really want to impress a pretty girl, do something about these." And she grabbed a handful of his locs.

"Yeah, yeah, yeah," he teased.

Tia was resting her head on my chest, clearly not happy with the turn of events.

"This is Tia?" Justin came closer, bending slightly so that he would be eye level with her. "I have heard so much about you." He reached out to shake her tiny hand. "How much do I owe you, Tia?"

She looked at him in laughing surprise. "You can't give me any money!"

"Why not? Didn't you take care of Sam for me?" By now both Tia and Sam were giggling.

"No, I'm too little! Mommy did everything!"

"Oh, well, then," Justin said, getting up and turning toward me, "how much . . ."

"My services can't be bought," I said haughtily.

"Well, seriously, thanks so much again. You really helped me out." He gave me a little peck on the cheek and squeezed my shoulder.

I was on delayed time for a minute, wondering if it was static electricity that caused the shock I felt when his lips brushed my cheek.

"Well, I guess we'd better get on across town."

"Jewel, I hope to see you again some time," Mrs. Baptiste said at the door.

"Oh, I hope so. Actually, there's something special going on soon."

"My party!" Tia started jumping up and down.

"Tia, don't forget there are people under us."

She stopped abruptly and crouched as if she had just been caught in a prison searchlight. And then softly she started again, "My party!"

"You're having a party?" Justin asked. "What? You taking a trip? Retiring from work?"

"No, a *birthday* party!" Tia explained.

"Oh, I see." Justin nodded as if that thought had never occurred to him.

"Mommy, can Sam come to the party?"

"What about me?" Justin chimed in like a little kid.

"Me, too?" Mrs. Baptiste asked. "I can bring my own paper plate."

"That's okay - there's plenty. Can they come, Mommy?"

"Sure. I was going to send them an invitation when they went out next week."

"Wanna see what I want?" Tia asked, moving toward the magazine she left on my desk.

"Tia!" I cried sharply, pulling her back against my legs, completely embarrassed as everyone tried not to laugh out loud. "Tia, let's walk everyone down to their cars. Then you and I will have a little talk about etiquette when we come back up."

We saw them off and headed back upstairs to get ready for the rest of the week. The apartment suddenly seemed so empty and quiet with the Baptiste family gone, but then it was business as usual with just me and my little straight-from-the-hip little girl (not that I would have had her any other way). After trying unsuccessfully to con me into letting her watch an entire movie, she settled down into bed and afterward, I listened to the answering machine again. I used to jump at the chance to find out if Malcolm had called, hoping to satisfy my heart by listening to his voice. But that behavior was becoming more and more infrequent. *"Could it be because of a certain detective?"* my head asked my heart. *Could be. Could be.*

CHAPTER 15

The balloons and streamers were everywhere. On the floor, hanging from the walls, some even trailing behind the fifty or so children running all over the place. The lodge hall of Malcolm's dad had been transformed into that sunny day, the place where the air is clean. The actors had really outdone themselves and the little guests seemed to concur. The big muppets had been kept to a minimum so as not to scare the toddlers. Big Bird sat on his "nest," greeting the children instead of chasing them down - to a small child, seeing the eight-foot bird on television was very different from having him up close and personal. The rest of the Sesame Street characters were holding conversations from windows or their trashcan homes, and the little children came up to shake a furry hand or just smile and giggle as the actors made the characters come alive.

When Tia first arrived and saw the then dormant Sesame Street set, she was shocked. Big Bird pretended to be asleep and snored softly as Tia and I timidly approached. I nudged Tia to say something to wake him up.

"Hello, Big Bird?" she said holding onto my hand, standing firmly by my side.

"Try again," I urged.

"Big Bird, wake up!" Tia tried again, this time stretching her neck out as far as it would go. The big yellow bird began making all kinds of snorting, waking up sounds as his eyes began to flutter open and closed.

"Tia?" he asked uncertainly.

"Yes," she responded, equally uncertain.

"Tia Stone?" Big Bird asked as if he were in awe of her.

"Yes."

"Oh, my goodness! Everybody! Tia's here! Come on, everybody!" Feathers began flying as he began calling out. Suddenly everyone started popping out from the big faux apartment building, all shouting "HAPPY BIRTHDAY, TIA!"

Lou released the balloons and confetti that had been tied up against the skylight dome, and the celebration began.

"Come on, Annette!" Tia cried enthusiastically, and she pulled Annette behind her into the sea of balloons, streamers and noise. Everyone had said I was crazy to invite Annette, but as I explained to Malcolm when I issued the invitation, if Tia was going to be spending time with her, then I had a right to get to know her. I hadn't been sure that he would bring her, but now I knew.

Watching Tia drag her off, I wished I could say my mind played tricks on me that long-ago January day - but no, my memory hadn't exaggerated Annette's appearance. She was gorgeous, and I felt stupid in the little sunsuit that Tia had insisted I wear to match hers. Annette looked so beautiful in a pleated, navy blue tennis skirt with a light blue polo shirt. Her long legs flowed into a pair of slip-on sandals that didn't exaggerate her height, just made her feet look good along with the rest of her. *When will my world stop going in slow motion whenever I see her, as if I need to imprint her every detail on my mind?*

I noticed Malcolm also watching Tia and Annette, and a feeling of foreboding washed over me. *The way he looked at them together - did they complete a happy picture for him?* I tried to recall Jazz's words on the issue of sole custody. My mind was filled with doubt, perhaps from seeing Tia with Annette for the first time or perhaps an irrational fear that my child would also choose the beautiful Annette over me.

Something needed for the party broke into my thoughts, and after busying myself with that, I ran into Tia and Annette again over by the cake table.

"Malcolm said that you needed a face painter?" Annette asked, giving Tia a little tweak on her stomach.

"Face painting?!" Tia squealed, and suddenly we were surrounded by a group of yelling voices all demanding "ME FIRST! ME FIRST!"

"BIRTHDAY GIRL GETS TO GO FIRST," Annette announced over the noise.

"Mommy, you go first," Tia insisted, so I reluctantly sat down and removed my glasses, hoping that for once my failed vision would benefit me and turn my successor into a big blur - but with my exposed face only inches from hers, I wasn't lucky enough to be completely blind. Every detail was there for me to see. A blue headband held her hair away from her face which was sheer perfection. The lips formed a small O as Annette carefully started applying the paint strokes to my cheeks. I could see her complexion was flawless, and it made me think about my own. *Maybe she'll play connect the dots with the little moles that came after Tia was born.* My doctor had told me they were brought on by my changing hormones. Funny how they never bothered me until now. I kept wondering why I never knew that this was the kind of woman that Malcolm wanted. *How much about Malcolm does she know? Does he confide in her like he never did with me? Or does she just take his moodiness in stride? Maybe there's no reason for him to be moody now that she's in his life.*

"Oops! I'm sorry." Annette's little cry of alarm brought me back from my reverie. She was looking for a tissue to fix a mistake she had made. When I looked down at her hands, I was shocked to see they were trembling. *She's scared!* I was amazed. Then it occurred to me that she wasn't the bad guy. She was just the right person for Malcolm, but she came at the wrong time for me. She probably had no idea that as far as I was concerned, Malcolm and I were still happily married when she came into the picture. In all likelihood, Malcolm started a relationship based on a lie, but that was on him.

Annette took a deep breath and tried to steady her hand, telling me with a nervous smile that she was usually much better at this. "There," she said finally, sitting back and reaching for the hand mirror.

I looked at the painting of the balloon on my cheek that read "Number One Mom." "It's great," I said with a smile. "Looks like you're going to be busy!"

Small faces were peering at me and then turning to Annette, asking, "Can you make a kite? Can you make a rainbow?"

I wandered away.

"She seems nice," Robyn said as I approached my posse.

"Well, unfortunately she is," I said with a sigh and avoided looking in her direction so she wouldn't think we were talking about her.

"How old is she, anyway?" Jazz asked, sizing her up.

"I think she's a little younger than me, twenty or so." *Does it matter?* "Let's tell everyone who wants their faces painted to do it now; otherwise, we'll never get to the presents and cake." Just my way of reminding my friends that this was Tia's day and we could discuss Malcolm's new love later.

"I'll do it," Jazz volunteered, and we all broke and headed in different directions to work the party.

For the rest of the hour, I was discreetly asked in a number of different ways if that was Annette, as eyes gazed over in the direction of the beautiful young lady who was laughing and painting faces. I had to steel myself to keep from shouting, "YES, THAT'S ANNETTE! THE WOMAN THAT MY HUSBAND LEFT ME FOR!"

Once, standing next to Mommy, I looked up and saw Malcolm give Annette a peck on the cheek.

"Now that is inappropriate," Mommy said, disapproval all over her face.

"Oh, Mommy, I'm not going to worry about that. We're here for Tia and to have a good time."

Mommy took her attitude with her into the kitchen and helped Quinton and Lou wheel out a huge cake on top of which were Sesame Street characters, smiling and waving. Malcolm and I each went to stand awkwardly on either side of Tia who was standing on a chair at the cake table. She placed her arms around both of our necks, as Lou turned out the lights and everyone began to sing *Happy Birthday!* Just then someone snapped a picture of Tia getting ready to blow out the candles, with Malcolm and me smiling at her, and I wondered, if once it were developed, would Annette be seen standing just off to the left behind Malcolm, smiling too. It would be so much easier if I could just hate her or him or both, but I couldn't, which made it all the harder to bear.

After the three candles were removed from the cake, I reached for the knife and began to quickly cut little squares. During a quick scan to make sure everyone had plates, I was startled to see Tia and Sam sitting together between Malcolm and Justin! I wondered what they were talking about, but didn't have time to think on it too long, before someone was at me, asking for more punch. Then it was time for the presents. Before I knew it, parents were thanking me for a wonderful time, as they headed towards the elevators where Mommy was dispensing party bags.

"Jewel?" Justin, Sam, and Justin's parents were coming to say their goodbyes.

"Thank you for inviting me," Sam said.

"Well, you are very welcome. Thank you for coming." I smiled down at him and rubbed his head. He was such a serious little fellow.

"Yes, thank you," Barbara and Clarence Baptiste said, almost in unison.

"Excuse me, Jewel, can I talk to you for a minute?" Malcolm had come up behind me with Tia in his arms.

"Sure." I turned back to the Baptiste clan and said, "I'll see you all soon, I hope."

"No doubt about it," Justin smiled as the doors began to close.

I turned back to Malcolm.

"Jewel, would you mind if I took Tia out for a little while? Just so we could spend a little daddy/daughter time?" *I hope he doesn't expect me to entertain Annette while he's gone!*

"Annette's going home with my parents." Funny how he could still read my mind while his was a complete void to me now.

"Sure. I'll give you a page when we're finished here. Did you have a good time?" I asked my now three-year-old baby.

"Yep, yep, yep!" She started to kiss my cheek but decided that she didn't want to mess up Annette's artwork so she kissed me on the lips instead. Malcolm and Tia headed toward the elevator, and I waved until the doors completely shut. *This is a feeling I am never going to get used to.*

CHAPTER 16

Kevin and I had agreed to meet after work down by the DuPont Metro station. People were rushing all around me, moving in and out from under the concrete canopy that covered the Metro exit. Trying to stay out of the way, I leaned against one of the heavy pillars. My eyes were drawn to the bank of payphones that stood nearby. I could just give Justin a quick call to make sure that everything was all right. Just to make sure that he hadn't been in an accident, and a broken arm and wired jaw was what had kept him from calling me ever since the party. But that's what had always got me in trouble with Malcolm. I would drive myself crazy when I hadn't heard from him when he said he would call or when I thought he should have called. Of course, I eventually found out what had Malcolm so preoccupied, and the thought of it stopped me from calling Justin.

I tried to stop thinking about Malcolm's infidelity and Justin's complete silence for the last week and scanned Connecticut Avenue looking for Kevin. I wondered if he was a chronically late person and started to get a little uneasy when I realized that I didn't know very much about him. I had often spoken casually with him at the lunch counter of an eatery we both frequented, and it was I who approached him on an impulse and asked him out a couple of days ago after Justin seemed to have disappeared out of my life. Kevin had called last night, but the conversation was stilted and halting - nothing like the natural flow with Justin. Or even Malcolm - his introverted personality had combined with my outgoing one to fashion a comfortable quilt of understanding that enveloped us whenever we were together - too bad I didn't see the tear in the fabric that ultimately disintegrated into shreds. Maybe if I had, I wouldn't be standing here now waiting for a man about whom I knew very little except that he worked real hard at being a cool player.

I checked the clock on my Walkman and noticed that Kevin was now ten minutes late. I looked up and down the street, thinking maybe I was at the wrong entrance - but I doubted that I was wrong. I decided to give it up, go home, and resign myself to the idea that my moment of love was past and that being alone was not so bad. After all, I still had Tia and my family and friends. Nevertheless, my eyes grazed the phones again, and the thought of calling just to leave a quick message on Justin's machine propelled my feet to begin heading in that direction when I heard my name.

"Jewel, whuz up?" When I turned around, Kevin was standing behind me, scowling slightly, as if I had been the one who was now fifteen minutes late.

"We did agree on this entrance, right?" I asked just to make sure that I wasn't really in the wrong.

"Yeah, yeah," Kevin muttered, looking up and down the street. *Who is he looking for?*

"Oh, okay." *He seems different than when I saw him last Wednesday. But he still looks good. Just like a chocolate drop come to life. His head freshly shaved and oiled.* His concern for his personal appearance was what got my attention when I kept running into him at lunchtime.

Because Kevin's everyday wardrobe was always right out of GQ, I couldn't tell if he had dressed up just for me - right now he looked great. His shirt, made of a soft, jersey-type material patterned with all kinds of things like clocks, chains, and some more stuff that seemed to float suspended on a sea of navy blue, slightly billowed as it disappeared, neatly tucked, into a pair of pleated navy blue slacks. A gold watch and chain around his wrist and a stud in his left ear were the only accessories that he wore. The only thing that threw me off was the fact that Kevin wasn't wearing any socks, opting for slipping his feet into a pair of soft leather loafers.

After just standing there waiting for him to say something, like apologize for being late or suggest somewhere to go, I finally made the first move. "So where did you want to go?"

"I don't know." He shrugged.

Okay, this isn't going to be easy. I could feel myself making an effort to go on. "Oh, we could head over to the seafood place down the street? Or we could . . ."

"Do you have your car?" he asked suddenly.

"Well, no," I said hesitantly. "Why, what did you want to do?"

"I was kind of hoping that we could catch happy hour over at that place that they're always talking about on the radio."

"Oh, right. I know that place - it's not too far from here, we could walk." To me, walking is one of the easiest ways to get to know a person. You don't have to worry about food flying out of your mouth during dinner or having to whisper through a movie. Walking is comfortable, and everyone knows how to do it. The expression on Kevin's face, however, said that I had lost my mind. "Well . . . I guess we could go and pick up my car and head back down here," I thought out loud.

"Yeah, they got free parking all night," Kevin announced as if that would be the bait that would get me hooked.

"Sure." After just standing there for a few more moments, I cleared my throat and said, "Well, unless my car's name is Kit, then we'd better go and get it." My little laugh faded off to die - either he didn't get my joke or it wasn't funny to him. We turned and headed into the tunnels of the Metro.

I found out on the train ride that he was late because he was on the phone with one of his boys and lost track of the time. He made me feel uncomfortable by pressing his leg against mine while he tried to make his sparse frame take over the entire seat from Metro Center to the Stadium Armory where my car was parked. He complained because the car was on the second lot. He wasn't capable of sparking enough energy to get a halfway decent conversation going, but when we got to the club, he showed some life as he practically pulled me down the stairs. But any hopes that things might improve were dashed when he told me that if I could do the door, he would get the drinks. I thought that he just meant me, but what he meant was for me to pay for both of us.

I followed behind Kevin into the club, and he immediately started roaming the building like he was on the trail of someone. We finally sat down at a table. First, he got an attitude because I didn't order a drink from the fifty-cent menu. And then pouted when he found out they had discontinued the free buffet after six on Fridays. It got worse. Kevin insisted on showing me his prowess as a pool player. Well, maybe he was able to play, but he was an ugly winner. Most of the fellas were there just to have a little fun. When Kevin acted like he didn't want to relinquish the table, I made my move saying I was ready to go. Then he started whining about how he needed a ride home, and I said that was fine. I walked out of the poolroom, forcing Kevin to follow, and I think everyone was grateful.

He gave me directions to his house, and I drove well over the speed limit, not caring whether I got a ticket - just focusing on becoming one with the hundred-and-thirty-five horses running beneath the hood of my Civic.

As we neared his house, Kevin asked me if I would stop at the Seven Eleven for just a second. I turned in and waited for him to come out, drumming my fingers impatiently. He came out carrying a little paper bag and five minutes later we were at his home. I asked him if he owned the cute little two-story house with the little front lawn that was strewn with bicycle parts and patches of grass.

"Naw, I rent out the basement from my brother and his wife," he announced proudly. "Naw, I wasn't going to stay and mooch off my Mama forever."

Well, maybe Kevin's getting himself together and trying to save a little somethin' somethin' for himself. That explains why he's so frugal. Can't blame a brother for that.

But any good thoughts I managed to muster up about him ended when he pulled out a bottle of Wild Irish Rose and a pack of condoms, and with a lopsided, sly grin, asked me if I wanted to come in for a while. I stiffly declined and put the car into gear. He didn't even have the gumption to put up a fight - just got out, mumbling that he'd see me around.

On the drive home, I wrestled with whether I should call Justin. *Will I wish that I hadn't? Is there a reason why I can't just give him a call? Of course not, we're just friends - maybe if I keep saying it, I'll actually believe it.*

Pushing in my cruising music, I allowed my nervousness to be soothed by the sounds I had put together just for that effect. I decided that I would just call Justin and leave a message that said I was thinking about him and that would be that. Maybe suggest that he call whenever he got the chance. It was no big deal.

* * * *

The sound of someone coming through my front door woke me up. "Who's there?" I called out.
"Jewel? Are you all right?" I sat up, surprised by Ashley's voice as she came through my bedroom door.
"Ashley? What are you doing here? What time is it?" Looking over at the clock it read nine forty-five. Groaning, I climbed out of bed. Ashley had invited me to go and work out with her at the gym, and I had completely forgotten about it.
"Girl, I've been calling you since last Tuesday. Why didn't you call me back?"
"Why didn't you leave a message?" I asked, running past her into the bathroom to get ready.
"I did - three of them. You didn't get them? Something must be wrong with your tape."
I rushed out of the bathroom into the kitchen and lifted the cover of the answering machine with my free hand while brushing my teeth with the other. The tape looked fine. I pulled it out, relieved to see that the machine hadn't eaten it, but perplexed as to what could be wrong with the stupid thing. I shrugged as Ashley reached over and took the tape from my hands.
"Well, here's the problem," she said, holding the tape up in the light. "The tape is twisted right here. Weren't you wondering why you suddenly became so unpopular?"
Then it hit me. "Oh, no!" I froze. *Justin never calls me at work, per my request, and maybe he's been trying to reach me and I . . .*
"What?" Ashley asked, looking up.
"I went on a date last night," I said with a sick feeling in my stomach.
"What? With Justin?" Ashley asked all nonchalantly, as if I hadn't just done one of the stupidest and most impulsive things in the world.

"No, with a jerk!" I cried.
"What are you talking about?"
Standing in front of the machine, I tried to think of something to do about the message I had left Justin last night. Like if I wished hard enough, one of those new features that the phone company was putting out to make our lives better would suddenly appear - if you want to remove a stupid message from a machine, press star eighty-two - star tb for take back.

I jumped when the phone actually rang. Snatching it off the hook, I tried to sound calm when I answered.

"Hello?"
"Good morning, Mommy."
"Hey, Lady! What's up?"
"Can I go with Daddy to ride the horses?" My heart jumped in my throat. *Horseback riding? What is Malcolm thinking? She only turned three last week.* "Let me speak to him."

Malcolm's voice came on the line. "Hello?"
I jumped right in. "Malcolm, she cannot go horseback riding."
"Oh, so now I'm stupid and irresponsible?" he snapped.
Here we go again. I tried to remain calm. "Tia called to ask me if she could go riding and. . ."

Malcolm abruptly cut me off.
"Don't you think I know that Tia can't go horseback riding? We're going to visit a riding camp - I was thinking of enrolling Tia next summer so she's not just sitting around all day with nothing to do." *Is that a stab at me?*

"I thought that we agreed she is too young to get involved in a lot of activities," I reminded him.

"That's why I want to take her now, so that she can get a feel for it and be ready next summer." Malcolm was speaking to me as if I were an idiot.

"So when were you going to discuss her plans with me?" I was getting really ticked because I never made a move without discussing it with him first when it came to Tia. On the other hand, Malcolm often did things like this - like when he took her swimming for the first time. I was furious, not because I didn't think he could keep her from harm's way, but because it was a first moment and I wanted to be a part of it - something

Malcolm was continually trying to deny me. He had even made a snide remark about how I was the one who got to see her every day - that *every* day was a first for her as far as he was concerned. That shut me up, but I could have reminded him that he had created this situation, not me. And I always tried to make it as easy as possible for both of them. I never demanded that Malcolm have Tia home by six o'clock on the nose or anything like that. Still I got treated like the enemy.

"Never mind, Malcolm. I'll see you all when you get here."

"Right, tomorrow evening," he said in his superior way.

I let it go and was ready to hang up when I remembered.

"Oh, just in case, there's something wrong with the answering machine."

"Uh, oh. If it comes with a cord, keep it away from Jewel!" It was the old Malcolm again. The one who liked to tease me. The one that I would like to have for a friend again, despite the pain he caused me.

"Ha! Ha! The tape twisted, and since I'm going to the gym with Ashley, you'll have to page me if you need me."

"Uh, Jewel, don't you think that in an emergency, if I couldn't get you on the phone, I would page you?"

I let it hang for a minute, because I didn't know which person I was talking to. *God, this boy should have been a Gemini for all of his good Malcolm, evil Malcolm.*

"We'll stop off and pick up a new cassette for you." *Ah, it's the good Malcolm.*

"Thanks," I said sincerely and we both hung up.

"That man makes me so crazy sometimes," I raved, heading back to the bedroom. "No matter what I do, it seems to tick him off."

"Well, Jewel, you do sometimes act as if he's Tia's weekend babysitter instead of her father. He can take care of her in any emergency."

"No, what I'm trying to do is make sure that he can contact me in case something happens," I said in my best "I'm trying to be civil about this" tone. "I *am* her mother."

"And he *is* her father and a very capable one at that," Ashley gently reminded me.

"Whatever," I said dully and started changing into something to work out in.

"You're not going to shower?" Ashley asked in a shocked voice as she watched me pull my sneakers on.

"Why should I get showered if I'm just going to the gym to get all funky again?" I grabbed some towels and toiletries for after the workout. "Besides, I took a long bath last night, so come on."

"And just why was a long bath required, Miss Thang?"

"Sorry to disappoint you, but I was terribly disappointed myself." And I told her all about the date on the way to the space age gym.

"So that's why you're so upset about Justin?" Ashley puffed as she climbed to nowhere on the stairmaster.

"Yeah! I left this message on his machine, kind of casually mentioning that I had just gotten home from a date, just so he wouldn't think that all I do is sit by the phone and wait for him to call."

"You know, Jewel, impulsiveness is definitely one of your downfalls."

"Can't help it," I said as the timers went off, signaling that it was time to let the next group on. We moved over to the rowing machines and started punching in the signals to start the simulated race.

"Oh, no, you don't!" Ashley reached over to readjust my level. "You are no beginner." She keyed in for intermediate, and despite my protest the gun sounded followed by the sound of what are supposed to be the oars slicing through the water as my cartoon opponent jumped out ahead of me.

"So what are you going to do?" Ashley asked, really putting her back into it.

"First up, we're basing this on the assumption that Justin has called at all." *Maybe he hasn't been trying to reach me.* That idea caused me to pull a little harder on the machine.

"Come on, based on the way he was watching you at the party, I would say . . ."

"What way?" I asked, slowing down and losing my lead on my computer adversary.

"His eyes hardly ever left you the whole time he was there. You mean you didn't notice?"

"No," I said wonderingly and absently finished the reps on the machine, my stomach fluttering as if I really were on water.

When the gun went off again announcing Ashley as the winner, she held her arms up in mock victory before falling over and gasping for breath. "Come on, let's do some strength and toning."

Obediently, I followed behind Ashley like the dutiful little sister, watching the way everyone, men and women, admired my big sister as she walked by.

My sister is tall and thick with curvy hips, long legs, and a butt that showed how hard she worked out. Her breasts are heavy but not too large, and since she never nursed they're still firm and round. By no means a size four, Ashley has the kind of body that can stop traffic. She is a beautiful black woman - not like the African queens from whence we originally came, but more like our later ancestors. Ashley's stature mirrors the strong back and arms of the women who picked cotton, carried bales of the stuff to be seeded. Thick legs that carried their tired bodies up and down the stairs twenty times a day or more. The graceful neck that despite all of the blows that were bestowed upon it, still held itself erect and proud. It never ceases to amaze me that artists always portray the strength of the black woman, even in slavery. The eyes may be downcast, but the head is only slightly bowed, not bent, almost as if in a silent nod of waiting. Waiting for the day that will allow her to raise it up in freedom. No, there was no way that type of strength could be hidden. And Ashley was the lucky one in whom those genes resurfaced.

"So what are you going to do when you're finished here?" I asked, looking over at my big sister, straining to keep my leg off the floor for the full count.

Ashley checked her watch. "By the time we get showered and changed, I should be able to pry Tamicia away from Mommy. Maybe we'll head over to the museum or go roller skating."

"Oh, don't go inside," I pleaded. "It's too beautiful outside. How about the arboretum?" I suggested, hoping that I would be invited to go along.

"Okay. Maybe we can take some pictures."

I leaned into my stretch, satisfied but unable to relax.

"You can just call him, you know?" Ashley whispered.

"No, I can't. I mean, you know how I would feel if I found out that he was seeing someone else. I just really don't know where I stand with him."

"Trust me, girlfriend, from all that you've told me, I don't think that you have to worry about his feelings for you," Ashley said as walked toward the shower room. "Maybe it wasn't such a bad thing."

"What?"

"The message you left him - maybe it was good to let him know that the grass doesn't grow under your feet."

"But I don't even want to get into playing games," I said and stuck my head under the hot spray of the shower.

"Well, then you're going to have to make a move."

"And what's that?"

"Tell him what's really going on and hope for the best."

"That's what I'm afraid of. How can I know what's going on with someone that I haven't really known all that long?" *And who's only kissed me on the cheek?*

* * * *

At the arboretum, the three of us took pictures, did cartwheels, and when we pulled up into my complex parking lot to drop me off, I was more than a little reluctant to let them go and made several attempts to treat them to dinner.

"Jewel, did you hit the lottery or something?" Ashley asked suspiciously. "Because you sure have been going through an obscene amount of money lately. What's up?"

"It's just some of my savings," I answered, suddenly very ready to get out of her car.

"You mean the money that you and Malcolm were saving to buy a house with?"

I started to squirm while my older sister made me feel like I was six again.

"Jewel, you can still use that money to get a house on your own. There are tons of programs out there . . ."

But I didn't want to hear it. "Don't worry, I've got it covered. Come here, Tamicia, give your Auntie a big kiss." I reached back and pulled the little sweetie pie through the space of the front seats for a kiss and a hug. I made her promise to check her social calendar to see if she could make space for a sleepover with me and Tia. She was still a little shy about being away from Ashley, but we let her know that she was welcome whenever she wanted to come.

"Well, thanks for the day, sister." Kissing Ashley on the cheek, avoiding her look that said "we aren't finished with this yet," I climbed out of the car and jogged up the stairs.

I knew that I'd been dipping into the house fund, as Malcolm and I used to call it, but what else was it good for now, other than to make me feel better by spending it? Together we had saved close to two thousand dollars for a house. Malcolm didn't ask for any of it when we separated. I guess he felt that he owed me. I knew that I could have continued to save and it was stupid to rent, but the idea of buying a house alone scared me.

So I went on spending sprees buying the latest clothes for me and Tia, promising that I would only nip at the interest, but that nipping had left me with only about a thousand - not much toward a place of our own where Tia could have a dog and some space to run around . . . and for things to break that I'd have no clue as to how to fix . . . and for strange noises in the middle of the night!

Shuddering at my insecurities, I put on my Kevon Edmunds CD, poured a respectable glass of wine and went to sit on the balcony. Tonight I was going to enjoy my own company for a change.

The evening trudged on at a snail's pace while I tried to occupy myself with studying but couldn't really get into it - just sort of flipping through the books trying not to look at the phone. Two more glasses of wine later, the beeping of the phone startled me out of my semiconscious state of couch vegetation, and I jumped for the receiver.

"Hello?"

"Hey, Jewel!"

"Hey, Justin. How's it going?" Nothing could have slapped the grin off my face or slowed my thumping pulse.

"I should be asking you, Ms. Busy."

"And, I guess the same could be said of you," I said in a joking tone. "Come to a party and we never hear from you again!"

"Oh, man," I heard him sigh. I was about to cut him off, my head reminding me that he didn't owe me any explanations but he just jumped in. "Sam got sick, an ear infection." My hand instinctively went to my own ear remembering all too well my last ear infection. It was when I was twelve. I woke up because I was sure that someone was jabbing an icepick into the middle of my ear. When I sat up, the pain eased to a low ebb, but no sooner did I turn my head than the icepick was back in full force. So all night it went - stab, ebb, throb, jab. To this day, I always wince when I hear that a child has an ear infection.

"I'm so sorry. Is he okay now?" I asked, completely sympathetic.

"Yeah, but it traveled from one ear to the other. I changed shifts and was home with him during the day and my parents kept him at night." The concern in his voice for his child reminded me of why my heart beat faster whenever I thought of this caring and gentle man. *But that doesn't make him your man, gentle or otherwise! Hey, head! Can't I be happy for just a minute?*

Justin said, "I called you several times to let you know, but I figured you were busy since you didn't call me back. I wanted to call your job but I know that you feel uncomfortable about that and I didn't want to page you because well, I didn't want you to think it was an emergency or anything." He was sounding a little embarrassed. "You know, just paging you to say hello."

"Oh, Justin, my answering machine's been broken. I never got your messages."

"Well, that explains it then." Justin sounded pleased. "So what are you guys up to tonight?"

"Tia's with her father," I sighed.

"Oh, I thought she was with him last weekend."

"Malcolm wanted to stay on track with the agreement, and this was his weekend according to the courts. I inadvertently threw in last weekend as a freebie." My repressed anger made the words pour out a little bitterly, but as I told myself when Malcolm called to let me know that he would be spending the appointed weekend with Tia, from now on, things were going to go by the book.

"So what are you doing with yourself?" Justin asked.

"Not much - I feel at such loose ends when Tias's not here - more or less trying to fill up the hours until she comes back."

"Really? I thought most mothers look forward to having a break from their kids."

"Sure, most of the time, *any* parent, mother or father, needs that little breather, but after about a half hour, you want the little critters back."

"Yeah, that's how I am with Sam when my parents grab him for a weekend. Funny that instead of relaxing at home, I wind up doing an extra duty at work."

"Well, maybe in a few years I'll be happy to hit the streets without a care, but for now, I just hate to be without her." In the beginning Tia had been my baby to protect, and now she was becoming her own little person - and what a wonderful person she was turning out to be. So good natured and mature that I loved every moment we spent together, and so did her father . . . which is why the conflicts arose!

Justin asked me again what I had been up to. "Catch me up on all that I've missed since our last conversation." I could almost hear him settling back getting comfortable.

"Uh . . . well . . . yesterday I went to work, then out with a fella I know. Then this morning, I went with Ashley to the gym and hung out with her and Tamicia all afternoon at the Arboretum." I was speaking quickly, hoping that he was preoccupied with Sam or only half listening, but I wasn't going to be that lucky. Justin asked quietly about my date.

"Oh . . . you know . . . it wasn't all that. As a matter of fact, it was a disaster!" I was trying to keep it light. I described the whole evening. It wasn't necessary to embellish the story to make it sound bad, because it really was.

"So you kicked the brother to the curb?" Justin asked, also keeping it light. He went on like it was just polite conversation, asking how I knew this guy. I realized that he was probably thinking back to Baltimore, and my cheeks began to burn.

"But you know I wouldn't have gone if I'd known you were still interested in me." *Did I just say that out loud - please, not out loud! The wine must have made it slip out.* I tried to clean it up, saying, "I meant interested in talking to me. I figured you and Sam must have had enough of me. I know that most people can only take me in small doses." I was rambling now, completely embarrassed, and ready to end the conversation.

"So is that what you thought?" Justin asked in a soft voice.

"Well, kinda," I stammered. "I mean, I had no idea that our evening schedule had changed. Not that, you know . . . not that you *have* to call every evening." *This is just getting worse!*

"Only if you want to." I poured more wine in the glass and then directly into me. The silence on the other end only confirmed to me that I was making a fool of myself.

"So are you and Tia busy next weekend?"

"Um . . . no, not that I know of."

"Then how about Sam and I take you two out for the day? Sam has been asking about Tia and you. What do you say?"

"Sure," I said, making a mental note that the operative words in this conversation probably were "Sam has been asking about Tia and you," and reminding myself that I was not going to make the same mistake I made with Malcolm, getting all caught up in a romance that wasn't there.

"Okay, then, provided that Sam stays infection-free, we'll pick you two lovely ladies up on Saturday for a fun-filled day of adventure and exploration. Does Tia have a hat?" Justin asked, and I laughed that she did, getting all excited about the idea of having a good time.

"Well, good, make sure that you both bring hats, and I'll let you go now."

I felt a pang of disappointment. I still had twenty hours to get through before Tia came home and one hundred and sixty-four hours before I would see Justin, but what could I do? We said our goodbyes and I went back to sitting on the balcony, still waiting, but somehow more serene than before.

CHAPTER 17

Saturday morning had threatened our day with summer thunderclouds, but by the time Justin pulled up in his huge black 4Runner with Sam, sunbeams were beginning to peek out from behind the dark clouds which were moving off toward Maryland's horizon.

"Hi, Sam! Are you feeling better?" I asked before Tia took him over completely. He said yes to me, while peering at Tia's favorite shirt with little yellow kittens chasing daisies and the jeans that were splashed with daisies on the knees and pockets. Putting on her sunglasses and her hat with another big daisy on top, she grinned at Sam who told her that she looked very pretty.

"Thank you," she said, nodding somewhat complacently. Soon they were immersed in their own animated conversation.

"So did we follow orders well enough?" I asked, as I placed my own big straw hat, complete with daisy, on my head and struck a dramatic pose. I was wearing a plain white tee shirt and relaxed, fitted jeans.

"Perfect," he said.

We drove for a while, sitting back and listening to the two only children in the back enjoying one another's company. A few times, I noticed Justin looking over at me while we sat at a light. "What?" I asked, reaching for the hat wondering if it looked ridiculous. "It's the hat, right?":

"No," he said and reached for my hand. "It looks fine." An impatient motorist behind us made Justin turn away from me and put both hands on the wheel.

Justin was wearing jeans and a navy blue tee shirt, the top of his locs hidden under a navy blue bandana. Sam was chipper as Justin's twin, only wearing a baseball cap turned to the back and sunglasses, looking very handsome indeed.

Our adventure took us to Roosevelt Island where I realized the importance of the hats - to protect us from stray insects, particularly ticks, looking for a new home in our hair. Once again I marveled that Justin seemed to think of everything.

After we explored every inch of the island, Justin took us to the airport park that sat across the river. We sat in the grass watching Sam and Tia run around until a plane would fly overhead and then they would either stand still like statues or drop to the ground like lifeless toys, their heaving chests undetectable from the planes above. Or sometimes they would run after the planes, waving their arms wildly, shouting "HELLO!" at the top of their lungs.

"So, can I ask you a question?" Justin asked, as I focused on the kids and squeezed off a round of pictures.

"Sure."

"That day in Baltimore . . ." Immediately I stiffened because we had never really discussed it before. " . . . you weren't looking for a serious relationship were you?"

"No, not really," I said, snapping more pictures. "Why do you want to go and bring that up?"

"Because I'm really curious as to what it was you wanted," he responded calmly. "What were you looking for?"

I hesitated and then said, "I had for the most part been with one man all my life, and suddenly I was alone . . ." I don't know why I was getting angry, but I was and Justin seemed to be oblivious to it. "So I wanted to see what I was missing and then if it was fun, I was going to take out some stock in condoms and make myself rich." *There. Now he can feel assured that I'm not looking to tie him down.* "Why?"

"Because I just needed to know," he said, still very calm. "And now?" he pressed. "What are you looking for now, Jewel?"

"Now," I sighed, looking at the kids playing like they didn't have a care in the world, "now, I understand that we don't have any control over what will happen in our lives. That things change. Why? Do you worry that I'm the same person? That I'll attack you? That I can't make responsible decisions - because I can. I was just in a bad place at the time."

"And now you're all right?" he asked, still unfazed by my short fuse.

"Yes."

"You're able to make what you would call good judgments for yourself?" There was a twinkle in his eye and a smile spreading under the mustache that was back again, along with the neatly trimmed, chestnut goatee.

"Yep."

"Then what do you say to seafood?"

"What?"

"Seafood!" Justin shouted, climbing to his feet and running after the kids. "Hey, you two? Y'all need some fuel?" They both stopped and looked at him as he came running toward them at full speed. He ran past them as the two small pairs of legs u-turned to catch up with the long lean ones that were streaking across the grassy field. Then Justin did a fake out, turning around and scooping them both up, swinging them around in circles as they laughed and shouted.

"SEAFOOD! SEAFOOD!" they all began chanting.

Smiling, I collected the hats, camera, and other little odds and ends and met them on the way to the truck.

Justin took us to one of the last all-you-can eat seafood restaurants in town. It was a Saturday night, and it was packed. We decided to wait patiently. A rather large group, large in every sense of the word, came in right after us, loud and ignorant, complaining about the line and their every other word was fuck this and fuckin' that. The kids with them had those blank stares from not having used their imaginations for some time now, and the littlest one just stood there with her thumb in her mouth while what I assumed was her mother sucked her teeth and rolled her eyes about the wait. Sam and Tia were staying within eye view, pretending to be planes landing and taking off. I couldn't help thinking that it doesn't take much to get little minds going, and it made me sad to look into the eyes of those children and see the sharp gleam of adulthood staring back, instead of the light of childish imagination.

When a couple was called ahead of people who had more than three in their party, all hell broke loose in the group behind us. "Was they heya before?" The mother who obviously couldn't decide on fingerwaves, spiral curls, or a French roll, so got all three, was addressing the question to Justin and me. I shook my head, ready to explain the situation to her, but the woman was already moving her heavy girth toward the highschool-age hostess.

"Hey! We was heya first!" She moved her elaborately hairstyled head to the side, a sure sign that she was ready to start something.

"Yes, I know," replied the young hostess, "but we had a table for two ready . . ."

"So? If you got more than two people you got to wait longer than someone who's got less?" the woman asked, oblivious to the fact that she had just answered her own question.

"Yes, ma'am." The hostess, used to this part of the job, sighed and tried to explain. "As soon as we have a table cleared to accommodate your party and your name comes up next on the list, I will be happy to seat you." The woman with the frozen hair stood there, making no move to leave.

"Dis is bullshit! What they need to do is get some more tables up in there. Dey know that it's gonna be busy on Satady!" The rest of her group noisily voiced their agreement. Then one of her kids started whining that he wanted to go and get a kid's meal.

"Shut up!" she practically screamed at him. Tia would be scared to death if I ever yelled at her like that, but this little boy just took it in stride, more upset that he couldn't get his burger than at the tone his mother was using. I noticed that both Tia and Sam had stopped in their play to watch the drama unfold.

The woman continued the floor show for us. "You get on my nerves! Always whining about something! You'd better get the hell outta my face."

A young man came to tell the hostess that a table was ready. She motioned for us, and we walked away as Ms. Stockholder in Spritz and her entourage watched. Again, she shot the hostess a look that should have caused the girl to double over in back spasms.

Finally, we were seated, and the kids started drawing on the placemats and playing with each other.

"Hey, man, what do you say we take a trip?" Justin suggested to Sam, indicating the restrooms. "Right after we let the ladies go and powder their noses."

Tia laughed because Justin was pretending to powder his nose and pat his hair down in place.

"Come on, Tia." We headed to the little girl's room. They were out of paper seat covers, so I had to line the toilet with layers of toilet paper before I would allow Tia to put her little bottom down. Then we shifted around the tiny space of the stall as she waited for me to go.

"Are you having a good time?" I asked, refastening my jeans.

"Yes. Can Sam sleep over?" I smiled and said maybe another time. We washed our hands and headed back to the table.

"Hey, what happened in there?" Justin asked, noticing Tia's slightly long face.

"She's a little upset because Sam can't have sleepover tonight."

Then Sam's face dropped a little too, but Justin stepped in, placing Tia on his lap and telling her kindly, "It was a very nice suggestion. And one that I will definitely think about when I have a little more notice, but Sam has to go to church tomorrow with me and his grandparents."

"Sam can go to church with me and Mommy."

"True, true, but I can't call my parents and tell them that the plans have changed, because they're out playing poker. If we aren't there for church, they'll think that something happened to us. Now you don't want them to worry, do you?"

Tia shook her head no. "Maybe another time," she suggested, and I looked over at Justin who smiled and said that it sounded like a winner and then said to Sam, "Let's take a little break. Ladies, excuse us." Justin deposited Tia back into the booster seat and took Sam's hand, leading him toward the men's room.

The noisy group from outside was in the house now, and chick was complaining that her table was too close to the front door. But their complaints didn't interfere with our appetites. We all started out with crab legs that Justin and I first broke open for the kids and made them a little mountain to eat. Then we moved down the list of the all-you-can-eat meals - shrimp, scallops, almost everything except for frog legs which no one felt daring enough to try. We finished it off with big sundaes, sitting back stuffed like ticks while we waited for the check.

"Next stop - home for Tia and her Mommy!" Justin announced after we had all buckled into the car. I had looked forward to talking with Justin on the ride home, but to my embarrassment fell asleep five minutes after the kids. The next thing I knew Justin was gently shaking me awake as we sat in front of my building.

"Oh, Justin, I am so sorry." I tried to push back the fog from my brain.

"Don't worry. It lets me know that you had a good time."

Oh, yes, I had a good time! "Do you want me to carry Tia up for you?"

"No, that's all right. You'd have to wake up Sam. Besides," I assured him when he started to protest, "I've done this a thousand and one times before." Opening the back door, I gently moved Tia who was sort of slumped over Sam. She stirred just a little before settling on my shoulder, snoring softly, not even opening her eyes.

"Well, thanks again. I feel that I can speak for Tia when I say that we had a great time," I whispered and turned away.

"Wait!"

I stopped and turned back, and Justin came around to my side of the truck.

"What's this?" I asked, taking the brightly wrapped package he was placing in my free hand.

"Open it when you get inside." Looking suddenly shy, he patted Tia on the back and ran around back to the driver's side.

I climbed up the stairs, and when I got to our landing looked out the window and saw Justin leaning out, looking up to make sure we had reached our floor safely. I waved down at him, and the truck started moving away.

Tia was knocked out. After getting her to bed and kissing her goodnight, I rushed back into the living room where I had left the package from Justin. Excitedly, I pulled the paper apart. Inside was a Day Planner and an envelope on which were written instructions to open the Planner first. Flipping through the pages, I saw that every page had Justin's large scrawling handwriting, reminding me that there would be a phone call from him each evening at ten o'clock except on Thursdays -

there the time was pushed back to eleven. Laughing, I opened the note which read:

Jewel:
I value all the time that we've spent together and I hope that you have too. Those nights that I wasn't able to speak with you, well, the days felt incomplete. I know that I don't have the right to monopolize all of your time, but if it works for you then I would be grateful for whatever days you could accommodate.
I am sorry if you got the impression that I had enough of you. Nothing could be farther from the truth. I wish that there were more hours in the day for us. And I hope that before you spend time with someone else you would first consider investing that time with me. I promise that I will try my best to never make you regret it.
Justin

And at that moment it didn't matter where this was going, I only knew for sure that I wouldn't have traded the experience for anything in the world.

CHAPTER 18

October greeted us with an early snowstorm to go along with the hawk's cold wind, and we decided to have a family night out at the ice skating rink downtown. Robyn and Frank with Nikki and Marquette, Jazz and Bryce with their brood, Justin and Sam, and Tia and me bringing up the rear. None of us were any good, some never having even tested the ice before, but we were all willing to give it a go.

I had left word for Malcolm at his mother's that I would be a little late but assured her that I would have Tia back no later than seven, an hour later than the usual time, not thinking it would make a difference. I was about to find out how wrong I was. Pulling myself up for the sixth time, I saw Tia and Sam hugging the wall as they trudged against the flow of skaters, both trying to get back to the opening that allowed people on and off the ice. I wondered why they were going in the wrong direction, and then I saw the cause of Tia's determination. Malcolm was standing on the outside of the wall waiting for the two would-not-be-Olympic hopefuls to get to him. Steadying myself and concentrating on gliding instead of the sawing shuffle I had been doing all night, I moved toward the exit. Just as I was getting into a rhythm, Frank came to a slamming stop in front of me crashing into the wall, and I went down for the seventh time.

"Sorry about that, Jewel," he said, trying to help me to my feet which would have been all right if he had been able to regain his own balance. By the time we untangled ourselves, my falling record was up to ten.

Finally, breathless, I carefully stepped out onto the rubber mat at the exit, grateful for the stable surface beneath my feet.

"Hey, Malcolm," I began, but then stopped. Malcolm was stooped in front of Tia, untying her laces, but she was crying so hard I thought she'd been hurt. She wasn't howling, just crying like her heart was breaking.

"What's the matter?!" I asked anxiously, clumping over to my despondent child, but her muted cries and sobbing were racking her body so badly that she couldn't get the words out.

"What is going on?!" I demanded, close to tears myself, as Malcolm continued unlacing the skate, not looking up at either one of us.

"Malcolm?!"

"I told you six o'clock, Jewel." His voice was tight as he determinedly worked at getting a knot out of Tia's laces.

"Yes, I know, but I called and told your mother that I would have her there by seven." I checked my watch and it was only quarter to six.

"Well, you should have checked with me, not my mother," he said tersely.

Okay, this is between him and me, I thought, looking down in despair at my child's bent head, her shoulders heaving with every sob that escaped her little mouth and floated up past her face in a white-plumed whiff.

"Wait, Malcolm. Let's talk about this."

"Look, I've made plans, and I'm not going to allow you to have us all dance to your tune." He was looking around for Tia's boots.

In what I hoped would be viewed as a playful gesture, I firmly pulled him up and away from the little face that was contorted in such agony. Breathing deeply, trying to keep this from escalating, I tried to get him to see that this was wrong. "Malcolm, she's only three years old. You're just going to swoop down on her and take her away without first trying to explain the situation to her?" I looked over his shoulder at Tia and gave her a reassuring smile - smiled so hard that it hurt.

"Hey, it was your idea to bring her here even though I specifically told you what time I was coming. It's in the agreement that Tia and I get to spend what the courts say is adequate quality time beginning at six o'clock."

"Okay, so because she doesn't want to go with you right now and she's hurt your feelings, you're going to be the big man in charge and force her to go with you right in the middle of her fun?" I gave Tia one of those crossed-eyed looks, turning my finger around the side of my head like this is just so crazy, and she gave me one of those hopeful looks, like Mommy can solve it all.

Malcolm's chest was all puffed out. Looking beyond his wounded pride, I saw the frustration, the anger that Malcolm felt at the courts for believing that children are better off with their mothers instead of their fathers who also care about them. *Maybe he's trying to understand just like I am how we ended up here - with me trying to get all the time I can get with Tia because even though I do have her almost every day, between work and school, my moments with her seem fleeting - and Malcolm now having to deal with the consequences of his choice to be free of me - seeing his daughter only on a part-time basis.*

Okay, take it down, Jewel. "I wasn't trying to usurp your authority, Malcolm. I made the plans before I talked to you, and I am sorry - honestly I am - but don't make her pay for my inconsideration. Just let her finish this session, and then I will pack her up and she'll be all yours. And to compensate, please feel free to bring her back a little late this Sunday. But, Malcolm . . ." I placed my hand on his shoulder, hoping that he would look at me and see that I meant no malice toward him, "please don't do this. You'll only be hurting her." I saw the stubborn face that I once loved so much looking over my head into the distance.

He finally looked down at me and although I knew the face, the eyes were completely unfamiliar. "We're taking her to see a play at the Kennedy Center, and the show starts at six-thirty. A play that my child told me she wanted to see months ago. And silly me, I went out and bought tickets because I depended on seeing her tonight . . . on time."

I looked over at Tia who was watching me while trying to stifle the sniffles that had her in their grip.

"Okay, well tell her," I began reasonably. "Don't just drag her off crying her little heart out."

Malcolm sighed like I was truly trying to sabotage his evening. "It was supposed to be a surprise. But I guess that I can't even do that without checking with you first." He was looking at me as if he really did hate me.

"Okay. I'm sorry. Just give me a minute to fix it," I said clumping past him to our child who I never imagined would end up like the baby in the tale of King Solomon - torn between two people who claimed to love her very much.

"Can I stay, Mommy?" Tia asked with those huge brown eyes turned up to me, tears clinging to her lashes, sparkling like the icicles hanging from the branches that encircled the skating rink.

"No, sweetie."

Her tears began anew.

"No, wait," I pleaded, stooping down to take the skate off her tiny foot, almost falling over as I tried to balance myself on my own skates. "Tia, everyone is getting ready to go." I would have paid a year's salary for the rink guards to come and force everyone off the ice at that moment because clearly my child didn't believe me. "Besides, you don't want to be late." Sam caught my attention out of the corner of my eye as I pulled the second layer of socks off her foot. He was heading over to see why Tia was crying, but Justin gently pulled him back and picked the little fella up, holding him close as Sam kept a worried gaze on Tia's face.

"Yes, Daddy has a big surprise for you. And, Tia . . ." I waved for Annette to come over, and she approached somewhat timidly. "You have a job to do later on," I told Tia. I pulled Annette's glove off and began to tsk. "See, Tia, look at these nails." They were perfect, but I went on. "This color is all wrong for her, don't you think?" Tia stopped that heart-wrenching, silent crying long enough to peek at Annette's outstretched hand. "Annette needs you to help her do her nails."

Solemnly, Tia looked at first Annette's face and then back at her hands.

I gave Annette a nudge, and she took the hint. "Oh . . . yeah - that's right! I was hoping after we went to . . ."

I put my hand up to that perfect mouth and whispered loud enough for Tia to hear, "Don't tell. It's a surprise."

Tia's eyes went wide with the mention of the surprise again. "I want to know," she began, her three-year-old thoughts now on another track altogether.

"Well, I don't know if we have time to tell you," Malcolm said, catching on to the game. He lifted Tia up on the bench. Annette reached over to tie Tia's bootlaces, then stopped suddenly, realizing she might be stepping on my toes, but I moved back, letting her finish the job. Listening to Malcolm explain to Tia how they needed to get to the surprise before both the big and little hand met at the six, I knew that we had made it over this hurdle, but my mouth was beginning to hurt from all the phony smiling.

I watched Tia jump off the bench into Malcolm's waiting outstretched arms. "Come on, Daddy! Run, so we won't be late."

"Okay, little girl! Hold on!" And Malcolm began taking off up the snow-covered embankment toward his car, Annette going ahead to open the door.

Tia didn't say goodbye to me, I thought, standing alone in the cold, dirty snow and half-melted ice that covered the blue rubber mats spread out to protect the blades of the skaters. The sweet peals of my baby girl's laughter came floating back to me on the wings of the cold winter's night breeze. I was just about to sit down and undo my laces, no longer in the mood to go back on the ice when I heard my child's voice call me, strong and clear over the music and the shouts of the skaters.

"MOMMMYY!"

I jumped up and turned, thinking Tia had changed her mind and if she had - well, tough for Malcolm. Let him take me to court. What I saw was her in the arms of her beloved father, waving excitedly, "BYE, MOMMY! SEE YOU SUNDAY!"

I waved back, not able to speak over the lump in my throat. *This isn't getting any easier.*

"I LOVE YOU, MOMMY!"

I could tell from twenty yards away that the smile I knew so well had lit up her eyes.

"I LOVE YOU, TOO!" I shouted back, my voice cracking a little.

Malcolm waved and shouted, "HEY! I'LL PICK UP HER CLOTHES FROM MY MOTHER'S HOUSE THIS EVENING!"

I nodded my head at the three of them as they piled into Malcolm's truck and stood there waving until I saw them head down Constitution Avenue, their taillights eventually blending in with the coal-red glow of the other cars and becoming one big red blur. Maybe it was from trying to stare too hard, or maybe it was because I was sick and tired of the whole situation, but my eyes began to water, and I felt a large teardrop spill over and begin sliding halfway down my face before the frigid air made it disappear into my cheek, only to reappear in my other eye like magic.

"Girlfriend, you are wonderful." Robyn came and put her red scarf around my neck.

"You really outdid yourself," Jazz agreed as she came wobbling over. "Whoa!" Both Robyn and I reached out to steady the Amazon queen, a complete klutz on ice-skates.

"Such nobility. You know, you really don't have to be so nice to that woman," Jazz said as the three of us sat down on the bench.

I started pulling at my laces. "Why not? I mean she's not the one who ruined my marriage." I pulled off the first boot with extreme difficulty. "Remember, she didn't even know about me." I gave each of them a dry look before bending back down. "Besides . . ." I huffed and started to undo the knot that had formed in the second boot.

Robyn suddenly realized that I was removing my skates even though there was still another forty-five minutes to go. "What are you doing, Jewel?"

"Yeah, what about Justin and Sam?" Jazz demanded. "You can't go now."

"I'm going to get my child's clothes over to her grandmother's house, and then I'm going home," I informed them, feeling very old and tired.

"So, what? Now you're going to go home and sit in the dark and feel sorry for yourself?" Robyn threw at me.

"Yes, as a matter of fact, I am. You know why?" I stood up and faced them. "Because I don't deserve this. Neither does Tia - or even Malcolm for that matter. I feel like we're all being torn apart. There's not always going to be a way to make it easy for everyone, and I don't know how I'm going to deal with life if this is how it's going to be." I wasn't sad, but I sure was pissed at the curve ball that was still wreaking havoc on our lives. I stood up and faced my friends. "But you know what? I have to. I don't have a choice. So yes, I am going home to collect myself while you stay and have fun as a *family*. And you go home as a *family*. And tomorrow, if the Lord loves you, you'll wake up as a *family*."

Robyn and Jazz looked at me and quietly accepted my decision. What else could they do?

"Please say goodnight to everybody for me." I bent down and gave each of them a kiss on top of their heads. "I'll call you all later."

I turned away and saw Justin still holding a solemn Sam in his arms and sighed. "Hey, little man," I said fingering a piece of his coat between my fingers, "I have to get ready to go."

His eyes clouded over, and I thought that I was really too tired to go through any more tears tonight other than my own so I improvised again. "But before I leave, how about we share a cup of hot chocolate together?" Reaching in my pocket and pulling out some tissue, I began to wipe his nose. *His mother just has no idea what she's missing.*

And suddenly it made sense. No matter how bad it gets, you still have the honor of being Mommy after all is said and done. No one can take that away from you.

"So what do you say?" I asked again, and I guess he sensed that I needed this and nodded his snowhat-covered head before saying, "Yes, please."

"Go ahead now." Justin set him down without saying a word but squeezed my shoulder which was just enough.

Sam and I made our way to the concession stand, and he stood by shivering while I ordered two hot chocolates.

"Do you like whipped cream?" I asked.

"I don't know."

"No matter, 'cause I don't think they have any." I carried the drinks over to the table and we sat down and watched the skaters whiz by. Marquette who was trying to be adventurous went gliding by, only to suddenly disappear behind the barrier when she fell.

Sam let out a little chuckle, or so I thought, but when I looked again, he was his usual reflective self. *Is this what happens when you don't have a mother's love?*

"Are you warming up, Sam?"

"It's too hot to drink," he replied, watching the steam float above the Styrofoam cup.

"Well, here." I reached across and moved the cup in front of me. "Let me blow." Which I did until I thought that the drink had cooled off a bit. He took a tentative sip and then with a grateful sigh began drinking in small gulps.

"Thank you."

We both sat quietly, enjoying our drinks and before I knew it, the rink guards were moving the skaters off the ice. Justin came up with the small crowd that were returning their skates, his own hanging by the laces in one hand and Sam's boots in the other. "Well, son, you ready to put these on?"

Sam turned around and began struggling to get his clunky blades off.

Moving on autopilot, I reached over and helped him. When he was all tied up and ready to go, I leaned over and told him that I hoped that he and his dad had a good time and that I would love to do it again sometime, maybe when Tia could stay longer.

Our goodbye was interrupted by the kids who were coming up the ramp. "Bye, Aunt Jewel!" Little people all piled around me, each one giving me a hug and a kiss goodbye before they went to stand in line to return their skates. I turned to Justin to say goodbye when all of a sudden, Sam shyly put his arms up. Confused for a brief second, I wasn't sure what he wanted. As he was slowly putting his hands back to his sides, it dawned on me, and I stooped down and gave him a huge hug. When I released him, I gave him a kiss on the cheek, said my goodbyes and set off for home.

CHAPTER 19

"This is a game of trust." Justin turned to face me with a blindfold in his hands - a little mask without eye openings. "Are you ready to play?"

"Okay," I responded, ready for another adventure. He had already surprised me earlier that day by taking me horseback riding of all things. We had been seeing each other for quite a while now and having a good time, mostly with one or both of the children in tow. Even though Justin as yet had made no move toward the realm of the physical, I still enjoyed our conversations and excursions around town - plus Tia and Sam were growing very close. It almost broke Tia's heart when she had to go away with Malcolm and couldn't take Sam with her.

"Okay," Justin said, slipping the blindfold over my head. As the car pulled off, I sat there feeling goofy and a little nervous.

"Did you finish with the case you were working on?"

"Uh, I'm sorry but that is a depressing topic, so let's move on to a new one," Justin replied.

"Well, I feel silly sitting here completely in the dark. Am I supposed to be mute, too?"

"Okay, why don't you name all the parts of the digestive system?"

Grinning, I started rattling them off.

"Unh-uh! You have to tell me where they are and how they relate to each other."

Groaning, I complied, trying to visualize the diagram from my textbook.

After a while Justin began chuckling.

"What's so funny?" I demanded, knowing perfectly well that I was faking most of it.

"Let's just say that you still have a ways to go before I let you work on me!"

The car made a turn, and after a few moments, Justin parked and turned off the motor. "Now, wait here while I come around and let you out."

I was enjoying the game until I tried to get out without releasing the seatbelt, almost yoking myself.

"Wait a minute," Justin said, reaching across to unfasten me.

I was laughing because I could envision what I must look like. Then I felt Justin's hand take mine as he helped me out.

"Watch your head," he cautioned. Still holding my hand, he led me up a slight incline.

I stumbled, getting a little anxious that I couldn't see where I was going.

"Wait here," his voice said, and he walked away leaving me standing alone in the dark. "Okay, now hold on."

I gave a yelp when he lifted me off the ground. He carried me up the rest of the little incline, and it seemed that we entered a building of some sort.

"Justin, where are we?" I whispered as he set me down.

"It's a surprise." The door shut with the sound it makes when there has been some swelling. "Now come this way."

I shuffled behind him.

"Here's a step," he said. "Keep stepping when I tell you to."

So I clumped one step at a time until he told me that we were on a landing and that I should turn left. We walked down what I thought was a hallway and then into another room.

"Here, sit down here." He guided me to a chair that I almost fell into because it was so low to the floor.

"You okay?"

I smiled because I could tell that he was concerned and not out to kill me.

"Yeah." I got comfortable in the softly padded chair.

"Okay, I'll be right back." Again I felt the open air of nothingness and waited. Then the sound of light clinking made me wonder what was up until I got the distinct odor of seafood, and my mouth began to water.

"Are you hungry?" Justin asked.

"Yes."

"Open your mouth." I tasted crabmeat which was saturated with butter on a little fork.

"M-m-m," I murmured, opening my mouth for more and sat there while he fed me until I thought that I would burst.

"Okay, now this is something to drink, so be careful." The familiar aroma of root beer tickled my nose even before the glass touched my lips.

"Want dessert?"

"Hmm - no, not right now." I sat back full from the delicious little meal. "So now what?" I asked, feeling completely relaxed.

"Well, we could talk." It sounded like Justin was settling down across from me. Then suddenly there was music - a piano concerto of Beethoven's coming softly from the right side of the room.

"What do you want to talk about?" I asked, feeling funny, but still at ease, kind of like being on the phone with your eyes closed. There was a pause, and I sat back waiting for him to begin.

"Do you still miss him?" I knew that he was talking about Malcolm.

"No, not really," I said thoughtfully.

"So do you feel like you're ready to move on?" Justin tried to make the words sound light, but my heart started to pound. I had a feeling that I knew where this was going.

"Yes," I said softly. "I don't feel now like I have something to prove to myself or that I have to get back at Malcolm." I knew he was thinking about Baltimore, and I wanted him to understand that I felt differently now. "I've accepted the fact that Malcolm has gone on with his life and that it doesn't include me. Yes, my pride is still a little hurt, but it doesn't feel like the end of the world anymore." When I didn't get a response, I wondered if Justin had left. "Justin?" I called, waving my hand out in front of me.

Catching my hand, his deep voice reached my ears. "I'm right here." His tone gave the words a meaning greater than just being physically with me.

"What are you thinking?" I asked, still holding on to his hand with both of mine.

"No, Jewel, it's what *you* think. I'll be right back." He disappeared again but this time I heard water running. Suddenly the room exploded with the smell of honeysuckle.

"Okay, Jewel," he said coming closer. "This is where the game gets intense. I have to know that you really trust me."

"You don't need to play a game or test me to find that out," I replied.

"But isn't this fun?" I could hear the grin on his face.

And so the game continued.

"Come with me," he said and pulled me up, so close to him that I could feel his warm breath on my upturned face.

"Wait. First sit down again." I did and felt him pulling off the boots I had worn for riding that day. Then he removed my socks before pulling me up again, and I stood there expectantly.

"At any time, you can tell me you want to quit." Justin's voice was very quiet.

"As long as you're not videotaping this for a private collection, it's full steam ahead." I tried to shake off my nervous eagerness.

With that said, I felt his hands go to the top button of my jeans. In one quick motion, they were undone. Next my sweater and tee shirt were being pulled slowly over my head and then I think that he folded them. I felt him descend to his knees and felt the tug at my jeans as he slid them over my hips and down my legs. He braced my hand on his shoulders where I could feel the material of a sleeveless tee shirt, as I stepped first out of one leg and then the other. So now I was standing in just my bra and panties . . . blindfolded . . . waiting.

Justin took my hand and led me into what I could tell was a bathroom from the cold tiles I touched.

"Stand right here." The water I had heard before stopped running.

"Give me your hand."

I held out my hand while he steadied me around my bare waist and placed the tips of my fingers into the warm water.

"Is this too hot?" he breathed in my ear.

"No. It's fine."

"They say that a good soak is what you need after a day of riding to keep from stiffening up." *Is there a bit of tension in his voice?*

"Okay. First we have to remove these." When he said that, waves of desire flooded my most private parts. Standing me with my back to him, I felt his hands undo the clasp of my bra and my breasts fall free. Still behind me, his fingers pulled at the elastic of my panties, and they began a slow descent down my legs. Stepping out of them, I heard him sigh.

"Jewel, you are so beautiful."

I felt beautiful. I felt desirable. The whole scene was taking my breath away - just his voice and hands along with the music coming softly from the other room. I felt weightless.

Justin took my hand and helped me step into a very deep tub. He held my shoulders as I steadied myself to sink all the way into the soft foam of honeysuckle.

"It's like stepping into a cloud," I sighed as I tried to lean back, looking for something to relax against.

"Wait."

One of those bath pillows was fitted behind my head, and I settled back. The next sound I heard was the rustle of clothes coming off, and the water moved higher up on me as Justin stepped in at the opposite end of the tub, which had to be huge because I was semi-stretched out and still couldn't feel the edge with my toes. I felt Justin coming toward me, and for a second I thought that he was going to kiss me, but he reached past me. I sank back, disappointed, and let the water wash over me.

"Don't be startled; I'm going to turn on the jets." The tub became alive with swirling propulsion, easing away all the tension I had in my body. Everything in the world was blissful, so much so that I must have dozed off for a minute because I heard Justin softly calling my name.

"Hhm? What?"

"You were dozing." The bass in his voice made a deep echo in the bathroom.

"No. I'm awake," I protested.

"Then why do you have this little puddle of drool on the side of your mouth?" he asked.

I sat up hastily, about to wipe it away.

"Here, let me get it for you."

I expected to feel a washcloth brush against my face but instead felt the tips of his fingers. Then nothing. I was truly aroused now and wanted to have him kiss me, touch me, to replace the water that covered me with his hands and lips. Then there was the sound of water softly splashing and the next thing

I felt were his hands lifting my leg out of the water, slathering on a creamy soapy lather with a soft cloth. First one leg and then the other.

"What's the matter?" he asked when I began to squirm a bit.

"I'm so ticklish on my feet," I said, fearing I would ruin the moment with a loud outburst of laughter.

"Don't worry, I know just how to handle that." As his palm lay flat against the top of my foot, his fingers applied pressure to my instep, and he lathered my toes without me going into conniptions. After moving to my arms, he sat me up and turned me around so that he could work on my back and neck.

I let out a small moan and let my head fall forward. "This is pure bliss," I sighed.

Justin didn't say a word as he stood me up and proceeded to finish bathing me. From what I could gather, he was in a kneeling position as I stood in front of him. Making small circular motions he soaped my torso and breasts and between my legs, not grabbing or groping, just giving me the feeling that I was a goddess whose needs he was attending to.

"Now stand still while I rinse the suds off." The water moved and I got the distinct feeling of a presence behind me. Rushing warm water sprayed my body, and his magical hands aided the water in slip-sliding the soap down my body, leaving a trail of fragrance to excite my highly charged senses.

When Justin turned off the water and asked me to stand there for a minute, I again felt self-conscious. I knew he would be able to sense just how aroused I was - how much of my body was pulsing in anticipation.

"Take my hand."

I let Justin lead me out of the water and into what felt like the largest, plushest towel ever. He began to vigorously dry me off. I think that Justin thought that I was cold, but I was shivering from desire - I just wanted him so much. My hands reached out for him, but he evaded my touch and placed them up over my head so that he could wrap the terry sheet around my waist.

"Can I take the blindfold off now?" I asked as he led me out of the bathroom and back into the room we were in before. I wanted very much to see his bare body.

"Don't you remember the story of Cupid?"

"What?" I asked, racking my brain, trying to make my head work while my body was almost aching with passion.

"Now, I know that you still remember your Greek mythology," Justin chided, at the same time pulling me down onto what I thought was the floor but was some sort of pallet. It was soft, too soft to be a sleeping bag, but it was very low to the ground. "Do I need to remind you?" He asked.

Then it came rushing back to me. The story of how the God of Love had fallen in love with Psyche, a mortal, and his mother tried to convince him that mortals couldn't be trusted. Cupid set out to prove her wrong and have this woman for his wife. Psyche didn't know what Cupid looked like. He would come to her in the middle of the night and leave before dawn's light. Everything was good until people starting putting doubts in her mind.

"Well, because you are so quiet, does this mean that you remember?" he teased, and I felt him loosen the towel while I eased back onto the pallet. "Turn over on your stomach," he said, "and let's hear it."

"Psyche lost trust in him and broke her promise not to try and look at him, " I recited. "One night, convinced that he was really a hideous monster, she waited until he was asleep and lit the bedside lamp."

Justin was smoothing a warm oil over my body.

I continued. "Cupid was so crushed because she didn't trust him that he ran away forever."

He began to knead the oil into my shoulders.

"So, Justin, are you saying that if I take this blindfold off that something horrible will happen?"

"No, because this is just a game . . . and I am not a god, just a man. But I would like for you to continue to demonstrate your trust in me."

Asking me nicely, with so much sincerity, how could I not?

"How did you get this scar?" he asked, smoothing the oil on my legs and paying close attention to my hamstrings.

"What scar?" I didn't remember any scars on the back of my legs.

"This one." He turned me over and ran his finger along the raised indentation on my knee.

"Oh, I got that when I fell off my bike - when I was nine."

"Did it hurt?" he asked, still stroking the scar.

"Yes." Then I jumped as if burned because I felt his lips against the gnarled skin.

"What about this one?" His voice was smothered as his lips traveled toward my shin.

My mind was racing in a million directions, spurred by sensation. "Same day." Again, I felt the warmth of his lips linger against my long-forgotten wounds.

He did that with every scar he could find on my body.

Then I felt Justin gently raise my left breast a bit, and then he kissed me right beneath it.

"There's no scar there," I gasped.

"You're right . . . not one that you can see - it's still healing." And he kissed it again. Before this I had been half out of my mind with desire, wanting, needing. But when he said that, I felt the tears well up behind my mask, and as much as I tried to suppress them, the sobs broke loose.

"Ssshh, Jewel." The voice betrayed a tiny bit of alarm. Justin lay down beside me and gently folded me in his arms. "I'm sorry. I didn't mean to make you cry."

Gasping between sobs, I tried to explain that it wasn't because I was sad but because I had never experienced such beauty. I wanted to say, "Thank you for giving me this." If I never saw him again and was destined to spend the rest of my life in an emotional desert, I could quench my thirst for a thousand years with this memory and never once feel so much as parched. That's what I wanted him to know, but every time I tried to open my mouth, the feelings would overpower me, and the words became useless noises in my throat.

Finally, I began to calm down as Justin continued to stroke my back and arms. I felt the softness of a flannel sheet coming up over me, and occasionally Justin would squeeze me and I would sigh. I wanted to tell this god who had put wings on my heart what it felt like to soar, but my eyes were so heavy and the feeling of contentment so strong, I just lay there thinking that I'll say something in a minute - let my senses slow down so that he'd know that what I would say was from my head as well as my heart. But when I finally stirred again, it was morning and I was alone in an empty room.

CHAPTER 20

"Now that is *truly* bizarre," Robyn agreed as we slid in through her patio door. "Whew! What is that smell?"

I sniffed the air. It did smell strange. Like there had been a fish dinner baked two days ago and the smell was still lingering. "I don't know. But anyway, back to the other night, I mean there is kinky and then just plain strange."

"So he's asked you to host a party?" Robyn was moving around her kitchen putting food away.

"Yeah. Now I've found out that Justin had just bought the house he took me to, but I still don't really know what's going on. I do know that he's going to have a party there."

"Sounds *so* romantic to me," Robyn sighed.

"Well, romantic, yes - but not very concrete, if you know what I mean. I mean, it was beautiful, but I still don't know where he's headed with me. I'm not sure, but I don't believe he was thinking about making love."

"Are you kidding? It sounds like that's exactly what he did! So, anyway, when is the party?"

"It's next Friday at . . ."

Before I could finish, Robyn let out a cry of alarm.

"Frank! Frank!"

I stood up and ran to the kitchen doorway just as Frank came up from the back room.

"Which one of my girls did you mutilate?" Robyn demanded.

"What are you talkin' about, woman?"

"This!" Robyn pulled a box out of the trash can. "Now I know what that smell is!" I peered around and saw the box of kiddie perm in her hands.

"I gave Marquette a perm," Frank announced, very pleased with himself.

"Move." Robyn pushed him aside and called for Marquette who came rather tentatively down the hall.

"What are you gettin' so upset about?" Frank asked, standing behind his daughter. "I followed the directions." He was getting annoyed at Robyn who was looking through Marquette's head. "I *can* read, you know."

"And just what *did* you do? Jewel, get me the neutralizing shampoo under the sink in the bathroom." Robyn was getting a towel from the linen closet as she soothed Marquette. "Don't worry, baby, it'll be okay."

"I was just trying to help you out," Frank said, clearly offended that his attempts had met with such a lack of gratitude.

"Tell me step by step what you did."

Sighing, Frank recited in great detail what he had done. When he finished, he took the box from Robyn's hands and pointed - "I did everything, just like the directions said. I can read." He turned and went to sit down at the dining room table to sulk. "I don't see why you want to keep spending all that money at the hairdresser."

Robyn pursued him into the dining room. "And when you made the four sections did you make smaller sections and apply the perm to the new growth of those sections?"

Frank jumped up. "It doesn't say anything about making smaller sections. See, it doesn't say anything about that." He held out the diagram of the cartoon woman with her head divided into four equal sections.

"Come on, Marquette." Robyn took the bottle of shampoo from Nikki. "Daddy meant well," she crooned as she lathered up the little head.

"I was just trying to help, Robyn," Frank bleated, standing stiffly in the doorway and praying that Marquette's hair wouldn't go down the drain. "It didn't say anything about making smaller sections," he said apologetically to his first born.

Robyn was checking the color of the suds to make sure they were white and not pink. "I only ask that you leave the perms to me, okay?"

"Weeelll," I said gathering up my things. "I'll just be going now." I patted Frank on the arm. "It was a sweet gesture. Robyn, I'll call you later." By the time I slid the patio door shut, Robyn and Frank were finding the humor in the situation - especially since Marquette's hair was still attached to her head when Robyn dried it with a towel.

"I just need some practice," Frank announced, and I heard him shouting for Nikki. "Come on, Nikki, do it for your dad!" And then Robyn's resounding "NO WAY!" came through the glass door.

I smiled before walking back to my car. *Families are beautiful things.* I wondered if I would ever experience it again . . . or if I ever really had. Then I went off in search of a caterer for Justin's party.

* * * *

"All right, you all stay downstairs!" I called to the kids who were playing on the stairs. Justin's new house was alive with good food and best friends, along with his new neighbors, and the fires that we had going in three of the fireplaces added a cozy warmth. The house was still unoccupied with almost no place to sit except stairways and window sills, but people managed, balancing plates on their knees, bending to pick up paper cups that sat beside their feet. In the corner of the receiving area, the portable sound system was getting a serious workout. I moved around making sure everyone had enough to eat and drink, relishing my role as hostess of this little soiree. Every now and again the crowd would part, and I would see Justin looking over at me.

"Well, how's it going?" Ashley asked, suddenly appearing at my side.

"Okay, I guess." I scanned the happy faces. "But I still can't figure out what's up with Justin."

"Why? He seems to be having a good time." We both looked over and saw him standing with Marcus looking as if they were in a deep conversation.

"No, something's up. Ever since last week he's been . . ." but before I could finish getting my thought, someone asked where the bathroom was.

"There's one right at the foot of the stairs," I directed, not wanting anyone to use the upstairs room where I had experienced my first and possibly last romantic interlude with Justin. Before I could turn back to Ashley, I noticed that something had changed. The music had stopped. The sounds of the conversations going among the small clusters of people still seemed content, and I wondered if the deejay had taken an impromptu break. Turning and heading for the entertainment center, I saw Justin had beat me to it.

Suddenly the room became alive with Luther Vandross serenading us with the melancholy sounds of *A House is Not a Home*. *Now why does Justin want to go and change up to this slow stuff?*

Justin came toward me, and I stood rooted to the spot, knowing that something was about to happen. Marcus caught my attention as he stood off to the side as if he too were waiting for some major event to unfold. He mouthed to me that I should listen to the words. Everyone became quiet as if they were extras in a play. Taking my hands, Justin held me in a formal fashion and began to dance. Nervous and more than a little embarrassed, I moved with Justin in time with the music, like a slow waltz, within the circle that everyone had gradually formed around us.

"Listen to the words," Marcus said as we floated by him.

> *A chair is still a chair*
> *Even when there's no one sitting there.*

My mind was going a thousand miles an hour. I looked up at Justin who was watching me intently while he moved me gracefully around and around as if he were totally unaware of his guests and the party.

> *But a house is not a home*
> *When the two of us are far apart . . .*

Okay, Jewel, there is a theme going on here - you just have to figure it out. Everyone seemed to know what it was because they were all looking and smiling, and I seemed to be the only dunce, other than my crew who looked just as clueless as I did.

> *I am not meant to live alone.*
> *Turn this house into a home.*
> *When I climb the stairs and turn the key*
> *Oh, please be there. Still in love with me.*

As the last notes faded away, Justin released my hand and there nestled in my palm was a key. I looked up, still not sure of the meaning. *Is he asking me and Tia to move in with him?*
"Justin I don't under . . ."
But Justin was smiling a little nervously, clearing his throat. "Jewel," he started as he kneeled in front of me, "please help me make this house into a home?" And he pulled out a box, opening it to reveal a beautiful diamond ring - not a Carnardly, but a gorgeous, pear-shaped diamond held firmly to a gold band with four gold prongs.
Staring at him, I moved my lips, but it took a few minutes for the words to come out. "But I'm not divorced!!"
There was a spatter of laughter throughout the room, and Justin let out a sigh. "I know that. I'm thinking about after everything is settled."
Trying to believe if this was really happening or if it were just some kind of joke, my eyes found Ashley's. Looking at me, she nodded toward Justin with a slight scowl like I was committing some sort of faux pas in the etiquette of proposals.
"Justin, we need to talk about this," I said, feeling a little panicked and slightly sick. *He has to be kidding. I'm still legally in a marriage that went wrong, and I don't even have a clue as to why.*
"Awright!" Marcus stood center stage, taking some of the spotlight away from us. "Everybody up outta here!" People started turning away, heading to deposit trash and empty cups into the trash bags we had set up in corners around the room. "Come on, people, let's give these two a little privacy to talk." Marcus began herding people toward the room where all the coats were in a big pile on the carpeted floor.
"No, please don't go!" I cried. Disengaging my hands from Justin who was still on bended knee in front of me, I pleaded with everyone, "Please stay, enjoy yourselves. We'll go out and be right back." Turning back to Justin, who was now standing with his hands folded across his chest, the ring box softly tapping against his forearm, I grabbed his hand.
"Come on, you," I said, leading him out the sliding glass door which put us onto the deck with only the stars to overhear our discussion. "Justin, what were you trying to do in there?"

"Oh, hey! 'Scuse me." Robyn came out of the house, ever the mother hen, with our jackets to keep us warm against the November chill, handing them to us without another word, but giving Justin a little punch in the shoulder before heading back inside. When the door slid shut again, Justin began.

"Well, we have bended knee, a ring, a question. Yep, I think that it's pretty obvious." He took my hands again. "A question of marriage. Will you marry me?"

I was about to answer him when I noticed that there was still a houseful of people just beyond the glass who were trying to pretend that they weren't interested in what was going on out here, but I knew at least my people were just giving an Academy performance. Groaning up at the stars, I turned and walked down the wooden steps, protesting that it was wrong to propose marriage to a person who was already married.

"Look, Jewel, no one knows better than I about your current situation, which means that I am more than willing to wait. I have no choice." He followed me down off the deck toward the sentinel of trees which stood guard at the entrance to the woods beyond.

"Justin," I began again, trying to get him to understand how impulsive this was. "Marriage is a very serious matter."

"I'm aware of that." He nodded.

"It goes way beyond the ring and the big day. A lot of couples break up just getting ready for that big day."

"That's a shame for those couples."

"Okay, wait." I took a different approach. "Here you are with this big new house for you and Sam, and we've been seeing each other for a little while now. Now you want me and Tia to come in and complete the happy family portrait." I was watching him to see if this was sinking in. "But we haven't really known each other that long to even be there yet."

"Oh, so you're saying that we have to have known each other longer?" he asked.

"Yes," I nodded. "Oh, Justin, you don't know me!" I practically wailed, because it was so heartbreaking to be the level-headed one in a romance.

"Jewel, how long did you and Malcolm know each other before you got married?"

The question took the breath out of me.

Softly, gently, he continued, "It was a long time. You grew into adulthood together, but it didn't seem to make a difference."

I knew he wasn't trying to be mean or cruel, but it seemed that the wound that I had been trying to heal for the last year was about to burst open.

"It's true that Malcolm and I had known each other for what felt like forever," I said quietly, trying to keep my composure, "but Justin, don't you see, I don't know what I did to ruin that marriage. I don't want another failure. I don't have the right to make the same mistake with your life, or Sam's, or Tia's." I sent out a silent prayer that Justin wouldn't want to stop seeing me. I wanted him to understand that it wasn't lack of feeling for him that was keeping me from saying yes - it was the fear that once again those feelings wouldn't be enough.

"Jewel, why do you assume that it was all your fault?"

That stopped me for a minute, but I still couldn't help but feel that Malcolm turned to someone else because I was lacking in something.

"As for me not knowing you? How can you say that?" he asked quietly, but clearly shocked. "I know that you are a wonderful, loving mother. Your favorite season is fall, because it isn't too cold, and in the evening you can come in and curl up under a nice warm blanket and watch movies or read. Your favorite dish is almost anything with crabmeat. I know that you can see a movie that will move you to tears and see the same movie a week later and start crying at the exact same time."

I stood listening patiently as he continued.

"I even know that you go through almost an entire roll of paper towels when you fix one meal."

This got him a little smile, but I was about to rebut him when he held up his hand to silence me and said, "Let me assure you that I know your faults as well."

I raised my eyebrows at that.

"Like you are awful with your finances - because you're always trying to help somebody out and would give them the shirt off your back if you thought it would do them some good. You also hold way too much in. You take the blame for a lot of things that aren't your fault. And if any of your faults drive me crazy, it's that one. But I accept that because it's part of who you are."

Justin's heart wasn't on his sleeve, it was in his eyes. "I can tell when a smile is just on your lips and when something has made you so happy that it makes your eyes dance. And when you really are excited about something, your whole face comes alive. And I can even tell when you call yourself being strong and in control even though you're afraid. Like now. But Jewel, I'm scared, too."

"Why?" I was so caught up in what he was saying that I forgot to argue the point.

"Because after all you've been through, I want to make sure that you get the very best, and I don't want to drop the ball once."

"Oh, Justin, I wouldn't ever want you to feel that way. It's no fun. Always afraid that your best might not be good enough."

"Then, is this a yes?" he asked hopefully.

I snapped back, "No. I mean you've gone on and on about me, but what do I really know about you?"

He looked surprised.

"That's right. You know every inch of me, but I don't have the same advantage," I said, faintly blushing at the thought of last week's surprise. *Why didn't I get to see him? Why didn't he even kiss me?*

"Oh, well, I can drop my drawers right here to satisfy that concern."

"No!" I cried as he began reaching for his belt buckle. "Don't be crazy. It's not just me that we're talking about, or you, either. There's Tia and Sam."

"Jewel, Sam wants you and Tia to be a part of our lives. Do you really think that I would consider this without discussing it with him first? Just like I know that if you say yes and Tia vetoes it, then . . . well, we'd have to wait."

A highly unlikely scenario - Tia loves her Justy to death.

Justin went on, "You know that I would do anything for you. I would never hurt you or Tia. I would respect her father, but if I could get away with it, Tia would always think that she had two fathers, I love her and would care for her that much."

It was as if Lou's feelings toward Ashley and me had just been put into words for the first time.

I was tempted to let go and throw caution to the winds. *For how long? An hour? A week before reality comes crashing in?* I turned and started talking to Justin over my shoulder because it was too hard to stand fast looking directly into his face. I tried to make it light, saying, "You know, come to think of it, I might be a terrible kisser. If that were so, you could love all those things that you said about me a few minutes ago, but you'd always be trying to find ways to avoid intimacy and then . . ." I was getting worked up again.

Justin turned me around. His lips curved into a sexy grin. "Romance. You didn't think it was anything like what you read in the books, and I've tried real hard to show you that it can be. And trust me, girl, it has been hard. I wanted you so *bad* last weekend." His voice had become husky as his arms slipped around me, and he began kissing the top of my head, "But I didn't want you to think that I was being swept away by kisses." Breathing heavily, his hands were caressing my back, pulling me closer. "I wanted you to know that there was more substance to how I feel than that."

His lips were blazing a trail across my heated face, and for the first time in my life I felt faint.

"Jewel, I wanted to kiss you the first time I saw you looking so lost and afraid at Union Station." And he squeezed me tighter as I nestled down into those strong arms that were quickly becoming so familiar. "But I also wanted to know that they were *my* lips that touched yours, not some imitation of someone that you needed to get over - *my* voice the one you heard at night when I called out your name." His fingers softly drifted along my throat. "I didn't want you to ever be confused as to who it was. And . . ." but he didn't finish with words. He began to kiss me - gently and then more passionately.

There are times when you kiss a person, and you are aware of how soft their lips are, of when you first encounter their breath passing into your parted mouth, and it becomes the sweetest experience you think that you'll ever have. This went far beyond. No explosions, no stars fell. It was more like with each breath from him, there was a balm that traveled past my lips and salved my aching heart. He was giving me a piece of his soul, and my heart drank as if it had just crossed a journey through a thousand deserts. The fires of pain, loneliness and suffering were quenched, replaced by something so calming, soothing, so far beyond description, it almost hurt. I recognized it without ever having really known it. This was love - unstinting, unadulterated. When Justin finally stopped exploring my lips, he continued tenderly kissing my face, my eyes, my soul, embracing me as he lifted me off the ground. When he finally stopped, I was dazed, and it was hard to hear his voice over the ringing in my ears.

"I love you. I understand if you need to think on this. But, Jewel ... I want you to be aware that you hold my destiny ... right here in your hands."

I felt myself slipping down his body, and my feet hit the ground.

"I'll wait a day, a week, a lifetime, Jewel. But if you send me away, you'll know that you are responsible for damning me to spend the rest of my life with the wrong person. Is that what you want? To have me go home to someone else? Go through the motions but never be able to give her my heart because I've given it to you?"

I didn't ask him to say those words. His heart was speaking to me, and my soul was crying. My eyes focused on his again, and I knew that no matter how long I would know him, I could only love him more.

"No," I said, and his face fell. "I mean, no, I won't let you ruin anyone else's life but mine!" This time, I was reaching up for him, giving him what he had so generously given to me just moments before. When I let go, there were tears in his eyes as he reached for my hand and slipped the big diamond on my trembling finger. I'm not sure if I was shaking because I was scared or from the realization that I was happy. And happiness was pouring from some fountain within me that I never knew existed.

When we entered back through the glass door to the party, the answer must have been written all over my face because there was a cheer that almost deafened me, as Justin held up my hand triumphantly. Suddenly, we were surrounded by everyone trying to see the ring and pat Justin on the back.

"Jewel!" Marcus shouted over the crowd, "you just don't know how happy you've made this man. And if it wasn't hard enough working with him before, now it's going to be downright impossible." Everyone began to laugh. "This is the only man who can show up on a crime scene whistling."

"Let us see!" And I was being whisked across the room by Robyn and my crew.

"Let *me* see!" Tia was jumping up and down. I stooped down and showed her the ring, holding my breath because if she wasn't for this, then back in the box it would go.

"Well, what do you think?"

"It's pretty," she stated, turning my hand over to see the whole ring.

"Do you think that I should marry Justin? I mean would that be all right with you?"

"Yes."

"Why?" I asked, picking her up and walking away from the noise of the wellwishers.

"Because then Sam can be my brother."

I hugged her close, smiling at her ulterior motive.

"And they make us happy."

Well, that was good enough for me. The rest I knew would be trial and error, but that goes for any new family.

"Justin, can we have a dog?" Tia asked, as he and Sam came up behind us.

"I take it that all is a go here?" he inquired as we traded children.

"I would say yes." I bent down to the ever-solemn Sam. "What about you, little man? Is it okay with you if I marry your Daddy, and me and Tia come and live with you?"

"Yes."

I hugged him and promised that I wouldn't let him down.

"Are we going to live here?" Tia asked.

"Yep!" Justin said as he bounced her up and down. "And you two need to see your rooms." With that they both scampered up the stairs with Justin close behind.

"Well, Jazz, how long do I have before I'm able to wreak destruction on someone else's life?" I was only half joking.
"You filed January twentieth - so really, only long enough to get a wedding ready!"
My God, what am I doing? But somehow it still felt right. Even with Justin out of my sight, I felt okay, my lips still throbbing from his kisses. But I also felt scared. Much more afraid than when Malcolm and I decided on marriage.

* * * *

When the party was over and everyone had gone home, Tia and Sam were upstairs wondering where their beds would go. I told them that we weren't going to move in until the house was finished but left them upstairs to talk about how they wanted their rooms to look.
"I was kind of hoping that we would make this happen a lot sooner, Jewel," Justin hinted, following me through the dining room back out on the deck.
I stood staring at the stars, wanting nothing more than to grab a sleeping bag and go back upstairs to the room where everything changed for us. To hold him and settle in his arms forever. Just to make it harder for me, Justin came up behind me, slipping his arms around my waist. I snuggled back, and he began nuzzling my neck and kissing the upturned ear that was offered as he whispered things that I wanted to hear.
"Jewel," he breathed, "I want to begin our lives together, tonight." Moving further back in his arms, allowing my head to rest on his chest, I thought yes, of course, as he turned me around and kissed me deeply. It's so untrue when they say that it's never as good as the first time, because when I felt the tip of his tongue touch mine, once more there was a shock that coursed through my body and left me trembling. Justin's arms went tighter around me, and I could feel the need that was growing between us raise its head like a hungry beast, demanding to be satisfied.
"Jewel, I promise that I will always make you happy," he breathed between kisses, and I believed him. I leaned my head back to look up at him and saw my own desire mirrored on his

face. Eyes glassy, unfocused on anything other that what was in front of him. The lips fuller and more deeply colored from the passion. I put up no resistance when he kissed me again.

"I'm not going to stop until you say yes," Justin said as he came up for air and then descended to my mouth again. Suddenly my legs went weak, and I felt that all of the air had left my lungs as I stood panting and shaking. Wanting to make love to him right now . . . *right now!* I managed to turn my head away. "Wait." I used the little ounce of strength I had to push against his chest, to push away from those kisses that took my mind. "We can't," I protested, my voice shaky with uncertainty.

"Why not?"

"Because it's more than just us. It's Tia and Sam," I said, feeling a sense of moral responsibility slowly seeping in and spreading little do-the-right-thing droplets like rain on the smoldering fire that had ignited between us.

"Well, they've both given us their blessings."

"Yes, tonight when everything is so . . . so electric. I want to show the kids that there's a right way to fall in love with someone and start a family. Not that living together is that bad - I just want to do the whole thing right for them."

I could see that I was getting through because Justin sighed and half leaned and half sat on the railing of the deck, still holding me in his arms, but loosely, protectively. "I guess you're right," he admitted. Then he said softly, "But Jewel, be honest, is this just about the kids or is it about you, too?"

"No, it's not just about Tia and Sam," I sighed, "but they are my main concern. I mean, Justin, it's been just the two of you for a while now and suddenly here comes not one but two new people in Sam's life."

"Hey, why do you think I planned all the outings? Sure, I fell in love right at the beginning, and if I hadn't put any thought into some of the things that you're bringing up now, then I would have asked you to marry me the first night we went out to eat. But I also understand that Sam and I knew what we wanted long before I let you and Tia know, so . . ."

"You mean you discussed this with Sam from the very beginning?" I asked wide-eyed.

"Of course" was his matter of fact answer. "You don't think that I would have pursued you if he wasn't down with it, do you?"

"And he said it was okay?"

"You're wearing that ring that he helped me pick out, aintcha?"

I sat there quietly letting it sink in, and it made a nice warm spot in my heart.

CHAPTER 21

Children laughing, people passing, full of holiday cheer. It was the season of Christmas. The time when we forget all of our petty problems and give thanks to God for giving us the most important gift of all - that is, unless you are one-half of the parental unit of a child whose father is obviously a lunatic.

"I don't know what you expect me to do." I was getting more than a little annoyed as I steered my cart around the last-minute Christmas shoppers.

"Jewel, it's Christmas," Malcolm said . . . as if that wasn't exactly what was causing our problem.

"I am very much aware of that, Malcolm, and I also know that this is awkward for both of us." As usual Malcolm and I were in another unplanned situation - our first Christmas as a separated family. Malcolm wanted Tia to come and spend Christmas Eve with him at his parents', and of course I wanted her home with me as was the norm . . . forgetting that nothing would ever be normal again.

"Look." I stopped and tried a new approach since we were both actually trying to be reasonable. "Why don't you just come over early Christmas morning?"

"How very gracious of you," Malcolm replied mockingly.

"Look, what else do you want?"

This time it was Malcolm's turn to sigh because he knew that I was being fair in another unfair dilemma.

"You're right. You're right. I'll be there at five," he said grudgingly.

I agreed, and we finished loading up the toys in his car.

On Christmas morning, Malcolm arrived as planned. He enjoyed shopping at the last minute and then wrapping each little present as if it had come straight from Santa's workshop. I was happily surprised when I noticed that some of the gifts still read from Mommy and Daddy, in conjunction with the other loot from St. Nicholas himself, and the morning was filled with "oohs and ahs!" as Tia found just about everything on her list.

"So did you get any sleep last night?" I whispered to Malcolm. He gratefully took a sip of the coffee I had poured for him. He looked bleary-eyed but happy watching Tia play with her new doll and crib set.

"I dozed off when I was putting the last bow on that fantasy fun house."

It felt strange to be sitting here in the apartment where we had celebrated the holidays just three hundred and sixty-five days ago as man and wife. Now I was engaged to someone else, and Malcolm was in love with someone else.

"So have you two set a date yet?" Malcolm asked.

"No. I'm not quite ready for that. I have to wait for . . . for . . ." I was at a loss for words.

"Things to get more settled?"

I looked over at Malcolm, and, for the first time since everything fell apart, it was finally sinking in that things were indeed moving on for both of us. We sat in silence for a little bit, lost in thought of the changes that had come to us in so short a time.

"Jewel, I wanted to let you know first, Annette and I are looking for a place nearby." I nodded because it made sense. My heart was breaking just a little, but I wasn't sure why. There was no doubt that I loved Justin . . . but there was something about closing the book on my life with Malcolm that was a little sad.

"Would you mind if I took Tia to my parents' for dinner?"

I knew that his folks always had a house full of people for Christmas dinner - but then again so did mine. In the past, we had divided up the holidays by visiting one family in the morning and heading over to the other for dinner. I didn't really want her to go, but I also understood that Malcolm needed to stay connected with his child who had no problems talking on and on about Sam and Justin.

"Sure, I think Tia would like that. Did you want her to spend the night as well?" I asked, even though I already knew the answer and was on my way to pack her small overnight bag.

"Mommy, what are *you* going to do?" Tia asked while I brushed her hair.

"Did you see all that paper and stuff in the living room?"

"Yes."

"Well, it will probably take me until New Year's to get it all put back together." She seemed to accept this as a reasonable assumption.

After Malcolm and Tia left, I set to the task of making space for the new things in Tia's room, feeling more than a little blue. Around three the phone rang.

"Hey, Mommy."

"Jewel, where are you and the baby?"

"Tia's with Malcolm, and I'm sorry, but I just didn't feel like coming out without her." There was a pause while I waited for my mother to say something like I was crazy to allow Malcolm to have priority over Tia on such a special occasion, but instead she just said, "Well, I'll save you some potato salad." And that was it. I was grateful, too, because it seemed like the right thing to do - Tia and Malcolm needed to keep the bond between them strong, and I did have her all to myself for the most part. So a little sacrifice like this wasn't too hard . . . or was it?

After watching *It's a Wonderful Life* for the fifth time, I was able to do the dialogue with the characters almost line by line and figured that I needed a break, so I pulled on my clothes and took a long walk around the neighborhood. Lights were twinkling and people were coming and going, full of Christmas cheer, which made me feel a little better when I turned the key to the door of my own empty little home. There were several messages on the answering machine.

The first few were from my crew, all wishing Merry Christmas and Happy Kwaanza - then there was one from Justin and Sam. Justin had the understanding to realize that this would be a difficult time for me and had stayed with his and Sam's usual Christmas traditions, figuring that we would have the rest of our lives for special occasions together.

The last one was from Tia who sounded so happy that I was finally able to put a real smile on my lips and in my heart as I sent up a silent prayer to God for giving me a little insight as to the real meaning of Christmas - happy that I had shared the most special part of myself with others who loved her most as well.

CHAPTER 22

Robyn and I were walking around the mall in search of things for the new house.

"Okay, we're in agreement that you're only going to work on one room a month," Robyn said, becoming the frugal and financially insightful person I'd always known her to be. "I think you should consider a room that is already for the most part done," she advised, and I nodded in agreement.

So far we had put together the bathrooms, since they were rooms we used whenever we visited the house. There were always fresh hand towels and soap put out, making them feel like the homiest parts of the house.

"So Malcolm and Justin are out together today?" Robyn asked.

"Yep," I said, eyeing an entertainment center that looked like it would take up an entire wall.

"No, not that one," Robyn advised. "You'll limit your choices of rearranging the room later on. Look for something like racks and situate them around the room. So whose idea was it to have this little pow-wow?"

"Justin's. Malcolm dropped Tia off a couple of weeks ago, and Sam and Justin were there. Tia scrambled down from Malcolm's arms and straight up into Justin's and sat there waving goodbye to a very sad-looking Malcolm." The situation still seemed way too awkward for everyone, except Tia who was oblivious to the possibility of bruising her father's ego.

"Seems like just deserts," Robyn commented.

And it was true. Malcolm didn't care about my feelings when Annette came on the scene and left it up to me to be the bigger person, but that's not how I wanted things to go between the two men in Tia's life. I wanted there to be an understanding, and I was in full agreement when Justin suggested to Malcolm that the two step out this weekend.

Robyn and I spent half the afternoon going from one store to another until I thought that my eyes would cross from looking at the colors and patterns. After a while I begged her to continue it next payday as my mind wasn't really focusing on the big picture. "Plus I want to see Tia before she goes off with Malcolm for the weekend."

As we pulled into Mommy's driveway, Tia and Sam came flying out of the house. I smiled because it amazed me how much the little boy had emerged in the last few months. What I once thought of as a shy and reserved child had now become a typical little five-year-old who always had a million stories that all began with "guess what?"

"Where's Quinton?" I asked, ready to jump on him.

"I'm in here."

"You'd better be," I said jokingly as we walked into the kitchen and found my aproned brother putting a sheet of cut-up cookie dough into the oven.

Quinton grinned. "Didn't I tell you I was a responsible sitter?"

"All right, brother man," Robyn said, "I just know you can burn! But I'm afraid I'll have to find out next time 'cause I gotta run."

Quinton blushed and busied himself with cleaning up.

I walked Robyn to the door and went back inside to wait for Quinton's cookies.

An inexplicable moodiness had been building in me, and now I felt distracted by it, even though I couldn't figure out why.

Tia forced me to focus. "Mommy, are you listening to me?" she asked in that exasperated tone she used whenever my mind started to drift.

"Hmm? What did you say?"

"Can we get a dog when we move into the house?" Tia repeated.

"We'll see."

Just then, Mommy and Lou arrived, followed a few minutes later by Malcolm and Justin.

The children barreled into their respective fathers chattering a mile a minute.

"So, little girl," Malcolm said, "you ready to hit the road? We have to get moving so that we don't get stuck in all that rush hour traffic."

Tia turned and looked at Sam, who in turn looked at her. *Exactly when is it that those two became inseparable?*

"Don't worry about Sam, little lady," I said getting her backpack together, "he's going over to see his grandmother." That seemed to make things a little better, and she walked around and gave everyone a kiss and hug goodbye. I watched Malcolm to see if I could read how his meeting with Justin had gone, but as was the norm, his face was closed and for the first time in a while, I really couldn't have cared less.

Justin moved closer to me as I sat on the elevated stone hearth absently pushing dust out of the grooves between the bricks while Sam went and said his goodbyes.

"Bye, Lou. Bye, Grammy." The first time Sam and Justin came over here, Sam tried to be on his usual best, polite behavior which was hard to do in my crazy family. Coming through the door, the poor boy was quiet and obviously nervous, but that didn't last long. First Sam was overrun by Chaka and once we got him off the floor, he tried shaking hands with Mommy and Lou remembering to greet them with a formal "hello, Mr. and Mrs. Britt." Mommy got down to his level and said that all people that came through that front door who couldn't reach the knocker were to call her Grammy, and despite Justin's small protest, Sam fell into letting the name flow off his tongue with comfort, easing into my family's life as easily as a knife cuts through butter that's been sitting out in a hot kitchen.

"So are you riding with us?" Justin asked, coming to sit beside me on the hearth of the fireplace.

"No," I answered, knowing that I would make awful company.

We sat silently next to each other for a little while before he asked how I'd gotten to Mommy's.

"Robyn dropped me off." I sat looking at the colors of the bright flowers arranged in the vase on the coffeetable.

"So is she coming to pick you up again?" I knew that I was acting strangely, with my monotone answers, but I couldn't explain it, not now. I just felt I was drowning in some funk and I had to work my way through it. My attitude was belligerent, as if daring Justin to say something about it. *If he wants all of me as he claims, then he'll have to accept the bad with the good.*

"I'll probably just stay here tonight." I knew that Justin wanted me with him, but I just couldn't go there today. It was getting harder and harder to ignore the sexual dynamics, and this would be the first time we would have been alone since he kissed me. *No, I don't think I'm up for that at the moment.*

Justin sat quietly for a minute or two, I guess trying to figure out what was wrong, and I avoided looking in his eyes, focusing instead on the blue border pattern that went around the large rectangular area rug. I knew that he was puzzled and would more than likely get an attitude due to my behavior, but too bad.

Sam came and stood in front of us, wondering what the holdup was. "Are you coming?" he asked, with his own backpack thrown over his shoulder.

"Well, little man," Justin said, getting to his feet, "Jewel is going to stay here for a while."

I was watching Sam, trying to figure out what he was thinking, but he was going to be just like his dad - a man who could respect a woman's space. I hugged Sam and promised to see them both on Sunday.

"Well, call me if you need or want anything," Justin said a little forlornly and bent down and kissed me on the cheek.

I sent a silent blessing to him for understanding something that even I didn't get.

Mommy found me still sitting in the living room about twenty minutes later. "What are you doing here? You didn't go with Justin?" she asked, dusting her hands off on the clothes she wore to work out in the back yard.

Shrugging my shoulders, I sat there moping while Mommy sized up the situation and came to a conclusion. "C'mon, we could use another pair of hands."

I got up and followed Mommy out to the garden where Lou was in the process of taking some giant tweezer-looking thing and stabbing it into the ground and then pulling it out again.

"You can go through the rows of collards and pull the weeds," Mommy instructed. We worked silently for a little bit before Lou asked if the new place had a big yard.

"Yeah," I said with very little enthusiasm.

"All right, Jewel," my mother started, tired of this already. "What's on your mind?"

There was a time that I would have beat around the bush, but today was not one of those days.

"Mommy, do you think that Justin could hurt anyone?" She stopped hoeing and looked at me sharply.

"Hurt who?"

"Anybody?" I answered evasively.

"Why, *has* he hurt anybody?"

"Not that I know of," I said, pulling at the weeds sharply and quickly.

"Then where is this coming from?"

"How do I know that Justin won't hurt Tia?" I blurted out. My question hung there like a huge cloud while I waited for my mother to say that she was waiting for me to come to my senses.

Instead she sighed and said, "Jewel, you have been through quite a lot over the last few years. You became a mother and wife. Balanced school and tried to keep a family together which, despite your valiant efforts, didn't work."

I sat, fingering a weed, waiting for her to finish so that I could explain to her that she wasn't answering my question.

She continued. "Now you've met what seems like a really nice young man, and you're looking at being a wife again as well as now a mother of two, *and* trying to put together a new home. It's staring you in the face and you're scared." She paused as she dropped seeds into the ground behind Lou who continued to dig quietly, listening to our exchange, "It would worry me if you weren't scared. It would mean that you weren't thinking this through, and that's when people really have problems."

"But how do you know that the man you plan to marry isn't some sort of molester?" I questioned, trying to get her to refocus.

Mommy looked at me for a minute before answering, like I hadn't heard a word she had said.

"You don't know. Look at how many women have been molested by their *own fathers*. A man doesn't have to be a stepfather to do sick things to a little girl or boy. There's no way anyone can tell for sure."

I sat chewing on this for a minute. My mind went back to that day at the zoo with Tia on Justin's shoulders and Sam up in his arms. Justin, the same man who kept an eagle eye on them as he guided them through the park, making sure that they didn't get trampled or pushed out of the way. The same man who pulled a quarter from Tia and Sam's ears for the gumball machine when we did our weekly shopping together. Mommy seemed to be saying that I was looking for an excuse to push Justin away. *Am I?* He had never done anything the least bit inappropriate that would suggest that he would hurt Tia in any way.

Looking at Lou, I felt more than the warmth of the sun shine down on me. It was partly because Lou came into our life that I was who I was, and there was no way I would have wanted to grow up without him. Plus, it's not like Justin and I are getting married tomorrow, I told myself. We wouldn't be setting a date until my divorce was final.

The sun bounced off the stone that I wore on my left hand; there was no question as to what I wanted to do.

A little less than an hour later, Justin pulled up in the driveway on his motorcycle. Stepping off he came toward me as if nothing were amiss while I stood waiting for him, happy that I had paged him.

"You didn't even call me back to see what I wanted," I said, as he put his arm out and caught me around the waist, causing me to walk backward as he went toward the back yard.

"That's because you might not have wanted me to come."

I laughed and slipped away from him a little to take hold of his hand, and we went to say goodbye to my folks.

"Hey, I thought you were staying?" Lou said mischievously, and I gave him a light punch in his well-defined arm.

After saying our goodbyes, we climbed on the bike and were off. Trying to peek over Justin's shoulder I clutched him tightly as he headed toward the Beltway. Putting my trust in his ability to maneuver, I closed my eyes and listened to the rushing wind and the roar of the bike, leaning against his back as we moved along with the traffic.

Soon I started noticing signs for Baltimore, and within minutes, we had driven into the Inner Harbor area. Justin slowed down and guided the bike into a parking garage. Taking my hand, we walked in comfortable silence; the only sound was the echoing of his boots as we climbed from the catacombs of the garage to the avenue above, full of rushing pedestrians. Even though I had taken the day off, the after-five hour had its usual magical effect. I felt relief that the week was over and reveled in the fact that the next forty-eight hours were timeclock-free.

Our wanderings took us to a billiard hall which was cool because I was a pretty good shot - taught by my grandfather at the tender age of ten the art of how to hustle. Justin paid for a table and came over carrying a glass of water for him and a frosty root beer for me.

"You want to break?"

"What makes you think that I can even play?" I asked innocently.

"Oh, no, you don't! Malcolm filled me in." He chalked up a stick and handed it to me.

"So how did that go?" I asked, leaning over the table, lining up the ball like the pro that I was.

"Girl, I'm scared of you!" he exclaimed, impressed with my skills. "It went pretty well, I think. I basically let him know that I respect him as a father and that as your soon-to-be husband, hoped that he would do the same for me."

"And?"

"That was about it." I gave him a look that said there had to be more.

"What? You expected what?"

I didn't know. Did I think that Malcolm would be as difficult with Justin as he had been with me? That perhaps Malcolm gave him some hint about my failures as a wife? I could see that Justin didn't really want to say anything more about the time he had spent with Malcolm, and I didn't press him for more, especially in view of the fact that he had been so understanding of my bad mood earlier in the day.

We played a few games, just goofing around, and then headed back to Baltimore, roaring toward home, feeling that contentment that comes from being with someone who really knows what you're all about.

* * * *

The long ride from Baltimore left me feeling chilled to the bone. Justin and I headed upstairs to my apartment where as soon as I got inside I headed straight for the shower. Lathering up, I called out to Justin, who was standing outside my bedroom door, "I think we should plan a dinner party at the house." It's funny that he'd never come in the bedroom itself other than the first time he was here, and I gave him the grand tour. When I asked him about it, he just said that he felt funny about being in there - like he didn't know what Tia would think about it and all. I understood and appreciated his sensitivity, but it was odd that he wouldn't even come in when Tia wasn't here.

"A dinner party?"

"Yeah." I dipped under the warm water, feeling for the faucet so I could add a little more hot because I was still cold. "For the grandparents and Malcolm, and Annette if he wants to bring her."

"Okay, but what would be the purpose of this gathering?" He knew me so well.

"To give everyone an opportunity to understand that we aren't cutting anyone off, that we are merely expanding." I was thinking of my ex-inlaws who were beginning to wonder what was going to happen now that Tia would be starting school soon. "I want everyone to know that our door will always be open."

"Jewel?"

"Yeeess?"

"Are you going to invite your father to this little soiree?"

"Well, of course I'm going to invite Lou." I wondered if he were making some kind of joke.

"No . . ." I heard Justin's voice just outside the bathroom door which caused my heart to start pounding. "I mean your real father."

"Lou is my real father," I said ducking back under the water not particularly caring about where this conversation was going, but knowing that it was unavoidable.

"Come on, Jewel."

"If you are referring to the infamous Angelo Webster," I said, turning off the water, "no, I can't say that I would want to invite him." I felt a towel brushing against the top of my head and looked up to see that, sure enough, one was dangling over the top of the shower rod. "Thanks." I grabbed and toweled down over the goose bumps that had popped out all over my shivering body.

"Hey, I'm going to start that tape." We had rented *Hoodlum,* the film that took you back to the days of bootlegging when the brothers were still in charge of Harlem. Stepping out of the bathroom, I wondered why the sudden shy act. I mean the man had not just seen but washed every part of me. Maybe he didn't like what he saw, but his kisses seemed to say that he did. Well, whatever, I thought, pulling on a pair of athletic socks to complement the sweat pants and oversized tee shirt. I went into the living room where Justin was kneeling in front of the VCR.

"Jewel, are you that cold?" he asked, seeing me curled up in the corner of the couch with my teeth practically chattering. "Come here." Justin came and sat on the couch.

I scooted over close, and he wrapped me up in his warm arms, vigorously rubbing my arms which actually helped quite a bit. "Let me see your hands." Holding them out, Justin took them in his own. "Jewel, your hands are like ice. Do you feel sick?"

He started touching my forehead but I shook my head no because I really felt fine, just cold.

"What did you have to eat today?" he asked, and I stopped to think. The mall, nope didn't eat there. Mommy's? Nope. And we didn't stop in Baltimore.

"Well, what do you know, I haven't had anything today." I marveled that I wasn't starving.

"What about yesterday?" Justin pressured.

"Come on, Jus . . ."

He cut me off. "Jewel, did you eat yesterday?"

"I think I may have grabbed something at work."

"Yeah, it must have been because you sure didn't eat when we met at the house after work, and you said it was too late for you to eat after I dropped you and Tia off at home." It was funny the way he made it sound like I had committed a major crime.

"So what are you saying?" I asked, enjoying the heat that I was getting from his body.

"That I'm worried about you. And I don't think that you're taking care of yourself."

I wasn't about to tell him that ever since I agreed to marry him, I had been frantic about my weight, believing that my pouches and pudge had caused Malcolm to take up with the svelte Annette and perhaps might drive Justin away too. "It's just nerves." I said, trying to placate him.

"What are you nervous about, Jewel?" His voice was low as he softly stroked my forehead.

"Nothing and everything."

"Well, that's not a good enough explanation."

"Well, it's all I've got." I replied shortly.

He was getting up, and I thought, oh well, we've finally found a breaking point for Mr. Understanding. Watching him walk around the couch, figuring that he was getting his shoes to leave, my curiosity was piqued when he started looking in the foyer closet.

"What are you doing?" I asked. Without saying a word Justin waved the yellow pages at me and went to the kitchen phone and started dialing. Not wanting to appear interested, I sat back and pushed the remote to rewind the tape, but kept my ears open.

"Yeah, I want to order a large deep dish with extra cheese and sauce. Half with onions and pepperoni the other half just extra cheese and sauce. And a large order of buffalo wings." Looking in the refrigerator, "Yeah, and a six pack of ginger ale." He gave my address and hung up. Reaching into the linen closet, Justin pulled out a light blanket and came back to the couch and draped it across me while I sat looking at him.

"Justin, I am not your child."

"I know that, Jewel, but you are a person that I care a great deal about, and I think that I can safely assume that you haven't had more than five hundred calories so far this week. It's scaring me 'cause I've noticed that you've lost a lot of weight lately, and I'm afraid that it's because of me."

That startled me.

"If I'm pushing you into this marriage, I'll back off."

"Stop being silly," I fussed at him. "I'm silly enough for everyone. I don't think that I've been this happy in a long time -

even when I thought I was happy, looking back and comparing it to what I feel now, it wasn't even close."

And it was true. All the time that I was with Malcolm I felt that I had to work at making him happy, but with Justin, nothing seemed to faze him in the least. It was like he was always the one who was bolstering my spirits . . . that thought made me stop short. What had I really given to Justin? I knew why I was always holding back. I didn't want Justin to be disappointed if I wasn't sexually appealing - Malcolm obviously hadn't been satisfied by me. Did I ever stop to think that while trying not to disappoint him, I was really hurting him?

Looking at Justin watching me, I did something that I hadn't done since I'd known him. Taking the initiative, I slowly pulled up on my knees, and then leaning toward him, watched the surprise on his face as I kissed him. He was so unresponsive that I figured that I must be doing something wrong and started to pull back, but then his long arms came around me, crushing my body into his as he began tentatively returning my kisses. Relaxing, I parted his lips with the tip of my tongue and started exploring the warmth of his mouth. And again when his tongue kissed mine, it was electric and my body went limp as I breathed deeper and deeper into him, while Justin's kisses became bolder.

Wrapping my arms around him, holding on tightly I couldn't think straight. Didn't want to. All I knew was that Justin was kissing me with a hungry fervor that matched my own. My nipples were brushing against the fabric of my tee shirt, demanding more than the soft material that was teasing them to hardness, sending impulses to the center of my desire. I moaned and ground my legs together as Justin kissed my neck and ears, breathing heavily, then ravishing my lips again. His embrace became tighter when he shifted me slightly, slowly pushing me back onto the couch while stretching out and carefully lowering himself on top of me. My legs automatically parted, welcoming his fit between them, and his hands began to move down my thigh, squeezing it in his large grasp, like he was trying to get past the sweat pants to the flesh beneath. My own hands were traveling up his back feeling the muscles that were bunching as he placed his hands under my bottom and pulled me closer, and I could feel him, what I really craved, dig forcefully into the soft folds of my body's center. Instead of pushing him off, I pulled him closer to me. I felt an overwhelming relief that my attempt to reach out to him had met with such enthusiasm, and I wanted more, much more.

Suddenly he stopped and looked down at me almost as if asking permission to go further, and that was all I needed to move me back to reality, all my fears dousing me like cold water. I tried to push myself up from under him, trying to slow this down a bit, but Justin was not having it.

"Hold on to me, Jewel," he whispered. He must have been feeling my heart beating a thousand beats per minute.

"We aren't going to do anything that you don't want to," he said, kissing me softly, and he was being so sweet and gentle that I started to cry. Not huge wrenching sobs but enough to release some of my turmoil. *Oh, you are a real freak of nature. On fire one minute and a turnoff the next. No wonder Malcolm left. Doesn't Justin have a right to know me as a lover before we marry?*

I stopped my internal discussion and began kissing Justin again, reaching for him, determined that he would get the opportunity tonight. And unlike Baltimore, he was responding to me, wanting me. Just as I was about to drown again in his fiery homage to my body, the buzzer rang out shrill, an unwanted intruder, and we stopped. Falling back down to earth as the pizza man made his announcement again with the buzzer.

"Guess that I should get that?" Justin asked, looking down at me with glazed eyes, panting heavily.

"Remember that the pizza was *your* idea!" I breathed just as hard and looked just as dazed as he did. Justin jumped up to get the door, and I sat wondering if this was divine intervention at work. Intimacy was the point of no return in a relationship, and I sometimes didn't seem really ready to commit, physically or emotionally.

The wafting aroma of the pizza tickled my nose, and I gratefully accepted the slice that Justin offered with a napkin and a soda.

"I was thinking - you asked me about my father, and I feel that you deserve an explanation," I said around a mouthful of food. "Angelo is in California, establishing a dynasty to leave us when he's dead." I took a swallow of soda and continued. "I haven't seen my father since he flew out for my graduation from high school." I always acted like it didn't bother me, but it did a little, because everybody wants to be daddy's princess. It would have bothered me a lot if it weren't for Lou's presence in my life.

"So he's never seen Tia?" Justin asked incredulously.

"Nope. He's sent presents for her birthdays and Christmases."

"And what does she think of them?"

"She's never received them," I stated, and Justin looked at me like, why not? Sighing, I explained simply, "I've taught Tia to never take gifts from strangers so I take them over to Children's House - you know - the place with the boarder babies?"

He nodded, and I sat back waiting for him to ask me more, but he seemed to be mulling the information over in his mind.

"So does he ever call?"

"Oh, sure," I acknowledged, "and the conversations are like a debriefing." I hated the long distance catch-up which always ended with the standard "well I love you and give Tia a kiss for me" line. Ashley endured the same. "If Angelo were to die tomorrow, I doubt if I would shed any tears. I guess that's why I allow Malcolm to have so much say with Tia even when he's being unfair to me. I mean at least he wants to do the right thing, ya know?"

I waved off the second slice of pizza that Justin offered. I was hungry, but not for that, and I felt a blush creep up my face as my thoughts took on a life of their own. Catching Justin's gaze, my mouth started to water as he moved the box out of the way and came closer. Just then his pager went off. Divine intervention again?

"I'll be right back." Grabbing the phone in the kitchen, his pager went off again while he was waiting for the phone line to connect.

"This is Detective Baptiste," he said in his authoritative voice. I heard him making sounds of acknowledgment while I put the leftover pizza and wings into baggies. Feeling a tap on the shoulder I saw that he needed something to write on. I handed him a notebook from the basket by the phone; he leaned on the counter and started taking notes while asking questions.

"Where?" Pause, write. "What time?" More writing. "Is anybody talking?" He stopped, and I could see that he was picturing something other than my kitchen as he listened some more, then told the other voice that he would be right there and hung up.

"I'm sorry, but . . ."

"You have to go, right?"

"Yeah." But he was already gone. I tried not to get too involved in his work because he seemed to prefer it that way. Moving behind him to the steps and watching him pull on his boots, a feeling of loneliness seeped through me, mixed with relief, which caused the pizza to sit like lead in the pit of my stomach. I wanted him to stay so that we could curl up and watch the movie, but in the back of my mind, I knew that it wouldn't end there, so I was kind of relieved that he was called away.

"I don't know how long I'll be," he said standing up, "I'll talk to you tomorrow." He gave me a kiss that fanned the fire of passion that was still burning in each of us, and then he reluctantly pulled away.

"Okay, but at least call me when you get home, no matter what time it is." I made him promise which he did and with one last kiss, he was gone. I walked through the apartment and went to watch from the balcony as he rode past on his bike. Watching the taillight disappear from the parking lot, I thought about the dangers of Justin's job and how at any time I might lose him. Suddenly, I knew my mind and that, despite my misgivings and fears, I was ready to set a date. I was ready to be awakened by his side of the bed dipping slightly to one side, announcing his return, and not by the ringing of a telephone.

This time when the shivers started as I climbed into bed, I knew it was because I wanted to feel Justin's arms around me again. Pulling the covers up close, I drifted off to sleep. When the phone rang, I drowsily answered, and the first words to escape my lips were the last thought I had before I lay down. I whispered, "November 10th."

Hearing Justin say that he loved me before I disconnected, letting the phone slip from my grasp, the pillow secured beneath my smiling face, I felt no anxiety or pressure, just peace as I slept better than I had in a long time.

CHAPTER 23

It was Halloween, and that meant Jazz and Bryce's yearly costume party. This year's theme was entertainment, and Tia and I were going to be clowns. On the way to the party, I stopped to pick up Ashley and Tamicia. Malcolm and Annette would be bringing Tia.

As soon as I saw Tamicia, I marveled at her costume. "Micia, that is beautiful!" The child who is way beyond gifted had taken a plain white sweatsuit and painted it with a collage of African-American performers.

As we drove off, Ashley remarked, "So Justin and Sam are in New Orleans."

"Yes, and I'm still ticked at Malcolm for not letting me take Tia down there for Sam's birthday."

"Family traditions are nice," Robyn mused as we threaded our way through evening traffic. "He and Sam go down there every year?"

"Yeah, it seems that there were a lot of them born in October so that's when they have their family reunion. Malcolm had better get used to the fact that there's one more family that Tia is going to be a part of now," I said with more than a little attitude.

"Well, you could have gone down there to meet Justin's family, and then Tia could have come to the party with Malcolm."

"No, I didn't want to go that far away from my baby... and ...and..." My voice faded. I could almost feel Ashley rolling her eyes at me. "What?"

"Jewel, stop thinking of reasons to make it harder to compromise. Don't just dig in your heels when things don't go the way you want. The fact that you and Malcolm are apart doesn't mean that you should stop considering his feelings."

"Well, what about my feelings?" I muttered as we turned into the driveway that leads up to Jazz and Bryce's community center.

"What did you say?"
"Nothing. Come on."
The wind yelled and forced us to run past the empty playground to the brightly lit haven that beckoned us to come in from the darkness. The party room in the facility was brightly lit with games and activities for the smaller children, while the adjacent gym in the Center was almost dark with a deejay blasting music for the older kids to do their thing.

"Jazz, this is great!"
"Well - ya know!" she shrugged.
"Like she is really gonna stand here and take all the credit," Bryce said, coming up behind her.
"Okay, all thanks to you, oh Great Creator!"
"That's much better," Bryce laughed. "Just don't forget it."
Suddenly, the world went dark and two small sets of fingers covered my eyes. I cried out, "Who is that?!"
"Guess!" And I laughed at the bass Tia tried to put into her voice.
"Hm-m. Could it be a goblin?"
"Nope."
"Could it be a ghost?"
"Nope."
"All right then, I give."
"It's a cat!" And she let go. I turned around and was shocked to see the striped face with black whiskers and little cat ears sticking out, all in orange and black fur, perched up in her father's arms. "Look, Mommy! Annette did it!"
"Ooh, don't you look pretty." I tried to throw some enthusiasm in my voice, but it came out flat. There was no way Tia would give this up for the clown costume that I had brought for her and which matched mine. I mean, why would she want to be a clown when she and Annette made such cute kitties?
"Look, Daddy's dressed up too." Sure enough Malcolm was in the tall, red-and-white striped hat, gloves, and bow tie of Dr. Seuss.
"It really looks nice," I said to Annette who stood with her arm linked through Malcolm's.
"Yeah, she can really put together a costume." *This is too much. An unsolicited compliment from Malcolm?*

"Well, it is my job, ya know." Annette tried to appear modest, but you couldn't slap the grin off her face as she basked in Malcolm's praise (not that I truly didn't want to try!).

"Well, you'll have to excuse me," I said, mostly to the air because Tia had already been whisked away by the kids, and Malcolm and Annette were so wrapped up in each other that I could have made myself disappear and they would never have noticed.

"What's up with them?" Jazz asked me when we got to the punch bowl.

"Oh, those two? I think they just finished getting their groove on."

"And this bothers you?"

"Bothers me? Please!" I was really ticked that anyone would have the notion that I would be upset over something that had been going on for more than a year now. "Come on, Jazz - I knew that Malcolm was having great sex from the beginning."

"I'm just asking." Jazz threw up her hands defensively, I guess because my voice was a little rougher than I intended it to be. But then again why shouldn't it be? Jazz knew that I was getting married in just ten days; I would never consider doing so if I still had feelings for Malcolm. I turned to see them watching Tia try to hit a balloon with her dart. *Did we ever look that comfortable together? Did we? Am I jealous?*

"Jewel, why don't you come with me for a minute." I felt Jazz steer me toward the coatroom while I tried to slow my breathing, caught in the throes of what threatened to be a serious anxiety attack. Once outside, I allowed the cold air to dry the clown makeup before it smeared all over my face. We walked a little ways in silence to an empty playground area.

Jazz sat down on one of the swings, and I did too. "What's wrong, Jewel?"

The words came tumbling out. "Why didn't Malcolm love me? I've done everything I can to get Malcolm to be just a little nice. Just a little. And he acts like I'm the one who cheated on him! Like I'm the one who ruined everything!"

"I don't think that's his problem. No, I think that he acts that way because you accepted his departure with dignity and class," Jazz explained patiently. "And for Malcolm, I think that just throws his callousness back in his face, reminding him that what he did was inexcusable. If he can keep you angry at him, then he can just tell himself that you're not really a very nice person and justify what he did. When you're nice, it's worse for him - shows him that he didn't have to treat you bad to end your marriage."

"Look, all I want to know is what I did that was so terrible that Malcolm felt that he had to go out on me like that? Why didn't he want to stay married to me?"

"Have you asked him?" Jazz asked mildly.

"No, but then again he doesn't seem warm to the idea of an open forum. It's like he's afraid that I'll tell him that he did all these things wrong when really I just want to know what I did wrong," I finished wearily.

"Jewel, don't think like that! You didn't do anything wrong. You and Malcolm were just wrong for each other."

"But . . ."

"But, nothing. Justin and Malcolm are two very different men. Jewel, Justin is a very stable person - he's raised his son alone for the past five years. By the way, he's also very attractive, and do you think that no one else has noticed because if you don't, allow me to say, WAKE UUUP!" And she thumped me lightly on the head. "No, Jewel, you aren't his first but he does want you to be his last and . . ."

"So what! Suppose the real reason Malcolm left was because I'm sexually dissatisfying?" *There! My secret shame is out in the open.*

"Why do you think that you are?" Jazz asked, slightly amused.

"I didn't used to think that I was," I admitted uncertainly.

"So has Justin given you the impression that you'll find a manual on your pillow for your wedding night?"

"He doesn't know."

"What do you mean, he doesn't know?"

"It means that we haven't done anything."

For a minute she looked surprised, but then said, "I see."

"I mean we do have two small children between us and are trying to set a good example . . ."

"Jewel, you two have been together for what - all these months - and you mean to tell me that during that time . . .?"

"Okay, okay, maybe I don't want to - I'm scared that I may lose him before it's even started because Malcolm was really the only man I'd ever been with, and he didn't want me. Annette must be a whole *lot* better in bed than me," I said bitterly.

Jazz responded, "Well, Jewel, when you love someone, making love is wonderful *always* because it's not just sex. It's like kissing. You never taste bad breath or onions and garlic when you kiss someone that you really love." *Hmm, that's true.* Jazz continued. "Justin loves you. It's obvious, so believe that he will love every part of you, in bed and out. And if you really are a lousy lay, I'll give your name to one of those discreet mail order places - you know, the ones with the plain brown wrappers."

I began to giggle hysterically. "Jazz, you are a crazy person!" But I hoped that she was right - there were only ten more days before I would find out.

CHAPTER 24

"I think that this thing is in backwards," I moaned, blinking furiously.

"You're just nervous, doll," Zora said as she worked on Robyn's makeup. It was wonderful to have Zora come by and help with this very special occasion. What was even better was that when I saw her at the same salon, looking for makeup for my wedding, she didn't even so much as raise her carefully arched eyebrows - as if to say, "What happened to that *other* marriage?" No, the classy person that she is, Zora just insisted on making everyone look glamorous.

"Take your time, Jewel. You may need to get used to them again," Ashley told me.

"No, I really think that it's in backwards." Dodging discarded clothes, plastic bags, boxes, and a ton of other wedding whatnots, I fled my cluttered living room, which despite the lack of furniture that had been moved to our new home, was still full of chaos and women all trying to get ready for a formal event.

"What are you doing?" Robyn asked as she waited her turn with the hairdresser who was working out of my empty kitchen.

"This thing is in backwards," I grumbled, removing the offending invader from my eye and holding it on the tip of my finger.

"How can you tell?" she came to look.

"Because it's supposed to curve like a bowl," I said and carefully inspected the little clear disk on the tip of my quivering finger.

"It looks curved to me." Robyn observed. "Did you just turn it over?"

"I can't remember."

"Well, then how are you going to know . . ."

The look that I half gave her since I could only see with one good eye at the moment, shut her up. With raised hands, she slowly backed out of the bathroom.

"Is it in, Mommy?"

Moving it around my eye for a few moments, I slowly focused on Tia. "My goodness, but don't you look just like a little woodland sprite!" I bent down and noticed that the light gloss on her lips was appropriate for the special occasion, but wondered if she was going to eat if off before the service. "Is Tamicia ready yet?"

"Almost." I pushed a little loose curl back from Tia's face and followed her into the living room. My baby was just gorgeous. Her long, curly, frizzy hair was loose but pushed back with a black headband. Attached to the band was a crown of faux fall leaves in full vibrant colors. Red maples, yellow oaks, and deep purple signature leaf colors matched her pretty flower girl dress. I love the colors of fall and chose the season for my wedding theme.

All the bridesmaids' dresses were deep multi-colors with long sleeves, plunging backs, and full tea-length skirts. The taffeta slips were made in the same muted colors.

"So when do we get to see your dress?" Jazz asked as she vacated the seat where Zora was working to allow Robyn to get her face put on.

"Soon." I walked over to Tamicia who stood quietly by the balcony looking at the same colors outside that adorned the inside. "Gee, but you look like you could run out there in the woods, and just blend in." I pulled her down with me on the floor. Her hair was loose but piled up on top of her head with her natural curls cascading over to one side, the other side pushed back with more leaves and a little baby's breath giving her the same nymph look that Tia had. Sitting with the girls, I suddenly realized that this would be the last time that I would be looking at this sight. That I would be leaving my view, my perch, my security. So we just sat for a while and let everyone else move in fast forward around us.

We were interrupted by Ashley demanding to know when she would see my dress. "You know that as your sister, I'm supposed to see this dress first."

"Well, if you could sew as well as Robyn, you would have seen it by now." Searching around but unable to find just the right dress had been pure hell for me. I envisioned the dress so completely that no substitutes would do. Robyn came to my rescue. One of our daily searches brought us past a fabric shop that had just the right material in the window, and together, we put my dream dress into play.

"The masterpiece will be unveiled at the appropriate time," I assured Ashley.

"Jewel, how in the world do you put these things on?" Robyn and Jazz both came out of the bedroom, carrying the little boobie lifts as I call them, one in each hand. I started laughing because I really had no idea. I bought them because none of our dresses could hide a bra strap and the fabric was too tight to go free.

"Well, if I remember correctly," I said, coming up and getting my own, "you just sort of stick it underneath your boob and, viola!" And as if by magic I was pleasingly lopsided showing that the device did offer some support. I put the other one on, and everybody followed my example.

"I hope these things stay on for at least the whole service," Jazz said, stepping carefully into her gown.

"Two down," I observed as I watched Ashley pull her arms through the sleeves and adjust herself. Robyn put hers on then, and I mock wailed, "You all look so gorgeous - nobody is even going to notice me!"

They stood preening and moving so they could make their skirts twirl, the taffeta slips rustling and swishing.

"I want you to remember how good I made you all look the next time some of you start talking about me."

Pulling my robe loose, I headed into the bedroom. Robyn followed and shut the door.

A soft knock on the door preceded Zora's deep voice. "Jewel, sweetie? I'm all done, and I'm leaving now. I'll see you at the wedding."

"Okay. Thanks, Zora."

"No problem, cherie. Ciao."

Fifteen minutes later, we heard the buzzer go off, and Ashley knocked to let me know that the cars were downstairs.

"Okay, we'll be right there." Robyn was fastening the pearl necklace that was the something borrowed from Barbara Baptiste.

"Jewel?" Ashley shouted through the door, "Where are the flowers?"

"In the refrigerator." She couldn't miss them because that's all that was in there.

"Okay, Robyn, where are my shoes?" We started turning over boxes and tissue paper until we found the errant shoe and the lace handkerchief. Finally I was ready.

"Well, what do you think?" I struck a pose. "Oh, no, you don't!" I said sternly. "You've seen me in this dress before! You made this dress, so don't cry now!" I pleaded, knowing that if she started I would be right behind her.

"But it's the first time that I've seen the whole thing put together," she sniffled.

"Damn it, Robyn." I stamped my foot impatiently, beginning to feel overwhelmed myself. "You're gonna make me regret not getting a joint for today. Come on! You can't cry because we have to go out there and . . ."

"Get you married." Robyn sucked in her breath and giving my hand a squeeze, opened the door. After making everyone close their eyes, she called me out and stood me in front of the balcony window.

"All right." She paused. "Open your eyes." Watching everyone's eyes fly open, I felt delighted when their mouths flew open as well because I knew that the dress was beautiful in it simplicity. A classic nineteen-forties ballroom replica, only tea length instead of sweeping the floor, so the matching dyed ivory shoes with the pearl cluster encrusted at the top could clearly be seen. Deep ivory color, with a corset type bodice made from a lacy material with carefully stitched-in pearls and tiny glittering rhinestones which stopped just before the full skirt that billowed out in clouds of tulle. More of the little rhinestones had been sewn throughout the skirt to subtly reflect the light that bounced around making the dress seem almost magical. Since it was my second marriage but first wedding we opted for a tiara-type headpiece that had a gauzy material attached and spilled out in a froth over my hair which was straw curled and then gathered into a loose topknot. The fabric wrapped loosely around my neck spilling down the back where the bodice dipped, the hanging material making for a nice filler. Pearls and elbow-length gloves finished off the ensemble.

"Girl, you look so beautiful."

Everyone was standing there looking at me, trying hard not to cry while the photographer who had just arrived took pictures. We heard a knock at the door, and the moment was broken as Lou came in looking rather dashing in his morning coat. At first I had told Mommy that it seemed stupid to be given away since I was already on my own and a mother, and I planned to just go down the aisle by myself. But when I saw how excited Lou was at the idea of giving away one of his girls and knowing how my parents felt cheated when Malcolm and I eloped, I didn't have the heart to burst their bubble again. Looking at Lou's beaming face, I was glad that I opted to go with tradition. He had indeed earned this right.

"You are beautiful," he said and gave me a kiss on the cheek. "I want to give you a hug, but . . ."

Smiling because I could tell that he was really champing at the bit to give me one of his signature bear hugs, I went over and hugged him close which triggered his natural impulse to squeeze. I didn't care what happened to the dress - we both needed this hug.

When he let go, I was not surprised to see him wipe a tear from his eye.

"All right," he said gruffly to Ashley, "I just want you to know that I can only go through this once every ten years or so."

And we all smiled at the soft heart that he could never hide from any of us.

"Shall we?" he asked, holding out the black velvet cloak on loan from Mommy, his tophat at a rakish angle on his head.

Everyone moved out the door, and I turned the lock, thinking that this was the last time that I would come here as a single woman - that in two hours, I would be a married woman again.

As we pulled off in the huge, black stretch limo, Lou reached into his inside coat pocket. "Okay, ladies, you all don't see this." Pulling out a silver flask, he carefully poured out a single shot and threw it back sucking in his breath. "Hair of the dog," he explained and then did a doubletake when he saw that we all had the heavy drinking glasses provided for just this moment held out for our own little nips.

"All right, but just a shot," Lou warned as he carefully poured each of us a round. "I'm not tryin' to have your mother kill me if you all go staggering down the aisle."

"A toast," I declared, and we all stopped and held up our drinks. "To the women that I couldn't love any more even if I were gay." And we all laughed. "And to my dad here who always has the foresight to think of everything including the peppermints that he has stashed in his other pocket."

"Salud!" he cried, and we all tipped back and took a collective intake of breath as the brandy spread throughout our bodies, making us feel mellow and warm which was easy to do, since none of us had eaten that morning. We each had two more shots and were sucking on peppermints but feeling no rush at all by the time we reached the site of the wedding, a former mansion that now catered to special events. The driver opened the door, and I scooted to move out when Robyn grabbed my arm. "Jewel, you can't be seen yet," she fretted.

"True." I sat back and thought for a minute. "Okay, you all get out, and I'll have the driver take me over to the gardens. Then when it's almost time to start, Lou can come and get me."

I had just under an hour to wander around the gardens which I was afraid would be a bad thing for my nerves. But either the brandy or the still expanse of hedge left me feeling peaceful, wandering around the outside of the maze on the stone path that led around the perimeter, afraid to go inside for fear I would get lost and miss my wedding! Just as I was about to head around the corner I heard someone on the other side and called, "Lou?"

"Jewel?"

"Justin!!"

"The one and only."

"No, don't come around! You're not supposed to be here!" I looked for someplace to duck but was afraid of stepping into the grass and ruining my shoes.

"Don't worry." His rich baritone voice came through the hedges to me. "I'll just stand right here and talk to you for a few minutes - if that's okay?"

"Okay."

And we talked on opposite sides of the hedge, smiling because we felt kind of silly but in a fun kind of way.

"How long have you been here?" I asked.

"About an hour. My mother wanted to make sure that everything was in place, but your Mom had it covered. I think that she's been here since eight this morning!"

Just then Lou, Justin's dad, Clarence, and the photographer came up and snapped a picture as Justin told me he too had considered going into the maze to see what was in the middle but was afraid to do so. "That would be just great," he envisioned, "having to send out a search party to find the lost groom in the hedges."

Justin's dad told him that he should head back.

"See you soon?" Justin asked.

"In about thirty minutes," I smiled back with my voice.

And we each went our separate ways to be united later for the rest of our lives.

* * * *

The main hall was overflowing despite having shaved the short list to just family and close friends. Our wedding ceremony stayed pretty much within the themes of the Catholic service, without the actual mass but including the readings. When the minister pronounced us man and wife and told Justin that he could kiss me, I turned toward him. He took a tear that spilled from my overfilled eyes, brought it to his lips, and then kissed me - letting that tear of happiness seal the love that we had pledged before everyone.

After the ceremony, we all assembled in the ballroom, which was perfumed with the fragrance of flowers and the aroma of cedar wood burning in a wall-sized fireplace, adding to the warmth of having family and friends share in our special day.

We were formally introduced as Mr. and Mrs. Justin Baptiste, and everyone commenced to meal down, Justin and I easily slipping into comfortable parent roles, with me cutting up Tia and Sam's food and Justin placing the napkins under their chins.

"So are you and Justin going to start a family soon?" One of my aunts asked as I leaned over to spear a piece of tortellini on Sam's fork for him.

"We already have a family," I explained.

"Well, I mean one of your own."

"But these are our own." *Why is she standing here in front of my children implying that they aren't enough?*

"Jewel," she began as if one of us was too stupid to let this issue drop, "I mean are you and Justin planning on having any babies together?"

I really couldn't believe that this woman, whom I really only saw no more than three times a year, now felt that she needed privileged information into my reproductive life. Grinning as politely as I could muster, I told her, "Justin and I are very happy with our family just the way it is." And I could see that she was going to open her mouth again, and there was no way that I would be able to keep from saying that she had only been invited out of respect for my grandfather, but my mother came gliding over and saved me.

"Aunt Dottie," she cooed, "you have got to try this gumbo. I think that it might actually rival your own." That was all Aunt Dottie needed to get her moving. I knew later that I would find her over by the gifts trying to figure out how much people spent. She had already mentioned to my grandmother that she didn't see the need to spend a lot on a second wedding.

"The nerve of some people," I sighed.

"Who was that?" Sam asked, pushing his potato salad around his plate.

"That, sweetie, is *your* dear Aunt Dottie. That's right," I assured him when he looked at me quizzically. "We all got married here today, so now everyone in here is family in some way or another."

This seemed to impress Sam as he looked around the room full of laughing people, all enjoying their meal as well as each other's company. We continued our lunch thoughtfully while I played with him by picking stuff off his plate - and he from mine. After a while, appetites satiated, Ashley came to the door to announce that the deejay was ready and the ballroom ready for dancing.

"You ready to go and get your swerve on, Sambo?" He just grinned and blushed.

"Come on!" I joked, "I know that you can dance. I saw you at Tia's party."

"Come on you two." Robyn who lives for these events pulled at Justin and me and steered us onto the dancefloor; we shared our first dance to *After the Love Has Lost Its Shine*. When the last notes died away, Justin leaned me back into a full dip; it took a minute before I realized that the rushing sound in my ears was from the applause of our dearhearts. Justin smiled devilishly, gave me a wink, pulled me up and spun me out. The skirt of my dress fanned out and before it could settle, the deejay had commenced to mixing.

After about a half hour of moving and grooving, Justin and I separated and mingled with wellwishers. I was talking with Robyn when Ashley sauntered over. "Methinks that someone is looking forward to later," Ashley singsonged. She nodded toward Justin who was standing with a group of fellas but staring at me in such a way that my heart began to pound. It was only for a split second, but all of his expectations for what would take place later could be read in his face, before he saw me looking and sent me a smile. Several times throughout the reception, I would catch Justin watching me with the same intensity, and my stomach would pivot, and I would feel close to hyperventilating. I was trying hard not to think about later, when we would be alone, praying that we wouldn't end up on some talk show saying, "Got off to a great start, and then we hit the sheets and it was all downhill from there."

Toward late afternoon, Robyn rounded up Justin and myself again and ushered us into the dining room to cut the cake and thank the guests for their gifts. Then we were whisked away upstairs so that Justin and I could change for our flight to the Bahamas.

"Okay, Tia," I said as Robyn unzipped me from my dress while Jazz helped pull off the veil, "you and Sam are going to stay with Mommy and Lou tonight and tomorrow, then Mr. and Mrs. Baptiste . . ."

"That's Grandma and Gramps," Barbara Baptiste interjected softly.

"Yes, Grandma and Gramps' for the other two days . . ."

Going over the schedule for the next five days and four nights, making sure that all was in order before leaving the same soil on which my child stood - no, correction, *my children* stood - had me more than a little panicked.

Malcolm had wanted to take Tia while Justin and I were away, but I stood firmly against it, explaining that it was important that Sam and Tia be allowed to feel comfortable as brother and sister especially after partaking of such a big event. When he got snotty and suggested that Justin and I stay if we thought it was going to be such a difficult adjustment, I told him that I didn't foresee any difficulty in the transition. I just wanted for them to see that there would be some changes and get used to their new grandparents. When he saw that I refused to back down, he quit giving me grief.

I didn't know what to do about Malcolm and Sam. I really didn't expect them to have a relationship - I supposed he would leave Sam behind when he came to pick up Tia for their regular visits. I would have to cross that bridge when I came to it.

After I changed, I went down to the landing to conclude Robyn's rituals, and the bouquet went sailing, gracefully arcing over the banister before descending into the melee below. It was like dropping a carcass into the middle of a bunch of alligators. Some of the blossoms became crushed under heels as each woman fought in a possessed way to get a hand on the bouquet. There was a large pile of dresses on the floor until they all started struggling up, straightening skirts and patting hair, and one of my cousins arose, triumphantly holding the mangled stems in her hand. Looking at the sad little thing that once resembled flowers I was grateful that my real bouquet was safely tucked away to be encased later, forever suspended in water and glass.

Once the field had been cleared, the guys slowly sauntered over, like they could care less about all of the hoopla. Justin came up to the landing and knelt down beside me. Looking directly at me, he reached under my skirt, delight registering on his face when he encountered bare skin above my thigh-high nylon. Then giving me a little smile, he very slowly slid the garter down the length of my leg, leaving a trail of burning goosebumps in its wake. He stood and kissed the garter before hurling it over the railing (which at the moment was the only thing holding me up). A cheer went up, and I smiled when the garter landed on Marcus, who quickly shoved it into Sam's hand.

Finally, Justin and I were ready to leave. We walked down the wide staircase to meet Sam and Tia who were sitting on the bench at the bottom. I went over the lists of things to bring back, and they looked so pitiful that I wanted to just take them with me. But then Tamicia came to the rescue. She sat on the steps with them and went over plans for the weekend, making both children seem like the center of the world.

"They'll be fine," Mommy assured me, trying to erase the crease of concern that furrowed my brows.

"I know." Really, it was me that I was worried about.

CHAPTER 25

Okay, I can do this. Standing in the bathroom that sat in the middle of one of the most gorgeous tropical settings in the world, I was trying to make some pretty major decisions. *Should I put the aromatic lotion on? Suppose it has a disgusting taste? Should I put the lacy panties on under the ivory silk gown that Jazz gave me at my bridal shower? All right, Jewel, take it easy. You can get through this, you're just nervous.* Then the giggles hit me. I was standing in the bathroom on my honeymoon trying to decide if I should wear panties and what I was really afraid of was that I'd be terrible in bed and have that poor man running for the hills. The idea of Justin running naked out of the room, screaming for an annulment, sent fresh peals of laughter erupting from my clenched lips. Grabbing a towel to muffle the sounds, I sagged against the sink shaking with hysterical mirth.

"Jewel?" Justin tapped softly on the door. "Are you all right?"

Taking a deep breath, I hiccupped softly before saying, "Yes, I'm fine," but a snort of laughter escaped through my nose which set me off again. *Get a grip, woman!* "I'll be right out."

Looking at myself in the mirror, the eyes wild and unfocused, I started to compose myself. *Wait. Should I put my glasses on? Should I look serious or smile when I walk out into the room?* And it was another three minutes until, with a shaking hand, I turned the knob and stepped out into the master room.

Justin had already showered while I was talking to Mommy on the phone to give her our number. Now he stood across the room in front of the balcony in a new silk paisley robe watching me.

"Oh, did the hotel send up the champagne?" I asked, moving toward the table that was set up by the doorway to the bedroom. Picking up the bottle, I tried to figure out how to open the foil when I felt him behind me, and he began kneading my shoulders.

"You look beautiful," Justin breathed into my hair.

"Thank you. Jazz gave it to me as a bridal present." My voice began to fade as he started pulling the pins out of my hair, running his fingers through the curls.

"Smell so good." His breath was warm on my neck, and he ran his hands up my bare arms.

"The gown's a little long," I started, trying desperately to sustain a conversation as I felt his lips on the base of my neck.

Justin turned me around and placed his hands on the sides of my face. Tilting my head up, he kissed me. Softly at first, tracing circles around my lips, gently parting them as I accepted his tongue and the warmth of his breath into my mouth, making it water as if a rich piece of chocolate were melting inside, the kiss was so sweet. So wrapped up in the delicious feeling, I didn't notice that the straps of my gown were hanging just above my elbows, until I felt the silk of Justin's robe brush my bare nipples. Wanting to postpone the actual moment, I tried to move the strings back up. To just continue to kiss. Kissing was safe. I knew for sure that he liked my kisses.

But Justin firmly moved my hands to my sides, the straps falling with nothing to hold on to, the gown floating to the floor. Instinctively, I tried to pull away, but Justin lifted me up and carried me, still kissing my cheeks, eyes, throat, leaving a searing heat in the wake of his burning lips. Carrying me over to the bed, he laid me gently on the cool sheets, pulled back either by the staff or by him, but it didn't matter because I was falling, swirling as Justin's kisses left me breathless and dazed. Shrugging off his robe, his muscled chest and arms tight as he pressed his body against mine. His strong hands holding mine, entwined, firmly gripping my fingers as I felt his leg slide between my own.

"Jewel, I love you," he murmured, kissing me, not allowing me to speak. *No! I need more time. I have to make this perfect!* But then I felt him. Sliding easily into me, because although my head was thinking one thing, my body was ready, receiving every inch of him as he began to thrust deeply inside of me. I felt so full as Justin's hands moved down to my hips, pulling my body to him, allowing him to go deeper to my very core, but I was stiff, wooden with anxiety. He moved my still body in rhythm with his own, whispering words of love and affection the entire time, until he too became still, clutching me tightly to him. *It's over.* Justin was kissing me softly as he shifted his weight off me.

"Are you all right?" he breathed. *No, I'm not all right. I'm frigid!*

"Yeah, I'm fine," I lied, playing with the sheets. Trying to figure out if there really was a book for women like me. I remember hearing about a cream.

"Jewel?"

"Yes?" *I have to find out where to order that cream from. I won't make the same mistake twice. And I won't cry.*

"Oh, baby." Justin pulled me close to him as the sobs came wrenching out of me, releasing the sexual and mental tension I'd harnessed for the past few months, at the same time expressing my bitter disappointment at letting Justin down. "Please don't cry," he pleaded. "Did I hurt you, Jewel?"

Hearing the panic in his voice made me cry even harder.

"Jewel, did I hurt you?"

He was trying to get me to look at him, but I kept turning my head away. *I am such a failure. Not even married for twenty-four hours, and I can already see that I have doomed this marriage to failure. Just like the first one.*

Holding me close, Justin allowed me to cry myself out. He deserves better than this, I thought morosely.

"Here, turn over." Justin helped me turn on my stomach and started massaging my back.

Okay, how do I let him off the hook? Oh, no, the children! What about the children? And I began to curse myself all over again. I was so wrapped up in self-pity I didn't even realize that Justin had been speaking softly to me until he whispered my name in my ear. "Jewel? Do you realize that you are a pretty bad liar?" When I didn't say anything, he continued. "And I hope that this will be the last time that Malcolm will ever be in bed with us."

"What are you talking about?" I asked, trying to be brave.

"You know Jazz cares a lot about you," he said. I sat up pulling the sheet up around me, and everything fell into place.

"Jazz told you how I felt?" I managed to ask calmly, even though inside I was mortified.

"Jazz didn't need to tell me - I already knew you were scared that you wouldn't please me. I knew this was going to be hard for you. But you're you, and that satisfies me."

"Oh, so this was great for you? This was all that you dreamed of?" I asked sarcastically. *I can't believe that this is my wedding night!*

"Yes." Justin nuzzled my ear.

"Now who's lying?!" I tried to get off the bed but he held me down.

"It was." When I refused to look at him, he went on. "Jewel, this wasn't sex or some romantic scene from a movie or a book, it was consummation. The first chapter of making love. That's what makes it beautiful." Pulling me back into his arms, he went on, "Jewel, it almost broke my heart to see how nervous you were all day. Knowing that you were putting yourself through all that unnecessary drama, just because you didn't think that you would satisfy me."

He kissed me lightly. "Making love for the first time with the person you love is like being a virgin all over again. No one is sure about what to expect, and you never forget it." He kissed my wet cheeks. "And for most of us it only gets better."

Again his hands found my tension points and caressed the tightness into oblivion. Soon my tongue was kissing his, and my body started to respond.

His hands were stroking my sides. "Can I show you how much I love you again?" His words were pressed into my throat, and his lips traveled down to my breast. His tongue making lazy circles around my nipple, before gently swallowing, pulling it taut and then capturing it again, over and over, and finally moving to devour the other.

Slowly, deliberately, he kissed under each breast, then my stomach, causing my arms to ache as they longed to hold him. The fire that was smouldering inside called to him silently, and he was drawn down as if on command. The tips of his locs whispered across my thighs, and I thought I would die. I cried out when I first felt the heat of his breath, then his mouth and tongue, hot, moist, kissing, suckling, passionately, making me writhe and moan. His hands held my thighs firmly to the bed because they were trembling and jumping, the pleasure at my very center was so mercilessly intense. I felt an internal explosion coming, growing as waves of spasms gripped me. Suddenly Justin pulled up over me and with one fluid motion his body was a part of mine again; this time, I was meeting each of his thrusts without any help from the hands that gripped my behind. And it was me who kissed and pulled him closer, wanting more until I exploded into a thousand ultrasensitive particles, then slowly drifted back down to the arms that I had been waiting for a thousand years.

"Are you all right?" It was my turn to ask. "Oh, my God, was I that awful?" I teased happily, wiping the tear that had escaped from the corner of his eye and was sliding down his nose.

Breaking into a grin, he kissed me deeply. "Girl, quit trippin'. Don't you ever doubt that you can make me happy - as long as you love me like that! And I have faith that you always will 'cause I'm going to do everything I can to make sure that you want to."

I welcomed his tight embrace until I couldn't breathe.

"I'm sorry," Justin apologized, shifting his weight off of me, but my arms around his neck wouldn't allow him to go far.

We lay cuddled together listening to the waves of the ocean outside our balcony window. I felt that it couldn't get any better than this but I was wrong. It did and afterwards, Justin declared that he had better give me his gift before I killed him.

"Gift?" I asked as I went to reach for him again, but he evaded my hands.

"Not that gift. That's yours by right." Despite my protest, he was getting up from the bed moving toward the sitting room.

"What are you doing?" I called out and reached over to put on my glasses. Justin came back into the room with a big package, and I wondered how I could have missed it.

"I had it sent down yesterday," he answered when I asked.

I told him that I didn't get him anything.

"Well, this is sort of for both of us," he said, sitting there looking like Sam in his excitement. "Open it."

Tearing open the package, I stared at the white hat box in the middle of the brightly colored paper. "Did you buy me a hat?"

He just sat there grinning.

Moving aside the tissue paper, I found there was no hat but a backpack inside. Holding the canvas bag up, but without understanding, I thanked him, leaning over to give him a kiss.

"My, my, how easy you are to please. Look inside the front pocket."

I pulled open the zippered front pouch and found some papers. "Justin, this is a class schedule," I said, looking at the courses.

He was beaming. "They're your classes, Jewel."

Looking them over, I figured it was a full-time load. "Justin, there is no way that I can take this many classes, work, and take care of a new family." I sighed because I had tried it before and found too much time was being taken from Tia.

"I know," he said quietly. "That's why I want you to quit your job."

"Quit?!" I was stunned.

"Yes," he said, holding up his hand to stop me before I even started. "Jewel, I know how important school is to you. I've put in a lot of overtime over the years, the house is not that much since I got it through foreclosure. You need to do this. It would make you happy. Now, you have a few weeks to save a little money of your own, because I know you'll always want to have a degree of independence, but Jewel, we are a family - one for all and all for one."

I sat there dumbfounded because this was what I'd wanted for so long - to be able to finally see the light at the end of the tunnel.

"And don't think that this is a free ride," Justin said sternly. "I expect you to study hard and graduate on time. That would mean in about two years."

I started to get all misty again realizing that he actually was aware of how much longer I had to go before graduation.

"I could cut it down further if I went to school in the summer," I relented happily.

"Well, part-time because I don't want you to burn yourself out." He smiled, leaning back to watch me.

Eagerly, I devoured the list of courses again, thinking about how my dream was going to finally come true, then looked at the man who made it possible. Pushing everything out of the way, I dove over to him, covering Justin's face with kisses while his arms wrapped around me.

"And C's are not acceptable," he laughed between my pecking, which became deeper with each meeting of our lips.

"Have you seen the view?" he asked huskily.

Shaking my head no, I moved my hand to his.

"Well, it's hard to see with so much light in here." And he reached over to turn out the light beside the bed.

This time when I put my glasses on the nightstand, we didn't see the view until two o'clock the next day.

* * * *

The hotel where we honeymooned was a resort with its own stretch of beach, a pool, and all sorts of activities. Two days before, when I had first entered the lobby and looked through the literature on display, I was really thrilled by the idea of taking an island tour via horseback, but there was no animal that could bring the secret smile of pleasure to my lips like the magnificent beast now lolling on the bed in our room.

"Justin, we *are* going out today," I informed him while standing in the bathroom doorway with toothpaste foaming around my mouth.

"Okay." He stretched his long body, his arms over his head.

"We've been in here for two days and have not picked up one thing on this shopping list or taken any pictures."

"You're right."

When I came out of the bathroom he was sitting on the side of the bed.

"And I really want to see the straw market."

"Anything you want," he agreed, watching me move across the room in his robe.

We had only left the bed to go to the bathroom, take a shower together, or to sit and have juice and fruit while the maid service changed the sheets. Yesterday I had every intention of getting out, but it started to rain and while we were waiting for the rain to stop, we kept ourselves busy exploring each other, slowly, sometimes playfully. By the time we woke up from a much needed nap, it was dark outside and Justin rationalized that it would be too dangerous to set out for town so late, and I wholeheartedly agreed as he pulled me into a sitting position on top of him.

"So, I'm going to get in the shower and you're going to eat," I commanded.

"That's just what I was thinking." And he came to stand behind me and pulled at the robe that I had tied securely at my waist. I turned to fend him off, backing up until I was sitting on top of the dresser.

"Justin, we *are* going out," I protested, but the combination of silk and Justin's fondling hands made me surrender as he lifted my legs adroitly, wrapping them around his lean hips, and I was transported to heaven again.

We finally did get out and took a cruise around the islands in a glass-bottom boat, which was somewhat of a disappointment. There was a glass section in the middle of the boat which was a little green, more than likely from not being cleaned, and it was a lot easier to see the brightly colored fish moving through the crystal clear water by looking over the side.

After the cruise, Justin and I strolled back toward our hotel by going the back route, walking past the hotels, lit up with the flourescent lights that adorned the balconies facing the blackness of the ocean.

We were both missing the kids.

"You know," Justin said somewhat shyly, "this is the longest and furthest I've ever been away from my son."

I nodded. We started telling each other war stories about parenting.

"So Tia's riding in the back seat, and I'm thinking that she's asleep, when all of a sudden, she asks, 'Where the hell are you going?' I had to laugh because she wasn't trying to be smart mouth, just being a Paula Parrot, but I did explain to her how inappropriate it was."

"Yeah, they can be a trip. I remember when Sam was about three weeks old, and I was going crazy because I couldn't get him to stop crying. I fed him, walked him, changed him three times in an hour, checked him from head to toe and that boy just cussed me out in baby."

I remembered all too well those days myself.

"I figured that he missed having a mother's arms or listening for her heartbeat. Finally, I held him up in front of me and told him that I was all he had."

"And he stopped crying?"

"Yep, but I think it was because when I held him under the arms with my fingers supporting his head, it wedged a bubble he had stuck in his little digestive system." And we both cracked up.

I told Justin, "Don't worry, we'll see them both very soon."

We started back to the hotel, and I asked him, "So what did you think of our first excursion out?"

"Jewel, you know the feeling that you get when you've finally gotten something that you've waited your whole life for, but just didn't know it?"

"Yes."

He stopped walking and stood in front of me, his hands at his sides. "I'm even happier and more complete than when I first held Sam in my arms. That's the thing about surprises. You never know how wonderful they are until you get them. But tell me, are you happy?"

"Yes, I am." And it was true. "I never imagined that I would ever be this happy."

"Good, because I want you to always feel this way." Then he became very solemn, "Jewel, if I ever drop the ball, pull me aside and tell me. I want you to always be able to talk to me."

"Of course, that's what makes me feel so secure. Because we've been talking all along."

Justin took my hand, and we continued back to the hotel. People smiled at us as we passed, and we smiled back because we were in love and couldn't help ourselves. And when we got back to our room we sat together on the balcony wrapped in the comforter from the bed just watching the stars, finally checking out the view and just feeling at peace. Kissing me softly alongside my face, Justin's hands roaming my body under the blanket, I knew that I didn't have to fear getting my heart broken. Laughing and kissing we stumbled into the room, getting no further than just inside of the sliding glass before desire overtook us again. Tonight, there was no urgency to our lovemaking. Just slow and languid as we gave and received the gifts that we'd kept from each other for so long. Our hearts rejoicing in their meeting. And when he called out that he loved me, exploding inside of me, I knew that it was me and not the act itself, and I held him close, both of us floating back to heaven because there was nothing on earth that could possibly be this good.

* * * *

The last night of our honeymoon, after dinner and dessert, we wandered along the beach, the moonlight as our flashlight. It was almost twelve so the beach was pretty much deserted, the waves lapping at our feet, the surf swelling and receding as it had for centuries. The late night swingers were doing the club thing, already hot on the dance floor, or feeding money to the all-night casinos; the early risers were already snug in their beds - both destined to pass each other in the early morning as they traded places of rest and recreation.

Walking along quietly, I was startled when Justin suddenly pulled to a stop, looking out into the inky black water.

"What's that?" he asked, pointing toward the horizon.

"What?" I was afraid that he had seen a shark or something.

"Right over there? See in the water?"

I didn't see anything except for the wooden pilings sitting silently in the water.

"What are you doing?!" I cried in alarm because Justin was removing his shirt. "Justin, what are you *doing*?!" He had unfastened his shorts and stepped out of them along with his underwear without missing a beat, moving purposely toward the water that in the darkness looked anything but inviting.

"Justin! Come back here!" But he was already diving in, his head disappearing under the oncoming wave. I had visions of sharks or Justin pulling up a dead body or worse, sending my overactive imagination into hyperdrive.

"Jewel!" Justin called from a few feet away. "Come here!" He waved to me.

"Justin, you come here right now!!" I shouted from the safety of the beach.

"You won't believe what I've found!"

"Come here and tell me." I tried to cajole him back to shore.

"Meet me halfway, you can see it before it gets away." Groaning, but willing to do anything to get him out of the Atlantic, I gathered up my dress and started walking carefully into the cold water. "Justin, it's freezing," I shouted over the waves, trying to keep my balance. I yelped and jumped when something whispered past my calf. "Justin, there's stuff out here!" When he didn't answer I looked up and for a minute I was afraid that I was out there all alone. "JUSTIN!!"

Justin turned up beside me in the midst of a rolling wave. Startled, I lost my balance and fell on my butt, soaking my dress. "Justin, if this is a trick to get me out here to do it . . ." I started moving toward the beach. "You are going to be very disappointed!"

"Hey, babe, I'm sorry. I didn't mean to make you fall, honestly. I just wanted you to see it before it got away."

"See what?" I asked turning around to look back at the emptiness of the night.

"The mermaid."

"The what?" *No, he didn't just say mermaid.* But he was shaking his head yes, and I wondered if he was one of those people who couldn't hold their liquor even though he'd only had one beer. "A mermaid?" I repeated.

"Yeah, I saw her break the surface and thought I could catch her," he explained, helping me back to the beach and his dry clothes.

"And what were you going to do if you caught this mermaid?"

"I did catch her!" he said excitedly.

Okay, he is crazy. I watched him step back into his clothes, wet body and all.

"I was trying to hold on to her until you could come and see but you took too long." He sounded like a disappointed little kid, and I stood dripping and shivering trying to figure out if I would need to have him committed.

"You don't believe me, do you? Why, because you didn't see her?" he asked, using one hand to push back his dripping locs.

"Well, that would probably be my first guess," I agreed, folding my arms across my chest.

"Okay, then where did I get these?"

"Get what?"

"These." Nestled in the palm of his outstretched hand were two small shiny things. Taking my hand he placed them in it. When I brought my hand closer to my face I saw that they were two pearl studs, each with a little diamond, that would sit flush against the hole of my earlobe.

"But since you don't believe me I guess that I'll just have to throw them back."

"Don't you dare!" I said, closing the jewels in my fist. "And this mermaid just happened to know that you needed earrings?"

"Yes, she knew that you needed a new pair because she could see that you had these holes in your ears and nothing in them." He put his shirt around my shoulders and started leading me toward our hotel. "She saw how beautiful you are and wanted you to have them."

I smiled in the darkness, because I had taken my old earrings out before the wedding - the ones that Malcolm gave me a lifetime ago - and put them away for when Tia got older. When Justin asked me about them, I vaguely said that they didn't go with my new life. He must have put two and two together, but leave it to him to find such a memorable way to bestow me with a replacement pair.

"You know I've never encountered such an event," I said.

"Really? You'd better get used to it, 'cause these kinds of things happen to me all the time. Like wishing on a star."

"A star?"

"Yeah, pick that one right over there."

Following his finger I found the twinkling orb in the velvet sky.

"Make a wish," he whispered, leaning close to my ear.

Closing my eyes, I silently moved my lips.

"No, I have to hear what the wish is."

"Well, then it won't come true."

"No, that doesn't apply to me. I've got my own connection," Justin assured me.

"Okay, then I wished that we will always be as happy and content as we are this very moment," I murmured, looking deep in his eyes, all joking aside.

Looking down at me he said solemnly, "Okay, as long as there are stars in the sky, I guarantee you that I will do everything I can to make that wish come true."

And we went back upstairs where he proceeded to keep his word.

CHAPTER 26

"MOMMY!" I had no problem hearing Tia's voice over the din of the crowded airport, and a glance in her direction found my mother and Lou holding on to both kids as if they were little racehorses, ready to jump as soon as the gates opened - not that I was any better, rushing past people, running down the exit ramp toward them. As the gap between us got smaller, the little dynamos could no longer be contained, and it ended up with us falling all over each other in excitement, and people milled past the tangle of our arms and legs.

"Hey, little people!" I hugged them both tightly, enjoying the feeling of their little bodies against mine. I could hardly believe that Justin and I had such a good time without them.

Justin said, "Well, we'd better get our luggage before someone else does," and reaching down, grabbed both kids by the back of their pants and carried them like suitcases.

"Put us down!" Sam squealed as he and Tia both tried to wriggle out of Justin's firm grip.

"We're not suitcases!" Tia cried, hovering over the floor.

"How do I know that you're not suitcases?" Justin asked lifting her slightly higher so that he could see her face. "I mean, you're waiting at the airport, right?"

Giggles.

"And I can carry you each in one hand, right?"

More giggles.

"And you both sound like you have stuff rattling around inside of you." And he gave both of them a little jiggle which set them off again.

"No! We're not the suitcases. The suitcases are over there!" Sam pointed to the carousel of moving baggage.

"Oh, then what are you?"

"We're kids!" Tia panted, as Justin began rearranging them in his arms.

"O-h-h-h," he said as if this could be a possibility. "Whose kids are you?"

Sam and Tia looked at each other across Justin with raised eyebrows and little smiles sitting in the corners of their mouths.

"Your kids!" Tia growled, pushing her forehead up against his in a little head butt thing that they had started.

"Is that a fact?" He turned to butt Sam who nodded, giving me a bashful look before wrapping his arms around Justin's neck.

After a very talkative, animated ride back to town, we dropped my parents off and headed toward our new home. Pulling up in the driveway, our neighbors, Darrin and Linda, came to their front door, with their son, Brandon, who was practically jumping up and down at the sight of Sam.

"Welcome home, finally!" And we all laughed.

"Yeah! We're here for good now," Justin called. Wrapping his arm around my shoulder we slowly walked over.

"I can't say that we missed the weather." And it was true. You could feel the hawk about to swoop. The wind gustier and colder than when we left.

"Well, we won't keep you all. Brandon just wanted to make sure that Sam was actually moving in tonight."

And we all laughed as we watched the two little boys run around, playing some sort of make-believe game while Tia stood on the sidelines, jumping up and down.

"Come on, Brandon." After just a few half-hearted protests and the promise of having a long time to play with each other, our new neighbors said their farewells.

The kids and I were in the process of opening the front door when Justin almost pulled the door out of my hands.

"Uhn-uhn-uhn!" He said waving a little finger in front of us. "We have to do this right." He scooped up the kids and carried them over the threshold.

"Justin," I said, leaning against the doorjamb. "We've been here before."

"But this is our first time as a real family," he whispered in my ear before lifting me up and depositing me in the foyer.

"Ooooh, the first thing I want to do, is get warm!" I said, rubbing my hands together.

Justin went out with the kids to get some wood off the deck to start a fire in the family room.

I turned up the thermostat and searched out the phonebook to find out who delivered in the neighborhood and called for a large pepperoni pizza.

When I came into the family room, Sam and Tia were sitting on the floor entranced, as Justin stuffed kindling for the fire which took off pleasantly popping and crackling. There was no television in this room but it did have a music entertainment center, and I put on some classical melodies to add a soft background to the otherwise quiet house.

"So did you two have a good time this week?"

"It was more fun when Sam came home from school," Tia said, looking at her new brother with little sister admiration while he just blushed.

Tia began a round of twenty questions. "Mommy, do I get a thermos when I start school?"

"Of course."

"Will I go to Sam's school?"

"Of course."

"When will I go to school?"

"Next September, but you'll go to camp this coming summer."

I noticed Sam eyeing the bag that had all their souvenirs, and when he caught me watching him, he looked away and tried not to smile.

"Well, Justin, I guess that we should get these presents out before someone just about bursts."

"What presents?" Justin asked looking up at me with a blank stare.

"The presents for the kids."

"Aw, man! Those were for *these* kids?" He put his hand over his mouth, eyes wide.

"Stop teasing," I scolded, taking the gifts out of the suitcase. When I got to the plastic bag of seashells, the salty, fishy-smell aroma that wafted up to my nose transported me back to the island where it was probably warm enough today to leave the balcony door open. But looking at Tia and Sam open their gifts, marveling at the bamboo games and the straw doll, and the logs on the fire giving off a nice glow, I was much more content to be where I was.

After the pizza was eaten and the children stretched out with their little bellies extended, I figured that the house was warm enough for baths.

"Tia, we'll let Sam take his bath first, and then I'll dunk you in."

"Why don't you and Tia use the kids' bathroom upstairs, and Sam and I'll shower downstairs in the guest bathroom?" Justin suggested. "Sam can help me lock up the house."

"Okay, I'll put your pajamas and towels out for you both."

And we went our separate ways. I knew that bonds need to be formed over time and not forced. Right now I felt confident that we were on the right track, but it was interesting that Justin needed his space with Sam as much as I needed mine with Tia.

After getting Tia bathed, lotioned and powdered down, we pulled out her pj's that still had feet in them, and I watched her wiggle into them.

"What are you going to wear, Mommy?"

"My pajamas," I answered, trying to help her fit her big head through the opening of the pajama shirt.

"I mean which ones?" came her muffled voice.

"I don't know. You can help me pick them out. "Come on, let's go. ER will be on pretty soon," I said, swinging her up on my hip.

"You're gonna to watch ER?" she asked, obviously surprised.

"Yeah, why wouldn't I?" And I watched her expression as she played with the curls in my damp hair. "Don't I watch ER every Thursday night?"

"Yes," she answered slowly.

"And isn't today Thursday?"

Tia bobbed her head up and down. "Yes."

"Well, all right, then."

The sounds of the sports channel came down the hall and entering the master bedroom, we found Justin and Sam already sprawled out on our king-sized bed, both wearing pajama bottoms, but tee shirts instead of the matching tops. Justin reached up and took Tia from my arms, and she settled back in the crook of his arm.

"Tia, I thought you were going to help me find some pajamas?" She just gave me this look, like "you know that I'm comfortable so be a big girl and do it yourself."

"Stinker," I said, tossing one of the pillows over at both of them.

"Mommy's just jealous," Justin whispered, and Tia giggled, nodding her head like she really knew what he was talking about.

The phone started ringing which kind of surprised all of us since it was our first real official phone call as a new family.

I picked up the receiver.

"Hey, there, Mrs. Baptiste!"

"Hi, Marcus. What's up?" I said, smiling into the phone.

"Oh, wait! I know that you don't think you're going to get your little detective back so soon, do you?"

"Come on, Jewel, you know he's the only one around here who knows how to make the coffee."

We both chuckled, and I said, "Well, the last I saw he was being held hostage by some tiny little people."

"Yeah, man!" Justin yelled, so that Marcus could hear. "I think you'd better call for backup! I may not make it out of this nice warm house alive!"

Marcus said to me, "Tell him he can say it to me in person tomorrow, and for what it's worth, Jewel, I am sorry."

I handed the phone to Justin.

"Well, I guess it's back to the same old routine," Sam sighed.

"What do you mean, Sambo?"

"It's back to work for Daddy." And he sounded so pitiful that I felt really guilty for taking his father away for five whole days. Pulling Sam into my lap, I stroked his head trying to reassure him by letting him know he had me.

When I asked them if they were ready for a story, both kids yelled a definite yes, and I directed them to their rooms. Pulling the big wooden rocking chair that sat in front of the window into position in the hall, right between their two bedrooms, I began reading from a book of Carribean folklore. My voice rose loud enough to be heard in the beginning and then faded so that it was more like a whispered suggestion as the steady rhythmic breathing of two sleepy children bounced off me in stereo.

"The kids asleep already?" Justin asked, pulling back the covers for me when I returned to our bedroom.
"Yep. What'd I miss?" My eyes were glued to the set and ER, while I reached down to pull off my socks.
"Here, let me help," he offered, moving his hands up instead of down my leg.
"All right now, you know the rules when it comes to ER!" We both concentrated on my program. An hour later I was surprised that no one had come to our bedroom door.
"I think that they're both asleep," Justin murmured as he nuzzled the side of my neck. Two seconds later, it began.
"Daddy? Can I have some water please? My throat is dry."
Then, "Mommy, I'm hot."
This evolved into "Daddy I have to go to the bathroom" and "Mommy, my stomach hurts." Each message wasn't just yelled down the hall, it was delivered in person, each time little eyes peeping into our bedroom. And each time, Justin or I would calmly lead them back to their rooms. But as the wind grew louder and knowing that it was still a new house for both of them, with no street lights to shine in their rooms, I knew it would be just a matter of time before we bent the rule of each person sticking to their own bed. So I said nothing when, after dozing off, I was awakened to find Sam's leg flung over my knees. Turning over, I saw Justin way over on the other side of my three-year-old who was spread out at the very top of the bed, taking up the entire middle portion.
Smiling, I went to get an extra blanket to cover Sam who was sleeping on top of the comforter. Tiptoeing, I gently tried to remove the remote from Justin's grip, but he scared me, grabbing my wrist in a vise-like grip, before realizing that it was me. When recognition filtered past his dreams, eyes closing again, he puckered his lips for a kiss, and our family settled down for its first night at home.

* * * *

The weeks passed, and we all fell into a natural groove. One night, Justin came home a little after seven, looking beat but perking right up when the kids came running to him. The way the light danced in his eyes, I knew without a doubt that this was the life he had envisioned for himself. I hated to burst his bubble.

"Justin, can you help me with this jar in the kitchen?" Leaving the children to go back to playing upstairs, Justin followed me into the kitchen where everything was all ready, my famous pasta and seafood simmering by request. "What's up?"

"Something's wrong with Sam."

"What? Is he sick?" The worry caused his face to frown. "He didn't feel warm when I picked him up."

"No, nothing like that," I interrupted, "I think it has to do with all of us. The marriage."

"Well, Jewel, kids need time to adjust." Justin's voice echoed with relief that it wasn't a physical ailment, but his tone was still worried.

"Watch him tonight and let me know what you see."

"You don't want to just tell me?"

"No," I said, dumping the pasta into the strainer. "Because I may be making a big deal out of nothing."

At dinner, we all sat around the table laughing and catching up on the day, and making plans for tomorrow.

"Hey, man, we'll be too big to leave the house if we keep eating like this." Justin gave Sam's hand a little nudge.

"Yeah," Sam agreed, sitting back patting his full stomach. "Grandma doesn't even cook this good."

Tia had opened her mouth to say something but all that came out was a huge belch that seemed to be too loud to come from a mouth so small.

"There ya go!" Justin said over our howls of laughter. "That's the best compliment of a good meal."

Later, after the kitchen had been cleaned up with everyone's help, we were set for the evening. The kids were watching the Friday night lineup that had all of their favorite programs while Justin and I sat talking softly in our room.

"Well, did you notice?" I asked in a hushed whisper.

"He seemed fine to me," Justin tried to reassure me. "He didn't even seem shy like you know he can be - seems very comfortable."

Wondering if I was making a big deal out of nothing, I said bluntly, "Justin, he doesn't call me anything." I felt that was a sign that Sam really didn't accept this union.

Tia had dubbed Justin "Justy" which came about the day we experimented by trading kids for a day to try and find out what they thought of our whirlwind romance. I thought that things had gone well with Sam and me that day, but now I was no longer sure that Sam's and my relationship was going to be successful. *Sam hates me.*

"What do you mean, Sam doesn't call you anything?" Justin asked.

"Well, it's dawned on me that he has no name for me." *Sam hates me.*

"I didn't really realize that, Jewel - I'm sure if I talked to him . . ."

"No, Justin, I'm sure that it will work itself out." *Sam hates me.*

Another week later and I was still no-name to Sam. I decided I really had to get to the bottom of it. Tia was with Malcolm, so I went to pick up Sam from school. As he and a couple of little friends approached the truck, I heard one of the children ask Sam if I was his mother. Watching the little boy who already had my heart wrapped around his tiny finger, I saw him glance at me and then focus on making sure that his feet were still moving in the right direction. I noticed with dejection that he didn't answer the child. I know Sam didn't even whisper a reply because his little companion kept asking until Sam said goodbye and ran to jump in the truck.

"Hey, Sam!" I leaned over to get my kiss hello, but he was staring out the window, deep in thought about the unanswered question no doubt. "What do you say that I take you to my all-time favorite place?"

"Okay." The voice didn't have its usual enthusiasm.

After driving in silence for a while, I tried to initiate a conversation by asking him about his day, but clearly the little boy wasn't leaving the inner conversation he was having, so I just drove on. Pulling into the entrance to Haines Point, I found a place to park and stepped out. "Want to go for a walk?" I asked. The park for the most part was empty - too cold for playing although there were still a few hardcore runners and some golfers waiting for the sun. After a short walk, we sat down on a bench and just watched the water go by. "Did you know that I love coming here? Especially when I have a problem."

"Why?"

Handing him a tissue for his runny nose, I explained.

"Because whenever I come and sit right here, I can see the water and the trees."

He nodded politely, and I went on. "You see how wide this water is?"

Following my finger, Sam looked at the water that ran through the channel before widening out into the bay. "So when I see how big this bit of water is and how it just gets bigger, it makes me feel that my own problems aren't really that big." I glanced out of the corner of my eye and noticed that he was listening. "Is there anything on your mind that maybe I could help you with?" I nudged gently.

"No, not really," he answered softly.

"Were those boys . . ." At the mention of his classmates, Sam's little shoulders stiffened. " . . . asking you if I was your mother?"

"Are you my mother?" he asked, looking at me with big brown eyes.

"Yes, if you want me to be." I wasn't sure if Sam had that space reserved for the woman who had never even set eyes on him. "But if you want me to be just a mom kind of person instead, then I can do that."

"Can I call you Mommy?"

My heart was singing, and it dawned on me that perhaps he had just been waiting for permission from *me*! That I had been mistaken to assume that he would set the tone for our relationship, and all the while he had been waiting for me - the adult. I wanted to dance, to shout, but trying not to go overboard, I said calmly, "Sure, if you want to." Waiting for his reaction, I continued, "Or you can call me Mama, or Moms . . ."

"I like Mommy." Sam looked at me intently as if he wanted to make sure that I wasn't going to change my mind - I could almost see the word rolling around his tongue.

"Sam, I want you to be able to come and talk to me about anything. There is nothing that you can say or do that will make me not want to be your mommy."

Sam slowly nodded his head before saying, "Okay."

"Good. Well, then the water has done its job. Let's go and fix something for dinner."

Falling in step beside me, I heard little sniffling sounds. The wind had brought a fresh stream of mucus flowing from Sam's nose.

"Here, blow."

And he blew his nose holding onto my hand to make sure that I didn't pull it away too soon. After wiping under his nose, I took his hand and we headed home.

"Who made dinner?" Justin asked when he got home.

"Me and Mommy did!" Sam boasted cheerfully as he stood tossing the salad.

"Oh, you and *Mommy* did, huh?" Giving me a wink and a smile over Sam's head, I turned my own cheesy grin toward him.

"Yep, so go and wash up and get out of our way." I started shooing Justin from the kitchen. Kissing me softly, he traipsed up the stairs to get out of his work clothes and lock up his firearm, while I turned back to finish making the gumbo and salad with my son.

CHAPTER 27

The music could be heard before the little light went on around the "P" for penthouse, and then the elevator doors opened onto scores of adults and children all dressed in their finery for the annual family Christmas party. The room was filled not just with our extended family, but with friends as well. Oldies were blaring from the deejay's table, and our elders were having a ball, delighting the spectators who stood on the sidelines laughing and clapping.

"O-h-h, see! Now you're just showing off!" Ashley shouted when Lou spun Mommy and came around to Barbara Baptiste, and Clarence Baptiste caught Mommy before her turn was even completed. "Look at these people. They act like they're young or something."

I turned to Ashley. "All right, you. What's with the glow?" Then my eyes got big, "Are you . . ."

"Don't even think it," Ashley said, blowing my theory away. "See that man over there?"

I followed her gaze to an older man who was talking to Tamicia, Tia and Sam. He was handsome with his salt-and-pepper mustache matching the nicely trimmed fade. He had the body of an athlete, but the easy charm of a boardroom executive as he listened intently to Tia who was no doubt explaining something of great importance.

"That's Dillon!"

"I recognize him from the pictures you've showed me."

"So how long is he here for? When did he get here?" I was all excited because I wanted my sister to have something more than a long-distance, e-mail relationship - to have the same happiness that I'd been riding on for almost . . . what? A new beginning ago?

"He'll be here until after the New Year, but that's not the exciting part." She was practically squealing.

"What?!" I asked, almost jumping up and down myself.

"Tamicia likes him! Oh, Jewel, you're gonna catch flies if you don't shut your mouth." I was shocked because Tamicia never took to anyone right away, but maybe the years of Ashley's love and support were having their effect.

"Come on!" And my sister pulled me out onto the dance floor where we danced with each other like Mommy told us girls used to do back in her day.

Laughing and having fun, I saw Annette as usual standing off by herself. She looked great in her Christmas ensemble, a red silk shirt tucked into tuxedo pants. Her very slender height made her look just like a model coming down the runway. I grabbed her hand and pulled her out onto the floor, where Ashley and I showed her how to do the mashed potato and the pegleg.

Everyone had a good time, and when Santa showed up, the kids went wild until he settled them by reading his rendition of Charles Dickens' *Christmas Carol* with an urban flavor. When he finished, he told everybody to go on to church to understand the real meaning of Christmas and then hurry home because he'd be paying a visit that evening. And laying a finger aside his nose, he disappeared onto the elevator. The kids were so excited as they watched the little lights flash until the elevator reached the roof from where the faint sounds of sleigh bells came drifting back to us.

The Christmas mass at St. Augustine was packed, and as always I was so moved by the service which was for me an essential part of the holiday season. Afterward, we all promised to see each other during the next twelve days of Christmas, and my small family walked to the car, Justin carrying a sleeping Sam, propping him up in the backseat so that he could fasten his seatbelt. By the time we got home, Tia was slumped over next to him. Each of us took a child to carry upstairs to bed.

"Hey, I think my necklace must have slipped off in the truck. I'll be right back. Can you get Tia's clothes off her?" I asked at the doorway.

"Sure. You don't want me to look for you?"

I was already moving down the hall to the stairs. "No, I'll do it." Slipping into the garage, I carefully popped the car trunk. Then taking a deep breath, I grabbed the red silvery paper, trying not to rip it as I pulled it out. Pushing open the door, I checked to make sure that Justin was still upstairs with the kids. My burden made it difficult to move through the kitchen and downstairs to the family room. Slipping on the first step of the landing set me down hard on my butt with a groan and a thud, which brought Justin to the top landing at the top of the stairs.

"Jewel? Are you okay?"

As I pushed my bundle down the stairs again, trying to hurry and get it under the tree, he called me again. "Jewel?"

I heard him descending and quickly ran back upstairs, surprising him as we almost collided on the landing.

"What are you doing?" he asked.

"Oh, just making sure that the tree's lit like Santa said and that the presents are all stacked up." Before coming to the party, Marcus had stopped at our home first, bringing the kids' toys which had been hidden over at his house.

"Come on, let's go to bed," I coaxed, pleased with my cleverness in pulling off his surprise. We peeled off our clothes and took a quick shower together, then settled down to sleep but ended up looking at the moonlight shining through the window. All we needed was some new fallen snow - the children were nestled and we were snug.

Looking over, I met Justin's eyes staring at me. "You are beautiful."

And I smiled because I truly felt beautiful. "You know it's funny . . ."

"What's funny?" he asked, kissing me before I could answer.

"Two years ago, I was in another marriage thinking that everything was fine. Now I'm with another man in another marriage, and I still feel that everything is fine!"

"So, your point is?"

"That I'll have to divorce you, find another man in Baltimore, then get married so that next Christmas everything will *still* be fine!" I explained serenely.

"Okay." And he laid back down.

"That's it?" I asked, giving him a little slap upside his head.

"Woman, if you think that you can find someone else who can make you as happy as I can, or love you as much, and want to spend the rest of his life with you and that little girl in there, well . . ." He let the words hang and closed his eyes again.

Humming, I wondered aloud, "Maybe I can put an ad in the personals tomorrow" and giggled when he tweaked my butt. Just then his pager started vibrating on the nightstand. "No!" I groaned. "No, it's Christmas Eve." But Justin was already dialing the number that showed up on the little screen while I pulled a pillow over my head. A moment later, I felt him slip out of the bed.

"I'll be back before you can miss me," he promised, removing the pillow to kiss my pouty lips.

"I doubt that." My eyes were closed, and I heard him walk out of the room, followed by the sound of the garage door opening and closing. "This really sucks," I muttered to myself as I tried to burrow into the bed to get comfortable. Throwing a pillow off the bed, I jumped when I heard Justin's voice, "Hey!" as the pillow hit him in the stomach. "What happened?" I asked surprised.

He started undressing again. "I told you I'd be back before you could miss me." Sliding his cold hands around my waist he settled back down under the comforter with me.

"So what happened?"

"Oh . . ." He feigned innocence. "That was Marcus calling from his car. He had one more gift in the trunk that he forgot so he just wanted to drop it off. Now come on and go to sleep because we have about . . ." Justin squinted at the clock on the nightstand. ". . .three more hours before we are summoned. I don't know about Tia, but Sam has a special clock at Christmas that goes off at five-thirty am sharp."

I knew he was up to something, and I lay down pondering what it could be, but my mind was invaded by sugarplums, and I fell into a deep sleep.

The next thing I knew Tia and Sam were pulling on covers, arms, legs, anything they could get hold of - begging us to get up since the rules were clear that no one could go near the tree until we all went together.

"Come on, Mommy!" Tia and Sam tugged at me.

"All right, all right," I yawned, reaching to shake Justin, but Sam was kneeling in his place. "Where's your father?"

"Right here." And opening one eye I saw the video camera catch me in all my morning glory.

"Ugh! Justin!"

"Come on, let's go, let's go! Give me passion!" he cried, moving around like a demented director. "Great! Fabulous! Now give me anger!"

"I'll give you anger, all right," I retorted, sitting up rubbing my eyes.

Justin moved in front of us, still filming, as we plodded down the stairs. My own excitement was growing, thinking of the present I had gotten for him.

Tia and Sam beat me to the basement, and I assumed that their howls of delight were for the two shining bikes, but I froze when I reached the bottom step and saw the real cause of their jubilance.

"What the . . ." Sitting under the tree with a big red ribbon around his neck was the biggest dog I had ever seen, his tail making a thumping sound on the carpeted floor. The kids were petting him while he sat there looking at me as if to say, "What do you think?" I looked at the dog, then at Justin and then back at the dog. "Justin, what in the world did you do?" I gasped.

Removing his eye from the camera, he said, "Jewel, this is Klaus. Klaus, this is Jewel." And as if on cue, the dog came toward me, stopping at my feet to hold out his paw.

"Justin, we never discussed this," I complained, absently shaking the offered paw.

"Well, of course we did."

"When did we discuss a dog?"

"Remember the night that . . ." And he stood scratching his head. "I'm sorry, I must have dreamed it. But isn't he wonderful?" And he bent down to rub the dog behind the ears.

The kids came running over, and Klaus offered each of them a lick for the little hands that stroked his fur.

"Okay, here's the story." Justin sat down with me on the bottom steps where I had sunk in shock. "Klaus here is two years old, and he was supposed to be trained as a police dog, but the poor thing was too playful. Couldn't keep his mind on his work. They sent him to be a guide dog, but he failed that too."

As Justin gave me Klaus' poor academic record, the dog was trying to get Sam to continue rubbing him behind the ears by putting his nose under his hand.

"So he's stupid?" I asked.

"No, far from it. Klaus, come." Immediately, the dog came and stood at Justin's right side. "Sit." And he did. "Down." And Klaus laid down on all fours. I was impressed. I knew the debate was over and said, "Well, take that stupid bow off him. It clashes with his collar."

Everyone started to cheer, including Klaus who sat up and gave a loud bark of appreciation.

"All right, let's open some presents!" Justin cried.

After the kids had gone through the packages of clothes, toys, and games, I moved around the pile of papers to drag out my gift to Justin.

"Open it!" I was practically jumping up and down in anticipation.

Justin pulled back the paper carefully, prolonging my agony, and I told the kids to help him. In a matter of seconds the canvas, sand-filled punching bag was lying limply on its side.

"What in the world?" Justin laughed.

"It's a punching bag!"

"I know that, and it's great, but what made you think of it?"

"I got it because it's the only thing that your gym doesn't have!" I knew it was perfect. I like to give gifts I know people will use, something they want but never get around to getting for themselves.

"Thank you. I truly love it." And he gave me a kiss to prove it. "Now for you." He disappeared behind the huge fir tree and pulled out a large package wrapped in silver and gold. From the way he carried it, I could tell it was heavy as he stepped carefully over the torn up wrapping paper. "Now, you sit there and let me unwrap it, okay? Sam and Tia, come here and hold the sides please."

The kids stood on both sides of the box that looked like a big screen television. As Justin carefully pulled the paper off, the first thing I saw was the frame, followed by the colors, until the gift was completely exposed. I sat back, my breath completely taken away.

"Mommy, it's so pretty." Tia and Sam came to sit with me on the bottom step and were as awestruck as I was.

"Do you like it?" Justin asked worriedly.

Looking up at him, the world went all watery, and all I could do was nod my head as my eyes went back to feast on the most magnificient gift I had ever received.

It was an oil painting illuminated by a huge full moon suspended over the ocean and surrounded by stars. Glowing beams were bouncing off the water, creating a rippled mirror image of the floating orb and the dancing lights above. The beach was deserted except for two people who looked just like Justin and I. They stood looking down at something glowing which the man was handing to her, their faces animated by their amazement at the gift. And then my eyes were drawn to the small figure in mid-flight, looking as if she were diving back into the dark water below.

"Mommy, don't cry!" Tia begged, patting my shoulder. Tears were streaming down my face, and I couldn't tear my eyes away from the painting, it was so beautiful, so alive. I was speechless, my feelings overwhelming. I got up and gave Justin a hug for our night, our beach, our beginning. "Thank you," I finally managed to say. For the artist to have captured the scene so perfectly from just a description, it must have been indelibly etched in Justin's mind and heart.

CHAPTER 28

I had done everything humanly possible to be fair and reasonable when it came to Malcolm and his relationship with Tia, despite the shabby way that he'd had me bend over, and without the aid of petroleum jelly, serviced me in the most brutal way. But for Tia's sake, I'd managed to grin and stand quietly by, waiting for everything to become more stable, trying to make sure that Malcolm didn't feel our newly created family as a threat to his relationship with Tia. That was before today. Today, the gloves were off, and as far as I was concerned, Malcolm had made his last backdoor assault on me.

The sound of the motorized garage door came to my ears as Klaus perked up. Justin came through the door, a smile on his face, flowers in one hand, his helmet hanging from the other while I watched balefully from my spot on the bottom step across the room.

"Uh-oh," he said, slowly reading the look on my face before looking down to check his watch. "Am I late?"

"No. But I've gotta go out so I need you to watch the kids for a while." Jumping up and shrugging into my leather jacket, I explained, "They've already had dinner and right now they're playing upstairs with Brandon."

"Whoa! What's the matter?" Justin came toward me, removing his jacket as I zipped up mine, and before I could answer the children came flying down the stairs to greet him.

"Daddy! Daddy!" Sam barreled into him, shouting, "Tia's going to Disneyworld!" *Like hell she is!*

"Wha . . .?" Justin glanced at me, as Sam and Tia in their delirium chattered on about Tia's soon-to-be-aborted trip.

"Can we go next time - all of us?" Sam asked in Sam's way. Not pouting or whining, just making plans for the future.

Justin met my flashing eyes, and everything was understood. "Well, that's something," he said carefully.

"I'll be back," I announced, stalking out of the house to the garage not able to hide the fact, even for the children's sake, that I was way beyond pissed. Climbing into my car and adjusting the mirrors, I didn't notice that Justin had come out into the garage behind me until he pulled open the passenger side door and got in.

"You're sure you want to do this?" he asked softly.

I breathed deeply. I didn't want to lose any of this fine anger, but I knew that the force sitting behind my clenched teeth was liable to hit an unintended victim.

"I have to do this," I said and was happy that it didn't come out as a hiss. Pleased that the heat of my scorn still pulsed through my veins but that I hadn't accidentally spoken too harshly to the wrong person. No, this fury was for one special person, and I didn't want to spill one drop of the rage that had been building ever since I picked Tia and Sam up from Malcolm's mom's house earlier that day.

I should have realized that something was up when Malcolm paged me to say that he would be picking up both kids today and taking them to his Mom's after running a few errands with them. And stupid me, thinking, "How sweet, he's even going to pick up Sam." *What an idiot I am!* My hands gripped the steering wheel, causing my veins to dance back and forth over the knuckles as my hands opened and closed in response to my anxiety.

"Why don't you come back in and talk about it before you head out there?" Justin suggested. "Or wait until the weather gets better?"

How lucky I am to have such a caring husband, but that won't stop me from pushing him forcibly out of this car if he doesn't stop talking and just let me go.

Sensing that this was a losing battle, Justin sighed and asked if I wanted him to go along.

"Thank you, but no - I've got it covered." My voice was tight and clipped. *Get out of the car, Justin. Get **out** of the car! GET OUT OF THE CAR!*

"Well, you should at least take the truck."

Hallelujah, he's getting out! I quickly reached back to grab the seatbelt to strap across my chest. "No, that's okay, I'm used to driving this in the snow." I started the engine, ready to back out and head over to Malcolm's and the showdown that had been a long time coming when Justin bent down and tapped on the glass. *I swear, if this man doesn't let me handle my business!*

"Yes?" My irritation was evident as Justin said in his most authoritative, working voice, "Look, don't let this get out of control. I understand your frustration, but don't let him provoke you into doing anything that you'll regret."

And his eyes were so soft and pleading that it made me feel bad I couldn't allow him to have any illusions as to how this was really going to go down. "Justin, he started this a long time ago, trying at every chance to drag me down to his level." My voice was rising as my blood started to boil at Malcolm's past and latest unfair treatment slapped me again. "And I'm going there, but believe me, if anyone has any regrets it's going to be him!"

Shaking his head because he knew that this was something that I needed to do on my own, my husband stood up, allowing me to back out of the garage. The car bounced into the street, wheels spinning slightly before the treads of the tires could catch. With a little wobbly fishtail, the car found its footing and became the metal mountain goat that had moved me through many snow-covered roads. Luckily for me, there was no Friday rush-hour traffic since most of the government workers had gotten off early due to the snowstorm alert.

I slammed my hand against the wheel. *What more could I have done to make that man happy?*

Here we go, I thought, as my head tried to take over. *Let's face it, you set no ground rules and the few rinkydink boundaries you did set up, you allowed Malcolm to cross whenever he felt like it, letting him flout your authority again and again. I tried to tell you, but I'm just your head. You'd rather listen to that overemotional heart that's always trying to make sure everyone is happy no matter how many times you get kicked.*

Hey, whose side are you on?
I'm just telling you like it is.
Well, I'm going to fix it all right now.

Yeah, right! We're probably just going to sit there while Malcolm starts in about how he's the poor father just trying to be a part of his child's life. Malcolm will get just what he wants again.

Shut up! Don't be so sure that you know everything.

And the part of me that very few people got to see, the part of me that only emerged when pushed too far, became silent, biding its time.

Turning up the steep street that I knew like the back of my hand, I saw a few cars spinning their wheels since the plow trucks hadn't been down the back streets yet. I was amazed at the irony that Malcolm and Annette would end up getting a place pretty close to where we used to live - a nice little two-story condo on a quiet street.

When I pulled up to the curb, I didn't see Malcolm's car but the lights were on inside, so I climbed up the iron stairs that led to their front door. I had never come here in the past, never having been invited, even though I had invited Annette and Malcolm over to our house on several occasions, trying to keep communications open. I rang the doorbell, standing on the landing protected from the cold as the wind whipped along out in the street. Ringing the bell again, waiting, impatiently shifting from one snowbooted foot to another. Then I heard the sound of slippers shuffling, the deadbolt turned, and the door opened a crack, a security chain in place. Part of Annette's profile came into view.

"Jewel?" And she was clearly surprised as she shut the door, the chain rattling its protest at being pushed aside until her wide and expressive eyes were staring at me. It took a minute before she realized that I was waiting to be let in and stepped back and allowed me to enter. "Please come in. Is everything all right? Is Tia okay?"

"Yes, she's fine. I'm sorry to come over unannounced." Again I pulled on the reins even though it was hard. "Is Malcolm here? I need to speak to him."

Staring at me for a moment, taking in my disheveled appearance and rushed demeanor, slowly she said, "No. He's gone to the store. Is there anything that I can do?"

"Uhm . . ."

We both turned toward the front door as the deadbolt turned again, and my ex-husband came through the door with a blast of cold air. "Man, you say snow and those people act like there'll never be another delivery of toilet paper, bread, or milk again." Seeing me, he paused for a moment before heading past me into the little galley kitchen, and I knew that this was going to get ugly. We were measuring each other the way boxers touch gloves before they try to kill one another.

"So what brings you out here on a night like this?" he asked, feigning ignorance.

"Malcolm, you know why I'm here. I came to see why you did it?"

"What?!" He acted as if he were really surprised. "Decide to take my daughter on a trip?"

"*Our* daughter," I corrected him.

"Right, our daughter," he agreed with a sneer. "I'm glad you've finally remembered that."

"Malcolm, why did you invite Tia to Disneyworld without even so much as discussing it with me first?"

He came out of the kitchen, moving past me to sit on the couch that sat facing the television.

When he didn't answer, I continued trying to be reasonable. "Malcolm," I started wearily, "I have done everything I can to make sure that you have access to Tia and her upbringing. I have included you in everything from where she goes to school to what doctor she should use. I've allowed you to take her on a whim because I understand how much you need to be a part of her life. I even listened to you and thought I understood why you didn't want her to go to New Orleans last year, but then you turn around and do this?! Why?!"

Malcolm's eyes had been glued to the television, but now he turned and looked at me as if I had committed some heinous crime. Then he started to applaud. "Well thank *you* so very much for allowing me to have some time with *my* child!"

His words were harsh and there was pain behind them, but this time I didn't care. He had drawn blood one time too many.

"What the hell is wrong with you?" I asked, thoroughly disgusted.

"You know, Jewel, you have a lot of nerve coming in here and demanding an explanation for me wanting to take Tia to Disneyworld, just as I had always promised her."

"Oh, give me a break! Malcolm, she wasn't even two when you started that." I leaned back with my hand on my hip like I couldn't believe it.

"Jewel, why don't you sit down and maybe we . . ." Annette started, but I held up my hand and closed my eyes. "Annette, I really don't want to hurt your feelings, and I appreciate all that you've done for Tia in the past, being a really good friend to her, but," and I turned to look straight at her so that it would be clear, "this is between me and Malcolm, so please . . ."

"Don't come in here trying to dictate!" Malcolm cried, jumping up to stand between me and Annette which was fine because this wasn't about her. "If you weren't always trying to have everyone dance to your tune, then there would be no problem!" And he went back over to the couch as if he didn't trust himself to be that close to me. As if he would just really push fate and try to swing at me.

"Dance to *my* tune?! *You're* the one who comes and takes Tia whenever you feel like it despite the fact that I'm trying to build a family."

"I'm her family!"

"Right, and so am I and Justin and Sam whether you like it or not!"

"But I'm her father!"

"Tell me something I don't know!"

"So," he shouted over me, "if I want to do something that will make her happy and as long as I'm within the limits of my visitations, I have every right to take her on a trip, and if that doesn't sit well with you and your storybook life that's just tough because we have *joint* custody." Then he spat out, "Sorry to break up your perfect little new home. Sorry that I won't allow you to just kick me to the curb, treat me like I'm some uncle or outsider! Sorry that I didn't live up to your expectations and be everything you wanted me to be. You know what, Jewel? You're just pissed off because for once, I'm not giving a damn about what you think!"

"What the hell are you talking about?"

"I'm talking about you!" His voice rose as he did a grotesque mimic of me. "Malcolm, you need to finish school because without a degree you're nothing. Malcolm, that first degree was good, but not quite enough - you'd better go back and get another because you can't support me and Tia on the kind of jobs you're out here hustling around for. Malcolm, you'd better step off because you ain't shit for a father."

My mind was swirling around trying to make sense of what he was going off about, but I just couldn't go that deep yet. "Malcolm, all I want to do is wait until we can all go together." This was my last ditch effort at being diplomatic about this situation.

"What? Like we were all together when Tia learned to ride a bike?"

The reins snapped. "AND WHOSE FAULT IS IT THAT YOU WEREN'T THERE?! HUH?!" I challenged him, leaning down to get all in his face. Placing my hands flat on the coffee table, keeping just enough control not to hurtle it across the room, I put it all out there, waiting for an answer, knowing that he didn't have one to give. "Who walked out on the family that we started?!"

Despite whatever he'd told himself about how we got here, Malcolm knew who took the first step down that path. I threw it at him. "That's right. You made the decision, not me! You want to talk about dancing to *my* tune? I'm sorry that I wanted you to continue your education! I'm sorry that I was trying to be supportive! Don't give me that bullshit about dancing to my tune because everything I did, I was doing for us. My tune? Give me a break. I don't recall putting on a dance number that said go and FUCK somebody else!!!!"

I was breathing hard as I pushed on, really hating him for the first time - no sorrow, or pity, just pure hate. "If you're not there when Tia goes to sleep or wakes up or if she looks like she's grown six inches since you last saw her, it's because you wanted it that way!

"And if you're pissed because you feel left out in the cold, get over it! You aren't the first or the last to be hurt." And I thought back to that January when I literally sat out in the freezing cold because Malcolm didn't love me anymore. "You ought to be grateful . . ."

"GRATEFUL?!" Now he exploded, but I shut him up.

"That's right. GRATEFUL that Tia's growing up in a house where her mother is *happy*! That she's growing up comfortable and secure in her life, surrounded by people who care for her as much as you do. And like it or not, she has a brother now and a man who loves her like a father." I hastened to add, "Not that Justin or I would do anything to try and replace you as her father - we respect your role . . . even though you surely don't deserve it!" And then my eyes swept him up and down, as the words continued to roll off my tongue, spraying acid in their wake. "And if you weren't always walking around trying to blame other people for the wheels that you set into motion, crying like a little BITCH . . ."

Malcolm moved to jump in my face, and I met him head on. "That's right, a little sniveling bitch, then you would see that you're not the only one who got hurt!"

Nostrils flaring, teeth clenched, Malcolm said very carefully, "*Fuck you!*" I guess that was supposed to hurt my feelings.

I responded, "You still do - every chance you get, you selfish bastard."

"Well, if you think I've fucked you before, Jewel, get ready for the assault of your life if you continue to try and cut me out of my daughter's life. I'm taking *my* daughter to Disneyworld, and *you* just need to get over it. Now get out of my house!"

I felt pretty calm. It was all finally out there. I moved toward the door, but turned back to him so that neither my words nor their meaning would get lost and said, "I will tie you up in court so long that those tickets will be useless by the time this is all over." Then I turned toward Annette who sat at their little dining room table looking as if she were in shock. Another casualty of war, I thought sadly. "Annette, for what it's worth, I am truly sorry." And I carefully let myself out, asking again the same question that I knew God was sick of hearing. *How did I end up here?* The wind came howling down slapping me in the face as if to say, "Stop asking that!"

Outside and alone, my resolve was more than a little shaken by what had just happened, and a little twinge of fear made my blood run cold. Certain various and unpleasant future scenarios darted in and out of my head.

My mind goaded me. *So you're actually getting scared!* As I climbed in the car, I saw the silhouette of my child's father, my enemy, standing in the window, and I assured my mind that I would stand firm and go to Jazz's office first thing Monday morning.

When I pulled inside my own garage, my resolve was still strong as I headed in, hate building in me all over again at Malcolm for making me be the bad guy by telling Tia that she would have to wait for Disneyworld.

I climbed the stairs and heard Sam's voice. "You find all the good rides so that we won't have to spend a lot of time looking for them when we go together. Okay, Tia?"

My heart almost broke as I listened to Sam who had nothing but love and hope that his sister would have a good time. Walking in, I was greeted by the sight of Sam, Tia, and Justin all spread out on the floor.

"Hi, Mommy!" both children said, barely glancing up.

"Hey, whatcha doin'?" I sat down on the windowseat and looked at the scattered pages from the computer all over the floor.

"Sam and Justy are helping me find the best places at Disneyworld so that when we all go later, I can be a . . . uhm . . ." She looked at Justin for the right word.

"Tour guide," he whispered in her ear.

"Right! A tour guide for Sam."

It seemed that no one else had a problem with this but me, so I sighed and sat back grimly while they continued making plans. Slowly, my resolve crumbled. I told myself that resigning myself to Tia going to Disneyworld didn't mean that Malcolm had won. Not really. Actually, it was Tia who had won. Sam appeared to be down with it, and I would find something special for my little man to make up for this slight, although he didn't seem to mind now in the least as he scrambled over to retrieve a paper that had floated away.

It still wasn't all blue skies and sunshine by a longshot. No, today showed me how low Malcolm was willing to go to be difficult, and I was no longer going to be swayed to bend the rules that had been decreed by the Court. Tonight, my heart had become as cold and hard as the glass of our living room window which reflected our happiness at the same time it protected us from winter's harsh attentions. I set my mind to be just as protective of the life I was trying to build and to guard against Malcolm Stone and his insecurities, knowing that I had done all that I could and been kicked again and again. But no more.

The more I thought about it, the more restless and dejected I became because in fact Malcolm *had* won again. I left the room and went to sit on the windowseat of Tia's room. Justin followed me and asked if I was all right.

"Tia's going, if that's what you mean," I said leaning my head forward against his rock hard stomach. *Yes, my rock.*

"Good," he sighed.

"*Good?!* What do you mean good?"

"It's just that I understand where Justin's coming from. Hold up," he said, taking hold of my hand before I could get started, "I said that I understood, not that I agreed with his methods. He should have discussed it with you first."

"It's not just that," I said getting all upset again, "he doesn't have as many rights as he wants when it comes to Tia. He lost those privileges when he walked out on us."

"No, Jewel, he walked out on your marriage - not his relationship with Tia," Justin said quietly, but for once, I was going to get my point across to someone.

"No, that man walked out on a life that allowed him to have carte blanche access to Tia. When Malcolm made his break for freedom from us, he should have taken into account that I was going to move on with my life and since Tia goes with me, that meant her too, and . . ." I was whispering rapidly so the kids wouldn't hear from across the hall. ". . . that means that Malcolm should have been ready to accept that fact and not live in this fantasy world where he can put me and Tia in and out of a box whenever he gets the urge to do the daddy thing."

"Jewel, do you hear yourself?" Justin asked calmly.

"What?"

"You keep saying when Malcolm walked out on *us*. You and Tia." Shaking his head he asked, "Are you trying to get back at Malcolm for leaving by using Tia?"

"How could you even ask me something like that?!" And this time I did hiss at him. *Has the whole world gone mad? Am I the only one who understands how wrong it was for Malcolm to just spring this little vacation? No, not just any vacation, a first. Her first trip to the place that most children dream of going to, and I won't be there. Won't be there for the first time she steps into that magical world of adventure. I wouldn't intentionally have done that to Malcolm. And I refuse to let Malcolm throw the bicycle incident in my face.*

What was supposed to be one of the most exciting times in my child's life, her first major accomplishment, evidently had turned out to be the trigger for Malcolm's explosive trip plan. Little did I know at the time that I would be the one to actually set it all in motion even though it was completely unintentional.

Christmas Day, Sam wanted to ride his new bike, and of course so did Tia.

"You don't have a helmet yet." And so the waterfall started which gets to Justin every time, and he went to pick up the crying little girl.

"Hey, no one is supposed to cry on Christmas Day," he crooned to her.

I jumped in. "Don't start that, Tia, because you know that your tears just move me in the opposite direction." But I grabbed a tissue to dab at her wet eyes, my tone becoming soft. "What did Justy tell you about safety?"

She didn't want to hear this, crying out passionately, "Why didn't Santa Claus bring me a helmet?!" Before burying her face into Justin's neck, I turned my head to hide my smile, because my child was beyond any acting award.

Sam came back down and seeing Tia so upset, offered to stay inside to play.

"No, Sam. Tia and I will go and get her a helmet tomorrow."

But he stood uncertainly, until snapping his fingers, he ran back upstairs, coming down with one of his old helmets. Justin tried it on and since it fit pretty well, Tia and Justin ran upstairs to get dressed while I started breakfast. I just wasn't thinking that she would master the bike so quickly, but my child was determined so after breakfast Tia dragged us all back outside while she tried again and again. I was freezing, standing with the camcorder, while Justin held the bike as Tia coasted downhill on our little driveway. Trying to stifle a yawn, I waved to Sam as he went flying past me, Brandon close behind on his new roller blades. Looking through the lens, getting shots of both kids, I realized that Justin was running alongside Tia with his arms out, but not really holding on. When Tia got to the end of the driveway, Justin still running close beside, he calmly told her to pedal. I was ready to start jumping up and down, but seeing the look of concentration on Tia's little face, I didn't. Instead I focused the camera on her progress as the handlebars wobbled a little before she straightened up. When Justin finally slowed her down, turning the bike around she was all grins as I ran over.

"You did it!"

And we started a conga line down the street where we met Malcolm as he and Annette were getting out of the car.

"Daddy, I can ride!" Tia called to her daddy, so proud of herself. Malcolm stood woodenly while Tia insisted on Justin coming to help steady her, and she took off again, this time with more confidence.

Standing beside Malcolm, I said boastfully, "That's your girl!" and when he didn't reply, I turned and saw him staring angrily. Before I really understood what was going on, Malcolm went and met the little cyclist at the edge of the driveway.

"You ready to visit Grandma?" And he picked her up, holding her in a close hug before reaching up to remove the helmet.

"Yeah."

"Come on." He moved toward his car with Tia in tow.

"Malcolm, wait." I had to jog to catch up. "Can she at least say goodbye?" Used to him getting his boxers in a bunch, I reached up and gave Tia a kiss goodbye, while she waved to

Justin and Sam who stood in the background. Justin was holding up her little bike.

I hadn't planned on disrespecting Malcolm. I had videotaped and everything. Besides, if he had gotten her the bike for Christmas, would he have waited for me? I didn't think so.

And now this Disneyworld mess. What was really hurting me was the way Justin had questioned me. I looked up at the man I loved with all my heart, not understanding why he wasn't siding with me. I stared at him for a minute, trying to make sure that I wasn't just being overly sensitive.

Then I moved past him calling Klaus. I went outside with my only true friend, and we walked for hours as I talked to him, trying to make sense of what was happening to my family. When we got home, the kids were sleeping so I just went downstairs to rest for a minute. Not ready to get into it with Justin again, I sat back on the couch and started channel surfing. I only closed my eyes for a minute, but three hours later when I woke up, I was too tired to climb the stairs to bed. I turned over and went to sleep, curled up and alone on the couch.

* * * *

Mommy gave me a long look in her vanity mirror. "Jewel, you have to understand that there will be times when everything won't all come together like you want, and there will be times when Malcolm is going to want to have Tia to himself. He's not trying to undermine you directly - he's just being desperate and a little bit selfish, but why not let him be happy. *You* should be happy that he wants to be there for her. Now, I know what I'm talking about because I've been there, only in reverse. God knows it would have been nice if your father had been like that." Mommy continued to clip my ends, while I continued to drive myself crazy.

"I understand all that, it's just that . . ." I was at a loss because how could I explain that Malcolm was hurting me beyond belief, treating me without respect. "Mommy, Malcolm sprung this on me without any warning."

"He didn't have to tell you at all, you know."

"What if he tries to steal Tia away from me? There are organizations out there that would be more than happy to help him." The thought had crossed my mind on more than one occasion.

"Now, you're just being paranoid."

"Am I? Do we really know anybody?" I was thinking about Justin as well as Malcolm. I would never have thought that Justin would let me down. There had been no communication between us since last Friday, and it didn't look as if there would be any time soon. I sighed as I thought about the domino effect Malcolm's impulsive decision was having on everyone else's life.

"So where are my grandchildren today, anyway?" Mommy asked, brushing the hair from my shoulders.

"Justin and Marcus took Sam ice fishing. Don't ask," I said, rolling my eyes because I didn't get it either. "And Tia is playing over at Robyn's."

"And you came home to pout."

"I am *not* pouting."

"Watch your tone, missy," Mommy said in a borderline warning, and I quietly sucked my teeth. It was time to go, I decided.

Home was still quiet when I pulled up, and after about five minutes of my own company had just about driven me mad, I set to really cleaning up the house. Stripping the beds, dusting, vacuuming - the heavy duty version of the light cleaning we do during the week. My music was blaring from the surround system that was set up throughout the house and Kevon Edmunds and I were crooning about not calling out any names until we were done right, so I didn't hear the kitchen door open.

"Hi, Mommy!" Sam called from the kitchen. "Come and see what we caught!" I walked into the kitchen and looked into the open chest that was filled with dead fish.

"Those suckers were really hungry," Marcus said pulling out a big catfish. He gave Sam an affectionate rub on the head. "But they didn't stand a chance against little Captain Ahab here."

"Can I go next door and tell Brandon about fishing?" Sam asked excitedly.

"No, I don't think so - it's dark out now."

"I'll walk him over," Marcus offered, hoisting Sam up over his shoulder like a sack of potatoes.

"Bye!" Sam waved as Marcus toted him out the door, his little laughter fading away as they crossed past the kitchen window. I bent down to get started with the messy, smelling fish, pushing Klaus away who stood practically drooling into the slimy ice water.

"I'll take care of those," Justin offered.

"Okay," I said simply and went back to my cleaning, turning the stereo up again.

About an hour later, I called to ask Brenda to send Sam home, but she convinced me to let him stay over. "He and Brandon can sleep in their skivvies, and we always have an extra toothbrush over here."

"Come on, Brenda, I can't let you do that. I know that you weren't even expecting it."

"Please, Jewel, you know how much we love having Sam over."

In the end, I relented. No sooner had I hung up the phone, than it started ringing.

"Yes, Tia, you may spend the night." And I heard her yell into the background that it was all right just before the line went dead. I smiled a little because I knew she was in a hurry to break the connection in case I changed my mind. Some time later, the sound of the shower running filtered through the music, as I was putting the kids' clothes away.

"Jewel?!" Justin called from the bathroom.

"YEAH?!"

"I NEED A TOWEL." Walking back to the linen closet, I pulled out a towel and handed it to him in the steamy bathroom.

"Thanks. Is Sam home yet?"

I mumbled something about the kids sleeping over as I headed back out to finish putting the stuff away.

A few minutes later Justin called again. "Jewel?"

"WHAT IS IT?" I singsonged back up the stairs. *I'm going to hurt you if you don't leave me alone.*

"CAN YOU COME HERE FOR A MINUTE?" *If it means that I can tie you up and gag you, sure.* Climbing back upstairs,

I found Justin, still wet, standing in front of the mirror with just the towel wrapped around his taut, muscular waist.

"Yes?" I asked tersely, trying to ignore the body that God had smiled so generously upon.

Turning, he asked if I would look at his arms.

I sighed, but came closer and looked at his arms. "What's the matter?" I asked, my eyes scanning for a rash or cut.

"They're empty!" And he grabbed me and wrapped me in a wet embrace.

"Justin, let go." I twisted to get free.

"Kiss me." He pressed me closer.

"No."

"Come on." He bent his head closer.

"No." I turned my head away.

"Come on." And he took his hand and placed it on the side of my face, steadying it before his lips found their mark.

"There. You happy now?" I asked tonelessly.

"No." And he leaned down to kiss me again, and I felt him harden beneath the plush towel.

Does he really think that after he offended me three whole days ago that I would be willing to just break down and make love with him? Just because his hands are sneaking up under my sweatshirt, his touch light and sending shivers up my spine? Just because his fingers are gently tugging at my nipples through the soft fabric of my bra? Or just because my panties are getting moister with each meeting of our tongues? Okay, so maybe it wouldn't be so bad.

I stepped out of my slippers, my arms snaking around his neck only to have them pulled up as Justin lifted the sweatshirt over my head.

He soon returned to feeding me more kisses which I hungrily accepted while his hands quickly undid the clasp of my bra. Moving back to the bed, Justin pulled at the drawstring of my sweatpants, pulling them down, my panties following as we danced slowly across the room. When my naked leg met the edge of the bed, I turned him around and pulled off the towel, pushing him back in one fluid motion. Slowly moving up his body, stopping to drop a kiss along the way, I climbed over top of him. Reaching down, I guided him inside of me sitting back until I was resting on my haunches. Moving slowly up and down, I looked down into his face which was slack with desire, and I started moving faster, my own passion taking control. We were both panting hard as Justin's hands reached up and gripped my shoulders, our cravings pushing us close to the edge. Then I was gone! My back arching, as my body contracted in spasms of orgasm that went on and on before Justin finally erupted with a growl of relief, filling me, leaving me weightless and exhausted. Shaking from little jolts of satisfaction that coursed through my still sensitive body. Instinctively, I collapsed against Justin's chest which was heaving as he breathed deeply, content.

"Where are you going?" he asked with some alarm when I slid off of him.

"To finish my work and then watch a movie downstairs." I reached for my clothes.

Justin sat up. "And I'm just supposed to be okay with that?"

I didn't say anything.

"Jewel?" He grabbed my wrist before I could step into my clothes.

"I thought I told you I wasn't a hit and run kind of man."

And he never had been, always holding me close after each passionate union, but I still didn't say anything, sitting with a stony expression like a mask over the one which had been so euphoric just moments ago.

"Talk to me?" he asked, turning my face toward him, the scent of my sex still on his fingertips.

"So, now you want to talk?" I asked.

"Hey, I never wanted to stop talking. You were the one who closed yourself off."

"Oh, so, now it's my fault?" My voice was irritable.

Justin pulled me down next to him on the side of the bed. "Look, I saw that you were upset, and I figured that the best thing to do was to give you some space. But I thought you knew that I would always be here whenever you were ready to talk."

"You hurt me," I said, sounding like a child, which further annoyed me.

"I'm sorry, but Jewel, we aren't always going to agree on everything. That doesn't mean that we're supposed to let anything come between us. I love you and hope that you will always love me too."

"Of course I will, but nobody seems to understand what I'm feeling." Taking a deep breath to squash the emotions that threatened to come to the surface, I went on. "Every time I mention Malcolm and Tia, everyone reads the wrong thing into what I'm saying."

"Maybe it's the way you're saying it."

Groaning, I flopped back on the bed.

"Really," he said, lying back with me, "try it again."

"Okay, Malcolm walked out on a marriage that I thought was perfect. Well, that is until I married you."

"Naturally." I thought he might not be taking me seriously, but when I glanced over at him, he appeared to be listening intently, staring up at the ceiling.

"Okay, so it didn't work out to *Malcolm's* specifications, but it had to mine." Taking a deep breath hoping that I wouldn't be misunderstood but laying it on the line nonetheless I said, "We would still have been married, and I would have been ignorantly happy if Malcolm hadn't decided that he wanted out." Afraid to glance at Justin, I went on. "But we aren't still married, and I love the life I have now with you." Now I did look at him but his profile was still relaxed as he listened. "But that life involves Tia, and I don't want to spend the rest of her underage life fighting, running to court every time he tries to undermine me. And I feel that if he could do it this time, then he'll do it again and again. Starting something and leaving me to be the bad guy because it'll probably be out of the question." That was it in a nutshell, and I became silent as I too studied the ceiling.

"Jewel, I understand that you want what's best for Tia. So does Malcolm, believe it or not, which is why he appears to go overboard. He just wants to be as involved in Tia's life as much as possible - more than what a judge and a bunch of lawyers decide is adequate. They can't put restrictions on his heart or the way he cares for her. That's why it won't get easier, and this is probably the first big battle of many to come - when should she start dating, wear lipstick ... how short should her skirts be ... what should her curfew be? The joint responsibility for parenting doesn't stop because you and Malcolm aren't together anymore. But you have to understand that you may have to back down because Tia isn't a prize to be won, and she would be the only one hurt right now if you and Malcolm decide to take it to the mat whenever you two don't agree."

"So, what? I'm supposed to just let him run all over me?"

"No, just give a little more. I know that you already have," he hastened to say before I could begin protesting, "but just make it a little easier for him until he comes to realize that he's not being cut out. And I know that he's the one who brought this situation about, but don't make Tia pay for it."

I turned my head to look at him. "Justin, how did you get so wise?"

He just shrugged. "You know it comes from someone who, until now, never had to share Sam's upbringing with anyone else. I can't say my words would make as much sense to me if Sheila decided to waltz into Sam's life, but if Sam wanted a relationship with her, I would try my best to allow it because it's about Sam and what he might feel he needed.

"And don't get me wrong . . ." and now he was looking at me, "I love Tia just as much as I love Sam, which is why I think I understand Malcolm so well. I know that I wouldn't like it if he came in trying to tell me how and when I could show Tia that I love her."

"You know, Malcolm is a lucky man to have you in his corner."

Justin corrected me. "No, it's not that I'm in his corner. I'm in Tia's corner. I know that for all of the shortcomings and faults that we see, the children don't. They love unconditionally."

"Yeah, I felt that way about my father once."

"Exactly. And you made your decision as to how your relationship with him would be, and from what your mother said, you did it with no help from her or Lou."

"True."

"And wouldn't you rather see Tia and Malcolm have a strong relationship, rather than one that was influenced by your feelings toward each other?"

"Yes," I agreed.

"Well, there you go. When two people commit to having a child, their differences have to be swept aside even when the marriage doesn't work."

"Well, then, why didn't you just say so a week ago?" I joked, and he tickled my exposed ribs.

"I tried to, but you weren't ready to listen."

I wasn't sure if I could follow the vision that he presented so clearly, but for Tia's sake I wanted to try. *Please Lord give me a taste for pride because I get the feeling that I'll be swallowing a lot of it in the years to come. But maybe, just maybe Malcolm and I can work through this together.*

"And, Jewel?"

"Hhm?" I answered still moving forward in my mind.

"Don't forget, that as long as you have me, you'll never face anything alone." I felt his hands intertwine in mine, completely extinguishing my tumultuous feelings as his words played back in my mind.

CHAPTER 29

It had always been a fear of mine that with time would come comfort, followed by monotony, boredom, and then that dreaded day when you look up and wonder what happened to your life. But with each passing day, I believed perhaps that was for ordinary people. It had been three years since we had met again, and Justin had provided me with extraordinary love that didn't seem to be fading in the least. True, his work took him away from home much more often than I would have liked, but I understood his dedication and commitment to try to make this world a better place.

And I too had found a commitment outside our home. After graduating as a brand new physician's assistant, my clinicals impressed the staff at Howard Hospital, and it was so gratifying when they asked me to come aboard. The work in the ER was exciting. You got the feeling that you were truly needed - to hold a hand, to calm the fears of a child. It made you feel great when you saw a patient walk past the nurses' station and wave goodbye to you. I loved my job even though there were times that it took a toll on my emotions.

Today, it had been so hectic in the ER that, almost before I knew it, it was time to pick up the kids from aftercare. When I arrived, I found Sam looking like the world had collapsed and Tia sitting beside him holding onto his hand.

"Hey, what's the matter?" I rushed over to them but neither said anything as I stooped down close trying to see what had caused the storm clouds covering Sam's face.

"Mrs. Baptiste?" Mrs. Cannon, the principal came out of her office. "May I have a word with you?"

"I'll be right back." I gave Sam's leg a reassuring pat before following the principal into her office.

"Mrs. Baptiste, I would like to know if Mr. Baptiste can stop in the office tomorrow before Sam returns to class?"

"What's the problem?" I asked, ready to solve whatever crisis there might be.

"I'm afraid that I will need to discuss that with Mr. Baptiste."

Feeling my temper rise, I calmly asked her again what was wrong, explaining that as Sam's mother . . . but she interrupted me.

"Mrs. Baptiste, you are married to Sam's father, but according to our records you are not Sam's mother."

Her words hit me like a slap, and I retaliated.

"I beg your pardon, but how dare you say such a thing! That is my son, and I have a right to know what's going on." My voice had gone up a few decibels, and I didn't try to bring it down.

Clearing her throat, Mrs. Cannon sat behind her desk looking at her clasped hands resting on the completely organized desk and intoned, "Mrs. Baptiste, in this day and age, there are many extended families, remarriages or just cohabitating without too much thought of the children." *What the hell is she talking about?* "But here at the academy we take the children's rights seriously. That means that we do not discuss their behavior or grades or anything else with anyone other than the parents or legal guardians."

"Oh, and what? I'm just Hazel the nanny who comes to pick them up everyday?!" *Bitch!*

"Truthfully, the comparison is correct. I would no more discuss your child's behavior with anyone other than you or her father."

"Fine!" I said, turning on my heel to walk out the door before I actually went across the desk to hit this person and her superior airs. Yanking open the door, I grabbed Tia and Sam, practically pulling them down the hall.

"I will need to see Mr. Baptiste before Sam can return," the Wicked Witch of the East called after me, and I had to clench my teeth to keep from shouting down the hall, "go fuck yourself!" *Not Sam's mother? Yeah, right!*

"Come on, kids." I ushered them into the truck trying to stay calm despite the veil of red rage that distorted my vision. *How dare she try to make me feel illegitimate!*

Together with Malcolm, Justin and I had picked this school because the curriculum was outstanding, the teachers warm and caring, the classes small. And now this!

I started getting ticked all over again, and the idiot that decided to cut me off didn't help my disposition as I leaned heavily on the horn. "Mirrors! Why don't you use them!" I shouted, something I never did in this day and age, especially with the kids in the car. Checking the rearview mirror, I saw the faces of my children, scared and sad, and I took a deep breath. We drove quietly while I allowed my emotions to go from raging to slow simmer, and then I pulled the truck onto the grassy strip at Haines Point. I took both their hands, and we walked over to the benches beside the rushing water and sat down. I asked them to explain what had happened today. Neither of them said anything. I breathed in deeply before exhaling. Then calmly I tried again. "Look, I'm sorry for the way I acted, but Mommy needs to know what happened so that she can fix it. I promise that I won't be angry with either one of you - okay?"

The thundercloud brewing in Sam's eyes broke, and the tears started to flow. Tia joined in because she hated to see Sam cry.

Holding them close, I whispered that it couldn't be that bad. "Remember the water, Sam? Look at the water. Come on." Gently urging them up, I guided them to the barrier at the waterside and stood behind them as Tia clung to Sam's hand. "Okay, see how big all that is?"

They stared silently at the water going by.

"I don't think that what you've got inside is as big as that, but let's hear it to make sure."

"Tia was swinging on the swings," Sam began, trying to get himself under control. "And Joshua came over and . . ."

"He pushed me out and made me hurt my knees!" Tia held up her little bandaged knee for emphasis. "So Sam came over and told him to apologize but he didn't. So Sam got mad and pushed him and then they started fighting."

Sam was hanging his head down, looking ashamed, and the tears dripped off his nose onto his shirt. "Then Mrs. Cannon came and pulled me off Joshua and told me to apologize." His little voice was bitter.

"But Sam said that Joshua started it!" Tia continued passionately. "But she said that she saw Sam push Joshua first. She wouldn't even listen when I tried to show her how Joshua made me hurt my knee!"

My first impulse was to congratulate Sam for defending his sister, but I knew that I couldn't condone fighting. Finally, I said, "Sam, I'm not mad at you." I held his chin in my hand. "I'm glad to know that you protected your sister, but you really shouldn't fight." It sounded lame even to my ears, but I went on. "I was angry because Mrs. Cannon had no right to say that I'm not your mother because we know that I am."

This brought a sigh of relief from Sam who stood a little taller.

"I will talk to your father, and we'll get all this taken care of, okay?"

"Okay, Mommy," Sam said with a sniffle.

"Come on, let's get home." I led the children back toward the truck. As we neared, the truck appeared to be leaning heavily to the right. "Oh, no!" I groaned, not needing to look but looking anyway.

"Mommy, something's wrong with the tire."

"Yes, Tia, there certainly is." Now, I am no damsel in distress, but I'd only changed a tire once in my life, and it certainly wasn't on anything this big. Grabbing my cell phone, I dialed Justin's office only to be told that he was out on an assignment. I racked my brain trying to think of someone else to call. Rush hour wouldn't allow Lou to get here until maybe seven. Although I didn't like my only other option, I had no choice and made the call.

Minutes later, Tia cried out, "Daddy!"

"Hey, little girl!" Malcolm smiled, catching Tia as she flew into his arms. "Hey, Sam." He gave Sam a little dap before putting Tia back down.

"Thanks for coming."

"I told you a long time ago that you should learn to do this."

"Yeah, yeah, can you please just do it for me now?"

"So what happened?" Malcolm asked.

"The tire went flat."

"Very funny." He placed the jack under the car. "I mean what upset you to bring you out here?"

"Just some stuff that happened at the school."

"What?" he grunted, as he pulled the tire off.

Going around to the back, I pulled out the spare, and explained what had happened.

"Good for Sam," Malcolm said, "but the woman may have a point."

I looked at him like he had lost his mind.

Malcolm caught my look as he lowered the truck back to the ground. "Jewel, you may want to look into it."

"Malcolm, would you want Justin to step in if you couldn't?"

Malcolm thought about it for a minute, before answering. "If ever there was someone else to look out for Tia as a father, it would be him."

I was pleased. "Thanks, Malcolm."

"Any time. Justin can get the rim put back on when he gets the tire replaced."

For a minute the old friend that I met years ago seemed a lot closer to the surface.

When we arrived home, the kids barged into the house, grabbing Klaus to take him for his afternoon walk. I headed for the phone.

"Hey, Jewel? What's up?"

"Hi, Bryce. Is Jazz home?"

"Nope, she's working late at the office. She's finally got a court date for that trial. You want me to have her call you?"

I stood chewing on my pinky nail, thinking about how important this was, then finally said, "No, that's okay."

"Are you sure?" Bryce was able to pick up on the hesitancy from my end. "'Cause she should be home before long, lugging all those papers - it's a good thing the dog knows where to do his business - otherwise, he'd be real confused." Bryce laughed, and I chuckled with him, tickled at his obvious pride in his successful wife.

"No, don't bother her." I could gather the information on what I needed to do to establish my status as a decision-maker in Sam's life, and if I ran into difficulties, then I'd make an appointment with Jazz. "I'll catch up with her later."

Just then I heard the commotion that comes daily with having five kids under the same roof and Bryce shouting for them to quiet down.

"Hey, I'd better let you go."

"Yeah, these rockheads seem to have lost their minds. I'll tell Jazz you called." And Bryce signed off with a very distracted goodbye.

Hanging up the phone, I was a little calmer than I was two hours ago but still pissed at that creature who headed up Sam and Tia's school. I was thinking of calling Malcolm to tell him I didn't want Tia to attend such a backward institution when I was surprised by the phone ringing and Malcolm's voice on the other end.

"Hey, did you get in touch with Jazz?"

"No." I was pulling leftovers out of the refrigerator while holding the phone against my ear with my shoulder. "She's getting ready for court, and I didn't want to bother her about it." Wrapping Justin's dinner with saran wrap, I put it on the back of the stove to be heated later. "But it's funny that you called, I wanted to talk to you about transferring Tia at the end of the school year."

"Don't you think that you'll have the same problem somewhere else?"

"Honestly, I don't think so. I think that woman was just being vicious. I mean the whole time I was growing up, Lou never had this kind of a problem, and he interacted with all my teachers even before extended families became so common."

"Maybe that's the problem."

"What do you mean?" I slowed my busy movements and waited for Malcolm to explain.

"Well, nowadays you have a lot of relationships that split up - not only marriages, but the 'my baby's daddy' group as well. Everyone gets new partners, and you can be wild about each other in the beginning, got your kids calling him daddy and whatnot, then the wind can shift and you and the guy aren't together anymore."

I couldn't resist teasing him. "Are you referring to me in particular?"

"Of course not - I'm just trying to give you her perspective. Now like I was saying, you and dude break up but he decides as he's walking past the school, the breakup was with you, not the kids. Now what do you think happens when Moms gets there and finds out that her ex has been filled in by Ms. Purdy about Bobo's latest escapade?"

I thought for a moment and then responded. "First of all, what man do you know wants to have anything to do with someone else's kids after he breaks up with a woman? Second of all, you do have a point and I really hate that because it shows that I took this way too personally, but she made me feel so insignificant." My frustration was building again. "I mean what do I have to do to make sure that this doesn't happen again?"

"That's why you should be getting in touch with Jazz."

"Yes . . . and I guess I should find out what we need to do so that Annette can have some status in Tia's life since that might come up in an emergency - you never know."

After a brief pause, Malcolm responded by saying that I should deal with one thing at a time.

"Okay. Well, thanks for the call," I said, slightly tickled at the ability of having a what? Yes, a friendly conversation with Malcolm.

"No problem. Tell Tia I'll see her Saturday."

Justin took Sam back to school the next day and sat down with Mrs. Cannon to explain our situation, and the witch still refused to bend, stating haughtily that if she made an exception for one family then she would have to do it for all and that extended family situations were too unstable. We called Jazz.

A couple of days later, although Jazz had drawn up a document that seemed to appease Mrs. Cannon, it was still bothering me. I was moving around the kitchen getting breakfast ready for the kids before they went their separate ways. "Justin, Mrs. Cannon may be taken care of, but I think there really is a problem. We need to start looking into making sure that we have rights with both children in case something should happen to one of us."

Before Justin could respond, Sam and Tia came sniffing into the kitchen, and I hurried up with the breakfast preparations.

After eating, we lingered at the table. Tia started talking about my twenty-sixth birthday coming up the next day, and Justin pulled a small, neatly wrapped package from his pocket.

I reached for it, but Justin stopped me.

"Ah, you can't open it now."

"Why not?" I inquired indignantly.

"Because it's not your birthday."

"Well, why'd you bring it out then?" I asked, reaching across the table again.

"Oh, no, you don't." Justin put the gift back in his bathrobe pocket.

"I don't think so!" I cried and moved around the table to wrestle my gift away.

"No, Mommy!" Sam agreed, "you can't open it until your birthday."

"But today should be my birthday," I tried to explain while struggling to extract my wrist from Justin's grip. "You see, I was late."

"But you still have to wait," Tia insisted. She came around the table to try and pull me back, and then pandemonium broke out as we all started wrestling for the pocket.

Justin took the package out and threw it to Tia, shouting, "Go hide it!" over the laughter and grunting as he and Sam tried to keep me pinned to the living room floor where our fracas had led us.

"Klaus! Klaus, go and find it!" I pleaded, but Klaus who was used to our ridiculous displays gave me a lick in the face before heading back to the kitchen. "Traitor!" I shouted at his retreating rearend, and to my surprise he stopped and turned back. I praised him. "That's a good boy." But he walked past me to the front door, letting out a gruff woof, just before knocking was heard.

"Come in!" Justin shouted from the floor where he and Sam were practically sitting on me, waiting for Tia to come back.

"Hey," Malcolm said quietly.

"I hid it!" Tia cried excitedly, missing the last three steps altogether as she came down the stairs and dove into Malcolm's arms.

"Hid what?"

"Mommy's birthday present!"

"Oh." Malcolm looked over like he was a little embarrassed.

"Okay, so like can I get up now?" I asked, no longer trying to struggle.

"Sure." And Justin and Sam pulled me up.

"Such gentlemen!" I said facetiously. "Tia, you ready to head out?"

She nodded emphatically. "Yes, I am." She got down from Malcolm's arms, giving everyone a kiss goodbye.

"Uh . . . Sam . . ." Malcolm said, "do you like baseball?"

"Yes," Sam answered slowly.

"Well, Tia and I are going to see the Orioles this afternoon, and I picked up an extra ticket thinking you might like to join us?"

Unless you knew our little Sam, you would think that he wasn't thrilled, but I could tell that he was. "Yes, thank you."

"Great, then," and Malcolm reached behind him and pulled out a baseball cap which he placed on Sam's head. "To protect you from the sun." Then as if remembering, Malcolm looked at Justin and an open-mouthed me and asked if it was okay.

"Sure. Have a good time, little man," Justin said and gave Sam's cap a tap.

"I'll have them back around nine if that's okay? I figured after the game, we'd get something to eat, maybe check out a show."

"Sure, that would be great. Have a good time," Justin replied and walked him to the door. We stood outside waving to Tia and Sam who had already climbed in the car, Tia putting on her own O's hat while they waited for Malcolm.

"Hey, Sam!" Brandon shouted as he and his sister came down their front lawn. "You wanna go out for pizza later?"

"Can't! Gotta go to an Orioles game."

And the adults all had to hide their smiles, listening to Sam try to downplay it, but you could clearly see that he was trying to impress.

"Well, see you later."

"Thanks, Malcolm," Justin said, shaking his hand.

"No problem," he responded with an embarrassed grin before jogging to the car.

"Well, that was a surprise," Justin said after they'd gone.

"You're telling me!"

"Maybe he's trying to atone for that last move of his."

About two months previously, Malcolm had petitioned the court, requesting that Tia divide her time between our two households. I knew he wanted the same experiences that I shared with her every day, but I also knew it would be completely disruptive for Tia. I appealed to Malcolm in a letter; I didn't trust myself to talk to him about it in person. Evidently, I was persuasive because, in the end, the petition was withdrawn. Maybe, just maybe, we were moving in the right direction.

Justin was ready to head out to the office, but first he grabbed me, pulled me back in a dip over his knee, and warned, "Don't even try to find your present because it's been hidden with magic." When I didn't respond with any kind of enthusiasm, he flipped me up and, his eyes clouded with concern, asked me what was wrong.

"Nothing," I sighed, slowly moving up the stairs. "I'll see you when you get back. "Come on," I called to Klaus who overtook my slow ascent up the stairs.

The shower was warm and delicious, but I was feeling a little down, facing a day alone with nothing to do. Snaking my hand around the clear shower curtain, I turned up the tape player and began singing along with Ms. Braxton. She needed to find her a man. I started really belting when she got to the part about how she's too wonderful to settle for anything less than incredible. Wrapping the towel around me, spraying some lotion onto my still wet skin, I went to the closet looking for something to wear. I was startled to hear Justin say, "I didn't know you could sing so well."

"What are you still doing here?" I asked with my hand over my heart, trying to slow it down.

"Well . . ." He came toward me slowly. "There are no kids, and the office can do without me which means we have a ton of time, at least eight whole hours, and you know how I want to spend them?"

I nodded.

After drying off and helping me to *get* dressed for a change, we rushed out of the house and hopped on Justin's bike - something we rarely got to do anymore - and roared toward town. We spent the day as tourists. First we went to the top of the Washington Monument, and after lunching at Georgetown's inner harbor, we moved on to pay a visit to Frederick Douglass' home.

"You know, it's a shame," I observed, as we walked around the grounds before leaving, "Malcolm's first film featured Douglass' Home and the Lincoln Memorial." I explained how I had helped Malcolm set up the shots of both historical sites for the two-day shoot and that the Lincoln Memorial was filled with people all day from sunup to sundown, while the Frederick Douglas Home sat silent most of the day.

"And when Malcolm edited it, he cut back and forth between the two, using black and white film for the Frederick Douglass shots while keeping the Lincoln in color. It was astonishingly sad."

My hands were stretched out, my fingers the lens, as I tried to convey the scene for Justin who was listening intently.

"That's sounds pretty heavy - Malcolm must have been proud of that film. And, I agree, it is a shame that after all the movies and books, the attendance at the Douglas house is still so poor."

I sent a silent congratulations to Justin who never tried to pretend that I didn't have a life before him.

Climbing on Justin's bike again, we rode off into the fading twilight, heading out to Rock Creek Park. It was wonderful enjoying the freedom of just being able to hang out. Not that I didn't love my kids, but sometimes you need that grown up time to help keep the magic alive. On the way home, we stopped at the video store, and we were watching the old classic, *A Raisin in the Sun*, and sharing a large bowl of popcorn when Klaus' tail began wagging his nose, and he rushed to the front door.

Justin followed and opened the door for Malcolm with the two children in his arms.

"Here, let me take him." Justin reached out to take a drooping Sam from Malcolm's arms.

"Wow, you must have worn them out!"

"Oh, we had a ball!" Malcolm said and handed Tia to me. "Sam's a great kid."

"Thank you for the game, Malcolm," Sam was trying real hard to keep his eyes open and his head from falling.

"No problem. Maybe we can go again when they have a Friday night game."

Justin started up the stairs with Sam.

"Bye, Daddy." Tia half waved, almost asleep.
"Bye-bye, baby." He turned to me. "I'll see myself out. Later." And he was gone.

After carrying our beloved bundles up the stairs to bed, Justin and I went back downstairs, grabbed the bowl of popcorn, and settled down to finish watching the movie, content to know that everyone for the first time in years, Malcolm included, seemed to have enjoyed a good day, and happy to feel that many more were a lot closer than they used to be.

CHAPTER 30

Our household had suffered through a double bout of the chicken pox, and upon their recovery the children had been let loose to make their rounds of the grandparents and give Justin and me a much-needed break. But it was Saturday now, and I was glad that Sam and Tia would be coming home today - the house had been quiet - too quiet. Walking past their empty rooms, I realized how fast they were growing up. Tia was now five and a half, and her room was beginning to reflect tastes which were independent of mine. And Sam, well it amazed me how easy it was for him to get his arms around my neck without me having to bend so far.

It seemed like the only time I got to baby Tia and Sam was when they were sick - which made me return to thoughts which had been coming to me off and on for some time now, and when I went back downstairs to the kitchen, I asked Justin impulsively, "What would you say if I wanted to gain some more weight?"

"I would say call for a pizza with pepperoni and extra cheese."

"Well, I was thinking of short-term weight gain."

"Jewel, are you saying what I think you are?" His eyes began to dance, as I nodded my head.

"All joking aside?"

I nodded again and watched his face.

"I say that we get started now!" And pulling me toward him, set me up on the kitchen counter.

"Not this minute, Justin! Get off of me!" And I pushed hard until he backed off, and I hopped down. "I just wanted to get your thoughts on the subject before I came off the pill. I mean the kids seem very secure now, and we're both doing pretty well in our careers, so . . ."

"Jewel, you don't have to convince me. I've been ready for a long time."

"So, why didn't you say anything?"

"Because I was waiting for you."

"All right then, it's settled. I'll make an appointment for a checkup, and we can get started. But of course I want to get Sam and Tia's view on this."

Justin agreed, moving closer to me. "But in the meantime, we can practice, can't we?" He started nuzzling my ear again.

"Justin, that's the one thing I don't think we need any practice on." But I allowed myself to be pulled into his arms and out of the kichen so that we could brush up on the procedure again until early afternoon when it was time for Justin to pick up the kids.

* * * *

"All right, I'm gone." Justin gave me a kiss goodbye and left to get the children, while I stood stirring my special sauce for dinner.

After dinner was ready, I moved around the house tidying up. Justin called to say they were on their way, and I could hear Tia and Sam laughing in the background. I told him to get off the line and get their little behinds home to me, which brought laughter to my ears before he said goodbye and hung up.

"You missed them, too, didn't you, boy?" I rubbed Klaus behind his ears, and he turned up eyes that said he did and then kept me company as I gathered wood for a fire. Sam and Tia loved sitting by the fire.

About an hour later when I was wondering where they could be, I was relieved to hear a knock at the door. I ran to open it, thinking that Sam and Tia had run on ahead while Justin was parking the truck in the garage. I was surprised to see Marcus standing there instead. "Marcus! Come on in. Justin isn't home, but he should be here any minute."

Instead of coming in, he said, "Jewel, I need you to come with me."

"But Justin and . . ."

"There's been an accident. I heard it over my radio."

Marcus was pulling me out the door, but I resisted. "No, I have to turn off the stove."

Marcus ran past me into the kitchen.

An accident . . . and if Marcus wants me to come with him then it must be . . . I spun around, my eyes begging Marcus to tell me I was wrong, but instead he grabbed my arm and pulled me out to the car.

I climbed inside as he ran around, jumped into the driver's seat, pulling his seatbelt over and starting the car at the same time.

"Marcus, what's happened?" My voice was calm, but my hands were trembling so much I couldn't fasten my seatbelt.

"There was an accident. A bad one involving Justin's truck. I don't know any details." He grabbed the twirling light from the dash and stuck it on top of the car, and the siren started screaming to match that of the police cruiser racing in front of us that I hadn't noticed before.

Marcus was hardly ever serious for long, but now he was hunched over the steering wheel, driving with a face of granite, and I shrank back in my seat. We pulled up outside the emergency room of a hospital just outside the Beltway. Both Marcus and I hit the ground running.

"Baptiste!" Marcus shouted to the nurse, as I went running toward the trauma room doors, only to be stopped by a man who almost knocked me down as he tried to prevent me from entering.

"Let go!" I said, starting to fight. "LET GO!" But he held me fast as Marcus came around the triage station with a nurse.

"You can't go back there," she uttered in a calm voice.

"Is my family back there?! Is the Baptiste family back there?!" I shouted.

"Mrs. Baptiste?!" A young doctor was calling me.

Looking over at him I tried to hear what he was saying.

"Mrs. Baptiste, there has been an accident." He was speaking carefully. "Your son was brought here. I'm going to take you to see him now, but you have to calm down."

Sam is hurt? Oh God! Justin must be out of his mind, and Tia's probably scared to death! I tried to compose myself. I took a deep breath, and the attendant, sensing I was a bit calmer, released his grip on me. The doctor led me through the double doors and spoke rapidly while we walked briskly past the curtained sections. "Now your son sustained some major damage, and we're trying to stabilize him so that we can operate."

"Operate?" I whispered.

He nodded and went on in that same precise manner. "I'll try to help you understand what's going on here."

"I'm a P.A." I said, the words passing through a mouth that was suddenly very dry.

"Good, that'll make it easier."

We stopped in front of a curtained-off section where people were moving in and out. I wasn't ready for what I saw. Sam was lying on a gurney, completely naked with tons of lines and wires connected to him. His neck was secured with a brace. I wasn't sure if there was a neck injury or it was just a precaution. The monitors showed some infrequent beeps, and the blood lines snaking down to his arms told me that he had lost a lot of his own. Moving closer, I could see that his head was heavily bandaged with more tubes coming from the top, his left eye completely covered. The splints on his left leg and arm looked grotesque and ominous. I had seen scenes like this hundreds of times before, sometimes on children smaller than Sam, but this was different. This was *my* son!

"Oh, Sam!" I cried, moving closer, reaching for his tiny hand. "It's okay, baby. Mommy's here."

"Mrs. Baptiste?" The young doctor called me again.

Kissing Sam, promising him that I would be right back, I turned to face the physician.

"Where is my daughter?" I asked before he could begin. "Where is my husband?" I was ready to step into my healing role because there was no doubt that they would need me.

The doctor looked strained, as he ran his fingers through his hair.

"Are they in the OR?" I asked, trying to make it easy on him. Letting him know that I was in control.

"Mrs. Baptiste, your husband and your daughter sustained extensive injuries in the crash." He paused, and I waited. "They were subject to massive injuries."

Why is he saying "were"? Just then Marcus came into my peripheral vision. His shoulders were shaking as he leaned against the nurses' station. Part of my mind was fascinated because I had never seen Marcus even so much as frown, much less cry uncontrollably. The other part was listening to what the emergency room doctor was saying. "They were already beyond our capabilities at the scene. I'm very sorry."

I stood blinking because I had heard this many times before. Hell, I had even said it myself. But again, this was *my* family!

"Okay," I said, trying to get this M.D. to understand something, and he leaned forward to listen. "They had injuries, and may have appeared . . ."

The doctor looked at me while waiting for me to say it.

I couldn't say the word. Instead I said, "beyond your capabilities."

And he nodded, as I continued, "But there are others, no offense, who may be able to help them."

The doctor closed his eyes and hung his head.

"I mean, I treat people all day and I understand that sometimes there are situations that go beyond my abilities."

I was trying to get him to understand, and he was reaching for my arm. "Mrs. Baptiste," he started, but I couldn't be stopped. Time was critical. "No, see," I rushed on, "there was a woman who everyone thought was . . ." (there was the need for that word again) ". . . gone," I gulped. "But she wasn't. Sh- she woke up in the morgue as a matter of fact." Then the thought of Tia waking up alone and cold made me shake. "Wh- where is the morgue?" I turned, ready to search her out.

"Mrs. Baptiste! Your daughter and husband are gone. The injuries they suffered would make it impossible for it to be any other way." He held my gaze, waiting for the madness of a lost mother to dissipate. "I'm so sorry, but right now we have to focus on your son."

Turning away from the young man's agonized face, I looked at Sam. Poor, broken little Sam. Then my mind did something - I can't decide if it was cruel or not - I saw Tia as a baby - the first time they put her in my arms after the long labor and delivery, screaming loudly, little fists flailing in the air; then I saw her walking toward me, taking her first steps, her eyes smiling as she toddled to me. *Her smile! What am I going to do if I can't see that smile anymore?*

My arms started wrapping around me, but they were cold. Not all soft and warm the way Tia's are when she folds me in her hug, her face leaning against my thighs. No, that's right, she comes to my waist now. I looked down at my hands. *I need to feel that little hand that fits so neatly into mine. The little hand that strokes my cheek when I hold her in my arms.* My own arms fell like lead to my sides - useless without that precious little body to hold in them.

"Mrs. Baptiste?" The nurse was speaking to me.

I responded mutely, looking at her as she stooped beside me. *When did I sit on the floor?*

"Detective Richardson gave us the phone number for your family. They'll be here soon."

Her voice was soothing, and I crawled over to sit next to Sam. "Hear that, Sam?" I said softly. "Grandma is coming and Gramps and Lou and Grammy. They'll make everything okay. That's what parents do. So we'll just wait right here, okay?"

But the only sound that answered me was from the machines.

"That's all right," I told him, reaching out for his hand and patting it. "You rest. I'll wait for all of us." And I sat and started rocking slowly, waiting. I turned inward, hoping that my inner self would help me keep this all together, but what assembled was of no use. The heart sat in the corner, alone and confused, no more than a muscle pumping blood through my body. The head was silent, no glib words to give me a boost. *No Jack today, ladies? No, not even Jack can help us today.* So we waited . . . listening to the machines that beeped and hummed, striving to keep Sam with me a little while longer.

Before long, the sound of footsteps approached, and I stood up looking for those that could make everything okay. But when my parents stepped around the curtained area, even in my unfocused state, I was stunned to see that Mommy and Lou looked old and afraid. Barbara and Clarence seemed lost. Everyone stood around looking from Sam to me. Their own pain meeting my pain. So I sat down, hoping they could help each other.

Now what do we do?

We wait some more.
All right.
And the ensemble became silent again.

"Mrs. Baptiste?" The doctor was back. "Sam has had some severe trauma to his head, and his brain is swelling. We need to alleviate that swelling."

I knew that Sam should have been showing some sign of movement.

"The problem is that Sam has developed a clot in his leg, and we can't wait for him to stabilize. We need to get it removed now." As the doctor spoke, people were gathering instruments and portable machines and placing them around Sam's still body.

I nodded because I knew they had to and moved from his side so that the nurses could begin transferring the tubing from the walls to the portable systems.

"What's happening? Where are you taking him?" I heard Mommy ask, and the doctor explained that if they didn't relieve the pressure now, Sam could suffer a stroke and they could lose him. I watched them move the big bed with the tiny body on it quickly and efficiently. *Don't bump the wall.*

Once the family had been settled in the waiting room, they started whispering and crying. I wanted to help but I couldn't.

The Stones, along with Malcolm and Annette, came in. My eyes drifted over to Malcolm.

Mr. Stone said, "We just came from seeing Tia."

Seeing Tia? Then there was a mistake! My heart stood up to sing, but Mr. Stone's voice broke, shattering me all over again. *Oh, Malcolm, why did you go and see her like that? Why?*

There are no words. There is just this empty space where your heart should be, but it feels like someone has ripped it from your body, leaving a great big, empty, bleeding hole. I moved back and forth between Justin and Tia - my hearts - my two broken hearts.

"Mommy, look, I can write my whole name!"

"Let me see. Oh, my! And it's so neat, too!" The star on the top page matched the ones shining in Tia's eyes that boasted of her accomplishments.

The Rest of Our Lives

No! Don't pick her up yet! You won't be able to see that happy face if her head is resting on your shoulder.

"Oh, so you hate the picture so much that you want to hide it here in the bedroom?"

His long, strong arms steady himself on the ladder to drive the nail through the wall, hanging his Christmas gift to me.

"No, silly, I want it to be the last thing that I see when I go to sleep at night."

"Oh, be careful - don't fall, Justin!"

"If I fell and killed myself, I bet you'd throw the picture out!"

"You silly! That won't happen. 'Cause what would I do without you?"

Oh, Justin, what would I do without you?

"Mommy, I fell off my bike, but I didn't cry."

She has so much self-confidence. Watch her shimmy up the monkey bars trying to keep up with Sam. Her body so far off the ground as she moves from bar to bar.

Let me kiss the calluses that are forming in your little palm. The sweet taste of dirt, sweat, and love.

"Justin, where are you going?"

"You'll see," he said secretively, struggling into his down coat overtop of his sleeping attire, slipping his socked feet into his snowboots. "I'll be back." And he's gone off into the garage.

"Jewel, come and see!" Getting my coat, I went through the sliding glass door to see hoof prints and sleigh tracks in the snow . . . and Justin grinning, proud of himself.

"Good work, Santa."

Putting his arm around my shoulder, he confided. "I've always wanted to do that for Sam. You know - before he got too big to believe?"

And you did, Justin. You did.

Sam was moved to recovery, but remained unconscious, and I sat with him . . . waiting . . . remembering.

"What would you have done if I hadn't been there when you came out of the station that day you had me arrested?"

"Oh, I don't know. Stalked you. Sang outside your balcony day and night. Sent you subliminal messages while you watched ER."

"You were that sure that I was the one for you?"

"Of course."

"How did you know?"

"Because I felt it in here." And his strong, lean fingers placed my hand over his heart. Then he kissed me.

And that kiss like so many others he gave me, I didn't savor it. The way his lips pressed against my forehead. Why didn't I sit and allow the warmth to melt me, instead of letting it escape on that summer breeze?

For days, people moved all around me, but I couldn't acknowledge them, locked in memory and remorse.

"I think she's still in shock."

I heard it whispered over and over. *No, shock would allow the mind to close down all together. It's kinder.*

"Mommy, why are the clouds blue?"

Why didn't you study her face? Imprint every image in your mind to last you for a lifetime? To last you forever.

"I am so sick of that pager."

Justin gathered his things off the dresser, preparing for another unscheduled day at the office. "I know and I'm sorry, but it's my job. I promise I'll make it up to you."

"Don't worry, Justin. I may complain and gripe, but it's not the end of the world - we have the rest of our lives to spend together."

The rest of our lives.

My memories were blocked out by the presence of the doctor. He expressed his concern that Sam was still unconscious, but said he felt that he would come around. He assured me there was no major damage to Sam's arteries in his arm or leg, but the break in his leg was bad, and as to the eye, they would have to wait and see.

After he left, someone else came to my attention.

"What are you doing?" My voice was now hoarse and flat.

"It says here that Sam is Catholic."

"That's right."

"Well, I am here to pray for him."

"Why?"

"We want to be sure that Sam is prepared to greet our Heavenly Father should he be called home."

I turned to look at my son who lay healing among the tubes and machines. "No, thank you, Father."

"But, Mrs. Baptiste, your son is very ill. Don't you want his spirtitual obligations to be fulfilled?"

"Look, Father, Sam is injured, and I have to speak for him. He's healing. So unless God Himself has told you that He plans on bringing Sam home, I don't think that we should give Him any ideas. Please go to someone who needs you. We don't."

And I turned back to Sam. "Don't pay him any mind. You just go ahead and take your time and get better. But don't take too long because these people keep telling me that the longer it takes for you to wake up . . . well, things will just be harder, that's all."

I heard the whispered voices. "We have to make arrangements."

"I've gone to the funeral parlor on Georgia Avenue. We picked out caskets for them . . ." Lou was speaking to my mother.

"No."

"Jewel? Did you say something?" Mommy asked.

Turning to my Mother and Lou, I repeated myself. "No."

"But, Jewel, we have to . . ." and her voice trailed off, and I gripped her hands to let her know that I understood, but also to make sure that I was understood.

"No, Mommy, not separate. She can't be alone in the dark."

Lou took Mommy by the shoulders, saying that he comprehended my meaning.

"And I want you to put this with them." I undid the clasp of the life bracelet that had been moving through my hands like rosary beads. The gift from Justin and the children that we wrestled over - a lifetime ago, the day Malcolm took Sam to the Orioles game. Now I pressed it firmly into Mommy's hand. No need to express that the life it represented was gone.

Two days later, I dressed at the hospital for the funeral, all the while talking to Sam's still form, reassuring him that I would be back. Ashley had brought me the clothes I would need. With shaky legs I walked over to Sam and kissed him. "I promise I'll be back very soon." *I don't want to go. I don't want to say goodbye.*

The hallway was bright, and it took me a minute to readjust. Days and nights were all the same in the intensive care unit. There were no windows, the only light coming from the fluorescents above the nurses' station. *How can anyone do well in there? It's no wonder that Sam hasn't woken up yet after four days.*

The car was waiting downstairs in the hospital driveway and with a deep breath, I climbed in, wondering how the sun could be shining on a world that didn't have my Tia in it, didn't have my husband in it.

Sitting in the back of the church, I watched everyone come and go. Jazz kept people away from me, as protective as a mother lion. Malcolm came in just as the service was to begin, supported by his parents who didn't look like they had the strength, but like all parents do, they dug deep within and found it for their only son.

And I sat alone behind my veil, not really there, staring at the beautiful, gleaming box at the altar. Then the music stopped. The viewing was over. Someone from the funeral home was asking Jazz if I wanted to say my final goodbye. I sat there frozen. *Go up there and look down at the faces I'll never see again?* All eyes had turned to the back of the church, watching me.

> Mommy, these are for you, okay?!"
> And Tia is blowing into the little wand, her lips slightly puckered as the soap bursts forward from the force of her breath, creating a trail of bubbles that explodes to float in the air all around us.

Justin scoops Tia up in his arms, and laughing and smiling, they watch the bubbles float off into the sunshine.

"No." And then before I could change my mind about seeing those wax-hard replicas of my most cherished dreams, they closed the casket. Malcolm's unsuppressed sobs were carried back to me, but my eyes were dry. *I have not shed one tear. I can't. If I start, then where will it end?* So I sat and waited as the service droned on. Heartfelt letters of sympathy from co-workers and friends. An emotional eulogy by a very somber Marcus. So many words, all meant to offer comfort and ease the troubled heart.

Now, the casket was rolling toward me, but I couldn't move. *What am I going to do?* Then the words came to me. The soloist's sweet, rich, alto voice washed over me. Something about how He knows how much we can bear. As the casket came near, I held my hand out to stop it.

I want to be with you both so much it hurts. But I understand that Sam needs me, and I can't leave him all alone, no more than God would leave me without him.

I tried to say goodbye. I tried so hard, but it just wouldn't come. Not to my mind, not to my heart. Instead I stood back and watched silently as the casket began to roll again - away from me.

I didn't go to the burial site. I couldn't. Instead, I went back to the hospital and straight to the doctor who was handling Sam's case.

"Mrs. Baptiste, there is nothing more we can do but wait and see what develops. Sam is holding his own and has been stable for the last forty-eight hours." This was some comfort after the week of downers and close calls.

"So it's just a matter of time . . . we just wait for him to wake up? Right? And then wait for him to heal?"

Not wanting to argue, the doctor nodded, and I went back to waiting.

"Jewel, I'm going to your house and check on Klaus. Is there anything that you need?" It was Ashley.

"Yes, a realtor."

"What . . . ?"

"Yes." I arranged Sam so that he would be a little bit more comfortable. "I want to sell the house. It has too many . . . *(memories?)* . . . stairs for Sam to maneuver."

Ashley said nothing, but headed out, allowing me to tend to my only reason for living.

CHAPTER 31

The next thousands of seconds were spent in a limbo of anguish, bouncing emotionally between praying for Sam to wake up and praying for the strength to do the impossible. Then as if my plate weren't full enough, my darkest demon came to visit.
"Mrs. Baptiste, it has come to our attention that you are Sam's stepmother."
"No, I am his mother." I was moving Sam's good arm and leg to keep the circulation going while the woman from Social Services tried to explain what I didn't want to hear.
"Mrs. Baptiste, I know that this is a very difficult time for you . . ." *a severe understatement* ". . . but the law is clear that the guardianship of Sam belongs to his surviving blood family. That would be his grandparents. From this point on, all decisions concerning Sam's care will be turned over to them."
I moved around, talking gently to Sam.
"Mrs. Baptiste, I have to be sure that you understand this," the harried-looking woman went on.
I whispered to Sam, "I'm going to step outside with Mrs. Blackwell so that I can straighten this all out. Don't you worry, Sambo, because Mommy is here." And I kissed his forehead, then turned, indicating for Mrs. Blackwell to follow.
Out in the hall, I began a barrage of questions.
"What do I need to do in order to become Sam's legal guardian?" I hated the term. I was his mother, not some provider, and he was my little boy and not some name on a form. They wanted to act like he was an orphan now. Wearily I thought for the thousandth time since Mrs. Blackwell called to say that she needed to meet with me, why didn't Justin and I find a real solution for this as soon as we knew it was a potential problem? *Because we were young and knew we had forever.*
"Look, Sam's birth mother abandoned him the day he was born and has never looked back," I informed Mrs. Blackwell

while shooting a look of daggers at the priest who was making his rounds.

"Does she reside here in Washington?" *That she's never once called to say hello seems to have no meaning for this woman.*

"No, she . . ." My train of thought was thrown completely off track by the sight of Angelo, my father, heading for the nurses' station. Seeing me, he changed course and started striding down the hall in my direction. "The last I knew she was in California."

"And she's never attempted to contact your deceased husband as to Sam's well being?"

"No."

"You're sure?" she persisted.

"Yes, because Justin . . . *(my sweet, loving Justin)* . . . would never have denied her access to Sam whenever she felt like coming to see him."

"Well, the best thing that you can do is get a lawyer to petition the courts for sole or joint custody of Sam."

Joint custody? Didn't I do that already? No, that was for Tia.

"Here's my card. Please contact me if you need my assistance." And she was off, no doubt to find her broom so she could fly into someone's else life and cast spells of destruction.

"Jewel!" Angelo moved to embrace me, but I stepped back involuntarily, causing him to turn the aborted attempt of a hug into an open arms gesture.

I didn't need any long, drawn-out drama, so I jumped right in. "What are you doing here?"

For a moment he stood stunned, but I was waiting for an answer.

"Jewel, you're my daughter and Tia is . . .was . . ."

This is too much. This man, to whom I send a Father's Day card every year simply to say "thanks for not flushing me down the toilet in a condom," now stands before me as if eight years have not gone by since the last time I saw him.

"Look." He sounded wounded. "I know that by your standards, I am not the father you had hoped I would be . . ."

"No, you weren't the father I *needed* you to be. You gave that up when I was five. The father that you should have been was an obligation you left to Lou."

He visibly flinched, but I wasn't done yet. "And thank God for Lou and his care, understanding, patience, and guidance that enabled me to know what it's like to have a real father." My words were stinging, but I didn't care, unaware that for the second time in my life, Angelo was performing a useful function; he was affording me the opportunity to finally vent the rage and pain that had been building inside me. Seething and hot, but contained just below the surface because no one really deserved it.

Now, looking me straight in the eye, Angelo accepted all that I had to offer. "All right, I had that coming," he sighed, "But allow me to do something for you now. To . . ."

"What? Make it up to me? Make it up to Tia?"

"I have a trust fund that I started the day Tia was born. If you need anything . . ."

Money. Always money and possessions with the man whose name occupies the father space on my birth certificate. Never time. No, because Angelo doesn't know that love can't be bought no matter how fat your pockets become.

"Thanks, I'm sure that it will come in handy for her now." I blinked hard and turned to go back to Sam so that Angelo wouldn't think that the tears that were gathering were by any means for him.

"Look, if you want to do something with that money," I said facing the wall, "do with it what I've done with all the other gifts you've messengered over for Tia." And now I did turn back to face him, my eyes sharp. "Give it to the infant home off Michigan Avenue. Hell, you can even give it in Tia's name. I'm sure that if you let the papers know, it will provide some free publicity as an extra bonus. Now if you will excuse me, I have to go and tend to my son, even though according to the courts, he's not legally mine. But I guess you could understand their point of view. See you don't even understand how to love someone who *does* have the same blood as yours running through their veins."

Angelo wasn't prepared for this, and the way he hung his head down turned the gap between father and daughter into a yawning chasm, each of us realizing it in our own separate ways. *Oh, if the people who trembled in the wake of the great Angelo Webster could see him now. Reduced to quiet tears by the truth.*

"Have a nice life." I reached out and brushed an invisible speck of dirt from the lapel of the designer custom-made suit. "You always do."

I wish I could say that after going back into the room of machines and hissing noises, I gave some thought to my father, but why lie? The moment he was out of sight, he was out of my mind. But then again I'd had years of practice.

I sat by Sam's side, filled with dread, trying to figure out where to begin to make Sam mine in the eyes of the agencies and the courts. Scared to death that his birth mother was just waiting for a moment like this to come swooping down to reunite herself with the son she'd never seen.

Suddenly, I was startled by the strange noise coming from Sam's bed. "Sam? Sam can you hear me?"

He was moving his head from side to side, his one good eye trying to focus on the room.

I tried to calm him while pressing the buzzer for the nurse. "Sam, it's okay. You're in the hospital."

But he continued to fight the tube that was running down his throat. I tried to get hold of his hand to prevent him from hurting himself any further, and then the nurses came into the room and moved me aside.

The one named Kindra spoke to Sam in a chipper tone. "So you decided to wake up?" Kindra was an island woman who would speak to Sam in her lilting tones, even though he was unconscious, as if expecting an answer. Her voice always cut me like a knife, bringing back memories of my honeymoon with Justin. The other nurse was checking the monitors, turning off the audio for the heart rate that sounded like the heartbeat of a scared rabbit instead of a child.

"Sam! Sam listen to me!" Kindra tried again to get Sam to calm down while we waited for the doctor to come and evaluate him before removing the tube.

Just standing around was hard, peeking at Sam over the shoulder of the nurse, trying to assure the scared little boy that I was still there. It was hard, knowing that I was qualified to treat him myself, but couldn't since I wasn't an employee of the hospital.

"Well, Sam!" Dr. Ambrose came into the room to assess the situation, his eyes sweeping over everything all at once. He was a tall African-American brother who looked as if he would be more content on a basketball court than in a hospital.

"With nine children and my father determined that we would all go to college, basketball is what got me through medical school." He offered the unsolicited information once during one of his examinations of Sam. "I figured I would do my Daddy a favor and give him a helping hand. Lord knows he needed it." When I didn't make any response, perhaps trying to draw me out of my anguish, he continued as if we were having a conversation. "Yep, I still play."

Now, he bent over Sam, brushing one maverick dread that fell across his face so that he could get a clear look into Sam's eye. The tapered fingers, which were attached to hands that looked like he could palm Sam's head, held up the eyelid. "Now, Sam, I'm going to do a real quick exam and then we're going to remove that thing that is making you so uncomfortable, okay?"

Sam nodded, a little calmer but still looking anxiously at me.

"All right, Sammy, get ready because it was much easier putting this in when you were asleep." Dr. Ambrose looked from Sam to his assistants before grabbing the tube and giving a huge pull, sending mucus spewing out of Sam as he coughed and choked, a sign that let us know that his lungs were functioning properly on their own. "Okay, I need you to lie back. Don't try to talk yet - just shake your head yes or no."

I moved to sit on the bed next to my son.

"Now, do you remember why you're here?"

Sam shook his head.

"Well, there was an accident, and you were hurt pretty badly."

I could see him trying to remember, and Dr. Ambrose continued.

"You have a broken arm, and your leg is in a cast." Sam reached up toward his face.

"Yes, you hurt your eye too, but Dr. Watkins thinks it's going to be fine. It's under a patch which is why it's hard for you to see now. Can you follow my finger?" Moving his hand up and down, and across Sam's line of vision, Dr. Ambrose was pleased with the results. "Good."

"I've called Sam's grandparents," Kindra whispered to me. "They'll be here shortly."

I thanked her and continued to focus on Sam.

"I'm going to go over you a little bit more just to see what's been going on since you've been asleep." Dr. Ambrose began his exam, explaining everything that he was doing. Bracing his long arms on the side of Sam's bed he told Sam, "You have what is called a catheter. This helps you to go to the bathroom until you can move around on your leg. Don't look like that," and he gave Sam a winning smile. "Lots of people have to use them when they stay here."

My heart flipflopped between rejoicing at seeing Sam's eyes open and alert and knowing that what we had to tell him would surely destroy him.

"All right, Sammy, you are on the mend. Do you know what that means? Well, it means that you are going to be fine." *No, Dr. Ambrose, I don't think that he will ever be the same little boy again.*

"I'm going to speak to your mom outside for just a second."

"I'll be right back, and Kindra is going to sit here with you - okay?" I kissed Sam's lips before pressing my face against his cheek, and for the briefest moment, my heart had wings.

Stepping outside, Dr. Ambrose said, "Sam looks good. He's stable and alert which shows that, for now, there's no sign of neurological damage, but of course we'll have to run some tests to make sure. I want to get him started on physical therapy as soon as we can. Those bones won't heal properly if we don't."

I could tell that he was speaking more to himself than me so I listened, patiently absorbing it all.

"Are his grandparents coming?"

"Yes, they should be here shortly."

"Good, because Sam can be told about his father and sister, but I want to be there in case he has to be sedated."

Just then, Clarence and Barbara came down the hall with Mommy and Lou close behind. Once they were assembled, Dr. Ambrose went over what he had just told me and finally said, "All right, I guess that we should do this now. It won't get any easier with time."

Sam was surprised to see everyone coming in which was a good sign because it showed that there was no obvious memory problem, but then he went on looking toward the door. *He's looking for two more.*

"Hey, little man." Clarence went to kiss him, followed by everyone else. Sam accepted the display of affection but was still looking at the empty doorway.

"Sam, I need to tell you something," I said, slowly easing down on the bed. "Do you remember the accident?"

And his eye got big as he shook his head yes.

"Well," and I cleared my throat, "you were hurt really bad, and Dr. Ambrose here, he and Kindra and the other nurses, they helped to make you better." And I burrowed down deep to find a smile for my little boy. "But there was . . ." and I was lost for a minute ". . . a big tr-truck hit ours. It hit real hard on the driver's side." *Please don't make me do this, God. Please don't. I don't want Sam to relive this.*

I stopped, looking to the others for support, but the eyes that looked back said I was doing fine. Taking a deep breath, I continued, "Your daddy and Tia were hurt, too. But they were hurt too badly for the doctors to fix them." I waited, allowing the words to penetrate. "And God didn't want them to be in so much pain so He sent angels down to get them and . . ." but there was no need to go any further. Sam's eye traveled around the room searching for the two he would never see again. Sam understood.

"Oh, Sam, I'm so sorry." I bent to hug him close, but he pushed me away. It completely tore my heart apart, even though I realized he was just reacting to his pain. "Sam, please," I begged.

Sam started breathing heavily, and he continued to look to the door. His breathing became deeper until great racking sobs caused his little body to tremble. I was still trying to hold him, but he was fighting me, still struggling to get back to the life he once knew. Then my baby opened his mouth, and with his voice raw from the tubes, the pain he was feeling exploded in one long cry. "DADDDYYY!!"

He would have continued thrashing about if Dr. Ambrose hadn't injected the sleep aid directly into the IV - not strong enough to knock him out completely, but enough that between my rocking and shushing, his body began to relax, then slowly go limp as I carefully laid him back onto the pillows. *My poor little Sam. I wish that I could tell you that it gets better, but I've had a jump start on you, and it doesn't seem to.*

Not taking my eyes off his sweat-drenched face, I asked, "How long will he sleep?"

Dr. Ambrose answered, "For a good little while. Long enough for you to go and get some yourself."

"Yes, Jewel," Barbara said, touching me on the shoulder, "get some rest. We'll all stay here with Sam." She helped me stand up. With one last look at Sam, I left his room for the first time since the funeral.

Even though it was only three-thirty, the day looked like it was about to come to a close. The slate gray sky loomed somber, ready to give in at any moment to the shroud of darkness. Losing the light made me want to step on the accelerator of the car, but I didn't because I would never want to cause an accident - to bring this pain to someone else's door. Not that the accident was anyone's fault. There was no drunk driver. The driver of the tractor trailer wasn't half asleep at the wheel. Not even speeding. Just an unseen patch of black ice lying in wait at the wrong time. The huge rig fishtailed wildly, becoming a metal monster that changed our lives forever.

The iron gates of the cemetery were still open, although the groundskeeper told me he would be closing them soon.

"Can you tell me where I can find this?" I held out the little slip of paper.

"Oh, sure, the marker people were by here earlier today. Those must be some very special people. First time in all my years that I ever heard of two people being together. Not even twins laid to rest together like that."

"Yes, they are very special." My words were said quietly, and his tone softened as he continued. "It's right at the top of the hill. See that big oak tree up there?"

I nodded, putting the car back in gear ready to head up the winding road, but the man stopped me. "Hey, my name is Mr. Rubin. You rest your mind. I'll take care of your people for you."

"Thank you." And I rolled the window back up and drove toward the oak tree. It was huge and for some reason, offered me a little comfort, looking at its bare branches reaching to the sky. Climbing from the warmth of the car, my stiff legs carried me up the somewhat steep hill. It was obvious right away that Angelo had been here, or at least had made his presence known. The earth was still fresh from being turned, but the tombstone sat tall, and I moved closer, kneeling down in front of it, reading Tia and Justin's names and the simple inscription below. *Heaven's joy now knows no bounds.*

Below that, in a specially made window, Tia and Justin's smiles greeted me. The photograph that sat behind the airtight window embedded in the stone was one that I had taken a few months ago at the Arboretum. Justin had just finished flying Tia in the air, and they'd both collapsed in fits of laughter. I called for them to look my way, and I was able to capture their happiness with the click of my camera's shutter.

My hands trembled as I reached out to touch their forever smiling faces. Alone up on the hill with just my aching heart for company, I knew that Tia and Justin were really gone. It must be so, because I would never have been able to form the words to tell Sam were it not.

My tears came out in a torrent of pain. I wept and prayed just as hard as Christ wept in Gethsemane. But I didn't ask for God to move me faster past the hour. No, I pleaded that he move me back just for a little bit, please, to ease for a second the misery in my body that yearned for the arms, both big and small, to hold me. Just one more time. Please, just to feel the brush of a kiss against my cheek. Or, please God, just the sound of my baby's laughter floating by on the chilly wind that was starting to pick up as the sun was setting. If I could just have that, I promised, I would hold onto it forever. I sat with my head cocked to the side, eyes closed, suppressing my cries, straining to hear or feel the slightest something. Anything. But there was nothing that matched the magic of my child's laughter. Just dead leaves rustling along the curb. And the only thing that touched my cheek was the wind's frigid breath. Just as the Lord had denied His only son in his hour of need, for what reasons we aren't supposed to comprehend, so did He now deny me as well.

"Ma'am," Mr. Rubin called out. "It's getting late." Then he added gently, "You should really think about getting home now. Maybe come back tomorrow when the sun's back out?"

I nodded gratefully. Funny thing was that I hadn't really wanted to come to the cemetery, and now I didn't want to leave. I heard Mr. Rubin call to me again. I reached out and touched the faces of those that I missed so much. "Gotta go and take care of Sam," I whispered. I looked at the tree that now rose up against a last burst of sunlight shining through the clouds, and the purple, red, and orange of that magnificent display gave me comfort. God must have been inspired by my baby's smile or Justin's warmth to produce such beauty. Maybe He was telling me that I had made it through this far without my requests being filled and that I'd make it through another sunset tomorrow.

CHAPTER 32

When I returned from the cemetery, the look that Sam gave me said he believed the story I had told him earlier. For two days, he really didn't speak much at all, and I allowed him his time to grieve. His grandparents were there every day, as were Lou and Mommy, but no one tried to cheer him up - I mean, how could you expect to cheer up a child who just wants to see the face that he first saw in life - to feel the hands that had always been there to steady him. It wasn't possible so we moved around him, trying to let him know that we were there for him.

It wasn't as if he had cut us off completely, he just had so little to say, but when he did, well, it showed just how hard this was for him. One day I was dozing in my usual position, my head resting on the side of his bed and my body curled up in the chair I always pulled close to his bed.

"Mommy?"

"Yes, Sambo?" I asked, lifting my head up, instantly alert.

"Why didn't I die, too?"

Our voices were quiet in the darkened room; the only light was from the moon that sat looking like a fat, bright ball.

"Well, it's like this." I had spent a lot of time trying to prepare answers for him that I hoped would suffice. "God does a lot of things that we don't understand."

"Like taking away my daddy and Tia?"

"Yes," I said slowly because I didn't want Sam to lose his faith in God, knowing that life is a lot better with it than without. "For some reason, He needs them with Him now."

"Didn't He need me, too?" Sam sounded hurt.

"Well, you know, Sam, I think that He did." And I started playing with his fingers. "I think He did plan on bringing you with Him, but your angel was late and when he was almost there, God realized that if he took you away, then I would be all alone. So He made sure that your angel stood over you to protect you so that you could stay here with me."

"Are you sad?"

"I'm sad because I miss your daddy and Tia very much." Sam wiped at the tear that slid down my nose, which was in total contradiction to the smile that sat under it.

"But right now, I am so very happy that I still have you. I would go out of my mind if I didn't." I kissed his fingertips, stroking his hand until I recognized the rhythmic breathing of his sleep, and I laid my head back down to join him thinking that we had made it through another moment together. Now all I had to do was make sure that he and I would have every day together. Tomorrow, Jazz and Mr. Lipinsky were coming to the hospital to discuss that very subject.

Bright and early the next morning, the old gentleman and I embraced warmly in the hall outside Sam's room. "Mr. Lipinsky. You didn't have to come."

Stepping back he looked at me warmly, "Not come? Of course I had to come for you." And he kissed my hands.

"Thank you. Hey, girl." I stretched up to draw some strength from Jazz.

"How you doin'?" she asked, giving my back a vigorous rub.

"I'm making it." I sighed wearily and it was true. After visiting Tia and Justin at the gravesite, I was slowly finding my place among the living again.

"Is Sam awake?" Jazz asked, peeking into the room.

"Yeah. He's playing with Tamicia."

"Of course."

Since he had regained consciousness, Tamicia had been Sam's lifeline, keeping him safe from the raging sea his world had become.

. "Hi, Sam," Jazz said brightly, coming in to the room. "Hey, Nurse Tamicia."

Both children looked over at Jazz, but there was no joy in their eyes. I knew the light would someday return, but for now it hurt so badly to see both of them like this. Ashley had told me how badly Tamicia took Tia's death - that she went kind of into shock crawling into her closet and sitting there for almost two days. Ashley hadn't planned to take Tamicia to the funeral, but the morning of the ceremony, she woke up to find Tamicia sitting in the chair by the front door in her prettiest dress, dress socks and shoes, a hairbrush gripped tightly in her hand. Once

Ashley was sure this was something Tamicia wanted, she finished getting her ready.

"Sam, Tamicia, it is wonderful to see you," Mr. Lipinsky said, "and I have something for both of you." Stepping out into the hall, he came back with a large box. A rare spark of interest appeared in Sam's eye. Scratching his head, Mr. Lipinsky sounded embarrassed. "Gee whiz, children, I don't know what happened . . . there was supposed to be something in here and . . ." He pulled off the top to show them that the box was empty. "Oh, dear, I guess I'll have to take it back to the gift shop. Here, Tamicia, come and give me a hand, please."

The little girl climbed off Sam's bed and went to stand in front of Mr. Lipinsky.

"Sweetheart, would you please set that outside the door?"

She went to move the box, while Sam settled back on the bed, the spark completely flickered out. Then the box rattled.

"What was that?" Mr. Lipinsky looked up from his briefcase.

"There's something in here," Tamicia said, jumping back a little.

"Is that so? Take the lid off and let's see."

Lifting the lid, her eyes narrowing in concentration, Tamicia reached in and lifted out a cage with slender silver poles. Both children were now staring wide-eyed at the cage.

"No, no!" Mr. Lipinsky said, holding up the cage. "There's something still wrong here." And he pulled a handkerchief out of his back pocket and covered the cage. Both kids peered at it and then jumped back when they heard a scratching sound coming from inside.

"Ah-ha! I think my guest has finally decided to appear. Sam pull that handkerchief."

But the cage was still empty.

Scratching his head again, Mr. Lipinsky muttered about how strange it was. Then he snapped his fingers, turning to grab his hat. Looking inside, he showed it to Sam and Tamicia. "There he is."

"Mr. Lipinsky, there's nothing there," Sam informed him.

"What? Of course there is, you just have to look harder." And the old gentleman reached in and pulled a little brown dwarf rabbit from his hat and handed the little twitching-nosed bundle of fur to Tamicia who carried it carefully to the bed. "I was hoping that you two could take care of him while I go and speak with Sam's mother?"

"We will!" And for the first time I heard laughter coming from the bed as Mr. Bunny decided to try and crawl up to smell Sam's face and Tamicia had to catch him since Sam still only had one good working arm. Not the deep pure laughter of children who don't have a care, but it was a start for both of them.

"Thanks, Mr. Lipinsky," I said gratefully as we walked slowly down the hall to the elevators.

"What? That? That was nothing. Rabbits and children always go together - besides I haven't figured out how to get a pony out of a hat yet."

And I felt my own lips curve into a brief smile as we all sat down around the cafeteria table to discuss strategy.

"Jewel, the first thing we need to do is arrange for the courts to serve this woman with papers," Mr. Lipinsky said over his tea. "Do you have an address for her?"

I handed him an envelope which contained the last letter Justin had written to Sheila. It was marked "return to sender," just like all the other letters Mrs. Baptiste had turned over to me after Justin's death.

Slipping on his reading glasses, Mr. Lipinsky read it through. "Jewel, I will myself make a copy of this when I return to the office this evening."

"Mr. Lipinsky, you don't have to work on this tonight," I started protesting but he just waved me off.

He shook his head. "This family has had enough tragedy. I will make sure to do all that I can to avert another. I'll be talking to you, Jewel." And he kissed my hand and then patted Jazz on the shoulder. We watched him place the hat that held a rabbit a few minutes ago back on his head before heading toward the elevators.

"That man is so sweet," I sighed.

"Yes, he is. And he really likes you. That's why he's working so hard on this for you. He really wants to see you and Sam together for life. Now . . ." she said, shifting gears, "did you and Robyn get together?"

"No, I spoke to Frank a little bit when he stopped by to see Sam. He was baffled by Robyn's behavior too, but said she wouldn't talk to him about it."

Robyn had avoided me ever since the accident, and after the funeral, I called her, knowing there had to be a good reason. But she blew me off, talking about how sorry she was for not coming by but she'd been real busy. At first, though stung, I let it go thinking that maybe Robyn had a thing about hospitals as many people do. For me, the hospital had become my home for the last three weeks. I showered in any vacant room I could find and roamed the halls in my slippers, looking like a permanent patient.

Jazz shook her head. "You and I both know she loves you. But I think she may be going around the bend herself. It's like she's always calling me and asking how you and Sam are doing - digging for every detail. Then she says she's going to come see you that day, but a minute later she says she'll visit when you come home."

"Home."

"I know, girl." Jazz squeezed my shoulder.

We stopped at the end of the hall and looked out the window. "You know, Jazz, I know that Justin and Tia are gone." It was still difficult to get words around the lump that seemed always to be rising in my throat. "But I'm scared to death to go home. I keep wishing that when we pack up all Sam's stuff we're really going *home* - that Tia and Justin will be waiting there for us because that's my reality. Not a new condo with all our things and no Tia and Justin." I leaned my head against the cold glass, still trying to grasp that Sam and I were going to be starting a new life, without a father and a sister, without a husband and a daughter.

"Jewel, you have to allow yourself time to grieve, and later on, find a support group - they really are helpful."

"Mrs. Baptiste?" We both turned to see Kindra standing in the doorway of Sam's room waving us to come closer. "Does dis here belong to either of you?" And Mr. Bunny was held by the scruff of his neck for a minute before Kindra brought him back down to cradle in her arms. "I know dat no one in dis room can possible know how dis here bag of fur got into my patient's nice, clean and disinfected room?"

Jazz and I followed her back in the room like two guilty kids watching while she handed the rabbit back to Sam.

"Kindra, I am so sorry."

"Of course you are," she went on, "and de next rabbit dat be coming through here is going to be sorrier 'cause Kindra won't be stopping at the market on her way home dat day." She moved to the bathroom sink to fill the rabbit's water dispenser. "Dat'll be the night dat I will be trying jerk rabbit." Standing beside the kids who were paying her no mind, Kindra looked up at me, "So what we gonna do with dis ding for de next few days?"

"What thing?" Ashley asked, coming around the curtain.

"Dat ding!" Kindra said, happy to have a new audience. The young Jamaican woman was like a burst of Carribean sunshine whenever she came around. Not that she was overly buoyant, just a very vibrant personality. She looked at Ashley sternly. "And I can't believe dat you have de nerve to bring in a pizza for my recovering patient?" And she bent Sam's head close to her heart, "Don't you know dat de dieticians go to great lengths to prepare de basic food groups so dat dis boy's bones can heal?"

Since there was nothing wrong with his stomach, Dr. Ambrose had given the okay for some food from outside.

Ashley came closer to the unconcerned rabbit who was now checking out his new, more confining environment. Ashley assured Kindra that she would take the interloper over to Robyn's house to become acquainted with Klaus. "I'm sure Robyn will love that!"

"Well dat will be best for de little hopper," Kindra said peering at him again. "What kind of pizza did you bring to feast on today?" And she pulled Sam's tray over to the bed, while Ashley started pulling out paper plates and napkins.

"Everything except anchovies. See, I didn't want to bring down the wrath of Kindra," Ashley said, imitating her lilt.

"Oh, you are a bad girl!" she scoffed. "You make sure to save me some of dat for my break."

* * * *

It took a week and a half before I felt comfortable enough to leave Sam again. Robyn's car was sitting in front of her townhouse. Marquette must have seen me through the window, because before I could knock, she swung open the door and fell into my arms.

"Aunty Jewel!"

I savored her hug until I was almost knocked down by Nikki. Bending over, I lifted the little body and held her close. "How are my girls?" I asked, the hurt not as bad as I had been afraid it would be.

Our chattering brought Robyn up the stairs. "Hey, girl. How are you?" She shook her head like she had just said something really stupid. "Never mind, you don't need to answer."

"Aunt Jewel? How's Sam doing?" Marquette asked.

I smiled down at her. "He's coming along."

Nikki had settled on my lap. "I miss Tia."

Robyn froze and then looked at me. I smoothed Nikki's hair. "I miss her, too."

Robyn reached down and removed Nikki from my lap. "You all go on now."

"But we want to see Aunty Jewel," Nikki pouted.

"And I really don't want to beat your butt, so go!" They fled, even though we all knew that Robyn would never have laid a hand on them.

"So this is how it's gonna be from now on?" I asked.

"What?" She tried to act all innocent. "I'm sorry that I haven't been by but I've been working on this huge networking job." She was rearranging little knickknacks that were already in place. "Oh, in case you wondered, Klaus is with Frank out in the garage. He's so sad without his family . . ." Her voice faded, and she looked at me in horror.

"Look, Robyn," I started, "I only have a little bit of time before I have to get back to Sam, so I'll make this quick. I've always considered you my best friend. Friends do a lot more than laugh together, they can cry together too. And I would *never* begrudge your happiness, having your girls with you every day."

Robyn whispered, "Jewel, I don't want to let you down."

"If I know you're there for me, you can't let me down."

"But what if I say the wrong thing?" There were tears in her voice, and I saw the anguish in her face.

"Robyn, right now I can honestly say that everything is the wrong thing." She looked up at me, and I exhaled deeply. "That's right, everything hurts, but there's nothing you can do about it except go through it with me."

I wiped my eyes and wrapped my scarf around my neck. "I gotta go." We hugged, and I yelled up to the girls before heading back to the hospital.

All I wanted to do was to get back to Sam and rest. Just put my head down next to his. Maybe find a tiny bit of oblivion and comfort in having his little hand in mine.

When the elevator doors opened, the nurse on duty, Danielle, stepped quickly from behind the desk. The sound of her voice caused me to tense. "Mrs. Baptiste?" The young nurse was flustered, and I was getting a very uneasy sensation.

"Danielle, is something wrong with Sam?" I was about to start sprinting toward his room, but she placed a restraining hand on my arm.

"Look," I said while trying to twist my arm free, "you can tell me on the way down the hall."

At that moment, we were joined by Dr. Ambrose. He put his large hand on my shoulder, and I felt all the blood rush from my head. Dr. Ambrose wasn't supposed to be here - I knew his shift ended an hour and a half ago. *Oh, my God. Sam is gone!*

Dr. Ambrose's voice was deep and full of sympathy. "Mrs. Baptiste, I need to speak with you." I started pulling away, shaking my head. *No, God couldn't be that cruel. He wouldn't take away all that I have left.*

My anguish must have traveled up Dr. Ambrose's arm, because his grip on my shoulder became tighter. "Sam is doing fine. He's sleeping right now."

My mind was confused. "Wha . . ." I croaked and shook my head a little to put my thoughts in order. "What's wrong. If Sam is all right, then what's wrong?"

Dr. Ambrose tried to steer me toward the lounge.

"No!" I want to know what's going on now!" *Why were they keeping me from my son?*

I started walking toward his room, but Dr. Ambrose's long reach pulled me back. I turned back to his grave face. "What is it?" I almost shouted.

Dr. Ambrose squeezed my shoulder. "Jewel . . . Jewel, Sam's mother was here."

The entire world shifted off its axis. If Dr. Ambrose hadn't still had a grip on my shoulder, I would have been on the floor. My heart was thudding in my chest. My voice came from very far away. "Did she . . . uh?" I couldn't finish that question and changed it to "Is she here?" Instead of waiting for an answer, I turned and ran toward Sam. My son. The only piece of my heart still left. Dr. Ambrose was calling after me, but I barely heard his voice over the rushing in my ears. My legs were tired, and the faster I tried to move them toward Sam's room, the longer the hallway became. The distance seemed to be growing like the space between the shore and a drifting boat. Finally, I reached the door and stepped inside, ready to interrupt any long lost moments, but no one was there except Marcus and a sleeping Sam. Breathing heavily, I asked, "Where is she?"

Marcus raised up out of the chair and taking my arm, growled, "Come on, let's go." Outside the room, he handed me a piece of paper and said, "She wants you to call her at that number."

I was afraid to take the paper. Looking up at Marcus, I tried to push back the tears. "Did she say what she wanted?"

Marcus shook his head and nodded toward the paper. "She just wants you to call."

I went off to the lounge to call. When I came back, Marcus and Dr. Ambrose were standing outside Sam's door. Marcus leaned back to peek in at Sam and then asked me, keeping his voice low, "What did she want?"

"She wasn't there. I asked the one question I'd been dreading. "Marcus, did Sheila see Sam?"

Dr. Ambrose was shaking his head. "No, she stopped by the nurse's station and said she was looking for you."

"She didn't ask to see Sam?"

"Nope, Danielle says she didn't even ask how he was doing."

What if she's on her way back down here? What if she tells the hospital to remove me? Before my mind could go any further, I heard Sam stirring and rushed into the room. I felt it was important that someone Sam knew and trusted always be there, especially when he woke up. When you wake up, there's always that small moment of contentment - everything is all right. Then a moment of confusion - something isn't right, and BOOM! - the truth slams into you and knocks you down. I always wanted to make sure that my arms were waiting to catch Sam when that happened.

Watching him struggle to wake up, my heart ached. "Hey, sweetie." I tried to smile. "You want something to drink? Something to eat?"

Still groggy from medication, Sam softly answered, "No." Instead he took my hand and held it under his cheek before drifting back to sleep. I held tightly to that hand and prayed like I never had before.

Marcus came up and whispered, "Jewel, I have to go."

I just nodded, too busy trying to imprint Sam's image on my mind.

Marcus whispered again, "If she comes back or calls, I want you to contact me right away."

Again I nodded. *I really never thought Mr. Lipinsky would find Sheila. My God, it's been seven years!* Okay, let's face it, I had prayed she would be just as disinterested in Sam as she was the day he was born. *No, Jewel, be real. You hoped she was dead!* That thought almost made my heart stop. *Oh, God, how far have I sunk?*

CHAPTER 33

The sun was streaming through the blinds of Sam's room. We were sharing a bowl of fruit but lost in our own worlds. Sheila hadn't called back last night despite the fact that I'd left three messages for her. The other five times I called, I just hung up.

Sam sat back staring at me. *Don't let him see how tense you are. He's been through enough. I really should ask him how he feels about this woman. This woman? You mean his mother?*

I forced a smile and asked Sam if he was full.

"Yes," he answered softly.

"So what would you like to do today?"

Sam just shrugged his shoulders and then looked up at me quickly and answered quietly, "I don't know." Then hopefully, "Is Tamicia coming?"

I smiled at that. "She'll be here after school and homework."

The phone rang, and I heard Marcus's gravely voice in my ear. My face froze as my brain processed his words. "Okay," he rushed in a confidential whisper, "the nurse's station just called and told me Sheila's holding for you on their extension. I'll talk to Sam while you take the call."

I managed to smile when I held out the receiver to Sam. "Marcus wants to speak with you." In a matter of seconds, Sam was patiently explaining to Marcus the difference between a certain comic book character and another.

I went out to the desk and picked up the call. "Hello?" *Good. My voice sounds strong.* The sound of rushing air filled my ears before a stilted voice, raspy and deep, came across the line. "Is this Jewel?"

"Yes. You must be . . ."

"I'm sure you know who I am. You've uncovered every fuckin' stone lookin' for me." I was taken aback by her outburst, but listened as she continued. "Well, you've found me, so what do you want?"

Okay, this is gonna be hard. No sit down over tea to discuss Sam's best interests. "Yes, I thought we should meet." There was a long pause. "Hello?"

"I'm still here." I waited for more. I didn't want her to come to the hospital, but before I could suggest anything else, she barked an order. "Meet me at the Grand Hotel in Georgetown at eleven."

I looked at my watch. "Two hours?" I couldn't just leave. They were going to remove the patch on Sam's eye that afternoon. I was sputtering and hesitating when she cut me off again.

"I don't have a lot of time." *Not a lot of time? That sounds promising.* Reaching over the desk, I grabbed a post-it and pencil. "All right. What's your last name?"

"Why do you need that?"

"Well," I said, bewildered, "to find you." *Hello?*

"Just come to the main restaurant," she commanded. "Give the maitre'd your name. Eleven o'clock." The line went dead.

Marcus came strolling into the sunroom an hour later. Poker face set. "Hey, man! Look at you, up and about!" Sam was indeed out of bed and sitting in a wheelchair. Marcus knelt down and folded him in a hug. "I hear you're going to get this eyepiece taken off today?"

Sam shook his head. "No, Mommy has to go and meet someone."

Marcus glanced up at me, and I nodded my head. "Yep, "I'm about to go out, and Sam here wants me to be the first person he sees with his healed eye." I kissed those dark honey-colored curls. *So sweet.*

Marcus told me he'd walk me to the elevator and told Sam he'd be right back.

I filled Marcus in on the details of my conversation with Sheila. Looking back into the sunroom, I studied Sam, his broken leg extended but for the moment forgotten. "Marcus, it's like I'm afraid to leave him alone to think." I could feel the stinging behind my eyes, and I blinked furiously. "He just can't be put through any more trauma right now." *No, I can't go through any more trauma!*

The elevator doors opened. I waved to Sam who gave a little wave of his own.

Marcus's words tried to beat the sliding doors. "I'll be right here with him 'til you get back."

* * * *

The hotel was just setting up for lunch. I walked up to the maitre d' and gave my name who in turn gave me the onceover. *Okay, so I'm not looking my best. My hair hasn't seen a curl in weeks, and my clothes are for comfort, not to impress.*

Waving his hand imperiously, he summoned a young Latino brother. "Hector," he said carefully, please show this woman to table ten in the atrium."

I followed Hector to the airy, windowed room that must have been the smoking section because there was a small cloud of smoke hanging in the air and a steady stream coming from the table we were approaching.

This has got to be a mistake!

The sight of the woman behind the dark sunglasses, who sat in the midst of the cloud of smoke, made me turn to question Hector. I was sure that he had brought me to the wrong table. Then I heard her voice.

"Another drink." The same raspy, deep voice from the phone.

Wide-eyed, I was glad it was my jaw that hit the floor and not my butt. She was inhaling from the end of one cigarette, lighting it from the butt of another. Hector retrieved her empty glass and disappeared.

I flopped down in the booth, obviously stunned.

"What?" the woman asked, smirking. "He didn't tell you?" She took several drags from her cigarette in quick succession.

Hector had returned with her drink, and I asked him to bring me a double scotch. Neat. I didn't care if he did raise his eyebrows. I wouldn't have cared if it was eight o'clock in the morning. On the many occasions I had wondered what kind of woman could walk away from her child, what kind of woman would never even so much as look back, never had I expected the face of that woman to be white!

"I understand you've been looking for Sheila Bryant?"

Staring at her, I stammered, "I'm sorry . . . I thought *you* were Sheila! Do you know her?"

"I think that the correct term is *did* I know Sheila, and the answer is yes." She settled back in her seat and removed her sunglasses.

"I don't understand. Are you saying that she's dead? How? When?" My mind was racing. Mr. Lipinsky had found nothing to suggest that Sheila had died. A death record would have been the easiest thing to find.

"She died almost seven years ago," she said, the red crimson lips compressed into a straight line. "You asked how?" She paused to take a sip of her drink and then, smiling triumphantly, revealed, "Under the hands of a competent plastic surgeon and a good beautician."

"Excuse me?" *This is not making any sense.*

"Yes, Sheila Byrant is dead, but I, Marcil Clipper-Ashton, have risen as the Phoenix from her ashes!" And this woman dramatically spread open her arms. Her artificially enhanced blue eyes bore into my own which were widening in total surprise. *This is Sam's mother! Thank you, Lord, for making her crazy instead of dead!*

I raised my hand for Hector. "Would you please bring me another of these? Thank you."

The tall, anorexic woman folded herself back into the booth like a praying mantis. Blonde hair and carefully made up face. Skin so translucent you could tell it hadn't been near natural sunlight for some time. The casual clothes that hung off her food-deprived frame screamed out designer wear. Some would consider her pretty, but there was something very hard about the eyes which transformed the rest of her face to granite, cold and untouchable. An ice princess.

"I understand that you've been looking for Sheila because of the boy?" *Red flag. This chick keeps referring to herself as someone dead and Sam has no name?*

"I . . .," but she waved me off before I could get started.

"Look," and the voice that sounded as if it had been trained under a voice coach became flat and tired, "I never wanted kids. I'm sure that his father explained the situation to you?"

I nodded.

"Well, since he wanted the baby so bad, there was little I could do to fight him, so I sat around for months getting fat and out of shape with that thing moving around in me all the time." She shuddered in revulsion. "Anyway, I walked away as soon as I was able. Left the package with his father and just kept going." Sheila stopped and looked at me, almost as if expecting me to congratulate her.

Then she leaned toward me like a conspirator. "Justin's gone, and you're stuck holding the bag, right? Well, that's the price you pay when you marry somebody with kids." *She thinks I want to give Sam back!*

I sat stunned while she continued. "I would say you have a problem, honey. Kids don't go with a career - even had my tubes tied *and* burned last time I was in Mexico. So why you would think I'd want to raise a kid I haven't given much thought to for seven years is beyond me. I mean, he's your problem by marriage, not mine."

I tried to interrupt. "Sheila . . ." but she kept on going.

"You know, I never wanted to go to school in the first place, but Daddy insisted that I could catch a good husband there so I could settle down and be a good girl. See, that wasn't the first time I'd had a little trouble, if you know what I mean." She gave me a little wink while I sat there hanging on her every word.

"But this time was different - real different. We couldn't let Mommy and Daddykins know their little girl caught jungle fever, now could we?" Another wink and a burst of laughter as Sheila aka Marcil took a twisted trip down memory lane.

She told me how the day she left the hospital she left everything behind, including her family. "Oh, I had a good time then, better believe it. I raised some hell and drove a whole lot of men wild!"

It was beginning to dawn on me. *This person who carried my precious son is a tramp, at best.* That was it, plain and simple, but I still sat at attention because I needed to know how this was going to end up.

"But that was then. Now I'm working steady and my star is ascending every minute."

Her star was going nowhere - I could tell. Staring at her for a half hour now, I could see that the natural aging process was coming on fast in her case. There was a harsh quality to her face, and her body seemed a little bit on the worn side. She obviously fancied herself an actress, but I'd never seen her in anything. I was just amazed that Justin had involved himself with anyone like her, but maybe when she was a fresh young thing, she had looked and acted a lot different.

Now a look of concern clouded her features as if some director in her head were calling for a new scene to begin. "You know, there's nothing to tie me to this kid - I never even signed the birth certificate. Maybe you think I can't walk away, but . . . "

"Sheila, let me explain something. I'm not trying to foist Sam off on you. I *want* to raise him."

This obviously surprised her, and she brightened up. "Is that so? Is that so? Well, that is something! Well then, you won't mind signing this - to give me some assurance, you know." And now she started digging through her bag. "I had my lawyer draw this up." I watched as a ton of stuff came falling out - cosmetics, crumpled tissues, vials of pills. "Here it is." She placed a single page in my hand.

Right away, I could tell that this was no legal document. Nothing more than some nonsense with some legal words thrown in. Folding the page, I asked carefully, "What happened to the paperwork that Social Services sent you?"

Her eager eyes seemed to falter, and she looked down and ran her hands through her streaked hair. "Oh, that, I never even looked at it - besides, I don't want anything to do with Social Services. Tony feels that could surface one day - tie me to the kid - I mean . . ."

"Okay." I held up my hand to stop her because there was no way I wanted to hear her say his name. I reread the document again to make sure that I hadn't misinterpreted its meaning. "You want to make sure by having me sign this that I will 'never contact you or the media concerning the biological status of the product produced from the results of Sheila Bryant and the paternal partner, expressed in any form'?" I swear to God that's just how it was written!

"Yes, see Tony says that this is just the kind of scandal those rag magazines look for in an up-and-coming star, and well, that stuff from Social Services would be kept on file and then if someone wanted to do some snooping - well . . ." She looked at me for understanding. "But this could be kept in a safe deposit box. One for each of us. But if I sign my name as Sheila, *everything* can be traced back to me."

She couldn't be a natural blonde. Only a person pretending to be a blonde would want to adopt the stereotypical stupidity that went along with it.

"Look, Sheila, I really think that before we sign anything we should involve an attorney, don't you?" She bit her lip for a moment, and I pressed on. "This is good, but we want something really binding and legal - you know what I mean?"

She chewed on this for a minute. "Uh . . . maybe you're right."

I could tell that she was doubtful. "Look, I'll call my attorney as soon as I see you out, and we'll set up a meeting for tomorrow. This way, you can get back to L.A. . . ."

"Beverly Hills," she corrected me.

"I'm sorry, of course." I placed the paper in my purse and began to rise.

Waving her hands in the air, Sheila stopped my departure. "Wait. I have this for you." And she reached back down into that bag, rummaging around until her fingers found what she wanted. "This is for you, but no one has to know. It's a little expression of my appreciation at keeping this discreet."

I opened the envelope she handed me and pulled out a check made out in the amount of five thousand dollars. I stared at what this woman believed to be the selling price for Sam. For a split second, I thought about taking one of the heavy candlesticks from the buffet and with one mighty swing, "Pow! Home run!" *No, too many witnesses. Maybe I should stick around until she leaves and then shove her under a Metro bus.*

"Where are you staying?" There was no reply, and I looked down and saw the suspicion on her face. "So that I can contact you about tomorrow?"

"Oh, right." She sighed but no information was offered.

"Shel . . . er, Marcil, I need to be able to contact you."

She was biting her lower lip, and I guessed that whatever establishment she was residing in temporarily didn't match with where she believed someone of her status should be, so I decided to save her sorry ass. "Why don't I give you the law firm's business card, and you can call their receptionist and make arrangements."

"What about the money?" she asked, as I stuffed the card in her hand, trying not to actually touch her.

"Bring it with you."

"But no one's supposed to know about it," she whined.

"I know, but we'll have to work out something so it won't resurface and have your fans wondering why in the world would Marcil . . . *(what the hell is her new last name?)* . . . be giving someone like me such an amount?" She stood looking down at me, and I wasn't too sure that my acting was any better than hers but after a minute, she took back the check and nodded in agreement.

"Right, better let the attorneys handle this since that's what they get paid for." She placed the sunglasses back on and started striding toward the door. I watched her leave and then felt Hector's presence behind me.

"Excuse me, madame?"

"Yes?"

Looking a little uncomfortable, he said, "The lady said you would be paying?" I took the extended folder and slid my credit card inside without looking at the bill. While I waited for him to return, I wondered again how this would really turn out. It sounded like I was giving her what she wanted. She never even asked about Sam. *Why does it seem so easy but feel so wrong?*

CHAPTER 34

Sheila never called. I hadn't heard a word from her since I saw her in the restaurant, and that had been almost two weeks ago. Then Sheila had given me the impression she was going to cooperate in making Sam mine. Now I didn't know what to think and was feeling terribly anxious. What was going on in that lunatic mind? Jazz told me we just had to work harder and faster, but I just wanted to stop and slow down for a minute. So much was going on.

Right after the shock of Sheila showing up, I learned that Malcolm had been to visit Sam. Marcus told me he looked kind of bad, but that he was obviously glad to see Sam.

"I think they both needed it," Marcus explained. "They just sat and talked about Tia for about an hour."

Then there was the uncertainty surrounding the removal of the patch over Sam's eye, but that was going to come to an end right about now.

Clarence and Barbara and Mommy and Lou were with me in the examining room. The ophthalmologist, Dr. Watkins, was seated on a stool in front of Sam, speaking in a low, soothing tone. "Now this may hurt just a bit." This was immediately followed by a small yelp from Sam and then a series of squeaks and ows.

I peered over Dr. Watkins' shoulder and watched him slowly peel away the tape from the area around Sam's eye.

"Okay," he assured Sam. "Almost there." When the first dressing was removed, Dr. Watkins told him, "Now, Sam, I'm gonna remove the gauze over your eye, but don't open it yet, okay?"

We all leaned forward and waited.

Dr. Watkins pulled off the gauze and gently felt around the contours of Sam's eyes. "Tell me if this hurts."

Sam sat still and didn't flinch once.

"The bone feels good," the doctor said over his shoulder. "Okay, Sam. I want you to slowly open your eyes."

I stared and prayed at the same time.

Sam's eyes started to flutter and after a lot of squinting and blinking, he looked around the room. My heart was hammering, and I almost lost my balance, but then he saw me. He saw me, and this time a light went on. I saw it. I felt it.

"So, Sam, how's the world look?" Dr. Watkins was asking.

Sam looked around again before saying, "It's fuzzy."

I bent down to stare anxiously into my little boy's eyes.

Dr. Watkins' voice calmed everyone. "That'll get better with time." Speaking to me, he explained, "He may need to wear glasses until his eye completely strengthens."

I nodded, not trusting myself to speak. The grin on my face felt so good; the light in Sam's eyes warmed my heart.

Dr. Watkins was preparing to perform a more thorough examination when there was a discreet knock on the door. Michelle, a nurse from Sam's floor, looked in at me. "Excuse me? Mrs. Baptiste?"

"Hi, Michelle! Come in and see how our man's doing!"

She hesitated before saying, "Uh, can you and Sam's grandparents step outside for a minute?"

The hairs on my neck stood up.

"We'll stay here with Sam," Lou offered.

"Sam, we'll be right back," I assured him and followed the nurse out. Once in the light, it was evident that Michelle was very upset. "I'm sorry, but there's a situation going on upstairs." She started rushing down the hall to the stairs, and we tried to keep up. When she stopped to push open the door to the stairwell, she said breathlessly, "There's a woman upstairs claiming to be Sam's mother. She wants to take him out of the hospital!"

No! I darted past her, taking the stairs two at a time, Michelle's voice trailing behind me. "We called Marcus - he's on his way."

I didn't hear anything more since I had already pulled open the door to Sam's floor. Wearing a black sheath dress, no stockings, and red, very high-heeled pumps, Sheila was pacing in front of the nurse's station, running her fingers through her hair.

I shouted, Sheila, what are you doing?" She saw me coming and turned her back to me.

"SHEILA?!"

Before I could turn her around, a large man stepped in front of me. "Excuse me, but I would ask that you stay away from my wife." The man was well over six feet and burly. Clean shaven, deeply tanned, with his hair slicked back into a pony tail, he stood between me and Sheila.

Clarence came up behind me and demanded, "Who the hell are you?"

The man seemed unconcerned. With practiced patience, he responded, "I'm Tony Ashton, Marcil's husband. Sam's stepfather."

I felt as if someone had slapped my face, and I stepped back. Clarence pulled up to his full six foot four and roared, "Like hell you are!"

Tony stood his ground. "I'm married to Sam's mother, and so . . ."

Clarence grabbed my arm and pulled me forward. "This is Sam's mother!"

By now security guards had appeared. I disengaged myself and stepped around to Sheila. "What are you doing?" I whispered, but she wouldn't look at me.

Her eyes darted everywhere but to me.

"Marcil, we talked. You said that . . . that . . ."

"I know what I said." The calm with which she tried to smother her anxiety was too thin, and her voice began to rise. "I've changed my mind. That is my kid and I have rights!"

Marcus strode up the hall accompanied by two uniformed officers. "All right, what's going on here?"

Their appearance just made for more shouting, and while everyone was yelling, I watched Sheila. The noise was beginning to get to her. I pushed again. "Sheila, please. You told me that you didn't want children - went to great lengths to make sure!"

She kept trying to move past me, but I wouldn't get out of her way, following her like an image in a mirror. "What about your career?" Desperately, I planted myself directly in front of her. "I don't understand . . ."

"Oh, I bet you don't!" she snarled. "Why should you get to keep everything?"

Everyone stopped and looked at her. Hair wild and eyes wilder, she ranted on. "I saw that place of yours! Your personal attorneys!" She spat, "What makes you so privileged? That kid, that's what!"

Tony yelled to her to shut up, but Sheila kept going. "You think I'm stupid?! That I don't know what's going on? Well, I know and trust me, I'm getting everything that you're trying to deny me."

I watched her eyes narrow, and the smile that split her face in two told me that there was no punch line to this sordid joke.

Tony turned to the rest of us. "Look, we don't want no trouble. We just want to collect the kid and go home."

This started a new round of confused shouting which was the scene which Dr. Ambrose came upon. "What's going on here? I know you people understand that this is a hospital."

Tony spoke up. "We're Sam Baptiste's parents, and we've come to take him home."

Dr. Ambrose was visually stunned and looked over at me and then said, "First of all, Sam isn't able to go anywhere. Secondly, we're going to take this drama out of the hallway. I won't have patients disturbed by this. Security, please escort everyone to the conference room off my office."

The guards formed a line, and the two police officers herded the group from the rear.

Dr. Ambrose turned back when he saw I hadn't moved. "Jewel?"

"I'm going to wait here for Sam to come up."

"I think you should come with us."

"No, I should be here waiting for my son."

When he didn't move, I told him I would use the time to call my lawyers, and this seemed to satisfy him.

When Sam was brought up to the floor, I stayed until he went to sleep before going down to Dr. Ambrose's conference room. Sheila and Tony were gone. Justin's parents looked shaken. My parents were pissed. Closing the door, the tension almost suffocated me. "What happened?"

Marcus took a deep breath before answering. "They thought they could walk in and just take Sam away - that Sam's mother has the right."

I nodded my head.

"Dr. Ambrose told them Sam couldn't be released due to his medical condition, but they still tried to insist on it. I persuaded them otherwise."

Barbara stood up, her chair slamming back against the wall. "No, they didn't give a damn that Sam has suffered a terrible loss. That he doesn't even know them." Her nose was red and there were fresh tears in her eyes. "No, they just wanted us to hand him over."

Marcus spoke up. "I gotta go and run a check on them. There's no way that I'm gonna just let Justin down like that. No way it's goin' down like that." His voice faltered, and he stormed out.

Dr. Ambrose came around the desk. "I told them that Sam would be in no shape to travel for at least six weeks and that he would be needing extensive physical therapy and other care as well. Jewel, I'll also want to get a child psychologist in and see what her spin is on all of this."

I thanked Dr. Ambrose, and he left to go back on the floor.

Looking at the Baptistes, I just had to say something to comfort them. "Look, Mr. Lipinsky will find a way."

I felt like I had to get away before despair enveloped me. At the door, I spoke to them again. "You'll see, it's going to be fine." *And if I say it often enough, maybe I'll believe it!*

I went and sat on a bench outside the hospital, letting my feelings overwhelm me. *I can't lose Sam - I can't lose him. He's all I have left.* I cursed Sheila and her creepy husband. Berated Justin and myself for not taking the proper steps to secure Sam's future. *Why did we think we had the rest of our lives to do that?*

Finally, an hour later, with my composure in tact, I went back into the hospital.

"Mommy!" Sam rolled down the hallway so fast I had to sidestep or be run over. Tamicia was right on his wheels.

I bent down and kissed Sam and then accepted a hug from Tamicia.

"Mommy, I tried to call you, but you didn't answer your phone!"

"Oh, I'm sorry." I pulled the phone out of my pocket. "Look, I didn't have it on." I started to laugh at my own silliness, but stopped. Sam looked terrified. "Hey, Sam, I'm not going anywhere."

He just nodded his head.

Ashley came up behind him and rubbed his head. "Hi, Jewel. Sam was just a little worried, that's all. Tamicia, can you take Sam to the sunroom for a bit? I want to talk to your Auntie."

The little girl, barely taller than the chair, pushed her cousin down the hallway.

"Oh, Jewel, Marcus called me to tell me what happened. I'm so sorry!"

"Well, Mr. Lipinsky says that we'll stall all we can, maybe try to change her mind, help the Baptistes prepare for a custody fight - I don't know, maybe that pitifully worded agreement she gave me will help."

We sat quietly side by side for a bit. Staring straight ahead, I told Ashley, "Sam gets released next week."

"Yeah, I know. That's why Tamicia and I were a little late - we stopped by your new place to get things ready."

I rested my head on her shoulder. "Thank you, Ashley." I felt her hand against my cheek.

The elevator doors opened, and a disgruntled Robyn emerged. Storming toward us, she started waving something around. "Your dog owes me a new pair of boots!"

I looked up into her outraged face and couldn't stop myself. I tried to swallow the first tickle. Then the giggle came snorting out of my nose and before I knew it, Ashley and I were on the floor.

"Hey, this is not funny!" Robyn went on. "Do you know how much a pair of Nine West boots costs?"

When I looked down the hall, I saw Sam and Tamicia solemnly watching us like we had truly lost our minds as Ashley and I tried to pull each other up. *God, it feels good to laugh even if it is the laughter of madness.*

* * * *

That night, Sam and I sat up discussing our plans.

"Is it a house?" he asked in the stillness of the room. Sam didn't like the television to be on. He missed the partner he used to laugh and joke with when they watched the tube together.

"No, it's a condo that we're going to turn into a home," I replied, looking at all the belongings we would need to pack up.

"What's the difference?" he asked somewhat confused.

"A house is a place that holds your stuff, and a home is a place that holds your stuff *and* your love," I explained.

"So we're going to make a home, just the two of us?" He sounded dubious.

"Sure. It won't be easy at first, but we have each other and Grandma and Gramps, Grammy, Lou, Tamicia, Ashley . . ."

"Marcus."

"Yes, Marcus, too. We'll be all right."

"Did I hear my name?" Marcus came through the door looking beat.

"Hey, big man." I patted his shoulder.

"Hey, Jewel. Hey, Sam, my man!"

Right away, Sam asked Marcus, "So what did you do today?" Sam always asked him to tell him all about his day - not letting him leave out even the smallest detail.

"I think that he's trying to see his father's daily routine through Marcus's eyes," Ashley noted after a few observations of this. I had never made the connection. Of course he would feel close to Marcus, who was, after all, his father's partner.

"Well, gentlemen," I interrupted, "I have to go and find out what the doctor wanted with me." I headed out to the nurses' station, looking for Dr. Ambrose.

"He'll be right back," a nurse named Peggy assured me. "We're sure going to miss that little boy of yours."

And I smiled because even though everyone had been told of my legal relationship to Sam, everyone on the floor referred to Sam as my son or my little boy.

"Mrs. Baptiste?" I turned at the sound of Dr. Ambrose's voice.

"Hi," I greeted him.

"I was wondering if you had a minute?"

"Sure." I followed him into the family waiting area. The room was empty, and housekeeping had been through recently to remove the discarded newspapers and magazine and find homes for the empty soda cans and cups that had been left behind on the little tables.

"Please sit down." We both moved over to the couches nearest the windows, Dr. Ambrose sitting across from me, his legs so long that his knees almost bumped into mine.

"Is there a problem?"

He rubbed his hand under his chin as if he were really considering his next words very carefully and I sat waiting, my eyes drifting to the window, my thoughts to Justin and Tia.

". . . so I was hoping that you wouldn't think me too forward in speaking to you like this?" Dr. Ambrose looked quizzical.

I hadn't heard a thing. "I'm sorry, but my head was somewhere else altogether." I confessed, and he dropped his head shaking it back and forth.

The doctor's eyes were kind and smiling when he lifted them back to me. "I was worried about offending you if I got a little personal with you," he repeated, but with an easy smile.

"What about?" I asked curiously.

"Well, I know about your loss and how hard it's been, and no doubt with time you'll find some peace," and I smiled at his thoughtfulness, "but until then I thought that these might help." He started digging into his deep lab coat pocket, pulled out a small stack of brochures, and handed them to me. I turned the brochures over in my hand reading the names of support groups for surviving family members.

"Gee, I thought I was doing a pretty good job," I said quietly. *Guess I haven't been fooling Sam or anyone else either for all of my bravado.*

"No, not at all." Dr. Ambrose sounded flustered as he leaned his face down into my view. "Everyone on the floor is amazed at how well you've held things together, not just for your son, but for the others - your father-in-law was just singing your praises the other day, saying that he and his wife would never have found the strength to get through this if it weren't for you."

I lifted my face and looked across at the good doctor whose face was full of concern. "Have you ever lost anyone close?" I asked curiously.

"No. And I don't know if that's a blessing or a curse, to be twenty-eight and still never have a personal brush with death. Maybe I get a break because I live with it day to day."

"Well, this is really nice of you," I said, holding up the booklets knowing that for now, it was just too soon. For some reason I just didn't want to share my mourning with anyone. *Right now, it's the only thing that's keeping them close to me.*

"And Sam is going to talk to my sister who's a child psychologist."

"Fine," he said, reaching out to pat my knee. "But don't neglect yourself. Sam may seem somewhat distant now, but he's leaning very heavily on you, and it's okay to look for extra strength to rely on."

I nodded.

"We're gonna miss you all. You're almost family," he said, reiterating Peggy's earlier statement. "We hope that you'll come back to see us soon?"

"Well, not too soon," I said with a small laugh while we stood in the hall waiting to go our separate ways.

"All right then, I'll be by to check on Sam a little later," he assured me, and he went right while I went left.

When I returned to Sam's room, he was knocked out and Marcus' head was in the middle of a dip as he nodded, trying to keep his eyes open.

"Marcus?" I said giving him a little shake. "Are you off for the night?"

I knew that there were times that Marcus would come to see Sam in between his shifts. I caught him in the hallway once, putting some drops in his eyes to remove the telltale red film of exhaustion. "Marcus, you don't have to come every day," I had tried to tell him.

"Yeah, I do," the big man said quietly, "Justin was like my brother, and I wouldn't expect anything less from myself."

I gave him a big hug, but still chided him, "If you wear yourself out, you won't be any good to anyone."

"Yeah, and when was the last time you were out of here?" he had asked, and I had to concede partial victory to him.

Now I looked to see if he were truly awake as he sat on the side of the bed like a very big bear rubbing his eyes.

"Naw," he sighed heavily, "I still gotta go back and type up some paperwork." And after making sure that he was up and alert, I walked him to the nurses' station.

"See you all tomorrow," he said with a grin and was off to head back to the life that I remembered all so well. I waved to him, wishing for the millionth time that I could wave just once more to Justin. *But you can't - can't ever, never.*

I settled back down in my usual spot next to Sam. The brochures that Dr. Ambrose had given me earlier sat staring at me from across the room. But for now I could close my eyes to them, content for the memories to come to me like visions taking me back to that place between awake and asleep. Between the sadness of reality and the distortion of dreams, I could be content. And I tried to hold onto that moment a little longer before my mind shut down, never hearing Dr. Ambrose come into the room for Sam's last evening exam, realizing in the morning that he must have been the one who threw the blanket overtop of me.

* * * *

Friday, the staff came past at different intervals to say their goodbyes. Not making a big deal about it, but letting Sam know that he had been the model patient. Neither Sam nor I said much, feeling tense and nervous about moving beyond these walls to face the world. Offering up little nervous smiles as we waited for Dr. Ambrose to come and officially sign Sam out.

"All right, Sam," Kindra began as she came in with a wheelchair. "I want you to remember to do those dreaded exercises so dat you can be playing soccer next year."

And Sam gave her a little nod.

"Dere you go!" Kindra helped him into the chair. "Dat's better because dat bed is needed for a sick child and you, Sam, are de image of a healthy little boy." She bent down to make sure that the wheels were locked in place. "Now you stay here while I go and find de doctor so dat you can enjoy some of dis weather."

"Sam?" Dr. Ambrose came flying in with some charts in his hand twenty minutes later. "I'm sorry that I'm late, but I'm running behind." He checked the leg that sat straight out in the chair. "Well I guess that you are good to go. Here's some samples that'll hold you over until you can get the prescriptions filled. Call me if there are any signs of fever, headaches, blurred vision - anything out of the usual. Are you driving you guys home?"

"No, my sister is coming . . ." And there she was in the doorway.

Ashley and I started gathering bags, as Kindra began pushing Sam out of the room. We were quiet as we moved down the very familiar halls, Sam waving a few times to staff who wished him well.

We got Sam into the back seat. The truck would have made things much better, but there was no truck anymore. Once he was in and settled, I set to buckling him in somewhat strangely since he had to keep his leg out straight on the seat. Then I went to climb up front, but Sam grabbed my hand.

"You want me to ride back here with you?" I climbed in, careful of his leg. We pulled away from the place that Sam and I had known as home. I reminded myself that things would be very different now. *Tia won't be at home, bursting to tell me what she did that day, and Justin won't be coming in late from a long day at work, crawling into bed for a kiss and hug before stumbling back down to warm up the plate that you won't be leaving out on the stove anymore.*

Before, I hadn't really had time to think about the future since I was so focused on the present, but now things were moving toward the inevitable, and my priority was to make a safe and secure life for Sam. I looked over, sure that I would find his eyes closed, but they weren't. They were wide open and darting back and forth across the slow-moving traffic. The sedative they had given him before he left the hospital seemed to have no effect.

"Sam?" I whispered, "Sam, are you okay?"

He nodded, but there was a thin film of sweat on his body, and the hand that took mine was trembling.

"Sam, are you sick?" *Oh! Jewel, you can be so dense sometimes. This is Sam's first time back in a car! The last time, the ride ended with the death of his sister and father. Damn it! Okay, okay, you can fix this. Just be calm.* So I sat and patted his hand which was ice cold while Ashley carefully drove through town until she pulled off the road and burrowed into the garage under our new dwelling.

Robyn greeted us at the door.

"Sit," I commanded Klaus for fear that he might bowl Sam over.

Klaus sat at full attention, only the sound of his tail on the hardwood floor showing how happy he was to see part of his pack finally come back.

Then I called him. "Yes, boy, I missed you too!" Against his training, I allowed Klaus to jump up. "Yes, you were lonely?" I asked, scratching him behind the ears as he kissed me all over.

Our new home had been put together by my friends and family, often working late into the night, staining, polishing, sewing, talking... healing. The windows which reached all the way to the cathedral ceilings were framed with lacy curtains, pulled back to allow the sunlight of the April morning to spill in, feeding my many plants, as well as my soul. Everything shone and reflected a little of both me and Sam. Sam's room held his telescope, computer, and a bunkbed that looked more like a spaceship.

"I painted the mural," Tamicia said proudly, as she helped Sam get settled in his new room.

"Oh, my God!" I was awestruck. We all knew that Tamicia was gifted in the art department, but this went beyond anything I would conceive of coming from one so small.

"This is the Nebula and the Milky Way," she pointed out. "And this place right here?" She pointed up in the corner of the room to a golden circular cluster of stars and space dust. "That's heaven." She said it thoughtfully and Sam sat watching her with such adoration that for a minute I was lulled into thinking that everything would be simple. That Tamicia would always look out for her Sam, and everything would be all right. But I knew that wasn't how life works and that I would have to stay on my toes.

"Have you heard from Jazz?" I asked Robyn, leaving the kids to adjust without me hovering over them. "She was going to call here."

"Yes, Jazz said that Mr. Lipinsky had sent someone down to this woman's hometown." I had reluctantly allowed Angelo to assume some of the expense involved in the efforts to make Sam legally mine.

Robyn walked me through our new place. I was amazed at how everything was so comfy and homey, even though it felt a little like I was in someone else's house, but whose favorite colors and styles were the same as mine.

"This is the gym room," Robyn said, showing me the exercise equipment that Sam would be needing - floor mats and weights, even those wooden things that he would need to learn for climbing. Then it caught my eye . . . and took my mind.

"Okay, okay, move out the way before you hurt yourself!"

"What are you talking about? It's a punching bag, and I'm punching it."

"No, no, you have to lean into it, put the force of your whole body behind it. Here, watch Sam. Sam, show Mommy how it's done."

And Sam came and stood in front of the big bag while Justin held it firmly. "Okay, go! *Oof!* Man, you got some muscle! Here, give another swing."

And behind his father's praise, Sam really went to work while Justin held the bag and poured out advice like a coach to his prizefighter. Then, "Okay, that's enough without gloves. You'll soon be able to take me out, boy." He laughed and started sparring with his son.

"We hoped it would be okay to bring it." Robyn's voice brought me back as I ran my fingers along the side of the canvas bag.

"Sure, of course," I said, my voice slightly hoarse. I moved out of the gym room and down the hall. "Robyn, the place is really beautiful." Absently, I closed the hall door behind us, sort of looking for something but not wanting to ask about it specifically.

"This is your room." Robyn steered me into a room further down the hall. "Is this all right?" she asked worriedly, sliding open the mirrored closet door.

"It's fine." I looked over at an alien bed. "Is this mine?" I asked, touching one of the heavy chains that held it suspended from the ceiling.

"It's your old bed set. The mattress and suspension are new. If you would rather have something else . . ."

"No. This is fine." I climbed up on it and found that the swaying was minimal. "So this is it?" I asked, looking around.

"Except for this." And Robyn moved aside to close the door slightly, reaching over to turn on a small light which brought illumination to the portrait of the two happy lovers with the mermaid in the background. Positioned directly underneath was a framed picture that Tia had made with her handprints in colorful bright green. Her favorite color.

"We weren't sure where you would want it, or if it would be too upsetting to look at, but . . ."

"No, actually, I was looking for it. I would say you all have gone overboard in spoiling me."

None of it would have been possible without my friends and family. Ashley had advanced me the downpayment on the condo, and my parents were making the payments on it, with Mr. and Mrs. Baptiste paying for Sam's tutor until I could get settled. I would be able to repay them once our old house was sold.

"Robyn, I just hope I can get myself together and take care of me and Sam."

She came over and sat next to me on the edge of the bed. "Of course you will, and in the meantime you will get sick of me hanging around like a mother hen."

I sat looking at the picture, the symbol of my former happiness which I longed to regain. But since I couldn't, for the moment, the love of my friends and family would have to sustain me.

CHAPTER 35

We had been home for a whole two days. The first night Ashley and Tamicia had stayed with us, and we all lay around listening to music in Sam's room. Ashley had given Sam a rotating lampshade that had little pin holes pricked in it so that when the light was turned on, the feeling of floating through space was so real you almost thought you were weightless. Saturday, which had always been a day of running here and there, was spent just sitting around, visiting with family and friends who stopped by in the morning. But in the evening, everyone went home, giving Sam and me a chance to not only get used to being in a new place, but used to getting along by ourselves.

"Hey, Sambo!" I said with mock enthusiasm, "You wanna play me in some video games?"

"No, thank you." He sat rubbing behind Klaus' ears. The dog had his head on Sam's good leg and stared up at him with big brown eyes that begged for a little show of happiness.

I understood all too well that death was very painful to deal with, but my heart broke over and over because nothing I said or did seemed to get through to Sam. After the first night, he hardly ever cried, and if he did, it was never in front of me.

Give him time.

I'm trying, but I don't want to see him drown in his own despair.

Give him time.

"How 'bout we take Klaus out for a little stretch? Come on."

A half hour later we were sitting on the bench of a little playground not far from our house while Sam caught his breath.

"Your trainer is going to be very proud of you," I said trying to bolster him up a little bit.

"Thanks." The word was so soft that I thought my hearing must be as good as Klaus's to have picked it up at all.

"Sam . . ."

Let it rest.
I can't.
"Things are going to be all right, Sam. Trust me, okay?" And I tilted his head up so that he could see me.

"I miss my daddy." Then his face just crumbled as he cried, and I gathered him in my arms rocking him back and forth. "I miss Tia!" Sam continued to sob, and I held and kept rocking him.

"It's okay, Sam," I soothed, holding him closer still, "you're supposed to miss them." We sat there for just a bit longer, until his sobs subsided to sniffles, and I waited for the big sigh that always follows that kind of release. "Ready?" I asked and felt him nod against my heart. "Come on then - I'm fixing dinner tonight." And pulling Klaus, we headed up the street, both agreeing that we were sick of takeout.

"Can Tamicia come over, too?"

"I don't see why not."

"Can she spend the night?" .

"I figure that's why you have bunk beds." Sam and Tamicia were two children, who for some reason that only God knew, both suffered ordeals which made them grow up a little too quickly, but would be among the few souls who never take anyone for granted.

Soon the house was full again with Ashley and Tamicia helping me with dinner.

"Jewel, what are you making?" Ashley asked, as I tore another shell that refused to be stuffed.

"Stuffed pasta shells, what does it look like?" I snapped, frustrated.

"Okaaay," she murmured and continued to grate cheese for the Caesar salad.

I pulled out a big baking pan and dumped everything inside. "Now it's a casserole," I announced and carried it to the oven before she could say anything.

"You know Angelo is still in town?"

"Really?"

"Yes. He wants to come by and see how you and Sam are doing."

"Why can't he just make his monthly phone call as usual?"

Ashley said quietly, "He is trying, Jewel."

"Too little, too late," I answered shortly and started viciously slicing a long loaf of garlic bread.

"Look, you need all the support you can get," Ashley said bluntly. "You've gone through the worst possible thing anyone should ever have to endure. You've lost not just one part of your heart but two and then had to deal with Sam's recovery. Holding onto your faith while you waited for him to get better. Baby, just the fact you've made it through that alone and without any drugs is simply awesome in my professional opinion."

"Ashley, I'm going to have to learn how to stand on my own."

"Jewel, I have no doubt you can stand on your own, but it's okay to have people stand beside you too." My sister gave me a big hug, and I hugged back.

Dinner was delicious and the company very much appreciated, but I pushed Ashley out the door so she could spend some time with her Dillon, leaving me kind of on my own again. The kids were whispering in Sam's room, and I sat talking to the dog.

"Well, Klaus, time to go to bed now - what do you think?"

Klaus looked at me like he understood but since I didn't speak German Shepherd, why should he try to speak English?

I waited for Klaus to ask me to play a hand of gin rummy or whist. Something. Anything. But he didn't, so I climbed into my new, gently swaying bed. I wanted to take one of the sedatives that Dr. Ambrose had sent home with me, but I was terrified that something might happen and I wouldn't be alert enough to wake up and take care of the children. I finally nodded off and woke to sunlight streaming in the room and the phone ringing. I stumbled off the bed, completely disoriented, my heart slamming in my chest as a thousand moments rushed over me.

"Hello?"

It was Mommy. "Jewel, are you all right?"

"Yeah, I was just waking up." *You're waking up in a new home without your husband and your daughter. You have a son that needs you and, girlfriend, you are floundering.* I pretended to be alert. "What's up?"

"I just thought that you should start getting the children ready for services." *Church?*

"Okay. Give us a half hour."

We hustled around to get ready and then rode over to the church with Lou and Mommy. From where we lived now, it was really just a short walk, but with Sam's fear of cars, I figured that short rides would help to acclimatize him.

St. Augustine was the most fulfilling Catholic church I'd ever attended. The choir was always uplifting and the sermons spiritually gratifying. But the best thing was the congregation, a multi-cultural mixture of souls all striving to live by the word of God. I had started coming when I was searching for a church where, as an African-American slave descendant, I could feel comfortable. St. Augustine had been founded in the basement of St. Andrews so that African-American Catholics could come together to worship with soul. Now services were held in a fine, huge church that was standing room only for afternoon Mass, but the spirit of St. Andrews was still present.

It felt good to be in church, closer to my Lord, and I checked to see if it affected Sam the same way, but his eyes were on the candles that burned in the alcoves off the altar. After the service had ended, we waited for the rush to head out.

"Did we light a candle for Daddy and Tia?"

The question caught me off guard for a minute before I answered, "No."

"Can we?"

"Of course we can." We moved over to the little vigil section, and I slipped a bill into the box for the poor before getting four matches, two for each of us.

"What do I do?" Sam asked, sitting in the front pew.

"I'll light the candle and you can say a prayer for your Daddy and Tia." I wondered if he was ready to go and visit their resting place. I'd been playing it by ear, waiting for him to ask.

"But I can't kneel." *My heart must be like a used up rag from all the wrenching of late.*

"That's all right, sweetheart. God doesn't mind."

And he closed his eyes moving his lips silently, as I followed suit.

God, Justin, St. Peter, please help to keep Sam with me and give me strength to do right by him. To raise him to be the kind of man his father was. And please Lord, Blessed Mother, please look after my baby for me. I know that she is riding high in her splendor because there was no purer heart than hers, but still, don't let her forget her Mommy. Amen.

* * * *

That night, about three am, I woke up, not sure why. Sitting up in bed, I tried to figure out if I had been pushed out of a dream when I heard Sam's voice coming farther than from his room, somewhere down the hall. Getting up, I padded out into the dark, following the voice to its source. My blood was getting colder with each step. Then I saw him sitting in the middle of the floor. For a minute I thought he was talking to Klaus who was there, whining softly.

"Daddy, when will Tia be home?" Silence. "Do you wanna play for a little while?" Silence. "No, I'll get the game." And Sam climbed to his feet, moving stiffly but moving. "I can't find it, Daddy."

My knees buckled underneath me as I realized that Sam was sitting on the floor, speaking in a normal tone of voice, almost sounding happy, having a one-sided conversation with his dead father.

"Sam?" I crawled over to look at his face. The light from the street shining in the apartment showed his big brown eyes were open, but they weren't seeing this place. "Oh, my God." I whispered and reached out to touch Sam's hair, but he just moved slightly as if my hand were an annoying fly.

"Do we have to go to New Orleans again this year, Daddy? I want to dress up and tricker treat with Tia." His head cocked to the side as if listening for an answer.

Crawling over to the phone, I dialed my sister. "Ashley! Sam is talking to Justin and he's . . . he won't respond to me, he's like sleepwalking, and . . ." But between trying to whisper and talk over the choking tears, I couldn't finish. *Please, God! Please, no more!*

"Jewel! Jewel, listen to me!"

"Oh, my poor Sam!" I sobbed into the phone. "Why can't I help him?!"

"Jewel, you are going to help him. but listen to me. You have to get him back to bed. Do that, Jewel! I'm coming over."

Still on my hands and knees, I made my way over to the happy child who was clinging so hard in this unnatural way to the memory of his father. Taking a deep breath, I tried to penetrate Sam's consciousness without alarming him.

"Daddy says that you have to go to sleep now," I whispered.

"Where are you going, Daddy?"

"Daddy has to go to work now. Let's go to bed and get some rest so you can play later." *I can't do this! This is too hard!*

But it seemed to work for Sam, and he let me carry him to bed, and I sat there with him.

Dead. Justin is dead, and Sam is talking to him. How am I going to help him? I can't even help myself.

A soft knocking on the door some time later brought me back. I turned the lock with trembling fingers and opened the door to what I hoped would be sanity because my mind was truly going.

"It's all right. It's all right," Angelo's voice said over and over. "Jewel, it's going to be fine. Did you get Sam back to bed?"

"Yes, but I think maybe he's having a breakdown, Daddy." I didn't even realize that last word had slipped from my lips. Angelo gently pushed me down on the couch, and I watched him stride down the hall and into Sam's room.

My hands were clenched in a death grip, and I felt angry. *What more are you going to do to me?* Waiting for an answer that I knew wouldn't come, I went on plucking at God's nerves. *You took away my life four years ago. Took me all the way to the bottom for what? Then You allowed me love, to think that life could be good.* My voice hissed into the dark corners of the house.

You brought me back to let me fall. Are You laughing at me because I haven't let go of my faith? Is that the kind of Lord you are? I really didn't believe this, but right now I was pissed and there were no answers for me, so I just kept it going.

You took my child but I held on. You took my husband, and I still held on. And now Sam. First You let Sheila come back into his life, and I live every day in fear because of it - and now this. Please, God, leave Sam out of it. Are You showing me how selfish I'm being in trying to keep him with me? Is that it? I'll give him to his grandparents to raise. I'll live the rest of my life alone.

"Here drink this." And there was the smell of alcohol reaching my nose before it hit my tongue, burning the sobs which refused to be quieted.

"Let that settle, and then we'll talk, but for now just try to relax. I'm here and won't let anything happen to you or Sam."

I followed Angelo's advice, the brandy not leaving much room for argument. For about two minutes.

"Daddy, I just don't understand . . ." I started, but he hushed me and told me to drink a little more. "Relax. I'm here and won't let anything happen to you," he said again.

I didn't question why he was here or how long he would stay. I didn't have it in me to curse him for never being there to get to know Tia or Justin, or even me, for that matter. He was here now, and I leaned my head back on his shoulder until I slept.

CHAPTER 36

"Hey, you two I'm back. Can't believe that it's been over two months since you went away. Sam sends more of his artwork and love. I don't know if it's healthy - it seems like he's giving them to me as if I'm really gonna see you." Pulling out my little shovel I started to dig a small hole at the base of the tombstone. "But then again I'm still looking for both of you everywhere I go." Stopping to look at the two smiling faces, my mouth began to spread into a tiny smile. "Can't help it. Every time I see your faces staring back at me."

Once the hole was big enough, I pulled out the drawings Sam made and held them up. "This is a picture of Sam walking for the first time without his crutches. You'd both be so proud of him. He's really getting it together . . . physically." I placed the picture into a large plastic bag, sealing it carefully, and then put it into the cold earth. The breeze was soft - the tree full and green.

"You know, I was watching television the other day and this commercial came on for some car. This couple was going to deliver their baby girl and all the way to the hospital, the mother kept seeing her daughter in different phases of her life. You know, ballet lessons, then graduation, finally her own wedding." I pulled at a blade of grass. "I just fell to pieces. Sam came in and stood for a minute. Held my hand. Man!" Just the vision of that night brought a heavy sigh from me.

"I've finally started going to a support group. And, Justin, I know you'll find this hard to believe - my father has been around a lot, and somehow it's been a big help to me. But, Justin, I don't know what to do for Sam. I don't think that mentally he's dealt with you and Tia being gone." I told Justin about Sam's episodes of sleepwalking. "The nights that he's up and talking to you are bad enough, but I think the nights he sleeps soundly are worse. I sit up and wait for him to start his conversations with you. And Sam is reverting back to being this polite little boy who acts like he's just visiting me. Maybe I'm too much of a reminder of what life was supposed to be. Maybe he thinks that I don't want him even though he's the one who's been saving me. But maybe he can sense that, and the stress is too great on him." The maybes were always going round and round in my head. "Maybe I'm just expecting too much from him."

"Maybe you're expecting too much of yourself."

"MALCOLM! What the hell are you doing?"

"Same thing you are." And he came from behind the stone monument.

"Why not just reach in and stop my heart next time," I said, trying to slow my breathing.

"I'm sorry, I just didn't want to disturb you," he replied apologetically, and then I really looked at him and saw that sorrow had a face. This was the first time I'd had a close look at him since Tia died. His hair was growing long and looked unkempt as did the beard that covered his chin and upper lip. Wrinkled clothes hung off his gaunt frame, making him look like a lost orphan. But it was his eyes that really bothered me. *Do my eyes look that - broken and alone? Could that be why Sam pulls away from me?*

"Hey, I'm sorry," I said in a softer tone. "I'll let you have your time." And I started to leave.

"No, please! Stay for a while?"

"Okay." And I sat back down. "How did you get here?" I didn't see his car.

"Walked."

"Oh. Do you come here a lot?"

"Yeah, it's really nice here, and sometimes it makes me feel closer. This was a wonderful thing your father did."

We sat quietly for a little while, each lost in our own thoughts about Tia but not ready to vocalize them. Each taking comfort from the other who shared in the creation of that little life we both loved so much.

"Jewel, it hurts."

"I know it does, Malcolm. How is Annette doing?" She loved Tia, too, and I felt no animosity toward her, but Malcolm was shaking his head.

"I thought that she would help, and I think that she thinks she is. But she's talking about having a baby. Like Tia could be so easily replaced. Like she was a . . . a . . ." He was at a loss, and I was horrified. *How can Annette be so insensitive?*

"And your parents? How are they holding up?" I thought it best to change the subject.

"Better than me," Malcolm said ruefully. "I sit at home and watch the videos of Tia that you used to send to me." His voice took on a happier tone for a fleeting moment, and I knew he was seeing some image of our baby. "There she is, smiling and waving at me. Blowing kisses." You could almost hear him strain to keep the happiness from slipping away that, like mine, visited for oh, so brief a time. Memories that get your attention, but fade when you try to focus too closely. I handed him a pile of tissues that I kept on hand.

"And her voice." *Why are you doing this to yourself, Malcolm?* "Once I fell asleep with the tape on and heard her say, 'Daddy, pay attention!' I jumped up and started looking for her before I realized what was really going on." Malcolm gave a little laugh through his tears. "And I could hear you in the background trying to coach her along, but you know how she could always do everything herself?"

I can't do this. Not now. Sharing those moments. "Malcolm, I gotta go."

"No, wait, tell me about Sam, maybe I can help." And he was begging, so I went on to tell him, thinking that maybe Sam's situation would somehow save us both from losing it at this moment.

"Maybe he's afraid something will happen to you, too."

"I guess you're right. I try to reassure him but not make any promises that I may not be able to keep. I can't say, 'Sam, I'll be with you forever' and then find out I have cancer or something, you know?"

"Maybe I can come by and spend some time with him?" Malcolm asked hopefully.

"That would be nice." I nodded and looked at my watch. "Do you need a ride home?"

"No, I need . . ." And he stopped. "I need you, Jewel."

"Wha . . ." Before I could finish, Malcolm gripped my shoulders and pulled me to him in a kiss. This was the first time Malcolm's lips had touched mine since he left for school right after New Year's so many years ago. When he let go and opened his eyes, they were desperate and pleading, but the slap that flew across his face changed them to an aching hurt.

"WHAT THE HELL ARE YOU DOING?!" I shouted. "You have the nerve to stand here and kiss me over the grave of my husband?!"

"Jewel, please." He started reaching for my hand, but I jerked it away as if he were a leper, taking a step back in revulsion, watching Malcolm fall to his knees in front of me where he started crying and rambling. "Jewel, please help me! I need you. I've lost my child, my wife, my life! But we can start all over again. We can raise Sam together! Just give it a chance?"

"Give it a chance?!" I hissed. "Malcolm you couldn't even love me when Tia was alive. What would it be now? Building on a foundation of painful memories and fear of being alone?"

"I know that I hurt you and I'm sorry, but I've changed. I swear that I have. I changed long before this happened, but you had already found Justin . . ."

"That's right and he loved me! He cherished what you threw away! Justin showed me what true love really is."

"But he's gone, and I can give it to you again. You won't have to be alone." *This is truly pathetic.*

"You think because Justin isn't here with me physically, I'm just supposed to pack my love away? No, Malcolm, I understand something that you never will. True love goes on whether you want it to or not, and I want my love for Justin to live in me for the rest of my life so that means that there's no room for you there. You've lost your mind all right. *You* lost a daughter. Guess what?" I stood ranting over his bowed head. "I lost her, too! As for losing a wife - you didn't lose me, you threw me away! And a life? Well, you made this one for yourself! Now live with it, but stay the hell away from me!"

I turned away abruptly and stalked down to the car, fuming. *Goddamn you, Malcolm, why does it always have to be about what you want and your selfish needs? We can't even mourn like two civilized people. I hope you learn to deal with this on your own because I am out of here - I don't need to add you to my list of problems.*

I revved the engine. I should have just peeled out, but no, I had to glance back. Malcolm was kneeling on the ground, aimlessly moving leaves around in front of the grave. His shaking shoulders were my only indication that he was still crying.

Jewel, he is mourning and needs comfort and like every other time in his life doesn't know how to reach for it. Help him. If not for pity's sake, then at least because without him there never would have been a Tia.

"Damn it!" I cried out and slammed my fist against the steering wheel over and over again.

I found myself back on the hill. "Malcolm?"

"Hmm?"

"Malcolm." And I knelt down next to him. "I want to help you."

"You do?" He sounded confused.

"Yes, but what I'm going to do is just give you a push in the right direction - the rest is going to be up to you, okay?"

He nodded, as I took his hand and placed the pamphlet in his grasp. "I want you to go there and let them help you, okay?"

He looked up at me instead of the pamphlet, his eyes still filled with pain. "After we separated, did she ask for me a lot?"

"No, Malcolm," and just when I thought that there was no way that he could look more broken, I found that I was wrong. Reaching down, I lifted his chin with my finger and said gently, "You never gave her a chance to miss you."

"I'm so sorry for everything." He started sobbing again. "I was so jealous. I know I was the one who messed up, but I didn't want to accept that I would lose those special moments with her. I didn't want to be just a sometime dad. But I hurt everyone, and I'm so sorry."

Pulling Malcolm into my arms, I tried to console him as best I could. "I know that you're sorry, Malcolm." *Lord, when did I become the shepherd over this lost lamb?* "And that you miss Tia so much you think anyone who was close to her will fill the gap. Me, Sam. Anyone who loved her. But Malcolm, it doesn't work that way. You have to learn to hold onto to her in your heart - not let the grief smother you." I wasn't sure if I was getting through to him as he sat in the circle of my arms. The other half of what made Tia whole.

"I'm sorry, Jewel," Malcolm said after a minute. "I didn't mean to tarnish what you and Justin had - anyone could see just how beautiful it was."

"No one can take that away from me." I pulled him to his feet and hugged him. "You're going to be all right, Malcolm," I whispered, holding him tight.

"Do you think that one day we can be friends again?" he asked, still clinging to me.

"No, Malcolm. There's too much between us to allow anything new to grow."

"Will you at least not hate me?"

"I don't hate you, Malcolm. Because of you, I had the happiest moments of my life." And I stepped back to look at him without malice or anger.

He nodded in understanding before hugging me again. We stayed that way for a long time, knowing that it would be the last time. Each replaying how things might have been different.

This time when I was ready to pull off, I didn't look back. My obligation to Malcolm, other than an occasional prayer now and again, was over.

CHAPTER 37

"Mrs. Baptiste!"

"Dr. Ambrose, hi!" And there was warmth in my voice and in his hand that he stretched out to capture mine in greeting as he stepped off the hospital elevator.

"How are . . ." We both started at the same time.

"I'm sorry . . ." Again our words bumped.

"What brings you down here?" he asked, beaming over me.

"The grief management sessions," I replied, and he grew thoughtful and concerned.

"I hope that they've been beneficial to you?"

"Yes, it's been pretty good."

"Who's the group leader?"

"Dr. Horan," I answered, wondering if he had heard of him.

"Oh, yeah, he's great." Dr. Ambrose crossed his arms. "Studied theology for a while and found a happy balance between that and psychology."

"Yeah, he's got some great ideas I want to turn my sister on to."

"So how is Sam doing?" he asked as we stepped into the elevator.

"Physically, he's doing pretty good. The leg has mended perfectly. The eye still gives him trouble sometimes but he wears glasses now and then to relieve the stress. We even go bike riding now on Sundays after church. You know, along Beach Drive?"

And he nodded.

"Yeah, it's nice since they block it off, and we don't have to watch out for traffic in between the trails."

"But?"

"Oh, you mean how is he doing otherwise?" I asked, following his thoughts. "Well, that's a little complicated."

"Well, if you aren't in a rush, maybe we could head to the cafeteria and talk about it. Uh, no go?"

"Sorry, no offense to your place of business, but I've had enough of that stuff to last a lifetime."

"No offense taken. Do you have time for a quick walk onto the campus?"

"How about we head to U street and the best chili dogs in town?" I suggested.

"Now, you've got a deal. And I am starving, so what say we meet in about fifteen minutes?"

"It's a deal."

Once we were settled in the booth and waiting for our chili dogs and fries, I told him about Sam's recurring nighttime conversations with his father, and that a psychologist Ashley had referred us to was working very closely with him.

"Wow, poor little guy! And, his mother - if you don't mind my asking - is she still a concern?"

"I'm afraid so - a big concern - the date you told them he would be able to leave the area is almost here." Ever since my last encounter with Sheila, I jumped every time the phone rang, every time there was a knock at the door. I never stopped worrying about what she might be planning, and now with time running out, it was becoming unbearable.

"Being the sort of person you are, I'm sure you'll find a way to cope," Dr. Ambrose commended me.

"Really?" I had to laugh. "I'm sorry, but sometimes I think I should just buy stock in Prozac and watch it skyrocket, because I'm going to start taking it like some people smoke."

We both laughed and went back to eating. After a while he caught me staring.

"What, did I make another mess?" he asked, looking down at his baby blue tee shirt.

"No," I said, embarrassed, "it's just that it's strange to see you sitting here like a regular person."

"Oh, I exist outside of the hospital. I even have a first name. Mine is Matthew . . . or Matt."

"Well, Matt, I'm Jewel." And we shook hands from across the table.

"I've got it," I said, reaching for the check.

"Oh, hey no, I've got it covered," he protested, but I wasn't letting go of the check as I reached into my bag.

"I seriously advise you to take advantage of this moment because these splurges won't ever happen again until I get a job," I half joked.

"Are you still not working?" he asked, reaching into his pocket anyway.

"Nope. I just can't do that one yet. I was working in trauma and every time someone would come in from an accident, well . . ." I found my wallet and started thumbing through it. "I just need to find something to do so I can pay the bills."

"Do you want to leave medicine altogether?" Matt asked, handing the waitress his credit card.

Giving him a look and putting the tip down, I responded, "I don't know. I think that I'm still in transition, but that I'll be ready to pull my own weight very soon."

"Hey, there are tons of options. I can tell you about them," he offered.

"That would be great, but I'm going to have to get back with you on that one. I had no idea that time had slipped by so swiftly. I gotta run." And I started sliding out of the booth. "Matt, I will definitely call you to talk a little more. I'm so sorry to rush off like this, but I've got to get to Sam."

"Sure. You know where to find me."

And I waved as I crossed the street to my car.

* * * *

I knew the house was empty when I arrived because no small body, followed closely by a large, furry one, had hurled itself into my arms. Placing my keys on the table, I checked the answering machine and looked. On the table stood a vase of lovely flowers and a note, written in Sam's carefully penned hand:

> *Mommy, I hope you like the flowers. Uncle Marcus took me, Tamicia and Klaus out for a little while. Be back soon. Love, Sam*

Before I could bend over and inhale the fragrance, the doorbell echoed through the living room. I threw open the door with a big smile which instantly vanished. "Oh!" I stepped back and allowed Sheila to enter my home. I hadn't seen her for over two months. Walking past, she muttered a thank you.

I anticipated another performance, but this scene must have called for something a little more demure than the last. The blonde locks were arranged in a tousled jumble, but the sunglasses were resting on top of her head, pushing her hair away from the unmade face. Her costume was less flamboyant - a pair of jeans and a plain, button-down red shirt. Her boots sounded loud and intrusive on my floors. I closed the door and prepared to do battle.

"Look, Sheila . . ."

"Marcil."

"Whatever." My eyes followed her to the window where she stood with her back to me. "I know you don't expect to just walk up into my house after the way you turned on me at the hospital?" With fear pumping through my chest, I knew what I had to do. If she really thought that I was just going to pack up my son and hand him over, she was sadly mistaken. If it came down to it, one of us might not be walking out of here, because that's just about what it would take for her to get Sam away from me. During the past couple of months, in preparation for the custody case, Mr. Lipinsky and Jazz had uncovered some very interesting information concerning this person. *No! No! Hell, no! Sam isn't going anywhere with her!*

Crossing back to the front door, I pulled it open. "You might as well just leave right now because I don't care what anyone says, you can't . . ."

"Look!" she interrupted. "You were the one who tracked me down."

Truth has its way of affecting people. All of the months of riding this emotional cyclone came to a head. Slamming the door shut, I advanced toward her. "*That's right!*" I yelled. "I tracked you down because Sam's father is dead, *not Sam*, and he has needs that must be met!" Counting off on my fingers, I let it rip. "Stability. Care. Love. He needs love! The love I can give him all by myself."

There was no reason to hold back, so I left myself wide open. "I needed your help. Justin is gone and so is any legal connection to Sam. School, hospital visits, anything that says parent or guardian, I can't do." *Calm down, Jewel.* "And I so *want* to do these things for Sam."

When she didn't respond, I tried to reason with her. "Let's be real. To you, Sam is an intruder. An extra puzzle piece that won't fit into your life. Sam already fits perfectly into mine."

I noticed that her shoulders were shaking. Moving slowly to her side so that I could see her profile, I saw that she was laughing.

She looked at me. "You know, you have a lot of nerve," she said, turning her attention back out the window. "You hunt me down - for what? To ask for something that you already had?"

"I had hoped you were dead." *Did I just say that? Well, I must have because it got her attention.*

Smiling, she spread her arms open wide. "Sheila is dead. I am but a vision!" *Oh, not this crazy mess again!*

"It's not that simple, Sheila," I said softly, trying to get a feel for where she was coming from. "You met me the first time and said that you didn't want anything to do with being Sam's mother. That you had your own agenda. Then you come right back - *a week later* - demanding your rights to him and putting me through hell."

Shaking her head vigorously, she mumbled, "That was a mistake."

My heart soared momentarily, before I remembered how crazy she was - she could easily change her mind again and again. "Oh, that's right," I said, moving away from her. "You wanted the rights to Sam's money." *I don't give a damn if I offend her or not.*

The more I thought about my situation, the angrier I became at this invasion. *Acting, my butt.* Porno films, drug and prostitution charges, wouldn't look good in family court. Together with Justin's parents, there was a chance at custody. And we still had that pitifully worded nullification of her maternal rights. Even if Sam's grandparents were the ones awarded custody, well, I could live with that. *I don't have to be nice to this woman one more minute, and right now I want her gone!*

"Please leave." I didn't want her here when Sam got home.

Instead of leaving, Sheila leaned her head against the window. "No, the mistake was listening to Tony." A rueful laugh crossed her lips, followed by a sigh that sounded like it came from someone whose soul was even more tired than mine. "Everyone wants to tell me what to do. First, my father." The carefully coached voice was gone and replaced with a gruff, southern twang. "'Now, honey, go on in the house and play with your dolls. Forget that acting. You'd better find yourself a good man to take care of you.' Then when I got to school, no one took me seriously. The guys who took me out acted like I was a trophy or something. No one ever asked if I was ready to go further than a kiss and a hug."

She turned to me for understanding, but I couldn't muster any.

"When I met Justin, I was at a party, and he came over, just being friendly.

I don't want to hear this. I don't want to hear the softness in her voice when she speaks of my Justin.

"Right away, it seemed like he saw me as a person, not some blonde bimbo. He made me believe that I could get good grades, that I could try out for parts I wouldn't have dreamed of before. It was wonderful."

Then her voice became hard again. "But then, just like everyone else, he changed. As soon as that little situation came up, he wanted to control me. He actually kept me a prisoner for all those months."

She extracted a cigarette and a little portable ashtray.

I didn't protest.

She took a long drag before going on. "Now Tony thinks that I'm going to allow him to run my life. He's the one who thinks the kid will bring us some money." She shook her head and grew silent.

I heard what she was saying, but there was a war going on, and I had to be careful of an ambush. The silence grew, but before it could overwhelm me with doubt, I shattered it. Smashing all of the uncertainty of that silence by asking, "So what are you saying?" Those words, spoken in a whisper, exploded between me and this woman. The debris was falling everywhere, but I didn't know where to run for cover. I had hit the detonator. She would decide how powerful the blast would be.

Sheila took another long drag on her cigarette, the ashes threatening to fall from the trembling of her hands. "I'm not a monster," she said. "Seven years ago, I decided not to live my life with someone else's life weaving in and out of it."

I watched her wrap the layers of self-preservation overtop herself.

She stubbed out her smoke and finally turned to face me. "I see no need to change that decision now. Here." She extended her hand. "Take it."

I accepted the envelope she held out to me. *Oh, no, not another pathetic document.*

"Everything's there that you need from me. The rest of keeping him is up to you."

Before I could break open the seal, Sheila was at the door. Turning back, she said, "Don't try to find me again. You have everything you want, so just stay away."

I looked at her closely. Somehow, the mask wasn't fitting just right. Was this the same look of grim determination she wore seven years ago? Did the tears welling in her eyes now get pushed away with the same impatient hand then? She placed the sunglasses over the windows of her soul, leaving me to forever wonder.

Facing the door, Sheila's voice was firm. "Despite what you think of me, I do have feelings." She pulled open the door and hesitated before finishing. "That's why I'm leaving him here with you. Tell him *that* if he ever asks about me."

The envelope in my hand and Sheila walking out the door should have brought closure, but it didn't. I was still afraid. Suddenly, the dinging bell in the hallway brought my sense of dread to fruition. *Sam! Oh, God!* I rushed for the door. Looking down the hall, I saw that Sheila was rapidly striding toward the elevator. Everything about her body said that she should be moving faster, but it was as if the air had tripled in density, preventing anyone from moving quickly.

I myself couldn't move. I could only watch as the events unfolded in front of me, like a rose opening to bloom. The doors to the elevator slowly slid open. Sam had his back to me, and

Tamicia and Marcus were listening to something he was saying. Klaus saw Sheila first and then our open front door. Sam was turning so slowly. In my mind's eye, it appeared that Sheila was moving in place. Sam looked down the hall, and my heart stopped. His face was in full view - that beautiful, innocent face that I knew by heart. Suddenly, for the first time, I could see some similarity in his face to that of the woman walking toward him down the hall. Now it seemed that Sheila's stride had quickened. *Oh, there's no way I can scoop Sam up before she gets to him!*

Brushing past Tamicia, Marcus looked like he was about to reach out and grab Sam; he lunged, but Sam was just out of his reach.

My Sam is coming toward me now, but will he stop when he gets close to her? Will there be a remnant of that severed bond - enough to light a spark? Just enough for them to glance at each other, perhaps enter into a tiny exploration of unfathomed intimations?

My hands reached out to protect Sam with my own maternal shield, but would it be strong enough against the real McCoy?

Now they were moving right up on each other . . . mother and son. . . for the first time ever. I couldn't breathe or look away, and then she did it. Without missing a beat, she strode past him, slipping between the elevator doors, just as Sam crashed into my arms.

"Hi, Mommy!"

I crushed him against me. Kissing his curls, his face, before picking him up and carrying him into the house.

Giggling, Sam would have let me eat him up if I wanted.

Instead, I sat down and held him tightly.

Smiling up at me, he asked, "Did you like the flowers?"

Snuggling into his neck, creating a huge stream of giggles, I replied, "No, I didn't. I *loved* them."

Sam settled back against my chest. *God, he smells so good!*

"They're supposed to cheer you up - sometimes you come back from your meetings looking sad." Sam looked over at Tamicia. "What's wrong?"

Timidly, she asked, "Has someone been smoking?"

Moving Sam off my lap, I went to the window and pushed it open. The cool breeze kissed my face, wafting the stale smell from my home.

"Yes, someone came while you were gone," I answered.

Marcus was casually looking around the apartment.

"Who was it?" Sam wondered, probably because no one we knew smoked.

Licking my dry lips, I leaned over the sofa. "Just someone dropping off some insurance papers. Now, let me see," I said, shifting gears before he could start, "it seems to me like someone needs a bath!"

"Aww, Mommy! Can't I show Tamicia my drawing?"

Before I could burst his bubble, the doorbell rang. I froze, and Marcus moved to the door.

"Hey, Mama!" Tamicia went to exchange kisses and hugs with my sister.

"Hey, y'all, what's up?" Ashley looked from my drawn face, to Marcus, then slowly around the room.

Marcus spoke up. "Jewel had a visitor while I was out with the kids. I took them for ice cream."

"Oh . . . ice cream. All right, Ms. Tamicia, we have to get going. Sam, I'll see you Monday?" I was grateful that Ashley could read a situation so well.

"Yes, Aunt Ashley." Sam doled out his kisses and went off to take his bath. "I've got some new pictures for you," he called over his shoulder. Klaus met up with Sam in the hallway and followed close behind him. The big dog enjoyed keeping Sam company while he played for hours in the tub, full of bubbles and little plastic men.

"Great, Sam! We can't wait to see them," Ashley responded enthusiastically. Speaking over Tamicia's head, she said, "I'll call you later," her eyes signaling her concern.

"Yes, you will," I agreed, walking them to the door.

Once they were gone, Marcus asked what happened. "Wait one minute," I said. Coming back to the living room with two brandies, I told him everything, and we both looked over the papers. This time they appeared to have been prepared by a real lawyer.

Marcus threw back the rest of his drink and asked, "So what does this mean?"

"I don't know. I'm going to call Jazz right now and see what she has to say."

Marcus rose, saying he had to leave. "I'll call you later."

I nodded, already dialing Jazz' number.

"See you, Sam!" Marcus called out.

"You still here?" Sam's muffled voice echoed from down the hall.

"Nope. I'm gone."

I waved as Marcus let himself out. Jazz came on the phone. We talked, and I promised to fax the contents of the envelope. We made an appointment to meet the next day.

"Hey, Jewel," she said before hanging up. "I'm sure it will be a help at this point."

"I hope so, Jazz. I really hope so."

CHAPTER 38

"Is Ms. Clipper-Ashton here?"

"No, your Honor, she had a prior commitment but supplied us with the paperwork so that we can go on with the proceedings," Mr. Lipinsky said respectfully.

"I see." The Honorable Judge Joan Griffin-Romwell reviewed the pages in front of her. There was just me, Mr. Lipinsky, Jazz, and the social worker in the small courtroom.

"What about Samuel Baptiste? Is he present?" she asked, looking around the room.

"No, your Honor," Mr. Lipinsky said, standing behind our table that faced the bench. "Sam has been through a very difficult period with the loss of his father and sister. The fact of the matter is that he is completely unaware of the proceedings concerning his parentage."

"That's very unusual." She pondered. "I prefer to hear from the children themselves since, in my court, I believe they should have a say as to their fate."

Sam's absence seemed to cause her Honor some discomfort, and I began to panic. But Mr. Lipinsky brought out the folder which contained reports from the art therapist and consulting child psychologist and another folder from the social worker and smoothly asked if he could approach the bench.

"What is this copy of a check in here for?"

The judge's voice startled me - she was raising a piece of paper in her hand.

"Your Honor, that was the monetary amount that Mrs. Clipper-Ashton offered to my client for not revealing the true maternal parentage of Samuel Baptiste."

Judge Harmon looked up, then sat back trying to make sure that she understood. "She was paying you five thousand dollars to take her son for a lifetime?"

The question was directed at me, and I nodded before speaking. "Yes, your Honor."

"And where is the money now?"

"There's a page there explaining that Mrs. Baptiste refused the payment and has signed an agreement to never seek Mrs. Clipper-Ashton under any circumstances whatsoever."

"Well, it must be nice to just throw away five thousand dollars when you have a son to raise alone. You are raising him alone, aren't you?" the judge questioned.

"Yes and no," I replied. "I have family and friends standing behind me. But I have a profession, and Sam has his father's Social Security until he's eighteen. That money will be set aside for his education. The rest I can take care of."

"And how will that be done?" she asked. "It shows here that you've been under the Family Leave Act since Sam's accident - do you plan to go back to your profession?"

"Yes, your Honor. I will be returning to work as a Physician Assistant." I had to resist the urge to fidget while she appraised me a little while longer.

"Mr. Lipinsky, is there anyone here who would contest these proceedings?"

"No, your Honor. Sam's next of kin would be his grandparents who are in full support of Mrs. Baptiste being awarded legal guardianship."

"Well, it appears that everything is here." Judge Griffin-Harmon said, closing the manila envelope on the stack of papers. "Because Mrs. Clipper-Ashton has relinquished legal guardianship to one Jewel Baptiste, it is the ruling of the Court that Ms. Jewel Baptiste be appointed the legal guardian of Samuel Baptiste, minor." And she went on and on, but all I knew was that Sam was mine! Legally and forever!

"He's mine!" I shouted, almost running out of the courtroom into the waiting arms of my sister and friends. I hugged Mr. Lipinsky and Jazz. "Thank you for all you've done."

"It was a pleasure, but Jewel I must warn you," Mr. Lipinsky said ominously, "she can still come back and try to overturn the ruling. Nothing in the judicial system is really set in stone."

But I wasn't letting go of my high.

"Mr. Lipinsky, you met that woman. You know her history. There is no way that she's coming back."

And for the first time since I considered Sam mine, I had documents to prove it. "Let's go and tell Sam!"

The Baptistes, along with Mommy and Lou, were watching Sam for the day. During the ride over, I thought about what I would say to Sam, my son. *God, that sounds and feels so good!* Ever since that day when Mrs. Cannon refused to accept me as Sam's mother, I felt like I was harboring a dirty little secret. That no matter where I went or what I did, someone would point their finger and say, "She can't take care of Sam. She has no rights."

I had told Sam that I was going to court to make sure that no one could ever say that I wasn't his mother. Pulling up into the driveway of the Baptiste home, I saw my father-in-law waiting on the steps.

"How did it go?" he asked as I stepped from the car.

"It's final!" I cried, holding the papers over my head, and he let out a sigh of relief, embracing me in a big hug before turning me loose, to call out, "Barb! Lou! Anna! She did it!" And everyone came flooding out of the house to offer their love which I basked in for a moment before looking for my most important person.

"He's back in the shed," Mommy told me softly.

I stepped through the little storage area that was filled with tools and garden stuff, picking my way to the back where I found Sam sitting astride his dad's motorcycle. I just stood there watching him for a moment, reliving my own memories of Justin and our rides together. "Sam?"

"Hi, Mommy. Tamicia and I cleaned off the bike." He lovingly ran his little hands along the handlebars. "Gramps said that he would save it for me when I get bigger."

"Just remember to wear a helmet. Here, I have something to show you." And I climbed astride behind him, feeling that this was the proper place to be for this and pulled out the paper, placing it in front of him while my arms provided a cradle for him. "See what it says here?" And I pointed to his name, "This says that Sam Toussaint Baptiste belongs to Jewel Baptiste."

"It doesn't say that, does it?" he asked, looking at the thousands of words.

"Well, in a lot of words that just what it says," I assured him.

Sam sat quietly holding the paper in his hands. "Can we show Daddy and Tia?"

"Sure, sweetie." I kissed his forehead thinking this was a big day indeed - the first time he ever talked about going to see them.

"Can we show them now?"

"Of course." And I helped him off the bike, and after taking one last look we covered it up before heading out.

"We've got good food inside here," Mrs. Baptiste said as she met us coming across the back yard.

"Well, keep a couple of plates warm for me and Sam," I answered her. "We have a visit to make. He wants to share the good news with his father and sister."

Her eyes were misty as she nodded her understanding, giving my arm a squeeze.

"Hey, Mr. Rubin." I waved to him at the gate. "This is my son, Sam."

"Hello there, young man." Mr. Rubin reached over to shake his hand, and after a brief exchange of pleasantries we followed the winding road to the top of the hill, Sam sitting up straight as he looked around.

"Do you want to go by yourself?" I asked, but he shook his head. So we climbed the hill together reaching the stone that I knew so well. The smiling faces still catching my heartstrings.

"Hi, Daddy. Hi, Tia," Sam said, moving toward the faces as I went to sit on the stone bench. "I really miss you both a lot." He dropped to his knees. "But Mommy says that we're a family and now the court says that we can be, too."

Everything became blurry as Sam continued the first real lucid conversation with his father, not like the nightly visits he made into the past from time to time. "Sometimes I wish that I could be with you." He looked up at the clouds. "But I know that Mommy needs me with her."

Oh, God, please make this all make sense to me one day but for now just give me a little more strength.

"I hope that you like the pictures I drew for you. I have some more at home, but I want to keep those." He looked over at me. I could tell there was no way that he could express everything in one visit so I told him we could come back any time he wanted.

He nodded. "We're gonna go now, but we'll be back. I love you both." And he reached up and kissed the smiling faces, before taking my hand, ready to go.

"Justin, I'll take the very best care of him," I promised. "You just continue to take care of our little Tia for me." And I also kissed the forever happy faces before turning to leave, taking Sam into a life that would be filled with as much love and security as I could bestow upon him.

THE END

WAVERLY HOUSE PUBLISHING

Dedicated to publishing quality books,
written and designed by African-Americans

Judge for Yourself! Purchase a Waverly House
book at your local or on-line bookstore.

❖ ❖ ❖ ❖ ❖

Crisis of Identity
by William A. Simms

Meet Gina:
An African-American woman who says:
*"Black men don't turn me on . . .
it's their hair, their lips . . . oh, I don't
know . . . just everything about them!"*

"A fast-paced book that's hard to put down."
Joe Wilson, Black Surburban Journal

Damaged! by Bernadette Y. Connor

Intriguing drama of the relationship of an abused teen and her psychiatrist, liberally laced with romance and suspense.

"Richly detailed characters and a great story line."
Marshall Lowe, LA Watts Times

Zuro! also by William A. Simms

A must read for those of you who always wanted to see us win for a change! Fascinating, controversial story of an African-American Independence Day.
"*Wow!*" says author Omar Tyree.

VISIT WAVERLY'S WEBSITE: WWW.NATSEL.COM

Waverly House, PO Box 1053, Glenside, Pa. 19038, 1-800-858-2253

To order these Waverly books, use order form on next page.

USE THIS FORM TO ORDER WAVERLY HOUSE BOOKS

FILL IN THIS FORM AND MAIL TO:
Waverly House Publishing, PO Box 1053, Glenside, Pa. 19038
For information call: 1-800-858-2253

Method of Payment (check one)
☐ Check Enclosed ☐ VISA ☐ Mastercard
☐ American Express ☐ Discover Card

Card Account No. Please list all numbers on card.   Exp. Mo.   Exp. Yr.

_____   _____
Customer Name   Customer Signature

_____   _____   _____   _____
Street Address   City   State   Zip Code

_____   _____
Day Time Phone (include area code)   Night Time Phone (include area code)

Your name and address must be filled in even if you're sending to another address.

Order #1 - Please send the following to the address below:

Qty	Description	Price	Subtotal
	Zuro! A Tale of Alien Avengers, softbound, 340 pages	$14.95	$
	Crisis of Identity, softbound, 266 pages	$12.50	$
	Damaged!, hardbound, 343 pages	$22.95	$
	The Rest of Our Lives, softbound, 370 pages	$15.00	$
	Add shipping and handling (see below)		$
	Add sales tax if required (see below)		$
		Total:	$

Ship to arrive week of _____

Ship to: Name _____

Address _____ Apt. # _____
             _____ Zip _____

Card to read: _____

You may enclose your own card or we'll enclose handwritten one

Remarks: _____
_____
_____

SHIPPING AND HANDLING; For one book, add $3.00; for each additional book, add $1.